Feldheym

Hall, Brian $18.00

The dreamers $18.00

6/98

13 ✓ 5/97
14 ✓ 11/16

the DREAMERS

the DREAMERS

a novel by **BRIAN HALL**

1817

HARPER & ROW, PUBLISHERS, NEW YORK

CAMBRIDGE, PHILADELPHIA, SAN FRANCISCO

LONDON, MEXICO CITY, SÃO PAULO, SINGAPORE, SYDNEY

2/13/9Ø
$18.ØØ
Feld

FIRST EDITION

Designed by Ruth Bornschlegel

Library of Congress Cataloging-in-Publication Data

Hall, Brian, 1959–
  The dreamers.

  I. Title.
PS3558.A363D74   1989   813'.54   88-24667
ISBN 0-06-016076-4

88 89 90 91 92 CC/HC 10 9 8 7 6 5 4 3 2 1

For my parents
And for Eric Kushner

CONTENTS

It was about this time that I began to have a strange feeling, that I have come to know since, and which I then innocently mistook for happiness. It seemed to me, wherever I went, that the world around me was losing its weight and was slowly beginning to flow upwards, a world of light only, of no solidity whatever . . . I felt extremely happy, if slightly lightheaded, under the faith, and took it as a foreboding of a greater happiness to come, a sort of apotheosis. The universe, and I myself with it, I thought, was on the wing, on the way to the seventh heaven. Now I know well enough what it means: it is the beginning of a final farewell; it is the cock crowing . . . The world around me was indeed on the wing, going upwards. It was only me myself, who, being too heavy for the flight, was to be left behind, in complete desolation.

—Isak Dinesen, "The Dreamers"

ADVENT

October 2, 1985

Brigham Fellowship Committee
Lehman Hall, Room 6
Harvard University
Cambridge, MA   02138

Dear Committee,

I arrived in Vienna ten days ago, and have spent much
of my time so far finding a place to live. As of yesterday,
my mailing address has become Pension Steiner,
Elizabethplatz 6, 1040 Wien.

There's little to report as yet: I've been to the state
archives to meet Herr Oberbichler (Professor Drury's
contact) and he promised to set me up with the
Verwaltungsdirektor, who can arrange for me to work in
the archive depository. Unfortunately, I've had bad luck at
the university. Universitätsprofessor Herr Doktor Steuer—
the man who had written he would get me a library pass
and a carrel—happens to be doing fieldwork on Java. And
of course he neglected to tell anyone that I was coming.
My documents generated mild interest but no noticeable
respect. Steuer won't be back until October 10th; until
then, I'm in limbo over there.

By the way, I should mention that my mother and I are
grateful to the History Department for the kindness shown

toward us during the past few months—in particular, the department's support for the proposed Rudolph Wiederholt Memorial Fellowship. Just saying "thank you" is not enough, but at this distance I can hardly do more. So, thank you all.

Cordially,

Eric R. Wiederholt

October 2, 1985

Dear Mom,

I just tapped out the first monthly report to the old farts administering the Brigham and thanked them, as you'd suggested, for their support of the R. W. Fellowship. You're right, of course. I don't know what makes it so difficult for me to be grateful to them. The suspicion, perhaps, that I was the pity candidate for this thing. But I'll stop biting the hand that funds me . . .

I thought you sounded better on the phone on Wednesday. How's the new Reconstruction seminar going?

The Big Knödel is as gray as always: how can the Viennese bear this dirty, oppressive place? Haven't they heard of soap, of paint? It may be the perfect city for black moods. You look around you and think, God, what have I got to complain about?

But really, it's thrilling to be back. Exasperating and depressing it may be, a city for Titans or for the enormous-gloomy stone buildings themselves—not for us poor mortals. But I still love it. I've been to the opera five times already, and the Belvedere Palace is only a hundred yards from my pension . . .

I'm in Elizabethplatz. Remember it? It's around the corner from the Turkish Embassy and Josh's apartment. A new sauna-massage parlor has moved in across from the church. Josh told me he went there once, dropped about fifty bucks, and was only given a massage, poor fellow.

Speaking of disappointments, Herr Steuer took off on a field trip a month ago without telling a soul at the university about my project. The letters from Drury and Steele failed to raise eyebrows to the stratospheric level I was assured they would. So I won't have the respect due one of my august education (nor even a place to set my derrière) until the Universitätsprof comes back in three weeks. I told Brigham one week, just so they wouldn't get in a tizzy. Nothing can be done about it, anyway.

For now, then, it's mainly the archives, the Nationalbibliotek in the Hofburg, the Landesbibliotek in the Rathaus, and a photo collection presided over by an Austro-bitch at the City History Museum. Just think, every time I enter the Nationalbibliotek, I walk under the very balcony from which Hitler proclaimed Austria's union with Germany—if that doesn't keep my nose to the grindstone, nothing will. (The balcony's getting sandblasted these days. Under the black, the stone turns out to be a pretty light cream.)

If Rick ever gets around to calling you, give him my love and try to get an address from him. I'm thinking of you, Mother. Please call whenever you need to talk—the front desk will give me the message.

Love,
Eric

October 18, 1985

Dear Mom,

Don't send any more letters to the Pension Steiner; I'll be moving out in a few days. I still don't know where to, but this place is too noisy to sleep in, let alone get any work done, and I don't think the day clerk (who gives new meaning to the word *Schlamperei*) is getting messages to me. Oberbichler claims he called the pension and left a time when I could meet the depository director, but I didn't hear anything about it and missed the meeting, which means another few days lost until we can set up another one. Arrangements in Vienna always take five times as long as in the rest of the civilized world.

Meanwhile, work is going slowly at the Nat. Lib. It's a

humongous collection—which relieves me, since I was half-guessing when I said that in my fellowship application. But it would help if there were a cataloguing system that post-dated Charlemagne. As it is, I have to spend my time in the subbasements, wading through stacks of papers and booklets in manila envelopes and rotting cardboard boxes filled with disorganized junk—letters, manuscripts, abstracts, newspapers, broadsides, posters—even decades-old school assignments. I keep expecting to discover some previously unknown Mozart juvenilia, or a letter in the king's English proving that it was actually Francis Bacon who wrote *The Sorrows of Young Werther.*

Your letter of the 9th arrived yesterday, and I thought you sounded pretty good, regardless. I think it's only natural still to be having bad spells. The worst thing is to burden yourself additionally with guilt, or doubts about your strength or independence. It's only been two months. A society that puts its old people into detention centers may expect you to forget sooner, but that's repulsive, in a Protestant sort of way.

In Vienna, some widows still wear black for a year, and I think the truism is true: the ritual of mourning externalizes the pain, allows it to be washed away gradually by tears. We Lutherans have a harder time of it, since most ritual embarrasses us. Not to mention emotion. We think we ought to be able to act normally. But then two months later, we still can hardly get out of bed, or we stop suddenly in a corridor of a university and don't believe we can walk the last twenty yards to lecture. *That's* normal.

Blah, blah. You know all this. I'll turn three times, and start again—

It's been an exhilarating day, with a sharp east wind driving the terns from the Danube into the Inner City, where they've been skreeking their little heads off. I walked about five miles, just remembering . . . I stopped at a stand on the Karl Lueger Ring and bought a *Polnischer,* with raw onion slices and hot mustard—I even drank a Coke, which still comes here in the old thick-glassed green sensuous bottles. Remember those? I'd forgotten how much of myself was bound up in this city.

I'll write again soon.

Love,
Eric

November 1, 1985

Brigham Fellowship Committee

Dear Committee,

I moved out of the Pension Steiner on the 25th, by which time the check for November-December had not arrived. I hope the check is not en route, as the odds of it being forwarded correctly to my new address are slim. The check should be sent (ASAP) to me, c/o Jutta Bechtler, Lazarettgasse 17/8, 1080 Wien, Austria. Frau Bechtler rents out rooms, but it is not a pension, and the check should not be addressed to "Pension Bechtler," as it might be returned for address correction (the Austrian post is like that). Unfortunately, there is no phone here.

Universitätsprofessor Herr Doktor Steuer returned to Vienna the middle of last month, and has finally gotten me a u. library pass and a carrel off the reading room. The u.'s collection of Nazi and opposition literature (and/or propaganda) is not as extensive as I had hoped, as much of what the university owns has been catalogued under two or three different titles, without cross-referencing. But the abundance of the National Library makes up for any disappointments there. A certain selectivity of material obtains in the years right around the *Anschluss*, not only in the libraries, but also, I've noticed, in the museums. No surprise, there.

The archive research has proven, unfortunately, to be far more complicated than I had imagined, the complications arising as much from bureaucratic intransigence as from disorganization of the records. The director of the main depository, a Herr von Eberhardt, is a difficult man to work with (or under, or near to, or by the grace of). He seems to regard the depository as his private

7

domain, to be guarded and protected from the public eye
as jealously as he guards the letters (which I would also like
to see) of his once-landed and now merely wealthy family.
(Beware the hobbyist, and his inexplicable passions!) The
work is still in too preliminary a stage for me to venture
any remarks on it. I don't want to prejudice my thinking.
Perhaps next month I will be able to report in more detail.
Cordially,
Eric R. Wiederholt

November 2, 1985

Dear Mom,

From the "city without a soul," I send you greetings on
a dark and windy All Souls' Day. I've never seen a city
with such a cult of death as Vienna. Yesterday, for All
Saints' Day, the trolley service out to the *Zentral Friedhof*
(a cemetery about the size of the Nevada salt flats) was
quadrupled, and when Josh and I went out there, we found
an enormous festival going on: thousands of people milling,
bratwurst stands and beer stalls set up, tables arrayed along
the avenue between the main gates and the Karl Lueger
Church. There were balloons for children, a lottery for a
keg, a band, bus service in and through the cemetery itself.
All this revelry amid the granite canopies, the scrolled iron
arches, the nouveau-riche mausolea as gilded and gaudy as
Hindu temples. Children ran all over the graves, chasing
each other. I saw a little boy, looking over his shoulder, run
smack into a black marble marker—Empire style, with a
bas-relief urn and grieving maid in robes—so hard that he
fell over and his balloon popped. Then two parents,
appearing like genies, and many tears . . . Singles were
putting lilies and red roses in the brass pots on marble
slabs. Couples strolled and read the names: Wittgenstein,
Beethoven, Schubert, Wolf, etc. (Many of them are only
"honor" graves—i.e., no stiff. They're there to boost the
necro-tourism. It's disturbing enough when you find that
Beethoven lived in nearly every apartment in the city; it's
even worse when you discover he's buried in every

graveyard.) Josh thinks it's all a bit gruesome, but I rather like it, this mixing of life and death.

I got your letter with Rick's address. How long has he been back in Boston? Have you seen him since he got back? I don't expect a letter from him, but if you see him . . . but perhaps I'll send him a letter.

Your letters have been talking about U. Mass., but nothing about how you're getting along. Are you OK?

Love,
Eric

November 20, 1985

Dear Mom,

I just received your letter of the 12th, and I don't know what to say, exactly.

To set the record straight: you made it clear to me in May (so, at least, I thought) that you *wanted* me to take this fellowship. It's what Dad wanted, anyway, and it never occurred to me that I wouldn't do what Dad wanted, at the end. Chances were nine out of ten in May that he wouldn't last the summer, so my taking the fellowship practically guaranteed that you would be alone in September. Right?

I *am* getting work done here. If you've got the impression from my letters that I'm blowing off the fellowship, then you must have been reading too much into a few snide comments about the committee. Of course I'm working! The research is progressing slowly but steadily (which I think is saying something, considering the condition of my material, and all the bureaucratic hassles I have to put up with).

I agree that it would be better for you to have me and Rick in Boston for the time being, and you know I would be there if I could. But Dad had his heart in this fellowship —you know he hated most of all to have to leave his work. What else could I promise him?

I've been writing to you at least once a week, and running up phone bills at the p.o. having heart-to-hearts with your machine. Where the hell is Rick? Can't you get him to come out to the house and stay with you for a while? He's only living five miles away, while I'm across the Atlantic Ocean. Maybe you could get him to tell you where he's been since June. That should keep him there for a while.

You will *not*, by the way, be spending Christmas at home alone. I know we talked about this, at least, before I left the U.S. I've had a flight booked for six weeks now for December 19th. I'll be at the house for 12 days. And if Rick doesn't come, I'll go out to Allston and break his door down and drag him home by his hair. And we'll all be together and we'll have a big cry. And perhaps we can persuade Rick to stay with you for a while after I go.

Love,
Eric

p.s. I also don't know where you got this ludicrous idea about Frau Bechtler. She's thirty-eight, and tremendously fat. She's a widow from the Tyrol. The boy you heard was her son, Timo—his father was an Italian, not a Nazi—and she is renting a room to me. We just happened to be at the p.o. together when I called. She is a friendly woman and we talk sometimes in the evening. OK?

December 10, 1985

Brigham Fellowship Committee

Dear Committee,

Sorry the report is a little late this month. I've been so busy the last few days at the archives that I haven't been home much; when I *am* home, it seems I just go right to sleep. It's only been in the past week that I've begun to feel I'm getting to the information I want. Because of the difficulties with the archivist Herr von Eberhardt, every change of direction in the research (e.g., I decide that I do, after all, need to be looking at military enrollment through district station records in the fall of '38 instead of through central administration records, because the latter have turned out to be too unreliable) has involved a substantial loss of time, since von Eberhardt must be notified and the proper permission obtained. I have been told over and over again how fragile much of this material is. I also made the mistake early on of assuming a couple of factors were constant that I discovered later were not constant at all. Perhaps an interesting discovery in itself, but one that required that I do a good deal of the research over again. I regret that mistake, but I suppose it goes with the territory. I never heard of archive research that didn't involve a good deal of wasted effort.

So the upshot is, I'm not yet willing to venture remarks in much detail. I'm hopeful, however, that the work of the next few weeks will yield more usable results than all that has gone before. As my work here is about to be interrupted by the Christmas break—I'm sure you all will understand why I have promised my mother I'll be home for the holidays, from December 14th to January 3rd—I will probably not be able to talk in more concrete terms until the February report.

The November-December check reached me at Frau Bechtler's on the 20th. I would greatly appreciate it if I could get the January-February check a little bit earlier, as my funds were practically exhausted by the time this last check came.

Merry Christmas and Happy Hanukah to the members of the committee!

Cordially,
Eric R. Wiederholt

p.s. On second thought, perhaps it would be more convenient for us both if I picked up the check in person at the department office while I'm in the Boston area for the Christmas holidays. I'll call the secretary about it when I get to the U.S.

Enough. Enough!

If I may pose a rhetorical question: can there be anything as weak, as pathetic, as a lie? To lie is to admit that you have lost control—to do what you don't believe in, or not to do what you yourself think you should. You are dead; un-human; an object being acted on, not acting.

By the last letter, everything was a lie. The "difficulties" with Herr von Eberhardt, the "fragility of the material," the "district station records" (whatever *that* means): I was making it all up.

There are lies in the very first letter, such as the claim to have visited Oberbichler at the city archives, when in fact I had only spoken to him, in the briefest way, over the telephone. But those, perhaps, are no more than the meat-scrap euphemisms that all procrastinating students toss at their ravenous professors. At the beginning, of course, I still expected I would actually do the research.

But things degenerate rapidly. The complaint about the noise in the Pension Steiner is pure fantasy—I wasn't getting any work done because it made me sick. The cataloguing system at the National Library was modern and convenient. And I managed to miss the meeting with the archivist (a patient, obliging man) without any help from the "day clerk," whose existence is doubtful—I just plain forgot.

At least some of the inventions are amusing. I like my references to Jutta as "Frau Bechtler." I can smile at the subconscious guilt, the fear of discovery, that drove me in the November 1 report to go out of my way to explain that, although "Frau Bechtler" hadn't a pension, she *was* renting me a room. As if anyone would suspect—or more to the point, care—that I wasn't paying Jutta, other than by helping her make the beast with two backs every night, while poor Timo waited in the hall.

But most of the lies are simply depressing. The juggling of dates shows a trivial-mindedness that surprises me. The lie about the telephone—Jutta had one, of course—was utter cowardice: I felt more protected knowing that no one could reach me unexpectedly. Some of the letters to my mother—I haven't reproduced them here—are just too painful to read now, too damaging to my image of myself. I should not even have copied them. But my father had taught me to keep a record of everything, and I somehow managed to stick to that lesson, like an automaton, even while I was busy jettisoning everything else he believed in.

Only one part of the correspondence rings true, and it stops me now, compels me to rethink matters. In the October 18th letter, I exhorted my mother not to blame herself for having trouble coming to terms with her husband's death. Those words remind me that I was going through as difficult a period as my mother, the difference between us being that she tried, and failed, to lose herself in her responsibilities, whereas I tried, and failed, to lose myself in irresponsibility. The words remind me that against my Lutheran, northern nature, I shouldn't perhaps be so hard on myself.

But—my own affairs can come later. There are other affairs to talk about first. I wandered in Jutta's soul as I walked the Viennese streets: taking a small and guilty comfort in contemplating what might have been my lot, but by the grace of God was not.

☐

One of the annexes of the National Library opens onto Josefsplatz, which lies along the edge of the old Imperial Palace, the "Hofburg." Approaching the annex on certain optimistic mornings, I would look up and see Atlas, who glowers down into the square from the palace roof, high above. My usual response was to identify with him—he with his copper-oxide wrecking ball, I with the literally tons of documents waiting for me behind those eighteenth-century walls. This particular Atlas looks like he is slowly dying from his efforts, and I would let him be a lesson to me. Scant yards from where I had been headed, I would decide not to take up the burden. Whenever I was more honest with myself and admitted that I would not be doing any work all day, I would head off for some other part of the city. But on the days I kidded myself into believing that *today* I really would do some work, just not this second, I was feeling a little sleepy and if I went in right now, the warmth of the reading room would send me off, better to wait a bit until I had digested my breakfast—then I wouldn't stray too far. And behold, across the square stand the stable doors of the Spanish Riding School. The workouts are cheaper than a cup of coffee, cooler than the library, and warmer than a park bench; and though boring, incomparably less so than the research I was supposed to be doing.

So it was that on the 25th of October I met Jutta. And on the 26th, I actually moved in with her. I had thought I knew myself better than that. But perhaps self-knowledge is founded on the realization that there are certain things one is just never going to learn.

That morning at the Riding School, a little boy wasn't paying attention to the workout. He was running back and forth along the balconies. He wasn't making much noise in his beat-up slippers, not

giggling or chattering—nonetheless, the row of elderly Viennese ladies sitting in their loden coats by the exit eyed him distastefully as he
flitted past. I could feel for the boy: Vienna wasn't the easiest town
to live in if you were a little kid with milk-chocolate skin and kinky
hair.

He stopped twenty feet away from me, surprised by my stare. Two
grave eyes. Those were the first things I noticed about him. Then two
other circles: the black of nostrils in a turned-up Caucasian nose. And
then the clothes: he looked as if he'd dressed by standing in the corner
and having people throw their old things at him. I decided to try
making friends. I gave him a Disarming Smile. I asked him how it was
going. He irradiated me for about two seconds with this utterly blank
gaze. Then he coughed. Then he bolted.

I watched him circle the hall. Every time he looked back, I
pointed at him and smiled. He started hiding behind pillars. After a
few seconds, he would look out, and I would point and smile again. I
meant him to realize it was a game: he was supposed to smile back,
or point back, or both. Or *something*. But he only stared gravely.

Opposite the hall from me, fifty feet across the basin of chocolate
dirt and white horses, he stopped by the side of a pale woman with
a spray of unkempt hair who was clutching the banister and staring
down at the big, graceful animals. He didn't speak to her, or touch her,
and she ignored him. But they were obviously a pair—she was the only
adult in the hall dressed the way he was. The boy knelt, half hiding
behind the stone pilasters, and he stared at me through them for the
rest of the rehearsal, kneeling close to the woman's parti-colored skirt
but not touching it—watching me as if I were some malevolent spirit
which he held at bay only through the power of his gaze.

Children and dogs are often said to be able to sense instinctively
if a person is good or evil. I thought of that famous sequence of photographs showing Adolph Hitler bending down to pet his own dog, his
German shepherd, Blondi. As his hand nears her back, Blondi begins
to crouch, and as he bends over farther, she crouches lower. In the last
photograph, she is prostrate on the ground, her ears flat against her
skull, as Hitler's hand finally touches her, strokes her. Perhaps Blondi
did somehow sense that this man would eventually poison her with
cyanide.

Anyway, I have a quiet, watchful demeanor that dogs and babies
usually like. Babies pull my wire-rimmed glasses off my face and put

them in their mouths. Dogs climb all over me. This, of course, means I'm a good person. I depend on such external evidence for my self-esteem. The boy had hurt my feelings.

By noon, when the workout ended, there weren't many of us left in the hall: hold-outs from a bus-load of Swedes, the old *Wiener* women—who always go the distance—the entranced woman, the suspicious boy.

I had nothing to do. Nothing except tons of research on Austrian Nazi Party members from 1934 to 1938, and that seemed to be out of the question. So on a whim, I followed the woman and the boy out of the hall. I was curious about this boy who could not recognize a good, kind person when he saw one.

They crossed Michaelerplatz and went through the arch into the Hofburg, then out the other side onto the open Heldenplatz. The woman walked slowly, seemingly in another world, while the boy darted around the statues of Archduke Karl and Prince Eugen, climbed and slipped and fell off Karl's plinth, ran ahead of her, behind her. He called to her, *"Mutti, mutti!,"* sometimes coughing, but she didn't answer. They crossed the Volksgarten, and I hung back, by the high, wrought-iron fencing, while they waited for the streetcar. A D came, and they boarded in the middle, I at the back. They switched at Schottentor to the #43. About a kilometer up Alserstrasse, past the hospital, they got off. I descended from the rear.

The boy spotted me immediately.

I did the only logical thing: I pointed at him and smiled.

Surprise, I could have accepted. Wonder. Curiosity. But terror? Of quiet, watchful me?

Yet his eyes widened and he backed up into the woman's legs, grabbing her capacious skirt behind him like a character in some bedroom farce about to disappear behind the draperies. She began to turn as I stepped forward to get out of the street, and her turning and my stepping, actions that were putting the two of us on a collision course, seemed to goad the boy into action.

He jumped off the sidewalk, took three coordinating steps, like a soccer player about to pass the ball, and kicked me hard just above the instep, with his ratty, brown, apparently steel-toed slipper.

"Well aimed," I thought, as I went down on one knee. I put a hand on the asphalt to keep my balance, so he kicked me again, with the same dismaying accuracy, in the funny bone. He drew back for another.

"Tiiimo!" A high drawn-out sound, falling on the last letter, like an air-raid siren. The slippers ascended out of range. Timo dangled from his collar. *"Timo, was ist denn los mit dir?"* The top button-hole ripped, and Timo fell back to earth, but bound by hands with cheap, silver-colored rings on third and fourth fingers.

"Timo, what is the matter with you?" She did not speak *Wienerisch,* the old German dialect of Vienna. "My God—" she said, as I got back on my feet, "my God—I just don't understand it! Are you all right?" She looked imploringly into my face. "I can't imagine why he —you're not hurt, are you?"

"No, not at all. I only fell because my ankle buckled. It does that sometimes even without encouragement."

The boy glared up at me. His skin was a curious patchwork of dark- and light-brown. It looked unnatural, like a skin graft—an argument for the Viennese miscegenophobes, I imagined.

"I still, I—I don't know what to say. He's never done anything like this before." Her voice was rather weak, with a soft rasping. I thought: She is a smoker.

"I must have startled him," I said. "We met already this morning, at the Spanish Riding School. Then we happened to get on the same streetcar, and off here, at the same stop. When he saw me again, just now, I suppose somehow it scared him. He must have thought I was following you." (Isn't that ridiculous, ha ha ha.)

She shook her head. "Television! He watches it all the time." She bent over the boy, still holding him against her legs, and surrounded him with her high, coaxing voice. "Timo, please don't be ridiculous, this man has nothing to do with us; could you please give him an apology?"

"That's unnecess—"

"No, he really must. I've got to get him to stop behaving like this. Timo?"

But Timo wouldn't say a word. The woman kissed him tenderly. "Please, Timo?" She stroked his hair. "Timo? Am I going to have to beat you black and blue?"

"Really, you don't—"

"Am I going to have to tip you upside down and drop you head first on the pavement?" She kissed him again, on the forehead, pre-

16

sumably where his head would split open. "Are you going to apologize, Timo?"

When he finally spoke, he was calm. "No."

She sighed and released him. Now angry at both of us, he ran a few feet ahead and stopped, turned toward the window of a coffee shop. He was a man out doing errands and hadn't the slightest idea who we were. "I'm sorry, sometimes he just won't listen."

"It's all right, really. This has happened before? You said you had to get him to stop behaving like this."

She surprised me by reaching out and touching my hand. For just a moment. She smiled ruefully, as if she were about to tell me that I had bad breath, or a weak chin, but didn't want to hurt my feelings. "He doesn't much like men. *He* is my man now, you know. But you are the first one he's actually . . . well, attacked." She said "men" and "one" as if referring to an alien species. "Do you live around here?" she asked.

"No, I'm . . . doing research. On the years just before the Second World War. There are records in the hospital about discharges from military service—for reasons of health—between the years 1936 and 1939 that I have to look through. Very boring work."

"But you've gotten off at the wrong stop for the hospital."

"Yes, I know. But I have to pick up a key for the records room. The archivist is sick today, and I said I'd come by. He lives up here, somewhere."

"What street?"

"I can't remember." I slapped a pocket. "I've got it written down. Up this way," and I pointed farther on.

"That's the way we're walking." She took Timo's hand. Timo looked away. I walked on her left, while Timo swung far out to her right. "You're a student?"

"Yes."

"So am I! Isn't that something!"

"Mmm."

"But you're not German, are you?"

I had thought my German was good enough to hide that. "No, I'm American. My father was German—Lübeck. And you, I think, are not Austrian; or at least, not Viennese."

She laughed, the rasp in her voice becoming more pronounced. The long, loose skirt spiraled, one way, then the other, as she walked.

A sexy walk. "I? No—not Viennese, thank God. But Austrian, yes. My real mother and I both grew up in the Tyrol, in Innsbruck."

We had reached a corner. "Timo and I turn here." Timo took his cue and began to tug her backward down the side street.

But this was a mistake—the woman pulled him up short. *"Tiimo!* Please! Don't boss me around!" Timo turned away, donning again his independence. He put his hand on the front of his pants, held his penis through the fabric.

There was a pause, and I waited. If she didn't invite me, I'd have nothing to do. Go back to the pension and masturbate, thinking about the walk, the swirling skirt.

She gave me a long look. She had deep-set eyes, a protruding lower lip, a smile that seemed to evaluate me. She said, "It's nearly 1:00. You're welcome to come have lunch with us if you would like to."

Immediately from behind her there came a whine. "Noo, Mommy. Pleeease!"

She might have been asking me in order to show the boy he couldn't decide such things—to put him on the defensive. "I don't want the boy to be unhappy."

"Timo? He has to get used to it. It does him good to have a man in the house."

"Mommy, he can't come to our house!"

"Be quiet, Timo!"

Actually, I didn't care in the least about Timo. This was all his fault for not smiling back at me in the first place, for kicking me when I was down. "Fine," I said.

"You don't need to pick up the key first?"

"It'll wait. I didn't tell him when I was coming."

I saw, as she turned away, a little purse of her lips, an expression of triumph. But whether she was triumphing over Timo, or over me, or over someone else who wasn't present, I didn't know. Timo repeated, unhappily, "Noo, Mommy!"

"Timo," she said brightly, "if you say that again I'll rip off your arms and beat you over the head with them. Understand?"

☐

"They are such beautiful animals, so strong. Did you see the way the muscles in their thighs ripple? Like milk. But best of all is the control.

All that strength balanced! It gives me goosebumps, it really does. I love control like that: so strong and yet gentle." Her eyes shone.

"Gentle?"

"Don't you think so? When they walk, like this—" she demonstrated on the table with her long-fingered hands—"the leg curled up, a pause at each step and then a hop. What could be more gentle? I used to visit them in the stables, before they were closed to the public. They aren't skittish or unpleasant, like thoroughbreds. You could stroke their muzzles and they would look at you very patiently, very quietly. Like princes."

I was intrigued. "Why not? Pure blood lines; white as the driven snow, and so on—"

"Although they're born jet-black, you know. They turn blazing white at three or four. It's almost miraculous."

"Like an apotheosis?"

"Well, they're pretty when they're black, too. Timo—aren't you going to eat your food?" She slid the plate closer to him. "And the people who work there are pleasant. It's a cosmopolitan place. The riders are Viennese, Czech, Hungarian, Yugoslav, even Gypsy. They've seen everything. Their love is the horses, anyway; they don't concern themselves about other people."

Meaning the boy?

We were on Lazarettgasse, behind the Children's Hospital, on the top floor of an old apartment house. Jutta and Timo lived in six shabby rooms with four others, all of whom were out at the moment. Toys and clothes were scattered across the floor. Dirty dishes piled up out of the sink and spread across the counter, while others huddled like refugees under the kitchen table. Out of the box on the fridge came Blue Danube Radio, the English-language station: practice for Jutta. Today's program was "How *You* Can Save the Vienna Woods." Timo, ignoring his food, played with a cigarette lighter, turning the little wheel to enlarge the flame. He coughed, periodically. I could hear the mucus whipping in his lungs.

"That's a bad cough," I said.

"Hmm? Oh, that." She glanced at the boy as if suddenly remembering his presence. "Yes, he can't seem to shake it."

"It must be hard to, when the weather is so cold and wet."

Timo spoke up: "Don't talk about me!"

Jutta gave me a sign that meant, "Humor him."

So instead, we talked about her. She was twenty-four. She was a student at the University of Vienna, where she was learning English and French. She was partly state-supported (because of her studying, and also because of Timo); for the rest, she worked varying hours at the day-care center in which she left Timo on her way to classes. Timo's father was absent.

"Oh, the key!" she exclaimed. "Hadn't you better get it?"

Not on your life—"He said I could come any time, any day. He's not waiting for me."

There was a knock at the door. Jutta returned with a mustachioed man, whom she introduced as Giancarlo. He sat with us, a slight, attractive man, between Jutta and Timo, his arm casually around Jutta.

Except for mention of the cough, I had been leaving the boy alone, but Giancarlo addressed himself to him. "Hey there, little fellah, what you got there?"

Timo ignored him. Flick, flick. He turned the wheel again.

"You shouldn't play with that thing, you might hurt yourself." His German had an Italian bounce to it.

Timo flicked again, and startled us all: the flame shot up, suddenly very high, into his face. He pulled his head back and cut off the flame. "What did I tell you?" Giancarlo tried to take it from him, but Timo slid away. He turned the wheel back, judiciously, and flicked again.

"Would you like more wine?" Jutta asked me, pouring herself another glass. "Giancarlo?"

One of the refugee glasses on the floor was rescued, dashed under water at the faucet, and filled for Giancarlo. He and Jutta smoked. He was a little nervous, a little uncertain. I guessed he was a new boyfriend. He continued to address his comments to Timo. Perhaps, like a coffee-table book or block-and-string puzzle, Timo was a convenient conversation piece for Giancarlo, as he groped for things to say to Jutta.

"You don't want to talk to me?"

Silence. Flick.

"That's all right. You don't have to. We have time."

Perhaps he had decided that the boy was the key to Jutta's heart. Or perhaps he only suspected that, whether the boy was a key or not, he would have peace in the apartment only if Timo accepted him.

But I had an idea that laying siege wasn't the right tactic.

I almost left. Goddamnit back alone on the streetcar and another afternoon with the door locked. This was driving me out of my mind.

But Giancarlo stood after a few minutes, kissed Jutta, and said he had to go. He shook my hand, and his quizzical look said, "Where do *you* fit in?" Jutta had not spoken to him much, and she took his kiss patiently. Did he have as much time to win over Timo as he thought?

Then he was gone.

"He's nice enough," she said, coming back from the door dreamily. "I met him last night in a discotheque."

He'd left his cigarette case, a dressy flat of gold on the table. Jutta took it up; again, that look of triumph. "We lay together last night, after the disco. And then today he thinks of me as his girl. With most men it's either/or. You lie with them and they think that changes everything. But—I think Giancarlo's not very confident." She put the case on a shelf. "He has to leave that behind so he can come back tonight." She sat again. "Timo, are you going to eat your food?"

"I don't want to."

"Men and their tricks!" She smiled, bemused. I enjoyed the way she talked about men. It was the way men talk about women—reductionist, making them all of a class. Jutta's talk accentuated the fact that she was, after all, a woman and I a man and that we might make something of that. It made me feel attractive, alluring. I wondered if that was how women felt when men treated them with similar condescension.

Then suddenly, she looked worried. "Giancarlo expects too much of me. We can be together for a while. Fine. I like him. But after a while, I get tired; no matter who it is. I want to be free again, to be alone, or to have someone else." She glanced at me coyly, and then away, smiling as if relishing the taste of something in her mouth. "Men are so sentimental about it: about sex. Don't you think?" She put her hand in Timo's curly hair, gently waggled his head. "Men say it's betrayal. They feel so violently! But you can't betray when you haven't promised. I don't want commitment; I want to have fun."

Timo coughed. Jutta took a corner of the greasy, plasticized table cloth and wiped his running nose.

"Italian men are the most sentimental: they come up to Vienna to meet the friendly Austrian women, to get away from the mothers and fiancées in Italy. And then they treat you like a wife! *Timo!* Are you going to eat your food, or am I going to have to ram it down your throat?"

"I don't *want* it, Mommy."

"Go play in another room, then."

Timo didn't move.

Jutta clenched her teeth and threw her head back, suddenly furious. "Timo, *please!* Mommy wants to be alone with Eric!"

Timo slid off the bench, sulking, and started out. Then he turned back. "Mommy?"

"What?"

"Please don't lie with him, Mommy."

"Of course I won't, Timo," Jutta said. She pulled him back to her and kissed him, on his runny Caucasian nose. The anger had left as quickly as it had come. "I promise."

He went out.

"Where was I?"

"Italian men."

"Oh, yes." She pulled the wild frizz of her hair forward over her shoulders, tugged meditatively on the straggling ends. "Something strange. I've been with four Italian men so far. And all four of them have wanted to butt-fuck me. Isn't that curious? They always say that I'll enjoy it, that I only have to relax. But I don't enjoy it. It hurts a little." She flipped the hair back again, and shrugged, smiled, sipped wine. "I suppose I don't relax enough."

Unexpectedly, a hurt expression passed over her face. "Why do men always demand? Why do they assume I want to do what they want? Why don't they ask me what *I* want?" A glint lined the bottom of each eye.

The suddenness of her moods startled me. There was a pause, during which I could think of nothing to say. I caught her eye, and she looked back at me. Expectantly? She was quite attractive, in a downtrodden and frazzled sort of way. Through the shout of hormones, I could feel the glimmerings of real sympathy for her, for what was probably not an easy life in this sexist and racist city.

Several seconds passed, the two of us motionless. The edge of her tongue ran along the protuberant lower lip.

I thought: Should I ask, should I demand? I reached out for her pale hand and she curled dry fingers around my palm. I leaned forward an inch. She didn't move. Her eyes were black, shining, agitated.

Was this what she wanted? I took her lower lip softly between my lips. Yes? A hand touched my neck, kept me from retreating. I could feel against my mouth, swelling, that dreamy slow exultant smile.

☐

First she had to take care of Timo, who had been promised, and the cough which she had previously ignored now became instrumental. From a city of bottles on the window ledge behind the kitchen sink, she extracted one of puce syrup. "It makes him sleepy," she told me.

After a few minutes—to be precise, twenty-three and a half—Timo was asleep, and we crept to Jutta's room. Her bed was a thin mattress on a raised wooden platform, surrounded by books and piled with clothes. The clothes we scattered, along with our own, and we paused on the mattress to let our bodies and the cool sheets warm. Now was the time, if not an hour ago—I finally summoned up the will-power to go through it all again, to set up my roadblock and only pray that she would run it.

Jutta, I had guessed, was not one who would sympathize with a digression. There had been no pause for a diaphragm, no mention of a condom—I'd noticed her pill-wheel on a bureau, and with its sober help she probably took her fucking as close to zipless as she could get it. She would no doubt have laughed at the cautionary "what does this mean" talk that I and my collegiate partners used to indulge in before sex. But oh God, how I wished I could wallow in that trivial crap, again! I had something else up my sleeve—

"I've tested positive for exposure to the AIDS virus. Most likely, I'm a carrier. Surprise!"

As the *National Enquirer* said to Rock Hudson, this was supposed to come before the kiss. Although the latest I had read was that kisses were all right. Then again, that was what they wrote in the articles devoted to quieting public panic. The pamphlets written expressly for the lepers still told us to keep our goddamned mouths shut. Until the next batch of statistics came in, anyway.

I belonged to none of the high-risk categories. I was asymptomatic. Still, the physician who had broken the news to me had said that I should limit my sexual partners. "Limit"! I got a kick out of that. Oh yes doctor, how about from five a month to three? Would that be enough? "Limiting" had turned out to be rather easy. I was honest

23

about the test, and partners ran like hell. I learned to accept celibacy like everything else I couldn't do anything about. I didn't so much as rub noses for months. But the insidious voice we all share grew slowly louder: You're a fool; nobody else is so conscientious; the test must have been wrong! And then all the news magazines told me it was really OK, after all, to stick my tongue in someone else's mouth. I finally chose to believe them. And here I was, in bed with a naked woman and an erection, and the surest six-word line under the sun for keeping the two permanently apart.

"You might get it from me." In my experience, things had never gone beyond that point.

But I had never met a woman like Jutta before. She delved her hands into my hair, as she had done with Timo. "Shhh," she said soothingly, beneath me. "Don't talk about it." She drew my head down to her breast, inviting me to be babyish. "It's all right," she said distantly, stroking my hair. "Don't worry about me. I want to lie with you."

I could have argued. But I wasn't that much of a fool. I did what I could to protect her. I produced a condom. She put on a look of disgust and laughingly pushed it away. But I insisted. By now, we were warm, and presently we began to sweat.

☐

I moved in the next day.

Jutta was waiting for me at the top of the stairs, with a sly smile that I couldn't read: a little contemptuous, perhaps, of these men who were so easily landed. An American Tourister filled with my books and papers went under Jutta's bed, a backpack was emptied into a couple of dresser drawers, my toothbrush found a niche at the sink, and I had settled in. I could move out just as easily the moment either of us wanted it.

Jutta's roommates—two other women—had accepted my indefinite residence guardedly, when Jutta had informed them of it at supper the evening before. They seemed used to men appearing out of nowhere and staying for a few days or weeks, emptying the refrigerator, doing nothing, but being coddled by Jutta. I had felt somewhat like a gigolo at that dinner, and had not been proud. Jutta had sat next to me and kissed me again and again, as if to show off her new acquisition from Masculand. But the roommates behaved well, as women so often do, even when men are blundering in on their territory.

Giancarlo showed up at eight, dressed for a night out, to reclaim his cigarette case. "Where do you fit in?" became "How did you do this?" and he looked so hurt, turning back down the stairs, that I almost reproached Jutta for her cruelty.

"Why don't you go out with him?" I said. "He seems like a nice guy."

She pushed out the lower lip, frowned. "Men will stick together for the strangest things."

"How *did* I do this, anyway? Why not Giancarlo?"

Jutta kissed me on the cheek. "You didn't want to butt-fuck me," she said.

Jutta's roommates were named Ulrike and Renate. Ulrike had a four-year-old son, Theodor; Renate, an infant daughter, Elizabeth. Theodor was big for four, towheaded, rather clumsy and slow, with the pouty sort of face that can make a child's gender debatable. A quiet boy with a penchant for hanging behind doorjambs, he had the deadpan expression of a dog I had encountered once on Corsica that had waited politely until I had turned my back before politely biting me. Like Timo, Theodor had a persistent cough, with which he seemed to experiment—for example, he would work his way through the kitchen spices, opening up each bottle and gravely coughing into the contents.

Elizabeth was tiny and slept a lot. She had fine black hair and a complexion like the Viennese *Melange* coffee. She, like Timo, had a black father. She did not yet eat anything but Renate's milk, so her diaper changing was not unpleasant: her urine was odorless, creamy, and good for her skin; her shit was thin and green and smelled exactly like a cultured dairy product available at the local supermarket.

Her mother was a nurse, on maternity leave from her position at the General Hospital. A slim, energetic woman, Renate came from the Burgenland, where people believed in plenty of fresh cold air for infants, so most mornings she took Elizabeth into the hills around Vienna, and spent the day pushing the perambulator among the vineyards of Grinzing or the acid-ravaged evergreens of Kahlenberg and Hermannskogel. ("Here's how *you* can help save the Vienna woods!") Afternoons, she read medical journals, baked bricks of whole-wheat bread, and knit jumpers and booties. Whenever the alarm on her credit-card-sized calculator tooted, she would drop whatever she was doing and rouse the baby for breast-feeding. A chart magneted to the refrigerator recorded five times daily the length of nursing time—that meant actually sucking milk, not falling asleep with the nipple lodged in the mouth; also daily, the number of shits and pisses, with comments; and weekly, Elizabeth's weight, which showed an abnormally slow rise.

"She weighed under two kilos when she was born," Renate told me, lightly pinching Elizabeth's cheeks to wake her so that she would take more milk. "My opening was only eight centimeters, but she popped out, anyway. They didn't even have to cut me." Elizabeth was resisting consciousness; she stirred at the pinches and slept on. Renate's nipple, poking out as big as a red thimble from under her sweater, shot out a filament of milk, then two, sprinkling the towel and the baby's face. "Oh help!" I ran for toilet paper.

Ulrike was actually married, the only one of the three. But her husband worked the family farm in a Carinthian village, while she studied psychology at the University of Vienna. On alternate Friday evenings, Ulrike and Theodor would take a train to Wolfsberg, where Ulrike's husband, Kurt, would pick them up and drive them out to the farm. They would return on Sunday night, Ulrike complaining that she hadn't done enough studying, Theodor looking tired and sore from having helped his father with the farm work. "He really blossoms on the farm," Ulrike assured us. "He wants to do everything! The city's not good for a farm boy." And Theodor would sit with his weary head on his mother's shoulder and say nothing.

The last member of the household was Ziu, a sleek black tom that Ulrike had named after the Teutonic god of war—inappropriately, as it turned out, as Ziu had grown into the mildest tom the world had ever seen. All the women loved him, especially Jutta, who praised his neatness and nonchalance. "I would love to be a cat," she said.

Meanwhile, each night I was rousing myself from the male response at about two and bare-footing it down the hall to the common-room futon, so that Timo, who invariably joined his mother in bed around three, wouldn't find me next to her, contrary to her promise. On the futon, later, I would start awake: the children's door had banged. Then a whine, half-asleep and receding to the back of the apartment: "Mommy!"

But of course our bald fiction lasted no time at all. One night, at some uncertain hour between the love-making and my intended creep to the futon, a knock brought us both awake. Jutta sat up with a wild, frightened expression. "My God, that's Timo!"

An unhappy voice, muffled by the door: "Mommy? Can I come in?"

"Wait, Timo!"

"Let him in," I said sleepily. "He knows I'm in here."

Of course he did. He saw the fondling during the day. He must have known it led to the bedroom. I was tired of the charade. The only arrangement Timo expected us to honor was that I be out of the bed by three, so he could have his mother to himself. He was early tonight, that was all. Once again, this was his fault.

I opened the door. I was naked. He was wearing his alligator pajamas and dangling his doll, Heidi, by her golden hair. I bowed him into the room. "She's all yours, partner," I said, and clumped down the hall.

The next day was All Saints' Day, and after I spent the morning generating horseshit for the edification of the Brigham Committee, I took a streetcar with Timo and Jutta to the Central Cemetery, to savor the Viennese death-fest. That day, Timo ran hard into a marble slab, and I was the first one at the scene, so I picked him up. I think it was the first time I had touched him and he acknowledged it, not by crying, as in the letter, but by punching me in the leg.

□

I wasn't doing any work, but for a while I continued to haunt the appropriate places. Josh was hoping that out of my research would come a fabulously popular and influential work—something "seminal," he kept saying—that would at long last tell the story of what Austria and the Austrians had been doing during the war. I quickly disabused him of the notion that I was going to change the world. But I did enjoy contemplating, with a certain morbid fascination, the city's monolithic amnesia. The bookstores had nothing on the war years, of course. There were plenty of books on *fin de siècle* Vienna, and on Schubert's Vienna, and Mozart's Vienna; and much hype was revolving at that time around a new coffee-table crusher entitled *Austria II,* which exhaustively detailed the history of the country since 1945, the year in which Austria ceased to have any historical importance whatsoever. More fun than the bookstores was the City History Museum, which claimed to cover Vienna "from prehistory to the present." By "present," the museum apparently meant 1920, after which I could find nothing except a single surrealist painting dated 1942, showing the interior of a room, its ceiling hung with webs, cocoons, and dead birds. Then there was the National Library catalogue, which listed all material on National Socialism, the *Anschluss,* and the war under "Occupation: Germany." But the biggest laughs in town were to be had down the hall, in the library reading room. There, bound in marbled volumes lining the left-hand wall, were the copies of all the Austrian newspapers, dating back to the early part of the century. There, just fifty feet from those thousands of three-by-five cards headed "Occupation: Germany," I spent merry afternoons reading the ecstatic prose of Austria's leading journalists, written during their nation's last days of independence in March, 1938: swooning accounts of the Führer, of every word he said, every gesture, every eructation, on his jubilant march toward the capital; endless reprints of Göring's speeches, plus descriptions of his handsome self; articles promising the "purification" of Austria, as though Austria were a love-sick bride, fearful that she wouldn't bleed enough on her wedding night. And in the corners of newspaper pages, the advertisements: "Café Weckler is now Café Berlin!"; "Herzmansky's Department Store: pure Aryan once more!"; and the notices: "All non-Aryan judges to be removed from their posts!"; "Jews Out of University Life!" After hours of perusal, I could cross the Ring and visit the university that still had virtually no Jews on the faculty or in the student body. Or I could shop at Herzmansky's, which, despite the fact that it no longer trumpeted the fact, was in all likelihood still *Judenrein.* Not because Jews were kept out, of course, but because there were no longer any Jews. At the time of the *Anschluss,* 180,000 Jews lived in Vienna. By the end of the war, 600 remained. "Clearly *someone* has to do this research," I said to Josh. "Someone has to tell this story." He nodded enthusiastically. I added silently, It's just not going to be me.

□

On the front door of Lazarettgasse 17, a brass plate identified the superintendent, but he lived in a different part of the city and never answered his telephone. In three years, none of the women had ever seen him.

The building had neither bathtubs nor showers. That was typical of these *Zinskasernen,* the shoddy and ugly "rent barracks" built in the 1880s. But the women had an illegal tub hidden behind a curtain in Ulrike's room. Ulrike's husband had built it without a license. He'd knocked a hole in the wall underneath the stairwell sink and run a branch pipe into the apartment. He'd attached a sixty-gallon water heater to the pipe and an enormous, green, claw-footed bathtub (secreted, at night, from a demolition site) to the water heater. Since he hadn't been able to run a drain pipe either through the floor or through the stairwell's stone wainscot, he'd been forced to place the tub on a platform higher than the wainscot—which was already halfway to the ceiling. The result was a tub that looked like a Rube Goldberg improbability: a high altar of cleanliness that happened to be poisonous green and sprouted pipes like large intestines.

The tub wasn't the only irregularity. My first job as Man Around Apartment was to open the door to the stairwell toilet, which had been jammed for weeks. An iron key protruded from the lock in the door, but the key was bent and immovable. After much struggling with a pair of pliers I finally succeeded in snapping the key, thereby rendering any further attempts futile. Ulrike, infuriated, suggested I split the door open with an axe. I suggested we continue using the toilet on the floor below. As no one had an axe, my suggestion prevailed. Unfortunately, the floor below was empty, and freezing air came through the broken window in the toilet. There was also no light, so at night one had to remember to bring a flashlight.

Half the building, in fact, was empty. It was slated for demolition, and as the tenants one by one moved out, no one was found to replace them. It was rumored that the General Hospital, which owned most of the land in the vicinity, was going to build an extension along the entire block. When, no one knew. All prognostications were doubtful, since the new constructions for the General Hospital lay at the center of the biggest corruption scandal in the city's history—which, in Vienna, was really saying something. Lazarettgasse 17 had probably been saved more than once by legal delays, as commissions went to court, politicians went to the dogs, and contractors went to jail.

The only tenants left in the building were a Turk, a Jordanian, a

Yugoslav family, and one old Viennese woman who would greet me, whenever we passed in the damp cold halls, as if she were Stanley and I Livingstone. As I came up the stairs at night, with Vienna's blustery winter wind moaning through the broken windows, the fluorescent hall lights flickering only half on, I felt sometimes as if I were in a story by Stanislaw Lem, or William Golding: that the stairs would keep turning up forever, from one dim and empty floor to the next, that I somehow knew I had to continue although I had no idea where I was or what I was doing.

The neighborhood, like the building, was poor and racially mixed. The establishments along Lazarettgasse had names like "China Restaurant Hollywood," "Café Habakuk," "Coiffeur Paola," or "René's Sex Boutique." A corner grocery was run by an Iranian couple whose surpassingly beautiful daughter rang up the cash register; occasionally, buying Iranian bread, I would fantasize about asking her to marry me. But the biggest establishment on the street—the closest thing Lazarettgasse had to a landmark—was the Fox Club, at the end of the block. The Fox Club was *"eine Piano Bar mit Séparée,"* in which a five-dollar bottle of champagne plus female company to share it with could be had for a hundred dollars. The club marquee was rimmed with rows of naked lightbulbs that flashed; display windows featured dusty champagne bottles wrapped in toilet paper; and flanking the door were two posters: a chorine with bared breasts about to put glistening lips around a banana, and an artful depiction of Stonehenge at sunset with, in the foreground, a woman apparently enjoying anal intercourse with a lion.

Just beyond the Fox Club lay the Gürtel, Vienna's outer "Ring," along which strolled many of the more desperate of the city's one thousand registered prostitutes. They appeared exactly at 9:00 P.M.; their legal hours were as strictly regulated as the stores'. I had found that walking the Gürtel at night was like running a gauntlet, and even the mention of AIDS failed to get the women off my back, as they usually thought I was joking. After all, I didn't look the part. In Central Europe, the conception of AIDS victims may be different from that of America, but it is no less primitive: not the musclemen in leather or the slim mustachioed dudes in flannel shirts and jeans who haunt the dreams of the Mid-West, but the garish transvestites who, from Berlin to Naples, bum a light from out of the evening shadows and then, as you lean close to cup the flame, ask if you want your cock sucked.

□

One morning, Renate was on the telephone.

". . . four point two kilos . . . It *is* going up, only slowly. . . . I don't want her back there. . . . I think she's doing fine."

Jutta, Timo, and I were breakfasting in Jutta's bedroom. Renate's voice floated from the kitchen.

". . . but that's not uncommon. I'll tell you when to get worried . . . what? . . . no . . . I said no. . . ."

"It's her parents," said Jutta, stirring sugar into her coffee. She wore a beat-up old silk bathrobe, something an earlier boyfriend had given her. It hung open at the front, giving me a long morning view of her heavy breasts.

". . . please, let's not talk about that, OK? . . ."

"Her parents always ask about Elizabeth." She buttered a slice of toast for Timo. Then she switched to English: "They hate Elizabeth, so they try to escape from their feelings by worrying about her health."

"They hate her because her father is black?"

"Of course." Then back to German: "I wonder, is that called displacement? Or compensation? I can't remember."

Timo had dropped his toast on the carpet, butter side down. English had that effect on him. "Tiimo! What am I going to do with you?" Jutta bent to pick up the toast, rubbed the pinpoints of butter into the rug with her bare foot. I picked Ziu's hairs out of the slice and replaced it on Timo's plate.

Timo had not yet spoken a word to me. Well no, that was not right: he'd told me to get out of the way, a couple of times. I hadn't spoken much to him yet, either. He seemed more comfortable with my presence as long as I channeled comments through his mother.

"I think Timo wants more milk."

"Do you want more milk, Timo?"

"Can I have juice, Mommy?"

And so it went: Timo cornered, I keeping my distance, and Jutta translating from Outsider to Insider and back again.

Renate had hung up, and was at the door. "May I come in?"

Jutta looked commiserating. "How are they this morning?"

Renate grimaced. "Oh—they mean well."

"Like hell they do."

Renate's look said don't *you* start. "Put yourself in their place—"

"Why don't they put themselves in ours? Why are we always the ones who have to understand?"

"Because they can afford not to understand. In their village, they've never seen—" she glanced at Timo "—anyone like Elizabeth's father. Jutta, they're trying."

Jutta raised her voice. "Trying? They won't even be seen in public with Elizabeth. What are they trying? Not to spit on her?"

"Jutta! They're my parents! And they're good people. No one would say otherwise."

Jutta pulled the bathrobe closer around her as if to protect herself from something unlovely. "That's the problem."

Renate shrugged. "Think what you like."

"Thanks, I will."

I cleared the table.

"Does Timo want any more toast?" I asked.

"Timo, do you want any more toast?"

□

" 'Timo' . . . It's not the German name, is it?"

"What?"

"Timo's name . . . I mean, it's the same as the old German name —but surely you're not getting it from there." "Timo" was a popular name with the Nazis—the German version of Timothy. The Nazis generally avoided Christian names, but perhaps they liked "Timo" because it sounded Roman. Emperor Timo. Field Marshal Timo. "Timotheos" was actually a Greek word, meaning "precious to God," but the Nazis were nothing if not sloppy in their thinking. Like "Adolf," the name "Timo" went rather thoroughly out of fashion after 1945.

"Oh God, of course not. 'Timo'! You know, I hadn't even thought of that."

"Where does it come from, then?"

"It's an Akan word."

" 'Akan' ?"

"One of the tribes of Ghana. Timo's father was an Akan. He was studying political science in Innsbruck—we met there."

"What does the name mean?"

"Isn't it terrible? I don't know! Joseph named him after his own father—to return to tribal names. He told me what it meant, but I forgot. My own son, and I don't know what his name means . . ."

"Where is Timo's father now?"

"He was killed in 1983, during a revolution."

"I'm sorry."

" . . . "

"*Should* I be sorry?"

"Oh, I don't know. Yes, of course you should. He was a very good man. But we only saw each other once after he left Austria. Timo and I went to Ghana when Timo was two. Timo didn't remember Joseph. He wouldn't speak to him, wouldn't even let him touch him. Joseph was terribly hurt. Timo was his only son. He wanted us to stay in Ghana. But I couldn't. I would never have been accepted there. The last I saw of Joseph was at the airport. He had wanted to hug Timo, but he only waved to him. The next year he was killed."

□

It was quite some time before I noticed the scars on Jutta's wrists. I took up her hand one night to kiss the palm and they came right up to my eyes: a dozen white lines crossing the veins. I kept myself from hesitating. But I immediately took up the other palm and kissed it, too. That wrist had the same scars. After that night, I couldn't imagine how I had missed them. As she reached out to hold me, they loomed: they seemed to glow in the dark, they were so white. From time to time, she would rub them, absently. Perhaps they ached. I didn't ask.

Then one afternoon we were sitting in bed, listening to the tape she had put on to accompany our love-making. (She was fond of mood music, of clichéd sultriness, even of beaver poses: was sex an escape into B-movie romance?) When Jackson Browne came on, with "Oh Won't You Stay," she laughed and said, "One time, listening to this song, I opened my veins."

I waited for her to go on.

Neither of us had said much yet about our private lives. We had come together purely for the sex; I with a desperate craving, she with more ambiguous motives. We had been like two strangers ship-wrecked together on an island, one with a knife and the other with matches. We knew that we needed each other, but we didn't know if we would like each other. Now we had to decide whether we wanted to grope our way into other, more important intimacies.

The song came to an end. Jutta sucked on her cigarette, stared into space with heavy-lidded eyes, and said nothing. The opportunity was passing. Then she said, "I was crazy. Stupid!"

It sounded like my cue. "Why did you do it?"

She shrugged. "I was trying to kill myself."

"You know what I mean."

Jutta turned to face me. I found her more attractive every day. I loved the paleness of her body, the thick brown hair between her legs and under her arms. "What kind of reason can I give you?" she asked, cheerfully, as if I were a child, wondering why the sky was blue. "I wanted to die. A man had left me, and I felt like a whore. I thought Timo would be better off without me."

"Who would Timo have, if he didn't have you?"

"That's what my therapist said. But I thought he'd be better off with nobody than with me."

"That's ridiculous—"

A tiny thing, an insect's wing, flashed in her eye. "Don't tell me what's ridiculous—you asked me."

"Sorry."

"It wasn't the only time I tried it." She offered this as proof: either on the logic that anyone who tried to kill herself several times could not be good for a child, or that if suicide had occurred to her several times, then it had to be the right course of action.

"How many times?"

She turned her eyes toward the ceiling and considered, matter-of-factly. "Six—seven times? Something like that. Let me see . . . No—eight, I guess. The first time I was going to jump off a bridge, but it's really too public that way. Too show-offy. And anyway, the police picked me up. After that, I always cut my wrists."

I wondered if anyone had ever pointed out to her that people who really wanted to kill themselves usually succeeded. "You said you were stupid. Crazy. You wouldn't try it again?"

"I've only changed my tactics. Now I sleep with men who have fatal diseases."

She was joking. But this wasn't one of the subjects I joked about much. I didn't like the idea that someone might consider me the hand of an angry god. "I've wondered why you were willing," I said.

My seriousness delighted her. "Eric, I was kidding! A danger like AIDS doesn't mean anything to me. It's too far in the future. I live my life day by day. I wanted you."

Yes, I thought, and you live your life day by day because you're unhappy and can't bear to look into the future. Sleeping with me is like your smoking, only better: inviting death to come in the back window, because you don't have the courage to jump out the front one.

She stroked my cheek, motheringly. "Don't worry," she said. "I don't play around with death any more. My therapist got me to see that I was only cutting my veins to get attention. I was so embarrassed! I thought I was making the most important, the most personal decision; but I was only throwing tantrums. That's over."

"So you won't slit your wrists again?" The thought of the blood revolted me. It made my own wrists ache. "You promise?"

Perhaps she heard the squeamishness in my voice and was offended by it; or heard the absurd hope that if I could get her to promise, it would somehow bind her. She balked. "I didn't say that. I meant, I won't do it again unless I really mean to kill myself."

"Timo would be—"

"Timo can't expect much. He's the son of a whore."

And as if to prove her point, a connection that I couldn't help but find unflattering, she put on a false sexy smile, wriggled her body against mine, kissed my chest, my stomach, my abdomen, took my penis in her mouth and sucked on it until I came, and then licked along the shaft and the balls, and rubbed her face in the pubic hair, murmuring and cooing. I had let her do it—but I cradled her head afterward and looked into her eyes, trying to see in there, somewhere, whether she had done it for me, or for her, or for some idea of herself that she loved, or hated, or both.

"You can't do that again," I said. "It might be dangerous."

I smelled my sperm, like mild white Camembert, on her breath. But when I kissed her, the taste, of course, was bitter.

I made her throw it up.

□

"Sometimes I bring men home, just to seduce them. Complete strangers."

"Like me."

"No. I had no intention of sleeping with you."

"Oh?"

"Don't look hurt! It's just that you're so young. Most of the men I seduce are in their thirties or forties."

"This is more whore talk."

"What do you mean?"

"I mean you run yourself down too much about it. What's wrong with sleeping with a lot of men?"

"Only a man would say that. For a woman, to sleep with many different men isn't a triumph; it's a failure."

"Let's not talk about 'man' and 'woman.' Let's talk about you and me. My case is so simple it makes me sick: I'd like to sleep with a lot of women, but I can't. If you want to sleep with a lot of men, then you should; that's fine. If you don't want to sleep with a lot of men, then don't. What's the problem?"

"You can't really believe it's that simple."

Of course I didn't. But I had inherited from my father the rational man's conviction that things *should* be that simple. And I got a lesson in how little that conviction had to do with reality every time Jutta and I had sex together.

The first time had been a shock. In a way, she had seemed to want it so badly. She had brought her legs up around my stomach, and I could feel against my stomach how wet she was already, how open. It seemed as if she was bringing herself to a climax just by rubbing against me. Then I slid into her: she gasped, her eyes fluttered deliriously, a look of utter fulfillment came over her face. It was as if she wanted no more; nothing more than to hold a man close to her, and feel him deep inside her. I was suspicious: her expression jibed too well with descriptions of sex in books; books written by certain male writers who exorcised in prose their own feelings of inadequacy—and it jibed with the way, later, she would lie back on a couch with her legs apart, the way she would tilt her head down and look up at me coyly along her forehead. She was flattering me, playing to the male ego. And at the same time, almost necessarily, she was playing the whore. She wanted me in her, wanted desperately to please me; to make me like her. But how much did she despise herself for it? And for what? For the whoring, or for the deep desire to make me like her?

Still in her, I brought my hand gently down, stroked her pubic hair. She shuddered, and I lifted my hand away. She responded to everything so strongly! As if she had no skin and I were touching directly on the tips of her nerve endings; like the jump of too-much, the involuntary pushing away of the hand when the sheath of the clitoris draws back and the white electric nub is touched. I brought my hand carefully back and laid it, unmoving, on the skin over her pubic bone. She shivered again, but less violently, and clutched me to her. My full weight was on her, yet she seemed to want more. She gripped me by the neck, pulling, pulling down, burying my face in the soft curve of her neck, digging fingers into muscle. And from there, holding me to her as if she wanted to pull me bodily, entirely, into her, my hand doing nothing but resting between us in the thick of her hair, the sliding of penis and vagina accomplished more by her bouncing on the mattress than by me, who had lost my balance, from there she began to spiral upward, with amazing swiftness, toward some kind of orgasm. "Some kind"—I still don't know, I never did know, or decide, in the hundreds of times we made love, *what* kind. I came to think it was not a physical orgasm at all, rather a different sort of paroxysm entirely—something purely emotional, something unhealthy. She released her grip on me and pushed me up. Her eyes were wild, her lips drawn back from her teeth. She began to fling her head violently from side to side, harder and faster, until I thought she would break her neck. Suddenly she said "No!," and yanked my hand away from her vagina, grabbed my buttocks and hauled me deeper into her until I could feel the head of my penis strike hard against the cervix, and she repeated softly, eyes turned up, as she forced me in, "No! no!" Then she stopped with a scream and clutched my arms so painfully that I cried out. Her whole body tensed, the blood drained out of her face, and she stared up, not seeing me, with an expression of terror. "What is it?" I demanded, frightened. "What's wrong?" She shook her head convulsively, continued to stare past me, through me, with eyes as blank and dead as black marbles. "For godssake, Jutta, what's the matter?" I withdrew. I gripped her. But as soon as I was out of her, the trance broke. "Don't stop!" In a moment, she looked human again. She even looked concerned. "Why are you stopping?" She guided me back in. I wanted no repetition of the fit, so I brought myself quickly to a climax. And as the pulsing began, her face took on the same look with which we had begun, with that kiss at the kitchen table: stillness, contentment, and a hint of triumph.

And *her* pleasure? As I would do a hundred more times, I wondered what had happened. Something too powerful to be pleasure, and disturbingly incomplete. Because she hadn't seemed to get where she had been headed. She never would. She would always seem to pull back at the last moment from a brink, as she screamed "NO!" and yet held me to her. The pulling back frightened me: the hard clutch, the empty eyes. Yet I began to fear even more her ever *not* pulling back. Whatever lay beyond that brink was stronger, more violent, than anything I wanted to face.

But we had months together—why couldn't we take things a step at a time? I tried. But Jutta could not, would not, slow down. She always forced the issue. She pulled me down on top of her, pulled me into her, flipped me over and held the penis up and sat on it. Fucking Jutta—getting fucked by Jutta—was like diving head first at night from a bridge I'd never been on before into black water.

And talking her through it? The problem was, she never remembered a thing. After I had rolled away from her, that first time, and after a decent interval had passed, I asked, "Are you all right?"

"What? Of course. Why do you say that?"

"You grabbed me. Really hard. You screamed 'no'."

She laughed, as if I were teasing her. "What? I did not!"

"You did."

She rolled and looked at me, smiling appreciatively at my wit. "You're crazy," she said affectionately.

Then a few minutes later, as if after thinking about it she had decided my kidding disguised a worry that I hadn't been impressive enough, she said, *"You* were the one who scared *me!* You were so wild!" She said it with a little oooh, the way a woman might jokingly say, "oooh! you're so *big!*" I searched her face for signs of sarcasm. But there were none. Impossible to know what she believed. Impossible to know at what point the thing she told herself she should say to please her man became an article of faith—unexamined and unalterable. I would remain always, for her, a wild man in bed.

□

None of the women ever cleaned the apartment, not even Renate, who in other things—her work and her child—seemed as orderly as I. None of them picked up anything, or washed the dishes until immediately before they used them, and even then not always. The dishes in the sink smelled like garbage.

The first time I washed up, I discovered a logistical problem: there was no place to put the dishes when they were clean. The only counter space in the kitchen was crowded with a vast array of spices, and the shelves served as the pantry. Pots went in the oven until the oven was used, at which point they went on the floor. I stacked the clean dishes at one end of the table. But there they collected coal dust whenever the heat was on. "Now you see why we don't do the dishes," Jutta said.

"Schlamperei," I said. A Viennese word, it describes what many consider a Viennese character trait: carelessness, slovenliness, laziness. One of the reasons Hitler had hated Vienna. One of the many. "No wonder Timo and Theodor have colds all the time," I said.

"They share colds because they sleep together."

When I was a child, whenever I didn't make my bed by 9:00, my parents called me a disgusting slob. In Lazarettgasse, Ulrike called me *Eric der Ordentliche:* Eric the Orderly. The epithet would have suited my father, whose favorite phrase for his favorite activity was "putting all his ducks in a row." The real haunting by the dead are those frightening family resemblances.

Some people hate neat-nuts, but my help seemed welcome here, even if the women found it comical. I persevered. Jutta was showing no sign of wanting me out, and the situation suited me fine, but the roommates could ruin it all—they had not bargained for so long a male presence. I did the dishes; I cooked; I picked up newspapers, sweaters, underpants, bills, shoes, socks, tampons, magazines, candy wrappers, glasses, blocks, bricks, dirty plates; I swept; I dusted; I washed diapers full of thin green shit and wrapped new dry ones with an extra twist because a doctor was concerned about a clicking in Elizabeth's hip joint. One night, at the end of a dinner that I had cooked, Jutta opened a discussion. The next day, I began paying a quarter of the rent.

That same day, I moved my books and papers to the desk in Jutta's room and set the American Tourister flat open in a corner of the kitchen. Clean dishes went into the Tourister, and when one side was full, I swung the other side over and closed it. "No coal dust," I said. No one seemed impressed.

I told Jutta that night I didn't want to move to the futon. "That will be hard on Timo," she said.

"He's got to get used to it," I replied, quoting her. "I'm a roommate now." When Timo appeared, we awoke, and the feeling came over me again that this was all some bedroom farce: there we were, our hair askew, propped on our elbows in our bed of sin, confronted by the injured party. Jutta looked as if Timo might whip out a blunderbuss and dispatch us on the instant. I remember the glint of wildness in her eyes, the worried droop of her lower lip. Timo saw us, but he kept coming, somnambulently, his doll Heidi clutched in front of him. Jutta sat up, the sheet falling away from her, and touched his shoulders as he reached the side of the bed.

"Mommy," he said, with a whine. Tough and aloof during the day, he showed his need for his mother only when his defenses were down. As with most of us, his defenses at three in the morning were very down.

Jutta tousled his hair. "Tiimo," she crooned, coaxingly. "Tiimo— Eric is going to stay here tonight, with me."

"No, Mommy."

"With both of you," I said. "Timo, come into bed."

"Noo," he said, sleepily. "I don't want to."

Jutta kissed his forehead, began to undress him. "Tiimo. Please, Tiimo. It's all right. Don't be angry with me." She pulled his arms out of the pajama sleeves. "You'll be just like us. Yes? We'll all sleep together." She undid the string on his pants, and pulled them down. "Eric belongs here too, now." She stepped him out of the pants. "Now we're all together. Nobody else. Just you and me and Eric." She lifted the blanket.

"Noo," he murmured again, as if in a daze. But he crawled in under the blanket.

"He can lie between us," I said. "It might make him feel better."

Jutta deposited him on my side and I moved against the wall to give him room. He turned his back to me and spooned with her, as he'd no doubt seen his mother's lovers do. Jutta kissed his hands. "You're such a good boy, Timo. You're my own special man." Timo snuggled, murmured, and was fast asleep. Soon Jutta too was sleeping. Pressed against the wall, not touching them, I listened to their sleep for what seemed hours. Then, through a dream about my father, I felt a tapping. I drifted up into consciousness. It was morning, and I was alone in the bed. Timo, in his underwear, was tapping on my chest.

"Mommy says come to breakfast," he said, and trotted out.

I sat up, dazed and depressed from the dream. Then I realized that Timo, for the first time, had spoken to me. He had finally confirmed for me that I was really there, living with Jutta in the apartment on Lazarettgasse. I was sinking further every day into an arrangement I had not quite willfully chosen. Who had he spoken to, who did he see? An American drifter, a layabout, his promiscuous mother's latest plaything.

□

Coming to Vienna had meant returning to memories of my childhood, memories tied up with my father and his passions. There had been a Guggenheim for the assistant professor in 1968, when I was five, our family living in a coldwater walk-up in the eighth district. Then much later it was just the two of us, the full professor and his younger son, spending summers in the Inner City, where we could always find one apartment or another belonging to a colleague who was in Baden or Salzburg until September. I did the straightforward reference work in the reading rooms of the libraries while my father researched the more creative aspects of his theories. I typed his drafts, I paid his bills, and I took care of his mail. I forged his signature so well that even my mother, back in Boston, couldn't tell the difference. My wages were experience: invaluable training for my career as a World War II historian.

Whenever I could, I wandered in the hot bright streets. And I understood why the colleague who owned our apartment had fled. The tourists sat at the outdoor cafés, crowding the Ring, the Kohlmarkt, Kärntnerstrasse from the opera to the cathedral, sat in the oppressive, unchanging heat in a daze. The Viennese were in the mountains, or swimming at the Gänsehäufel; the Philharmonic was in Salzburg; the Symphoniker was on tour; the opera houses were closed. Three nights a week something called the Vienna Strauss Orchestra played an unchanging program of waltzes and polkas in the Musikverein, sold tickets in blocks to the tour groups, and hawked the rest at merciless prices. Every concert was sold out. There was nothing else to do. I remember the long nights, while my father slept, his door barricaded, that I spent walking, driven by hormones and unexpressed resentment. I lost my virginity to a prostitute who picked me up on the Gürtel and kindly, professionally, talked me out of my embarrassment. I had a brief affair with an Australian woman who looked like a man and who threw me over when I said I wouldn't swim naked with her across the Danube canal because it was dangerous and illegal; in fact, I was afraid that someone would steal our clothes. I slept, eventually, with another man, a slim and pretty twenty-year-old—I was seventeen, and pretty, too—who worked one of the bumper-car rides in the Prater amusement park. I wavered for a while, wondering what I really liked, before I drifted away from bisexuality, without really having made a decision.

Many writers have lived in Vienna, so it has earned many well-known nicknames. One of them prevalent at the turn of the century was "The City of Dreams." Perhaps it was a reference to Vienna's burgeoning population, to the Czechs, Magyars, Slovenes, Slovaks, Croats, Italians, and Rumanians—Austrian subjects all—who came from dying villages, dreaming of a better life in the capital. Or perhaps a reference to the city's own illusions, its pompous Ring, its attempt to look like another Rome, even while nationalism was tearing apart its empire. Or perhaps it was a bow to Freud, who was living at the time on Berggasse, just a few blocks from the Schotten Ring, and whose *Interpretation of Dreams* was already his most famous work.

The City of Dreams was also my dream, the unsettling kind of dream that you forget as you wake, no matter how hard you try to hold on to the details, knowing only, as a certain trance lingers, that it was important. And the city was also my father's dream, but a different kind, the kind that recurs, always the same, every detail remembered so that each repetition is marked by a feeling of inevitability and horror: an obsession.

His was the morbid fascination of a foreigner. My father had been born about as far away from Vienna as you could get, both geographically and spiritually, and still be in the German-speaking world: Lübeck. A northern city of merchants, bankers, and shippers; Lutheran, hard working, honest, introverted. The city of Thomas Mann, and so of *Doktor Faustus,* that moral fable on ambition and intellectual rigor. Compare Vienna: a city of cafés and prostitutes, Catholic, indolent, gregarious, corrupt. And Vienna's writers? Arthur Schnitzler, dwelling on sexual obsessions and suicides. Karl Kraus, expounding with a lunatic's exuberance and vitriol on the last days of mankind. And Robert Musil, whose ambiguous, amoral masterpiece, *The Man Without Qualities,* manages after a thousand pages of prologue to go nowhere and is about being nothing. In that book, Vienna—all of Austria —is given another nickname: "Kakania." Shitland.

When my family came to Vienna in 1968, I was put in a kindergarten at an English-language school, even though I had grown up bilingually. "I didn't want you speaking that atrocious dialect," my father told me later.

But my mother claimed there was more to it. "It was Vienna that started your father behaving as if the world were a plague ward. He never admitted it, but the Viennese frightened him."

"Why?"

"They gave him vertigo: a view into that deep, black well of laxity. He used to dream about falling, forever." It was in Vienna that my parents began to sleep apart.

Two memories stand out from that first year. I remember riding the giant wheel in the Prater with my mother: we were alone in the big wooden cabin, and I was frightened as it rocked in the wind. I remember my mother's hands on my shoulders, a window in a splintered frame, and a view of Vienna below us, a bluish noisy corrugation sprawling outward to vineyards and hills. And I remember eavesdropping from the extension in my mother's study on the call from the United States offering my father a professorship at Georgetown. I couldn't sleep that night for fear of where we were going, and I finally went to my mother's bedroom. The distant voice on the phone had said, "I should warn you before you accept the job—I'm at my house in Bethesda and through the window I can see a red glow across the whole horizon. Washington is burning. I can't promise there'll still be a city here when you come." And my mother sat up, and took me in, and I admitted I'd listened on the phone, and said I didn't want to go live in a city on fire. And my mother explained that there had been a man named Martin Luther King, and that he had just been murdered, and the burning was anger, but the anger would end, or at least it would stop burning, before we ever saw the city. That same night my father came to my mother's room. "Eric is with me, Rudolph," my mother said. And: "So now we will live in Washington." She seemed to be angry at him.

My mother was born in Wisconsin in 1936. Her parents had just emigrated from Munich, and the three of them lived with her maternal uncle on his dairy farm. From this haven her parents watched their homeland go down in flames. There were two radios on the farm, one in the kitchen and one in the barn, and they would listen to reports of German defeats, of the bombing of Munich and the advance on Berlin, from wooden stools by the soft udders, or at the formica table, where, years later, I would sit during holidays and eat *Schweinshaxe* and *Sauerkraut,* a slice of *Schwarzwälder* and a glass of milk from Blume, or Rose, or Lorelei.

My mother grew up in this old-world atmosphere, speaking German better than English, and listening to stories from her parents about Munich, about Weimar, and about the harrowing flight from Germany: harrowing not because of the Germans, who in 1934 were glad to be rid of anyone who wanted to go, but because of the other nationalities, in particular the Americans, who made it very difficult for anyone to enter their countries. "Thank God we weren't Jews," her father used to say. "For the Jews, it was almost impossible to get visas."

My mother's parents were self-educated; they demanded that she go to college. She went to the University of Wisconsin at the age of sixteen and majored in American history. Then she did graduate work at Harvard University and got her doctorate when she was twenty-four. That year, she met my father at a department party when she heard him speaking German, and they were married three months later. An accidental pregnancy in the first year put my mother's brilliant career on hold. In 1961 she gave birth to Helga, my older sister. She never quite forgave Helga for forcing her to turn down an assistant professorship at Brown; she would have been the youngest assistant professor in the university's history. Instead, she was a young mother. Twins came two years later: Richard and, fourteen minutes later, me.

□

My father saw little of us during the first three years of our lives. He was working on his dissertation, which weighed in, in 1966, at 1,830 pages. When he submitted it, no Harvard professor wanted to read it; a departmental fracas ensued, instigated largely by my father, who showed up at a faculty meeting and attacked what he considered the intellectual mediocrity of the department. Much later, when he was a professor in the same department, he would say that at least Harvard had learned that it was easier to pay him a salary than it was to fight with him.

The dissertation was on Nazi Germany. It had begun as a study of the Wehrmacht: the role of the common German soldier during the years of Nazi rule. My mother always claimed that my father had been drawn to this subject—had been drawn, in fact, into academia—by the memory of his own father, who had been a brick-layer in Lübeck: neither a Nazi nor a thinker, my grandfather had never doubted his duty to his country, had been drafted into the Wehrmacht, and had spent four hellish years on the eastern front before catching a bullet in his head at Stalingrad. My father was ten years old when that happened. Lübeck was already a smoldering ruin.

The scope of his dissertation broadened after the Eichmann trial in Jerusalem. The prosecution's case brought a vast amount of Nazi archival material to light. Ever since his father had died, my father had been obsessed by the idea of "explaining" the war; that was the phrase he often used, although no one could ever quite figure out what he meant by it. Now there was this mountain of new material, and he was determined to gain its summit and there plant his explanatory flag. It took him five more years, working eighty hours a week, to do it. The dissertation was a treatise on ethics disguised as a demographic study of German men of fighting age between the years 1933 and 1945. No one but a German would have attempted it, let alone produced it: as ponderous as it was ambitious, it managed, through its tendency to leap from minutiae to mysticism in a single bound, to obscure both to its readers and to its author that the main arch of its argument could not stand for the lack of a few important stones.

But no matter. The study became famous anyway, because of what struck certain other historians as both its underlying assumption *and* its conclusion: that Nazi Germany could have happened anywhere. Other people, of course, had claimed that. My father differed from them only in that he actually tried to prove it. That was perhaps not surprising for a self-taught working-class kid who had entered academia out of reverence not for its intellectuality but for its power: the power of marshalled facts. Most historians born to the jargon don't claim they've "proved" anything, no matter how dogmatic their views; my father, more dogmatic than many, claimed it all the time.

When the dissertation was published by the University of Chicago Press, in three volumes, it stirred a controversy in academia over its methodology: the aforementioned charge of tautology. Everyone agreed, however, that my father had done some immensely important research. But then he sold a much shorter version (one without the charts) to a New York publisher under the title *The Nazi Soldier,* and in this form it aroused a vastly greater controversy in the general press, in which the consensus seemed to be that my father was an apologist for the Nazis. The controversy boosted the trade edition onto the *New York Times'* best-seller list, prompted harrassment from the Jewish Anti-Defamation League, and led to a trickle of hate mail that was somewhat less disturbing than the torrent of anti-Semitic mail that accompanied it.

My father insisted—quite justifiably—that this second controversy could not possibly have been maintained by anyone who had actually read his book, even the shorter version. He had not, he repeated, cast the smallest doubt on the sin and guilt of the Germans. What he had done was to analyze what that sin and guilt had consisted of. And he had done it with facts, with numbers, in a cautious way. This only prompted the media to call him a coward, not willing to argue the issues that he himself had raised. Then a magazine printed my father's "life story," including comments from a psychiatrist about his need to explain away the guilt of his Nazi father. (The author of the article seemed to think that the Wehrmacht was an organ of the Nazi party.) My father did just the wrong thing: he sued.

His background had tripped him up again. He actually thought his works might change the world; therefore, he viewed the general public, not academia, as his real audience. He felt he had no choice but to get into the arena and fight. Of course, he didn't stand a chance. From the newspaper and magazine articles, from the sixty-second television spots, he came out looking, to the great world of fools who followed his "story," like a fool.

Much of what he wrote for the rest of his life was provoked by that first, stinging controversy. His tenets never changed. The sin of the Germans from 1933 to 1945 was the sin of us all: weakness in the face of an evil minority; ignoring the only moral standard—private conscience—out of fear or for the sake of an ideal of obedience. The terrible lesson of the Nazis had never been learned. People said "remember, remember"; but they meant "remember Germany, remember the Germans." That was the safe memory. It should have been, "remember human weakness."

Whence the charge of apologist. The critics had assumed that as soon as he started talking about universal weakness, he was talking about forgiveness. But nothing could have been more wrong. He was talking about universal culpability. Universal sin. This, I suppose, was his "explanation." His arguments could be subtle, but his conclusions were simplistic and uncompromising. Obedience was inherently evil, he would say, for example. If a soldier believes in what he is doing, then he is not obeying orders but listening to his conscience. If a soldier does not believe in what he is doing, then he is wrong to do it. My father's ideal seemed to be a world without idealism, without dreams: a prickly and raucous anarchy in which no one could do too much harm because no one believed in anything but his own integrity. It was a mess and he knew it.

He had become a preacher, a zealot. He required that his readers recognize themselves not only as weak, but as unforgivably weak—in short, contemptible. Of course, as the years went by, he lost more and more readers. It was increasingly said that his obsession had unbalanced him.

Perhaps so. My father saw weakness everywhere, beginning with his own family and expanding outward in waves of disappointment to encompass institutions, governments, the world. Vienna struck him as a symbol of weakness *par excellence:* the wild enthusiasm with which Hitler was welcomed there in 1938; the slavishness the Viennese showed toward this psychopath who hated them, who considered them a mongrel, degenerate people; the fact that Austria had done even less than Germany to come to terms with its past, had tried none of its Nazis, learned none of its lessons, had rebuilt and forgotten and lied and lied and lied. My father saw this as an example of the worst of which man was capable: laxness, self-contempt, escapism. *Schlamperei.*

By the time of our summers in Vienna, his eccentricities were manifest. He was claustrophobic. At the same time, the slightest noise disturbed him, so he had to shut himself in for quiet. He could only sleep in enormous bedrooms, with the door and windows barricaded. He was perpetually cold, so he wore a fur cap, gloves, and overcoat throughout the summer. He was plagued by allergies.

I was his secretary. On the return address of every letter he had me add Karl Kraus' epithet for Austria: "Research Laboratory for World Destruction." Once he was brought home by a policeman; he had been haranguing a crowd on Kärntnerstrasse. Sometimes, late at night, alone in his bedroom, he would rant. But his basic research was still much respected. I worked my tail off and I feared his opinion of me. In fact, he approved of me. He rather doubted I would go on to do great things, but as he told me, "at least, with you, there's a chance." By implication, there was no chance for my twin brother, Rick, who was a biochemistry prodigy and used his talents to custom-design hallucinatory and mood-altering drugs for himself. Nor for my sister, Helga, who had married young and rashly, who had broken with the family, and whose whereabouts were not known. It was an example of just that complexity of human nature that my father did not often acknowledge that although he said, "obedience is evil," he demanded from his children absolute obedience. And he got, I suppose, what he deserved: two outright resistance fighters and one collaborator who did not actually believe, but was only waiting until the war was over.

When my father died, I and five of his graduate students were the pall-bearers. Three hundred people came to the funeral. Before that crowd, my mother and I were tearless. We knew where Helga lived by then, and I had written to her about the funeral. But she did not come. Neither did Rick, who had himself disappeared some three months earlier, when my father's illness had turned grave. As we drove home from the funeral, my mother said, "My family was always very close." She did not elaborate.

□

November 20. I was banging out a letter to my mother. Jutta had just come home from an English class at the university. Inspired to practice, she looked over my shoulder. "Are you lying to your mother?"

"No." Before I could stop her, she had zipped the page out of the typewriter. "Don't read that!" I made a grab for it, but she danced away, laughing.

"Guilty conscience?"

"Come on, give it back." She started quickly to skim it. I got up and she backed away playfully, still reading. I wasn't in a playful mood. "All right, read the damn thing, then."

"You *are* lying to her! The poor woman—and she's all alone, too—"

"I'm just trying to make her feel better. She's worried—a letter came today accusing me of all sorts of things. Not working was the least of it."

"Oh really?" Her voice sharpened. "What else?"

"She's guessed we're sleeping together."

Jutta crossed her arms. It was her arguing pose. (Significant that even in starting a fight she took a defensive pose; less vulnerable people quarrel with arms akimbo, as if ready to strike.) "And what does it matter if she knows? She doesn't want her little boy sleeping with loose women? It's none of her—"

"—business, yes, it isn't. I agree. *But.* You yourself just pointed out she was all alone. Why should I hurt her unnecessarily by telling her—"

"Eric, she's not your girlfriend. You're ashamed of me, aren't you?"

"No. All I'm saying is, she's going through a very bad time. It doesn't matter to her whether you're a 'loose' woman, or a schoolgirl, or a nun, or a transsexual scuba diver. She feels like her family is deserting her—I'm the only child she's still on good terms with."

"So what? She's *not* your girlfriend." Jutta smiled bitterly. "We both know she's not going to lose you to me."

"*She* doesn't know that—"

"Only because she doesn't know what a worthless bitch you've picked up—"

"—and besides, we—what? what are you talking about?—we *don't* both know she's not going to lose you to me; I mean, me to you—"

"And if you're so fucking worried about deserting her, why aren't you in Boston?"

"This conversation is not getting anywhere, as far as I can tell." I said that, of course, because she was right. My only excuse for being in Vienna was to do work—which I wasn't doing. If I cared about my mother's problems, why didn't I go home? If I didn't care, why conceal my affair with Jutta? As I'd said rhetorically in some other argument: What was the problem? "I'd rather be here," I said lamely. "I'm not doing much work, and I do want to make my mother happier. But I can't help it. I'd rather be here." Don't my preferences count for anything? Finally?

"Why don't you just tell her you're not interested in the fellowship any more?"

"Because it's my father's work, and I promised him I'd do it. She would be very disappointed." Wrong. She had admired but never been devoted to my father's work. She had resented the way he'd monopolized me, turned me into *his* kind of historian, had me be his secretary when she could have used a secretary herself. As an adolescent I'd often felt like Ganymede, the beautiful boy cup-bearer, fought over by Hera and Zeus. Ovid never wrote, nor anybody else, about what Ganymede wanted to be doing. But it sure as hell wasn't trotting around spilling nectar on his sneakers, or bending over at the first sign of lightning. "And because," I added, holding up a check, "this also came in the mail today. Where do you think my rent money comes from? How do you think I help you with Timo's clothes?"

"We can do without the money."

"Bullshit, we can."

"Well, why don't you just *do* the work, then?"

There. She'd finally asked it. She'd probably been waiting for an opportunity. "It would be easier to explain if I'd actually lost interest —but I suppose the real question is why I was offered this fellowship in the first place. And then, given my lack of interest, why I accepted it. The answer to both questions is: because my father died." The committee, pitying me, offered it. And I, pitying my father, accepted it.

I had arrived in Vienna determined to work, still straining not to lose his approval. But then, wandering through the streets on the second day, I had made a strange discovery. I was on Naglergasse, just off the *Graben*, and I passed an apartment building that my father and I had lived in one summer. I looked up at a second floor window that had been his bedroom. When we lived there, the window had two huge green wooden shutters that each night he would swing in and lock with the usual little hooks; then he would push a fat iron bar through their handles. I looked up, and I saw that the apartment had been converted into office space. The shutters were gone. Through the glass—a single pane now—I could see the back of a computer terminal.

And it finally sunk in: my father had died in America; but he was dead in Vienna, too! The bald, shrunken body had gone, but it had dragged with it the other body: the nervous presence in the archives and libraries, rooting, mumbling to itself, breathing an aah of discovery. His work was dead with him. Now, it was . . . my God . . . it was *my* work now. *My* work? And a shiver of revulsion came over me. That work left me utterly cold, longing to go to sleep. *My* work? As if a child had been laid at my door with a slip calling me the father —a child that looked nothing like me, that didn't have my temperament, or my blood type, or my chromosomes—a child that the court, nonetheless, had ruled was mine, my responsibility, no one else's, for the next eighteen years. But he was dead! He was dead in Vienna, too! I didn't have to obey the court. To put it snidely—the court had adjourned. I'd already lost my father's approval. I'd lost it that last night, a week into his coma, the moment his convulsive, child-like suckings on his plastic oxygen tube stopped.

Jutta asked, "How did he die?"

"Lung cancer. He smoked. Like a factory, as they say. Although less than you do." I looked back over the letter to my mother. "They'd string me up by my balls for what I've done already. I might as well enjoy myself as long as I can, and get strung up by my balls later."

"What will happen?" Jutta asked.

"If I'm lucky, I might last until May. Then the department will expect a detailed report. Say, forty pages of notes, outlining what would later be a long article, or the kernel of a dissertation. They won't get it. I get bounced out of the department so hard I fly right over the spiked walls of academia. No other department in the country will accept me. My mother's spirit curls into its non-corporeal version of the fetal position. My brother, Rick, welcomes me at last as a fellow deadbeat and loser. I start sharing Rick's custom-designed drugs, and we float arm-in-arm into the sunset and beyond, into complete indifference and irresponsibility. Twins at last."

Perversely pleased with this last image, I reinserted the letter in the typewriter. Jutta sat silently on the bed, her coat still on, her hands hugged between her knees, lost in thought.

"P.s.," I typed, "I also don't know where you got this ludicrous idea about Frau Bechtler . . ."

"Eric?"

"Yes?"

"Why go back at all?"

"Hm?" I tapped out the final words and turned back to her. "What was that?"

She licked her lips nervously. "If you're going to get into so much trouble, why go back to America at all? Why not stay here?" She would not meet my eyes.

I saw, as now I always saw, every time I looked at her, the scars on her wrists, peeking out of her coat sleeves. The long lines, curved a little at the ends, crossed each other to form runes. And the runes spoke to my father's son, saying "weak." I thought: For chrissake, it's been less than a month. Groping for something to say, I switched to automatic: "Stay here?"

And with a sharp intake of breath she hid her face from me and jumped up, speaking with sudden harshness: "Oh forget it!" She ran, and the sound of the door slamming behind her reverberated throughout the apartment.

□

I hid the letter. But later, Jutta rummaged through my things and found it. She was incorrigible that way. She saw nothing wrong with confirming her worst suspicions.

She confronted me with the evidence in her hands. I thought for a moment that she was furious. But she surprised me: the trembling of her mouth turned out to be suppressed laughter. "Thirty-eight?" she shrieked. "And a widow?"

I was properly sheepish. "Don't forget tremendously fat." I loved her laugh—a throaty gasp—even though I didn't always believe it. "I pulled the age out of my hat. And my mother would identify with a widow." Not to mention having respect for one, as she did not for unwed mothers.

"And why is Timo's father Italian? Is America like Austria? Is your beloved mother as bad as my parents, that you can't admit Joseph was black?"

Yes, I thought. "No," I said. "I picked Italian because if you were really a widow, chances were better it was with an Italian." Wha-at? What was I talking about? "Anyway, it also made sense because 'Timo' happens to be an Italian word."

"Is it?" Jutta was intrigued. "What does it mean?"

I knew what she was thinking. Jutta had a superstitious instinct: that back-door sort of superstition that characterizes so much of modern thinking, such as having the technology to get people into space and then not being too terribly surprised when Apollo 13 is a disaster, or publishing an important scientific treatise and then refusing to speculate about the Nobel prize on the grounds that it might bring bad luck. When Jutta read a horoscope for the day, she would laugh at it; but later she would be able to recite it word for word. She had read my palm, also as a joke, but then had seemed truly gratified to find that my lines were like hers (short life, filled with sorrow). She was at her most superstitious on the subject of Fate: she believed people got what was coming to them. The fact that Timo's name meant nothing to her was a bad omen. Did that mean she would lose him? That she would never understand his true nature?

"I'm afraid it's not a very important word. 'Timo' in Italian means 'thyme.' The herb. When I first heard his name, that's where I thought you'd gotten it."

But Jutta loved it. "Thyme!" she repeated, laughing. She cooked with it frequently, throwing in handfuls, until the whole floor reeked of it. "Small, earthy, curly-headed—and it smells so good! Just like a little boy!"

It made me feel good to see her happy. So I hastened to point out the kind of felicitous association that she would find significant. "The Greeks and Romans associated thyme with strength and happiness. A woman in the Middle Ages would embroider a sprig of thyme on her knight's cloak, to symbolize his courage and valor in the Crusades."

"Well, Timo is a strong boy. Stronger than I am. And it means happiness, too?"

"Yes. And for that matter, in Greek, it means 'precious.'"

"Ohh! But this is wonderful!" She grabbed me and kissed me.

I was smart enough to stop there. Akan, Greek, Italian, and Latin too: I couldn't think of another name that had so many possible interpretations. But Jutta would have been aghast at the Latin word; a word, coincidentally, that in my eyes evoked the boy better than curly-headed thyme, happiness, or preciousness. I thought of the dangerous toys he played with, of the cough that never got better; I thought of the succession of men who planted themselves like colossi between him and his mother. Surely the Nazis weren't thinking of this when they named their little blond field marshals "Timo." In Latin, "Timo" means "I fear."

□

Our love-making was usually instigated by Jutta, and she did it often. She liked to compel me to make love to her two or three times in as quick succession as my body would allow. It delighted her that she could always take me, but that I often couldn't take her. Afterward, she would be brimming with energy, and I—I would be in the condition she loved best: receptive and gently sleepy, like a friendly dog, wanting to be nowhere except in its mistress' lap.

At these times, Jutta was talkative. She'd sit up and find a cigarette among the junk around the bed. She'd stare in front of her, slightly up, at her own thoughts, and squint as she took a deep drag, and blow giant smoke rings toward the foot of the bed. She would talk about herself. I would come up between her thighs and rest my neck against her pubic bone, my head on her slanted belly, and breathe in the smoke. I didn't smoke myself, and not having really dated until I was in college, where I'd mixed with my own Cantabrigian, health-conscious kind, I'd never had a girlfriend who smoked. This blue haze, which settled like fuzz on my teeth, came to mean simply Jutta's breath to me. In kissing her, more than anything else I remember removing the cigarette first—she held it cocked with her lower lip, like a defiant middle finger—and holding it while I took that swollen lip between my own lips until her mouth opened. My brother Rick had begun smoking at the age of eleven, because the girls he was then kissing (I was in awe of him, because he Frenched—does anyone say that anymore?—whereas I hadn't kissed anybody, open-mouthed or otherwise), these girls smoked, and Rick said kissing a girl who smoked was like eating old cigarette butts, unless you smoked yourself. But delighted by the novelty, I liked the dust-dry, acrid taste of Jutta's mouth. The bitterness of her kisses turned in my mind until they became the taste of my feelings for her. Regret.

She was born in Innsbruck and raised in one of those colorful cuckoo-clock houses that the tourist sees by the thousands in the Tyrol. Her father taught mathematics at the University of Innsbruck and went on long, lone hunting trips during his holidays. Her mother was a typically hard-working Austrian housewife: she cleaned, gardened, baked, sewed dirndls and *Lederhosen*, brewed Wilhelm-pear and apricot schnapps, and kept the window pots overflowing with flowers.

Jutta was the only child in the house. She played alone in a walled-in garden and saw nothing of the outside world. A few days after she started school, a teacher put a hand on her head and called her a pretty girl. She would never forget that moment, and her confusion—who was the teacher talking to? She knew very well she was ugly. Her mother had always told her so. "My mother liked to contrast me with Princess Stephanie of Monaco," Jutta said, "who was about my age. I always lost."

When Jutta was twelve, her mother told her that she and her husband were not really Jutta's parents. Actually, they were the parents of Jutta's mother. They didn't know where their daughter was living. They didn't care, either. Jutta's real mother, her grandmother said, was a whore. "And she said I would be a whore, too," Jutta said.

"What about your grandfather?"

"He didn't concern himself much with me. I was part of the housework. My mother's domain."

Jutta continued to call the middle-aged couple, and to think of them as, her mother and father. She differentiated the other two—reviled, but never seen—from her "mother" and "father" by calling them her "real mother" and "real father." This helped make her stories rather confusing.

Her grandmother refused to talk in any detail about the missing mother. Jutta sometimes went to the extraordinary length of asking her grandfather, who would turn from what he was doing and look down at her, puzzled and preoccupied, as if at a stray dog. Then he would turn back to his business without a word. Asking the neighbors was out of the question: the Bechtlers were such intensely private people that Jutta didn't know any of them.

She might never have learned more, but for a stroke of luck. She happened to make the acquaintance of an elderly man who was a physics professor at the university. He also happened to be a former friend of Jutta's grandmother. Eventually, the old man took pity on the lonely and awkward girl, and he told her what he knew. He was a suspect source: an estranged admirer. But his would be the only account Jutta would ever hear.

"My father was born in 1920," Jutta told me. "My mother, in 1921. They met in Vienna, in 1938." She laughed. "Of all places, on the Heldenplatz, on March 15."

That was the day Hitler stood on the balcony of the Hofburg and addressed over 100,000 people: frenzied, fulfilled; Austrians no longer. Photographs show a dead white sky, a sea of arms raised in the Hitler salute, people clinging to the statues of Prince Eugen and Archduke Karl, the heroes who had defended Austria in the past from, respectively, the Turks and the French. When he had entered Austria on March 12, Hitler had had no intention of annexing his homeland. But the rapturous welcome he had received along the road to Linz and in the provincial capital itself—a hysteria unparalleled in Germany—had convinced him that nothing less would satisfy the demands of destiny. In his speech, he struck precisely the note that Austrians wanted so much to hear: "I believe I shall be able to point with pride to my homeland before the whole of the other German people." Today, Austrians refer to the *Anschluss* as "the rape of Austria."

Heinrich Bechtler was there, having hitched from his village in the Tyrol to Vienna. A Protestant in a predominantly Catholic country, Heinrich was used to being separate, to looking down on his fellow Austrians. From his parents he had learned an attitude of hopeful devotion toward Berlin after 1933. Anything but Vienna, which even after the Fascist take-over in 1934 was an unruly and incompetent city, run by corrupt and soft Christian Socialists—that is, Catholics—and wealthy Jews. In the melee on the Heldenplatz, a big bullying woman from a working-class district of Vienna was pushed into him and knocked him down. Although Martina was Catholic, when she married Heinrich in 1939, she converted to his religion: Protestantism no longer, but a mystical Nazi mish-mash which referred to God as the "Higher Bearer of Meaning." Other than her anti-Semitism—which since the 1890s could be found in virtually all Christian Austrians, like some *a priori* mode of perception—Martina's political views were not pronounced. But she revered Heinrich and so she took his views, whole cloth. Like many converts she brought to his views the more passion precisely because her appreciation of any complexities was slight.

The war years brought Heinrich leadership of an Einsatzgruppe, then an important position at the Mauthausen concentration camp, and the rank of Hauptsturmführer in the SS. They also brought Hildegaard in 1940, Hermann in 1942, and Brigitte in 1944. Heinrich had always wanted children: he believed in the decisive power of genes, and he believed the world would benefit from more minds like his own.

"The loss of the war embittered my father," Jutta said. "It was the one personal thing I would hear him talk about. He absolutely *hated* Himmler, who he said sold Hitler down the river."

And the children? These now superfluous little Aryans, denied the *Lebensraum* for which they had been sired?

"The post-war world was all opportunism and decadence, and the children were part of it. I remember him staring at me at the breakfast table. I hung my head. He said to my mother, 'Each generation is worse than the last.'" An apocalyptic view: the despair of a man whose faith in the power of genes was broken.

In 1949 Heinrich moved his family to Innsbruck, where he became a professor at the university. His Nazi past was not an obstacle. Left behind in Vienna was a certain physics student who had loved Martina. It wasn't until six years later that he, too, moved out to Innsbruck—he chose a position there over Graz to be near Martina again. But by then, his relationship with the couple had grown so distant that he only saw them every two or three months. "All poor Berthold could tell me was that my mother had changed. He was convinced it was my father's fault." Berthold was sure the old Martina, the lovely and volatile girl he'd admired in Vienna, was hidden still inside the brittle, angry woman he saw in Innsbruck.

"The rest is brief. Berthold almost never saw my parents' children. In 1958 Hildegaard—my aunt—married an itinerant Catholic tool-and-die maker. My parents threw her out. Berthold tried to trace her two years later, but unsuccessfully. In 1959 Hermann was also thrown out, although Berthold never knew why. Brigitte lived alone with my parents for two more years. Berthold saw her now and then and said that she looked just like her mother. She was pretty, with long brown hair, and she had a mole on her chin. She dressed neatly. She was very polite whenever he greeted her. In 1961 she got pregnant."

Jutta smiled sadly, as if remembering her own pregnancy. Never having seen her real mother, she felt, perhaps, that this early indiscretion was something that bound them together, across the years of silence. "About that, my mother *would* talk to me. It had to do with my being a bastard, and my real mother a whore. But my real father was the worst of all. For one thing, he was American." She glanced down at me apologetically. "My parents *hate* Americans. And for another, he was nowhere to be found."

The only thing now known about the man was that his name was Hank. "A name like the sound of vomiting, my mother said." Like a chewed piece of gum picked up from the sidewalk, Jutta came from

God only knew where. Brigitte's parents hanked, and she and her mongrel bastard were spat out.

"My real mother put me in an orphanage and disappeared," Jutta said. "She had no way to support me. My parents found me there and took me out."

"Why?"

"The orphanage disgusted my mother. I wasn't being fed and clothed properly. I wasn't clean. It was her Christian duty to take me home and raise me decently."

"Oh—Christians again?"

"Of course. My mother, anyway . . ."

"Decently . . ."

"They never abused me physically. My mother did feed and clothe me well."

Jutta, perhaps, was Martina's revenge: a revenge on the three unworthy children whom she had chased out of her reach. A revenge especially on Brigitte, the last hope of the family, who had lived neatly and politely with her parents for two years, who had looked so much like her mother, and who had turned out to be the worst of all.

Jutta stared straight ahead, entranced by the drifting cigarette smoke. "They never hugged me, you know. They never kissed me." She pulled on the butt, lodged cockily between her lips. "Not once in seventeen years." Her voice shifted down, from its rasp to a low tremble. "All I ever wanted was for them to love me. Is that so much to ask?" And she cried.

I thought: My parents never touched me, either. But I didn't say so, because that was different. After all, my parents never touched each other, and that despite the fact that they were in love to the end. At least, I thought they were. With my family, it was always a bit hard to tell. Signing letters was as far as we ever went with the word "love."

Jutta grew up, learning her lessons well. She hated herself, and she fooled around with older boys. *They* never seemed reluctant to hug or kiss her. But she was still a virgin at fifteen, when a big property owner in Innsbruck, the father of a girlfriend, offered her a ride home from school, drove her into the woods, got her drunk, and raped her.

Jutta used the word "seduced."

"Did you want it?"

"No, but—"

"Then he raped you. What did you do?"

58

Why even ask? She had learned her lessons well. She felt guilty, and did nothing. Later, he would call her and tell her where to meet him. She would always do exactly what he said. She never told anyone. She was always hard and dry. None of it surprised her. She was a whore. Eventually, the man tired of her, and the meetings stopped.

Jutta called it "my first affair."

Then there was the black man. Jutta, at 17, unerringly hit on the one thing that could actually lower her grandparents' opinion of her. In the provincial Austrian mind, sleeping with a black person is not far removed from bestiality. It was as if she were saying, "You want to see whore?"

"Paul was an American. He worked at a ski resort, where I was a waitress," Jutta said. "He was a wonderful man—one of the kindest men I've ever known. I wanted to marry him." But then the grandparents found out. "My father said he would shoot Paul if he came anywhere near the house. Paul did come. Of course, my father didn't shoot him. But he called the police, and the police took Paul to the station and beat him up. They broke his nose and a few ribs. We didn't date after that."

And so it went. Many more boyfriends. Many of them black. Then Jutta met Joseph and became pregnant. She had affronted her grandparents many times, but they had been waiting, perhaps, for just the right moment. When Jutta reached her ninth month of pregnancy with Timo, that moment came, and with the delectation of true connoisseurs, they turned her out of the family house. Joseph's visa had run out two months before, and he was back in Ghana. Jutta could think of nowhere to go. She went and sat on a bridge over the Inn, and watched the fast gray water until the police picked her up.

□

"I'm allowed to visit them twice a year," Jutta said. "Christmas and Easter. But I can't bring Timo. They won't talk about him." She went on defensively: "I can't help it. I know I should hate them. I know with my mind that they are terrible people. But I still want to be loved by them more than by anyone else." She shrugged resignedly. "Everyone wants to be loved by their parents, right? That's only natural." Jutta used to be in therapy, and I thought I could hear her therapist's influence in that last sentence.

"Of course it's natural," I said. "I understand." What I didn't understand was why Jutta's grandparents invited her. Perhaps they were getting lonely in their old age. "But if I could somehow reach into your brain and turn off a little switch," I said. "Because other than your parents, who thinks poorly of you? Timo loves you, and Renate and Ulrike. If only that switch could be turned off, so that you would no longer care about these two unimportant people; just two cruel people in the whole world."

Therapy *had* gotten Jutta to feel better about herself, at least intellectually. Which was an achievement, since what I had said was utter crap—most Austrians would, in fact, revile Jutta. That was why, when she'd come to Vienna, she'd moved in with Renate, who was then dating Elizabeth's black father. No one else would live with her. ("You can't escape provinciality by moving to Vienna," Josh says. "The Viennese have practically enshrined intolerance and xenophobia. They call it 'tradition.'")

Jutta loved Timo. She knew her grandparents were wrong about him. She knew her grandparents were wrong about *her*. And if emotions were math problems, you could say Q.E.D. But they aren't, and you can't. "If my parents said tomorrow that they would take me back, with Timo, I would go running back. No matter what they called me."

I did not believe this. Jutta sometimes exaggerated her own weakness in order to sharpen her sense of self-contempt. But at least she acknowledged what her attitude should have been. Therapy had gotten her that far.

She had, by the way, also slept with her therapist.

"I could tell he wanted it," Jutta said, "and I liked him." They dated for a month, and then ended it amicably. Jutta stayed on as his patient. But now she was seeing no one. She couldn't afford it. And her old therapist, who would have continued seeing her for free, had committed suicide last year.

□

Der Rosenkavalier was at the opera house. Opera bored Jutta, so I called Josh and we met under the house's neo-Renaissance loggia, out of the December drizzle.

"How's work?" I asked.

"Enh. I got tough licks coming out my ass."

"What pieces?"

"Dvořák Cello Concerto. Then Beethoven's Sixth, for godssake." He rolled his eyes. "I might as well shoot myself during the storm."

Joshua Kohler was a couple of years older than I: a tall, stooping Georgian with prematurely graying hair and a rich basso profundo voice. His family had moved to Boston in the seventies and we had met on the chamber music circuit—he as a hot new horn player, I as a snot-nosed reviewer for a Harvard rag. Like a lot of American classical musicians, Josh had come eventually to Europe to get a job. He was currently playing first horn in the Tonkünstler Orchestra, the same orchestra that Mozart used to conduct.

"You mean the opening of the fifth movement?"

"You got it, Junior. Hardest lick in the whole literature."

It seemed that every week some piece came along containing the hardest lick in the whole literature. Josh always complained, and he always worried. The afternoon before every performance he slept, to prevent himself pacing in his apartment or practicing too much and blowing his chops. His cupboard was stuffed with various teas, left over from fruitless attempts to settle his stomach. He usually forbade me to attend his performances, because he didn't want me to hear him screw up. And yet, after most concerts, he was satisfied. Josh worried, but he was a superb horn player. The rest of the horn section, Viennese all, ostracized him: for being first horn, for being good, for being American, and most of all, Josh was convinced, for being a Jew.

"How's your own work going?" he asked.

"All right."

"Kick ass," he advised, with a power salute.

"Will do."

The ticket line began to move. "Look at these guys," Josh said, as the brown-jacketed guards marched up and down the line, prodding this group forward, pushing that group closer to the wall. "I've heard the opera sends all its job applications to p.o. boxes in Argentina." Then he added with a frown, "Actually, I suppose postage to Argentina wouldn't be necessary. Jews were shocked when Reagan laid a wreath at the feet of dead SS at Bitburg—but every state visit to Austria entails shaking the hands of live, happy SS officers."

"You know, Bitburg was the occasion of my father's last tirade. He was really pissed off at Elie Wiesel. After a lifetime of saying 'remember, remember' and 'take a strong stand,' what did Wiesel do? His committee didn't resign, he accepted the congressional medal, and he gave a very polite, respectful speech. My father said he should have thrown the medal in Reagan's face and told him to kiss his ass."

"Your father was a laugh riot."

"You're telling me."

Between the first and second acts, we looked at an exhibition on the ground floor covering the history of the opera house. Josh spent some time admiring a photograph of the house in flames: in March 1945 a bomb had come through the roof and touched off a blaze lasting two days. "They didn't even get bombed much," he said. "The Germans were getting the shit kicked out of them by then and the occupied cities, too. But fervent, fascist Vienna? Now and then a bomber back from a run to the Rumanian oilfields might heave a couple extra bombs overboard, but that was it. Why are they such lucky bastards?"

"Lucky and unlucky. What about that incident the Viennese talk of, the lone bomber?" A single American plane, returning from a routine rubbling of Budapest, casually took a pass over Vienna. It dropped its three last bombs blind. The first bomb hit the cathedral. The second hit the opera house. The third hit the General Hospital.

"I don't believe it," sneered Josh. "Third-rate Viennese melodrama. The cathedral, opera, and hospital aren't even in a straight line."

Back in the balcony, I was smiled at by a woman returning to her seat. Josh whispered, "I think there's something in that." This was the only phrase he uttered more often than "hardest lick in the literature."

"I don't think so."

"I can tell, Junior. She thinks you're adorable." She had taken up her position next to another woman. "There's two of them! Eric: they're ours. It's a sign from the Higher Bearer of Meaning."

In the end, Josh had to introduce us himself. He was not a good-looking man. He would have been, perhaps, a good-looking ferret. But he was supremely confident of his ability to attract women, and his confidence had the usual effect, at least among shier women, of in fact attracting them. Indeed: when the opera was over, the two women, American tourists, walked with us out from the spot-lit loggia and we headed into the Inner City to find a bar. Josh took us down a flight of steps, under a brick arch inscribed with medieval doggerel, and we found ourselves in a vaulted cellar. He collared a waiter and ordered wine, in his best and most incomprehensible Viennese. He was showing off.

I was along solely to watch Josh in action. It always amazed me how well his charm worked. I knew how artificial that charm was, how easily he flicked it on and off. I was always tempted to take his conquests aside and conduct a poll: what did you see in him? did you actually believe *that?* which "no"s meant "no" and which "no"s meant "yes"? would you describe your feeling afterward as "very satisfied," "satisfied," "unsatisfied," or "completely duped and fucked over"?

Of course Josh had sometimes been rejected, too. I'd heard women say things to him that would have left me impotent for the rest of my life. (E.g., "What on earth makes you think I want to talk to an ugly geek like you?" Submitted by a Boston University senior in a bar on Comm Ave.) But that sort of thing bounced right off him. He would smile impenetrably and try someone else.

In any case, neither of tonight's women looked like the free-wheeling, self-destructive type who would listen nonchalantly to my timely mention of a certain HTLV-III infection. So on our way up out of the cellar, two liters of wine later, I excused myself. Josh wasn't surprised. I had done this to him twice before. As he didn't know anything about the results of my blood tests, he had to assume I was crazy. But his infuriation with me had mellowed when he'd ended up, after my departure in the second instance, in bed with both women simultaneously. The added piquancy had been that they were sisters. Later, to punish me, he had regaled me with a detailed and wholly incredible account of their triangular maneuverings.

We parted on Kärntnerstrasse. Josh had hooked his elbows with both women, and the three of them disappeared up the pedestrian zone that way, Josh with his head back, intoxicated with his own charm, the two women laughing. His wife, in all likelihood, would not see him until dawn.

I took off through the dark side streets, emerged eventually at Schottentor, and caught the last #44 for the night. I stared out at Alserstrasse, at the old hospital, the shadow of my head in the streetcarlight sliding over its long façade of dirty gray stucco. I felt like a plague. Hell, I most likely was a plague. My body was a research laboratory for world destruction. I thought: I should count myself luckier than I have any right to expect. I have Jutta.

When I let myself back into the apartment, I found Jutta still awake, sitting at the kitchen table and smoking. She had on a skirt and stockings. I put my hands out and went to kiss her. She looked up at me with a concentrated expression, her eyes seemingly drawn together to the center of her face, and buried the lit end of her cigarette in the flesh between my right thumb and forefinger.

I howled, yanked back the hand, stepped back into a chair, stumbled, recovered. "What—" I said in English; "what in hell—?"

"*Wer war sie?*" Who was she?

"What? Who?"

"I saw you with her—"

"Who?"

She screamed, "Don't *lie* to me!"

I went to the sink, knocked a dirty pot out of the way, turned cold water on the spot. A purplish blister was forming. "What—just tell me what you're talking about. That woman this evening?"

She mimicked me, simpering: " 'That woman this evening?' " She came up to me at the sink, her chin out pugnaciously. "Where were you going with her?"

"With *them.* Two Americans who didn't know the town." The icy water numbed the pain. "Josh and I were just going to get—to have coffee with them." Mistake.

"I can smell the wine on your breath!"

"Wine—yes, so what? So I had wine too—big fucking deal."

"With her?"

"With *them.* With Josh and the two Americans—"

"What, was she good-looking—?"

"No—"

"I *saw* her!"

"For chrissake, Jutta, what are you *asking* me for, then?"

"She was pretty—"

"Was she? Good for her."

"Did you lie with her? You liked her tits better than mine?"

"That's vulgar—"

"I saw those firm young tits—"

I turned on her, away from the water, and blew up. "Will you shut up? What's the matter with you?"

She was crying. Water dripped from my fingers onto the floor. The hand was smarting again. "Jutta—"

A stirring came from the children's room. "Mommy!"

"Go to sleep, Timo! It's all right." She sobbed.

"Jutta—this is ridiculous. Believe me—"

She pulled in her lower lip, skewered me with a look of blank hatred, and turned away. She grabbed the edge of the table and pulled it over, crashing, sending a school of spoons and an ash tray skittering. At the end of the hall, her door slammed.

Christallmighty.

I sat and tried to calm down. She wanted me to come to her. To sit on the edge of the bed and talk, apologize, plead, accuse—it didn't matter what, really—or not so much. Not so much as that I simply come, sit next to her. But I couldn't; not yet. Jutta blew and then broke. But the murderous instinct in me took longer to dissipate.

I found some antiseptic under the sink and painted the puckered skin and blister brown with it. I turned the table upright, crawled and found the spoons, swept up the butts and ash from the fallen ashtray. I ran hot water in the sink, pulled a rubber glove over the injured hand, and washed the dishes. Dried them, stacked them in the suitcase on the floor, shut it. Would I be packing that suitcase with my books tomorrow? Wiped the table and the stove. Nothing so dramatic. Right now I wanted to, but in the morning I wouldn't. I was damned lucky to have Jutta. Brushed and flossed my teeth. Picked up toothbrushes all around the sink and deposited them in the cup where they belonged. Put the soap back in its dish. Just another way to calm myself down.

I locked the door. Turned out the lights. Felt my way through the hall to her door. Here I come, dear. "Jutta, may I come in?"

"Go away."

Bu-ullshit. "Please Jutta, can't I come in? I want to come in."

A pause . . . eight, nine, ten. Then, sulkily: "All right."

She was lying on the bed, turned toward the wall. Dutifully, I sat next to her. But when I saw her face, the mockery drained out of me. She looked lonely and frightened.

"Jutta, nothing happened." She sighed, keeping her eyes fixed on the wall. "Josh met a woman at the opera. He wanted to go out with her afterward. She had a friend—"

Jutta stiffened, shook her head. "No, I don't want to hear—"

"You *have* to—"

She brought her hands to her ears, like a child.

"Please, Jutta—"

"No!" I tried to pull her hands away, but she shrugged me off. She spoke softly. "You can . . . *fuck* other women, if you have to. I can stand that. But I can't stand to hear you lie."

Christallmighty. "I did not fuck anybody. I'm sorry if you think that's a lie, but it's true."

"I should throw you out of here. I should just throw you out into the street. But I can't. Isn't that terrible? I hate you right now, but I don't want you to go. Eric, I'm so weak!"

"That's not the point, though. The point is—goddamnit the *point* is, there's no reason to throw me out. I haven't done anything."

"I was so shocked. You should know how much you hurt me. I came to the opera to surprise you. I'd thought we could go dancing —or just to the Augustiner. We haven't been out much; I thought it would be so much fun! I dressed up. And then I saw you with her. I felt like I was going to faint. My heart was knocking against my ribs. I just watched you walk away; ignoring me."

"I didn't *see* you—"

"It's so scary, Eric! You know you could kill me, if you wanted to. If you left me. If you were mean to me. You must be careful. Don't let me find out what you do."

A great weariness had come over me. Why was she alluding to these things as if I already knew about them? When had this dependence become acknowledged between us? There was nothing I could say now that would not make things worse.

"Ulrike and Renate were furious when I told them what you'd done. They told me to throw all your books and clothes into the hall. And they had begun to like you, too! But I told them—I said I couldn't do it. They know how weak I am; they've seen the way I throw myself at men, like a nymphomaniac. They weren't surprised. They told me they would throw you out themselves. But I said no. I know you must despise me for taking you back. Men are cruel that way. But I can't help it."

I sighed, and got up from the bed. I felt like punching a hole in a wall, or throwing a chair out the window and watching it splinter in the street, five floors down. I contented myself with picking up a couple of Jutta's blouses and putting them in the hamper. Then I undressed. Turned out the light. Crawled into bed.

"You know," Jutta said, "in a way, I feel better. I was in awe of you before. You seemed too good, too much in control. Now I know you're a man, just like all the others; you do bad things too, just like I do." She took hold of my injured hand. "Your poor hand!" She kissed it, and the pain flared again. "I'm sorry, I didn't really mean to do it. But you had hurt me so much, I had to hurt you back." She snuggled against me. I stared up at the ceiling. A note of approval came into her voice. "You were very angry! You were like a wild man! When you knocked the dishes over and yelled at me. I was frightened!" She kissed the hand again, and pressed it to her breast. She loved me to hold her breasts, she had said; it made her feel safe, she had said.

I was frightened, too. I felt misunderstood, vastly over-rated. What had happened? When had it happened? Somehow it had become important to me to make Jutta happy. And I was frightened that I wouldn't be able to do that: that it would turn out that in her life, a life filled with terrible things, I was the worst thing that had ever happened to her.

□

Jutta slept late the next morning.

Timo had gotten up first, and I caught him in the hall, naked, with an iron bar in his hands. He was swinging it around wildly, whooping like a Basque Separatist.

"Where did you get that?" I asked, dodging to save my knees.

"I found it."

"Where?"

"Outside."

He twirled, and the end of the bar hit a door frame. Paint chips fell on the linoleum. "For chrissake, Timo, be careful with that." I glanced around to make sure Theodor wasn't lying in one of the corners, bleeding from the ears. "You're going to hurt somebody."

"Mm." To show that he'd heard and didn't care, he pounded the bar a couple of times against the floor, and laughed.

"I think you'd better give that to me." I reached for it.

"No!" He swung it behind him.

"Timo! It's dangerous. Give it to me."

He was really too good a kid to try to hit me with it. He backed up, and I trapped him against the wall, took the bar out of his hands. It weighed about fifteen pounds. *"No!"* He reached up after it, whining. "Give it back!"

"I'm not in the mood to talk about it, Timo. I'm sorry. You might break something. All right?" He slugged me a couple of times and then turned away, sulking.

"If you get your clothes on, I'll make you some breakfast, OK? Where's Theodor?"

But he wouldn't answer, except to say, "You stink."

"Suit yourself. If you decide you want breakfast, let me know."

It seemed no one was talking to me that morning. In the kitchen, Ulrike was boiling water. Renate was reading a journal. Elizabeth sat round-eyed at the table, propped up in a high chair. In the last couple of days she had discovered her stomach muscles, and she now happily bounced forward and back, forward and back, her tiny thin arms almost straight out, the fingers grasping at the air.

The two women glanced up as I came in, pointedly went blank, and returned to what they were doing. I brought a finger within Elizabeth's sphere of influence and she immediately guided it toward her mouth.

"I just took this bar away from Timo. Didn't you hear him knocking it around?"

Silence. Elizabeth rocked back and forth, holding my finger for balance.

"Hello? Earth to roommates . . ."

Ulrike said, "He wouldn't hurt anyone, Eric. He never has. Let him do what he wants."

"He was knocking the paint off the walls."

"*Our* walls," Renate said, without looking up. Ulrike dropped a bouillon cube into a cup of hot water.

"I pay my share of the rent—"

"We all understood that to be temporary, Eric." Neither of them would look at me. All three of us were embarrassed. "Don't you think you owe it to Jutta to leave? Haven't you realized how easy it is to hurt her?"

Ulrike went out with the bouillon and a dish of cottage cheese. I tried to find something to say to Renate. I put on water for coffee instead. Then: "Is something the matter with Theodor?"

"He's got a temperature this morning. He's in bed." She put down her journal and finally met my eyes. "Eric, she's not going to ask you to go. She already likes you too much for her own good. Why don't you go now, instead of later? It will only get worse for her."

"What makes you so sure I'll leave later?"

She looked disgusted. "Don't talk nonsense! Everyone leaves Jutta—"

"Oh?"

"She's too good for them. Men are shits—this is just a fling for you. Like that woman last night, only Jutta's a bit more convenient. But it's not a fling for her."

"She told me it was she who left her men."

"Well it hasn't turned out that way, has it?"

Ulrike returned.

I said, "I *know* she likes me a lot. I like her a lot, too."

"It's different. She's dependent on you," Ulrike said, as if she'd never left.

"I know that, too. But why do you assume I don't care for her?"

They were both outraged: "Starting with last night—"

I shouted them down: "I didn't *do* anything last night!"

"You don't have to get violent."

"Look—just assume for the moment that I am telling the truth, and nothing happened. Let's just assume it. Now in my position, how am I supposed to prove it to you? I could have Josh tell you, but you won't believe him. Jutta sees me for five seconds, walking with Josh and two women on the street—five seconds! Try to imagine what it's like for me to come home and find Jutta in tears and this morning you two sharpening the steak knives when I *haven't done anything.*"

"You had your arm around her," Renate said.

"What?"

"Jutta said you had your arm around her."

I was nonplussed. "But that's not true." It wasn't.

The two women looked at each other.

Timo appeared, in T-shirt and army-green shorts. "I'm hungry!"

"I swear, it's not true."

"Jutta wouldn't lie."

"I'm hungry!"

"I'm not saying she lied. She was very upset. She told me she almost fainted—"

"Yes! You see how much you can hurt her?"

"Goddamnit, I *know* how much I can hurt her. That's why I *didn't* have my arm around the goddamn woman."

Timo was pulling at my hand. "Eric, you said—"

"Right, right—what do you want for breakfast?"

"It's just your word against hers."

"Ice cream."

"No, it's just *her* word against *mine*. What, Timo?"

"I don't see the difference—"

"Ice cream."

"You can't have ice cream for breakfast. Look, we can ask Jutta again when she gets up—"

"You said I could have anything I wanted!"

"She might not be able to say it in front of you—"

"I did not."

"Yes you did!"

"Then ask her when I'm not there. If she sticks to her story—Timo, will you let go of me? when did I promise you?—then I'll leave."

"When you took away my—"

"Timo, let go of him—"

"—I promise, I'll flush all my clothes down the toilet, throw my books out the window, and jump head first after them. Are you satisfied? Timo, LET GO OF ME!"

"Enh. Enh enh. Enh enh unh unh unhunhuhuhuhaaaaannnnnh!"

"Now you've made Elizabeth cry."

"Yes! I know! *I'm* the bad guy! I made the baby cry and I cheated on Jutta and I stole Timo's toy iron bar and I promised him he could have anything he wanted for breakfast just so I could force him to eat shit later, and I never do the dishes and I never clean up the apartment and I don't pay any rent and I—"

Jutta was at the door, sleepy-eyed. "What's all the yelling about?"

□

I could see where it would lead. My infidelity would become another of Jutta's myths, no longer producing anger but much repeated, as enduring an illusion as my wildness in bed, or the frightening rage I had displayed when Jutta drilled her cigarette into my hand. At breakfast, she held the hand, with its bandaged blister. She had forgiven me. But I had not forgiven her. In my family, grudges sublimated slowly, like frozen blocks of CO_2; they would kill us if we tried to swallow them.

But anger is unseemly. So instead of fighting with Jutta, I kissed her and left the apartment. I went for a long walk. It was snowing: the wet, dreary, Viennese snow that can come down day after day without ever collecting more than an inch—an ever-renewing white slime. The Christmas decorations had been hung across the streets and they cast their usual pall of good cheer, like smiles set in rigor mortis. I walked for hours. Eventually, I found myself at the opera. I called Josh, but he wasn't in. I got in line alone.

As Jutta went to the Spanish Riding School for consolation, so I went to the Vienna Opera.

"Control," she had said, so long ago, when all I could think of was how she would look when I pulled her blouse up over her head, unhooked the bra and took her breasts and fleshy nipples in my hands. The white horses, so beautiful, and big, and beautifully controlled. Power used gently: an ability rarely found in Jutta's world, where power meant brutality. Maleness and purity, the two judges of her inferiority, combined in the Lippizaners: lords that let her stroke their soft muzzles.

In a way, it was the control of opera, too, that comforted me. Or rather, I suppose, the control of so much of classical music, a lean discipline of harmony and motion, the precise measurement of time. I like my music structured, demanding, austere; what in the past would have been called "masculine." Beethoven, Berg, Bruckner, Mozart, Wagner, Haydn, Schumann, Schoenberg: it is no coincidence that these names are all German. To my mind, Western classical music is fundamentally a German invention and achievement. And the contemplation of this German achievement is comforting to me. It reassures me that this race to which I belong *has* accomplished something truly magnificent, in between its attempts to take over the world and kill everybody else.

"I fell in love with Vienna when I first came here," Josh once told me. "To a musician, this city is Jerusalem and El Dorado rolled into one. Beethoven died a few blocks from Lazarettgasse. Schubert was born in Grinzing. There's a greasemonkey's garage there, now—the Schubert Garage. You can hear Brahms at the Musikverein, where the piece was premiered while Brahms listened, then you can walk to the Hofkapelle, where Bruckner was the organist. Another short walk gets you to the Science Academy, where Haydn first conducted the *Creation*, and Beethoven conducted his third, fourth, and seventh symphonies. On the way to hear *The Marriage of Figaro*, you pass the

71

house where Mozart composed it, and the performance is in the opera that Mahler directed for years. And when Mahler died he was buried in the neighborhood of Schubert's birthplace, and his friend Arnold Schoenberg painted the scene!"

Josh's father, a composer, related an anecdote once which made a great impression on me. He had been showing me his dog-eared Viennese photocopy of the Mozart Requiem manuscript; we had turned to the "Lacrymosa," where on the top of the first page someone had written that Mozart had died, and on the following page you could almost *see* his death: the writing dwindled from a four-part chorus to just the soprano line, and then broke off in the middle of a phrase. "It reminds me," the composer said, closing the book and returning it to the shelf behind his Bösendorfer, "of another time, years ago, when I was studying a Mozart manuscript. It was 1954, and I was serving in the American Army as an interpreter. I had been in Salzburg on leave, and I was returning by train to Vienna, where I was stationed. I found myself in a second-class cabin with three others: a big man, about thirty-five years old, and then an old man with what looked to have been his granddaughter but who I was pretty sure was his mistress. Thus setting the stage for Austrian provincial scumminess, as it were.

"So we were talking, I with the score open in my lap, dressed in my threadbare tweed suit; the others in pricier clothes. I mention the clothes because, since I could never afford to dress well and my accent was a mite odd, I was always presumed to be *Volksdeutsch:* some bumpkin from an area none of my interlocutors had ever been to. Often Hungary. Which is amusing since my family *is* from Hungary, although much farther back. Anyway, the old gent and the middle-aged man had started in on the usual war complaints—deprivations, delays, and so on. The middle-aged man, it developed, had been an officer in the SS. Soon the conversation spread to bombings, street fighting, deaths—and then to the "unnecessary" involvement of the United States. Finally, the ex-officer said, 'If it hadn't been for that damned horse-faced woman—' and I realized he was talking about Eleanor Roosevelt. So I spoke up and said, '*Entschuldigen Sie mich bitte, aber ich bin Amerikaner!*'

"A startled silence followed—the old bugger in particular looked as if he'd just delivered himself of a thunderous fart. But the ex-officer was unfazed, and he neatly changed the subject. He began to talk about the Jewish problem. This went on for a few minutes. Eventually, he lamented that it was still a problem, and how unfortunate it was that things had gotten derailed . . . At which point I spoke up again, and said, *'Entschuldigen Sie mich bitte, aber ich bin auch Jüdisch!'*

"Well, at this point the old man was so embarrassed he simply grabbed his young mistress and fled from the cabin. So the ex-SS officer and I were left alone. And I told the man I'd never met a confessed Nazi before, and I was curious to hear his side. Which he then proceeded to tell me, in a completely reasonable way, you know, as if I might learn something. Yes, the camps were too much, he conceded that; but there had been a problem of absentee Jewish ownership. For example, a glass-making factory near his home town had laid off hundreds of workers during the depression. That would not have happened if the owner had been on the scene, if he had been some other Austrian provincial instead of a rich, Viennese Jew. There was probably nothing wrong with Jews *per se* but their enormous influence in a society to which they did not, could not, really, belong, was enormously damaging. It was a pity that more of them hadn't listened to Herzl and gone to Palestine—they'd been free to, why hadn't they? They hadn't because there was too much for them to gain by remaining in Europe, and everything they gained, by necessity, was taken away from Austrians and Germans who had worked for it. I pointed out, of course, that England had limited Jewish emigration to Palestine; but that only made him repeat the old Nazi chestnut—that it proved, in effect, that no one really wanted the Jews. He was sorry to say it, and he knew there were exceptions, but the fact remained that Jews were inordinately concerned with amassing wealth, and usually through financing and banking rather than production. He had learned from hindsight that the death camps had been an overreaction. A better solution would have been preferential taxation—i.e., a sur-tax on Jews—and confiscation of all their property rights. That would have been less costly, and infinitely more workable. Not to mention more humane.

"I even remember thanking him, afterward, for presenting an unfamiliar point of view. God, what a patsy I was! I still had the student's *Weltanschauung* then, in which all words are only information, and all events are simply experience. Let that be a lesson to you, Eric. I've been yelling at that Nazi in my dreams for thirty years. I usually wake up at the moment I begin to throttle him . . .

"At Linz, he got off the train. I was alone in the cabin. And I remember looking down at the score in my lap, which I had been studying before all this had started. It was Mozart's 'Jupiter' symphony—" a look of pain came over the composer's face—"and the page was opened to the great fugue! I felt as if everything were tumbling down on me: I was in Mozart country; the train was pulling out of Linz, which then was a center of unrepentant Nazism, and also the birthplace of Bruckner. In a few minutes, we would pass Mauthausen, and follow the same tracks that the trains followed in the war when they left the Mauthausen concentration camp, packed with Jews. I was on a train heading east! The sublime idealism of the music, the lunatic idealism of the camps . . .

"My stomach heaved. I jumped to the window and pulled it down, and I stuck my head out and vomited."

The composer sat at his Bösendorfer—the big Viennese piano in his study—and played a few bars of the "Jupiter" fugue. He smiled mischievously. "I'm afraid it was an affair of the head, Eric; not of the stomach!"

He went on to other Mozart, skipping around: the A major concerto, a sonata, the C minor fantasy. "Robert Musil captured the German spirit best," he said, "while referring to the two great emotional urges of pre–World War I Vienna: pacifism and racism. He called this duality 'the alternative of either loving *all* one's fellow-men or first of all exterminating some of them.' Very well put, don't you think?"

He switched to a Schubert impromptu, and then a sonata. "I've felt so much like playing Schubert lately," he explained. "I keep coming back to him." He hummed quietly as he played. There were tears in his eyes. "This is a wonderful piano," he said.

□

Jutta and Timo took the train with me to the suburb of Schwechat for my flight to New York. For security reasons, they couldn't accompany me into the boarding area, so we sat and waited together in the airport lounge, hard by the ticket counters. The lounge was patrolled by the usual complement of guards armed with submachine guns. *"Man gewöhnt sich daran,"* the Viennese said, with a shrug: "you get used to it." Outside the embassies, the airline offices, in the old Jewish quarter (where the synagogue, in 1981, was blown up), on every street corner during state visits: the big, green-coated men and their boxy Uzi machine guns were as common a sight as the Turks selling newspapers. In the first few weeks, I had been unable to pass them on the sidewalk; I had crossed to the other side of the street, instead. Even now, whenever I came within a few feet of a guard, I would see only his gun; and I would imagine the man turning toward me, with a little frown, and firing a short burst: ten, twelve bullets that would rip like a drum riff across my chest and leave me on the sidewalk, draining blood into the gutter. It was something you got used to, they said—but I hadn't gotten used to it.

We had plenty of time in the lounge, as I had insisted on leaving the apartment early. "You never know what might delay you on the way there," I had said. And Jutta had mocked, "Eric, this isn't earthquake season." And nothing had delayed us, and here we were, and they hadn't even posted the gate for my flight yet. Plenty of time—in which I could worry about terrorists, who scared me even more than the police did.

Timo sat speechless between us. Like me, he grew subdued in public places. He coughed. "Are you sure Timo and Theodor don't have TB?" I asked. Tuberculosis had been on my mind for the past week. A study had just come out identifying TB as one of the infections that frequently presaged the development of AIDS. Theodor had taken to clinging silently to me like some reproachful barnacle, and he coughed in my face the same way he coughed earnestly into our jars of food. I dreamed about waking with a cough that would never leave me.

I pulled out a tissue, gripped Timo to keep him from squirming and wiped his nose. "He's old enough to do that himself," Jutta objected.

"Yes, but he doesn't."

"If he doesn't want to, why not just leave him alone?"

"Because it's disgusting. It gets all crusted around his nostrils. Timo, blow." Timo blew. He really was a good kid. He was too wild, and the games he played were dangerous. But all his genes were in the right place.

"It's just a cold, I think," Jutta offered.

"It's a pretty damn long one."

"Well, that's Vienna. A lot of people here have colds all winter. And influenza. It's so windy." She changed both the subject and the language. "He hasn't any friends, you know," she said in English.

"What?"

"Timo. He hasn't got any friends. He already knows what kind of country he is growing up in."

Timo hit her leg. "Speak in German, Mommy!" She held his fist and kissed it. She continued in English.

"Theodor has his white father, and his white relatives. Everybody is Catholic, and everybody votes for the *Volkspartei*. But who does Timo have?"

The boy in question struggled with her. Especially when he heard his name in English, he grew angry. "Stop talking about me!"

"I won't talk about you any more, honey," she promised. And then in English: "I asked him who his friends are—I meant at the day place, where I keep him. But he had no friends there. He told me names of two cousins of Theodor, who came once to Lazarettgasse. He met them only once, during one day, more than a year past. And he tells me they are his friends! Nice white friends like Theodor has!"

Timo was livid: "You promised! You promised!"

"Mommy was talking about Eric's family, Timo." She kissed his forehead.

I resumed in German. "It's not just Austria. There'd be the same trouble anywhere. Even in Ghana. You said you'd never have been accepted there."

"But I was a foreigner. The boy is Austrian."

"And my sister's husband is American. But my family still broke with her over the marriage."

"Even in America . . ." Jutta mused.

"Europeans used to say *only* in America. 'What's wrong with you Americans?' they used to ask, so smugly. Before all the Commonwealth immigrants, before the North Africans came into France, before Germany and Austria ran out of jobs for their *Gastarbeiter*. Now everybody's guilty." The gate for my flight had appeared on the monitor. I stood up.

"There's still plenty of time," Jutta said.

"I know. But I want to be on the plane. I want to know that nothing else can go wrong." Schedules did this to me; the thought that a plane would leave whether I was on it or not.

Jutta shrugged, hurt. I took her hand and Timo's, and we crossed the lobby. Even now, Timo would only occasionally allow me to walk or sit between him and his mother, and then, only for a few minutes.

Eventually, he would seem to think better of it, and he would cross me, break our handhold and insert himself into the gap. Today he knew I was leaving, and this made him generous.

In the crush of people by the metal detectors, I hugged Jutta. I could feel her full body through the overcoat, the pressure of her big breasts against me, her big round butt beneath my hands. I felt a sudden strong rush of tenderness for that body, and for the woman who inhabited it. She had forgiven me on the morning after *Der Rosenkavalier.* But I realized that I was only now forgiving her, for shouting at me, for hurting me: only now, as I was leaving her. Because I knew I would miss her. I didn't allow myself to be angry at people who, I had to admit to myself, I needed. I would dream all Christmas of Jutta's throaty voice, of her sweat, of the nipples that I sucked like little thumbs, completing the circle from childhood. Suddenly, I wanted to spend my last few minutes not safely buckled on the plane, away from the chance disasters of the world, but with Jutta and Timo.

And yet I couldn't bring myself to tell her I'd changed my mind. It seemed too—too what? Too weak? Too emotional? And my rush of affection, combined with regret—regret for her that she had me, that she found herself with someone who couldn't even turn back for her, because he felt the momentum of a decision pulling him on—made me want to make it up to her somehow, and I spoke, almost blurting it out: "I'm so sorry, Jutta."

"What?" she asked.

"I've been so distant with you."

"You have?"

"It's just that I've been worried about going home."

Jutta was as surprised as I was. She pulled back. But I buried my face in her thick hair and held on to her against the current of strangers pressing past us. And it came up out of me, boiling up through embarrassment and reticence: something I had never said in my life, and wasn't sure I meant now, but wondered as I said it what extraordinary thing it was now that caused me, for the first time in my life, to say it: "I love you." And though it had come up reluctantly, once it was out it didn't sound wrong. What, I thought, astonished, does that mean?

Jutta was shaking her head. "Don't say that. You don't have to say that."

"But—"

Tears welled up in her eyes. "I only want you to come back. All you have to do is promise."

"Of course I'm coming back—"

Through her tears, there was anger: "Don't pretend I haven't a reason to ask."

"Jutta—" I looked at her earnestly. "I promise."

I shook Timo's hand, man to man, and even he asked me if I was coming back, and when I said yes, he didn't say "oh good," but he didn't say "too bad," either.

And then I let the current of strangers carry me through the electronic archway. And I had a strange feeling. That I was not only going home, but also leaving it. And my thoughts ran on ahead to that other home, and the worries sprang up again—what in God's name I could say to my mother, who would ask about my work; what I would say to Rick, who despised his twin brother; whether I would see Helga at all, who had married a black man herself, thereby sparking off just the sort of prickly, raucous anarchy in our house that my father had written so warmly of, although he had not, finding it in the safe bosom of his family, seemed to appreciate it.

Home! I buckled up on the plane as I would gird my loins, and we took off into the breach.

FASCHING

WHITE PINPOINTS TWIRLED DOWN from a gray sky. The city was black. A torrent of cars swept past the station, fouling the cold and raw air. I hoisted my pack and walked into the snow. I felt as if I had never left.

I clumped down into the concrete stomach of the road, where the gases mingled and stank. The city train looked like a string of decommissioned buses, coupled and perched on rails. We rustled under the streets in our lighted box—whites, Latinos, Asians, Africans—the international denizens of all big cities. Refugees all—if not from the politics or the economies of other countries, then from families or communities in this one. Seeking the refuge of anonymity. Or the refuge, simply, of noise and confusion. Away from the sheer boredom and emptiness in the countryside, obliterating emptiness in the heart.

From below, the train emerged into the gray light. I got off at my stop and stumbled down again to the street. I bought a magnum of champagne.

The familiar street, black and shining. I went up the stairs. I opened the door. A voice from the next room—"Eric?"

And Jutta came running: "Why didn't you tell me when your train was coming in?" And all I could see was the way her body moved beneath her clothes and I hugged her and pushed her, back into the hall and down the hall to her door, and I pushed open the door and pushed her into the room, dropped my pack and the champagne and pushed her onto the bed and while she was kissing me, I began to take off her clothes until she was naked and I pressed my face into her and smelled the fresh whiff of sweat in her hair and kept smelling her and tasting her until she had gotten off my clothes and taken my penis in her hands and I stopped her while she laughed to rip the square of foil and roll down the film that might save her life and then she slipped me greedily into her, into the wetness that seemed always to be there. As if I had never left.

And Timo, too, was there in the room, but he had seen us make love before and he had always known his mother did this and actually seeing it made no difference to him, although he had seemed surprised to see me again. He never came to lie between us until it was over, and so after my climax and after Jutta's frantic grappling with her climax, while I lay with my head in Jutta's lap, her damp pubic hair mingling with the hair on the back of my neck, he got up from the pile of junk he was playing with in the corner and undressed and crawled in naked with us, and I let him have his mother to himself while I went out, pranced down the freezing stairs to piss in the bathroom below, came back up through the kitchen grabbing Jutta's cigarettes on the way, put a cassette in the machine, and handed her a butt as I crawled back into bed with the champagne. As if I had never left.

□

The air outside had grown blue with evening and the bedroom was in shadow. The brightest point was the glow of Jutta's cigarette. From the other room came a babble about experiments with white mice. Timo had left us and glued himself to the tube. Jutta sat up. We were both drunk. In the blue light, her pale skin glowed. She was like a ripe blue fruit. I slid into the cave made by her butt, her spread bent legs, and her forward-leaning torso. I felt a great urge to lick her vagina, but she was too sensitive there so I kissed her inner thighs, her abdomen, turned on my back and took one breast, then the other, into my mouth. I wanted to consume her entirely, to suck her with one great pull into my mouth and swallow her, so that she could right herself inside me, put her eyes behind my eyes, slip her arms and legs down the channels of my arms and legs. I found the thought of it very satisfying. Then we could have our disastrous Christmases together.

Jutta had gone to Innsbruck for Christmas to visit her grandparents. Timo, of course, hadn't been allowed to go with her. Jutta had pleaded with her grandparents over the phone about that, but they had remained firm. They were nothing if not principled. So Timo had gone with Theodor and Ulrike to the farm in Carinthia.

"He'd never been there," Jutta had told me, as we each had held up our first glass, Timo squirming between us. The champagne was terrible. "He was very excited. He wanted to pat a cow and ride in the tractor." And Timo had had a good time. When he saw his mother again, he talked on and on about what he had seen, people and other children he had met. He told me about it, too, from his snuggled place in the blanket under the two bubbling glasses, his eyes sparkling happily. He said he was going to be a farmer when he grew up. He said he wanted to visit his friends there again soon.

After he had trotted off, Jutta told me more. Ulrike had come back to Vienna in tears. She was furious with the villagers, who had clucked their tongues at her when she'd taken Timo with her to shop. People she knew had laughed uncomfortably and thrown up their hands, as if to say, "well, it's none of *my* business." One of the shopkeepers, an old acquaintance, had told her point-blank that if she couldn't leave the city behind her, she shouldn't come out to the country. Fortunately, Timo was still young enough to have missed such things. So he prattled to his mother about friends while Ulrike cried to her about humiliations.

"Now she knows what it feels like," Jutta said. "Pretty little married girl—she's used to everyone pampering her. Now she knows."

Both reactions seemed strong to me: Ulrike's tears, Jutta's scorn. But something else had happened over the holiday; something Jutta wasn't telling me.

"Kurt, her husband, never wanted Timo down there. Kurt's not crazy about the way we live here. He always thought of himself as an upstanding citizen, and little black bastards didn't fit into that. Ulrike was always much worse when he was around—playing the darling wife. Then Renate and I weren't worth two groschen apiece."

And life in Innsbruck?

"Ohhh . . . ," Jutta let out a long sigh. She flopped back on the pillows and a dotted line of surprised champagne twinkled from her glass to her belly. "They don't look a bit older. They'll both live to be 125, I'm sure. My mother said I was getting really fat."

"Fat?" I said, and rubbed her wet stomach. "This stuff isn't fat. This is *substance.*" Jutta's midriff reminded me of Michelangelo's *Last Judgment,* in which his Christ has the taut, broad, muscled stomach of a stonemason. I used to prefer boyish builds. I couldn't fathom what had come over me.

"We didn't say a word about Timo. Or about you. As soon as I mention a boyfriend, they tell me I'm being disgusting."

"What *do* you talk about?"

She stared at the ceiling pensively. "Not much . . . My father hardly talks to me at all. If it were up to him, I'm sure he'd be just as happy never to see me again. My mother talks about the house, or about a dress she's making, or about prices . . . She nags me. My table manners are awful. I can't cook. I look like a mess. Nice, huh?" Her voice cracked on the last word. Talk of her grandparents upset her with a suddenness that still surprised me.

"Don't you think it odd that they have you come only to be unkind to you?"

"Oh, it's not for me. They invite me because it's Christmas, or Easter. My mother says those are family holidays. Even families that have 'had their troubles'—that's how she puts it—should come together on those two days. It's a time of Christian forgiveness, she says."

Yet the real children, Jutta's aunts and uncle, did not come to be "forgiven." Perhaps Heinrich Bechtler had been right. Perhaps each generation *was* worse than the last. At least Brigitte, Hildegaard and Hermann had the self-respect to stay away. Only Jutta returned for these ghastly parodies of family celebration, not only to suffer abuse but to let it sink deep, and in doing so she left behind her the only relative who loved her: her little black bastard.

"Have you ever considered telling them you weren't coming?" I asked. "Could staying away possibly be worse than going?"

"I know it's despicable, Eric, but I just can't—"

"I didn't say it was despicable. It just seems . . . unwarranted." I'd almost said "masochistic." But Jutta would have thought that just another way of saying "despicable."

And in a way, I would have, too.

But then, why didn't I despise Jutta?

□

Perhaps because I was coming from my own humiliations.

I had spent the holidays lying. About Jutta, for one thing; I had not been able to tell my mother about her, although I had promised Jutta

I would. Not because I had thought better of the idea (or at least, not much), but for a more shameful reason. In an early letter, I had called her thirty-eight and obese, and Timo Italian. Back at my mother's house, suddenly confronted—how had I not foreseen this?—with the recipient of my letters, I realized that to talk about Jutta I would first have to confess to earlier lies. Before I quite knew what I was doing, I had lied more, and with every lie it became less conceivable that I would pull up short and say "Wait a minute! Excuse me—everything I have said up until now is a lie." *Schlamperei!*

And my work! Thank God my mother's subject is nineteenth-century America and not World War II. I tried to be as vague as possible. I was helped by the fact that she wanted to be reassured. She convinced herself she was satisfied after I made a few noises about the membership of the *Heimwehr* and the Tyrolean Anti-Semitic League. (Both of which actually existed although I knew about as much concerning their membership as I did of Mozart's Masonic lodge.)

One of the myths of my family has me cast in the role of the utterly truthful son. In my entire childhood, my parents never caught me in a lie; not because I never lied, but because I only lied about those things that no one could check, such as my feelings and desires. My mother perhaps would not have minded Jutta so much. She had to concede, at least rhetorically, that that sort of thing was my business. But I could imagine the disappointment over the lying in her face— the crumbling of that vasty temple erected to my honesty—and I couldn't bear the thought of it. Recent events had shown me how much my character was not only formed but actually held together from moment to moment by my parents' ideas of me. My father had breathed life into my career and his death had as surely sucked the life back out of it. My mother's involvement with me had always been more moral than professional. Whereas I had studied and thought like my father, I behaved like my mother. I feared, in some obscure way, that if she lost her faith in my truthfulness, then I would cease to be, in anything, truthful. Somehow, as long as I lied and she didn't know it, I felt I was only a step away from the truth and could make that step back any time I wanted to.

But Rick knew. "You're blowing this off, aren't you?" he had asked me, after a few minutes' scrutiny.

"Yes," I said. I could trust him not to say anything.

He shook his head, smiling incredulously. "I knew this would happen to you some day." Rick had always known.

"Rick" and "Eric": one of those irritating name-pairs that twins sometimes inspire even in serious parents. From the beginning, we were dressed alike and treated alike and adults declared themselves unable to tell us apart. For a while in school we were even called "A"-Rick and "B"-Rick by waggish teachers who took their cue from my name: *Eh*-ric, get it? All of this taught us an early disrespect for adult perspicacity because it was obvious to both of us that we were very different, if not antithetical. Rick was brilliant, quick, rebellious. If anything, *he* was the honest one, but his honesty was obscured by his rebelliousness, which often expressed itself through lying.

We were different, and we disliked each other, but we knew each other better than anyone else did. Rick had always been the only one who could see my resentment as I obeyed, or the apathy beneath the enthusiasm when I agreed that yes, I wanted to do the work my parents suggested. I envied Rick's freedom, his happy appropriation of a position below which he could not go. I also thought he was a selfish and inconsiderate brat. He, on the other hand, thought I was weak, of mediocre intelligence, and a coward. And meanwhile adults told us, into our teens, that we were mirror images of each other.

So Christmas was a laugh a minute, between worrying about betraying myself and enduring Rick's silent derision; between trying to comfort my mother when comfort only discomforted her and being reminded of Helga, my vanished older sister, now that I was once again across the hall from her old room.

Good God, families! Josh, though largely oblivious to other people's concerns, styles himself a natural psychoanalyst. He likes to say, "I find families infinitely fascinating!" I'm afraid I found the subject, from the vantage of that rumpled bed in the blue light, with the blatter of television drifting to us, in the melancholia of an empty magnum, infinitely depressing.

I burrowed into Jutta, into my warm blue cave. I said, "You know —after a lifetime of politics, utopias, polemics, Aldous Huxley said when he was an old, old man that the only thing he believed any more would really help the world would be if everybody just tried to be a little nicer to each other."

"Hm?" Jutta murmured, all around me.

"But I would ask, 'Why isn't it enough to be nice? Why do we have to be strong, too?' "

Jutta didn't answer. She had fallen asleep.

☐

Brigham Fellowship Committee

Dear Committee,

Greetings! I'm back from my vacation in the U.S. of A., ready to reapply my proboscis to the proverbial grindstone—

Well, the holiday hadn't been a complete bust. I had discovered, purely by accident, something important.

I had gone to the Harvard history department on December 20 to pick up the Brigham check for January and February. I'd chosen the day carefully: the 20th was the Friday before the Christmas break, and there wasn't a snowball's chance in hell I would find anyone at the department except for the secretary. As an undergraduate, I had learned early the two cardinal rules of college life: for happiness in the dormitory, make friends with maintenance; for success in the department, make friends with the secretary. The latter had been easy. Pat was a sweet, sad woman whom most of the professors treated like a scribe, a wife, and a galley slave rolled conveniently into one. All she wanted for her work was politeness, gratitude, and a little patience— and as an undergraduate, I had showered her with all three. So when I showed up among the cyclamen, geraniums, and "You don't have to be crazy to work here but it helps" posters, she looked up from a Danielle Steel novel and greeted me warmly. And while we were shooting the breeze—kvetching about the latest *seconda donna*s on the junior faculty, wondering how the mediocre dullard I had had for German social history had managed to get tenure—Pat casually mentioned that no one in the department was reading my monthly reports. "I open them myself," she said cheerily, swiveling to a cabinet and pulling a folder out of a drawer, "and file them away immediately." And there they were, spread out on her desk like low-life suspects in a police line-up. "If anyone looked at them, I would know about it."

I picked them up.

"*I arrived in Vienna ten days ago, and have spent much of—*"

"*The archive research has proven, unfortunately, to be far more complicated than I had imagined—*"

"*I've been so busy the last few days at the archives that I haven't been home much—*"

Pat said gently, "Eric, you know how they never get to things like that—not for anybody." She had misread my blushing as anger.

"No, it's all right," I said. "I know." I handed them back to her, and she hid them away again. But I *hadn't* known. Which I realized had been grossly naive of me. After all, it was common knowledge that the professors had to be virtually handcuffed to their desks before they would read the theses and dissertations each spring, and those were far more important than my progress reports. Yet somehow, I had assumed that the department would want to keep track of its seven thousand dollars. "But if no one reads them, how have the checks been getting to me?" I asked.

"Oh, *I* read them," Pat assured me. "I look for an address change. It's also nice to find out how you're doing."

I had agonized over those letters. I had sent each one off, terrified that one of the professors on the committee would find a mistake, would perhaps notice my mention of "district station records" and would check to see if anything called "district stations" actually existed in the Austrian *Heimwehr* or the *Schutzbund* in 1938. But what could I have been thinking of? Only my father would do that kind of thing. On December 20, in the office of the history department, it dawned on me: Pat filed my reports away, and at the end of the year she would take them out for the few seconds needed to attach them to my final report, and then she would ship the package of monthly and final reports to the fellowship office, where some other secretary would file them away, and later I could rework the report into an article, or I could expand it into a masters thesis, or I could put it in a plastic bag, swing it around my head, and squawk like a chicken for all Harvard cared. Of course Harvard didn't care! It was seven thousand dollars, but it was money Harvard couldn't touch for any other purpose. If the money didn't go to me, it would just go to some other clown blowing off some other project in some other country.

Now I was curious. Between Christmas and the New Year, I went to the Harvard fellowship office and checked through the records of the Brigham. I read the final reports of previous recipients; the dry pages rustled crisply in my hands, as paper will do after years of lying undisturbed. One report was about dancing in an Israeli ballet company for the deaf. It was utterly uninformative, but it did gush at length about the inner nobility of handicapped people. Another report took a long, serious look at the quality of health-care provided to minorities in central Europe; throughout it, Iranians were referred to as "Arabs," and the German word for *hospital* was consistently misspelled. But my favorite report concerned, of all things, the effect of Arabic culture on Russian sacred music in Tunisia. Most of the report was devoted to transcriptions of Slavonic hymns, with arrows pointing everywhere, and the text in the remainder incorporated a suspiciously large amount of Cyrillic and Arabic script, rendering it safely incomprehensible. A trip to the atlas confirmed that all the Russian churches mentioned in the analysis were located near celebrated Tunisian beaches. A follow-up letter from the author—one Stanislav Al-Hazeh—revealed that he had gone on to a medical school in the Caribbean. The letter was written on the back of a restaurant menu.

In fact, in the entire history of the fellowship—thirty-two years—only one recipient had actually managed to lose his funding. His name was Charles Wigginton Whitehouse III, and his project had concerned rural depopulation in southern France and its effect on the powerful French farmers' lobby. His monthly reports were lengthy, enthusiastic, digressive, and often nonsensical—clearly written under the influence of controlled substances. Also, they had all been mailed from Monte Carlo. A cursory investigation revealed that Charles Wigginton Whitehouse III was using the Brigham funds for gambling. Even after this discovery, he might not have lost his bi-monthly checks but for the fact that he seemed to be winning enough at the table to support himself. (He had made a promising demographic historian because he was good at statistics, and the talent seemed to serve him equally well at blackjack.) Harvard, therefore, could cut off one of its own without leaving him adrift like an ordinary ne'er-do-well.

I walked out of the fellowship office feeling as if a weight had been lifted from my shoulders. So the shit wouldn't hit the fan unless I applied for graduate school in history, and thus gave someone a compelling reason to haul out my report and read it. And I had no intention of doing that, in any case. I had finally admitted to myself that I was through with history. Perhaps I could switch to comparative literature and read novels all day. Or art appreciation. Or hotel management.

I might get away with it! A startling thought. A dizzying thought. I had learned since infancy that breaking a trust brought punishment, humiliation. I had seen that principle operate inexorably with respect to my siblings. It had never occurred to me that this year of lying and throwing away Harvard's money would not end in public disgrace. By God, I just might get away with it!

Even my mother would accept my leaving history. She had not really had her way with me from the beginning. My only remaining fear was that she would find out about *this* year. This year, she would take as a slap in the face. She would never forgive me for it. But why should she find out? She had her own work to do, her own troubles.

January 5, 1986

Brigham Committee

Dear Committee,

Greetings! I'm back from my vacation in the U.S. of A., ready to reapply my proboscis to the proverbial grindstone. Having finished my research on the membership of the *Heimwehr*, I'll be moving on to the finances of the *Schutzbund*. The state archives on Kandlgasse have a large amount of material on the sources of the funds for the Left, both within the political apparatus and without. A curious thing that I've discovered so far is that the Jewish banking interests tended to fund the *Heimwehr* more than they did the *Schutzbund*, despite the fact that the leadership of the *Heimwehr* was openly anti-Semitic, and their stated aim for the private army was the protection and promotion of the interests of the Catholic peasantry, particularly in Upper Austria, against the encroachments of urban capital (which was largely seen to be in Jewish hands) . . .

And I had so dreaded this moment. I had thought that by January, at the latest, I would have to start saying *something*. I might even have been forced into the library, in order to look something up—a ghastly thought. But now I knew it didn't matter what I wrote, so long as I filled up a couple of pages. Pat was an excellent secretary, but she hadn't the slightest interest in history. Bless her heart, she could re-member that World War I preceded World War II only because of the happy fact that they were numbered.

□

Meanwhile, I was passing a milestone in my emotional life. I thought I was in love. And might that not be the same as being in love? If so, then I was in love.

The world was weightless, a great bird taking wing. Events were accompanied by a feeling of impermanence, of fragility. "This is it! here! now!" my spirit shouted, as each minute floated like a soap bubble in the particulate mist of the one that burst before it. All causality had disappeared. Responsibilities, consequences, the claims and feelings of other people: for the first time in my life I pulled myself to my full height and cried "Avaunt!" to them, and sent them from the field. Rick would have been proud. I never knew whether I was proud or ashamed.

I asked Timo today what he remembered of that time and he responded with a blank look. Then his face lit up and he said, "Taking a bath!" So I will begin there.

□

In the mornings, often, the three of us bathe together. It is usually Timo's idea, but when he runs the water there is no telling what the temperature will be, so if he wakes us up and says "Bath, Mommy!" one or the other of us rolls out in the gray light and pads with him down the hall, picks through the children's room ("Timo, this is an unbelievable mess" "It is?"), and on into Ulrike's room, where the bed is already empty and made, through the curtain and up the three steps to the side of the enormous ugly green enamel bathtub, where Timo reaches as far as he can over the green void and turns the chintzy chrome faucets and watches fascinated and pleased as the water foams out and splashes for a few seconds to no effect, then coalesces into a pool edging menacingly outward. After a minute the gas fwoomps under the ancient water heater and the fwoomp is the signal for Jutta or me (whoever it is) to tell Timo to go get the other and, as soon as Timo goes, Jutta or I adjust the faucets until the water comes out the way Jutta or I like it. When I do it, the bathwater is hot, and Timo complains at first and looks worriedly at the rosiness burning up through his brown skin. When Jutta does it, the bathwater is scalding, and Timo and I both complain—Timo hopping in and back out and in again and I wondering if I am being sterilized—while Jutta just lies back with the steam rising around her, her breasts floating flat-topped and flaming pink on the surface, her nipples pale and deflated, and murmurs to us somnambulently not to be babies.

Timo loves these baths, I think, because the tub, though large, is not quite large enough for three, and we are a tangle of limbs in it. It is here, unlike in the bed, where he can touch us and press against us and slide around us more than we can with each other. Here in the tub there isn't that mysterious other tangling that in bed makes both Jutta and me, no matter how good a boy Timo has been, utterly forget him for a while or at most react with intense, inexplicable annoyance if he tries to interfere. Here he is the center of attention, slipping about us, glistening—like a seal, I think, searching for a better simile and not finding one. We soap him up and twirl him around and pour water over his head out of a yellow plastic bucket. I wash Jutta's hair and she washes Timo's hair and Timo washes Heidi's hair or sometimes he asks me to do it, and the golden-haired doll stares inscrutably at a point a few inches in front of her up-turned nose as her fine plastic strands are rubbed with shampoo. Near the ceiling as we are, in such a tiny enclosure, the steam gathers in a dense fog around us so that we can hardly see the walls. We are alone in our own warm wet world.

□

Breakfasts are late and slow. There are no classes at the university.

"There are *never* classes at the university," I say. "The courses didn't start until mid-October. And then they knocked off three weeks before Christmas."

"It's interterm now," Jutta explains. "Second semester begins in March."

"No wonder Germans are taking all the important jobs in Austria."

"Yes we're nothing like you hard-working Harvard students."

So except for her work at the day-care center, Jutta is free. She practices her English by listening to Barry Holtzman on Blue Danube Radio. She practices her French by reading *Le Monde* and a leftist weekly called *La Révolution*. She catches the five-minute French news report on Austrian Radio in the morning and at noon. She also tries to practice her English with me. But she is a different person in English, clumsy and crude. She makes quaint mistakes. She tells stupider jokes. Her English makes me uncomfortable, as if I'm seeing a side of her personality otherwise hidden. Timo and I conspire to force her back into German. "You're not helping me!" she complains. "I help you with your German—"

"My German doesn't need any help."

She sneers. "Maybe your *Hochdeutsch* doesn't. You sound like a goddamn newscaster."

It's true. She's improving my gutterspeak. But since we are all *Nichtwiener,* none of us speak Viennese. Renate is from the Burgenland, Ulrike from Carinthia, Jutta from Innsbruck. One gets the feeling that the true Viennese are an endangered species, their natural habitat of wine cellars and whorehouses threatened by the recent wine scandals (anti-freeze was a favorite additive) and the flashy new incurable venereal diseases. So the slang I am learning is a hopeless mélange. Shopkeepers have begun to ask me, doubtfully, where I am from. Now I am a *Volksdeutscher,* too. I answer Argentina, *Ost-Friesland,* South-West Africa, Hungary. I make up stories. Until a Hungarian baker in a rough neighborhood takes offense at a joke and offers to knead my face. I think, forchrissake, I meant no harm. *"Bassza meg!"* I say to him, it being the only Hungarian I know. It means something on the order of "shit" or "fuck you." And in the second granted me, during which he looks stunned at my familiarity with this phrase, I flee. Then he bursts out onto the sidewalk, 250 pounds in white, and chases me. I thought storekeepers, like dogs, recognized certain limits to their territories. But he keeps after me into the next block, and when he reaches me, he clouts me on the back of the head so hard my glasses fly off. He would probably do more, except that I go down, arms around my head, and curl up. (Like grizzly bears, Hungarians have been known to leave people alone in this position.) After teaching me a few more Hungarian swear words, he stalks off. An Iranian student hands me back my glasses. Then he asks if I would like to give him money to fight Khomeini. I go home with a bruised ego and a headache.

□

Elizabeth is going to be a tiny girl. At breakfast she gums the bottom halves of home-baked Renate-rolls and dribbles her rice on the table with a proud Bronx cheer. The light-skinned Renate puts a tiny shower cap over her head when the sunlight is strong. "She doesn't need that!" Jutta guffaws, taking one of Elizabeth's coffee hands around a finger. "Do you, Bizzie-wizzie?" Now she can sit up on her own, so I find her in the middle of a blanket on the floor, a brown egg, a flannel Humpty-Dumpty, encircled by plastic toys that she has pushed just beyond her reach. My new fears are that Timo will trip over her, or hit her with one of the bricks—real bricks—he plays with (piling them into precarious towers), or light her hair on fire with his Bic, or pour sulphuric acid over her. (I'm sure he has a stash of sulphuric acid somewhere.)

The weather has become too cold for Renate's day-long walks and Ulrike, like Jutta, is between terms, so all of us are together for these late breakfasts. Ulrike's color is enthralling in the chill air—the apartment is never warm—her very red lips matched by lively reddish cheeks, her pure white forehead framed by the black hair and thick black upswept eyebrows. Next to her, Renate looks washed-out and bony; Jutta is a frowzy yellow-gray. Contemplating her husband, her white boy, and her up-country milk-maid looks, I can understand why Jutta is jealous of her. Ulrike, I think, could leave this fellowship of misfits any time she wanted to.

But there is the obvious question, and one night I ask it of Jutta. "If her classes don't begin until March, why isn't she on the farm with Kurt?"

"Oh . . . ," she sighs, as I brush her hair, "I was hoping you wouldn't ask." *Au contraire,* she looks as if she is delighted I finally have. "Ulrike didn't want me to tell you."

"Oh. Well then . . . Of course, you shouldn't—"

"But I suppose it's all right. Kurt . . . has never been very faithful to her. She's always known that. He tries to be good, but—" She makes a dismissive gesture with her hands. But you know men, is what she means. The dears can't help it. "This Christmas, while Ulrike was down there, she found out that Kurt had been lying with a girl who did the housework for him." She pauses, whether out of genuine delicacy or for dramatic effect, I can't tell.

"And that was the last straw?" I ask.

"Worse!" she exclaims, deliciously. (The latter.) "The girl is pregnant. That's how she found out. The whole town knows."

Jui-cy. And worse (and juicier) still: the girl is only thirteen.

Kurt, you devil.

"So Ulrike had a lousy Christmas, too," I say. "And she doesn't even have someone to commiserate with."

Jutta gives me a sharp look. "I'll bet you'd love to commiserate with her."

Unfortunately, that's true. "I'm not that stupid, Jutta." Fortunately, that's true, too.

"She doesn't seem upset," I say.

"Ulrike is very good at hiding her feelings."

Perhaps that is why I find myself so attracted to her. Ulrike and I have the same deadpan non-stop way of lying. "So now what happens?"

"Everybody waits. The girl's family is poor; uneducated. They may not go to court if Kurt pays them enough. And he'll have to pay for raising the child."

It is an Austrian custom that a farmer's son doesn't marry until he acquires the farm. For this reason, rural Austria is full of illegitimate children. The girl's child won't be stigmatized so much for that. Pedophilia is not uncommon either. Kurt's behavior would be seen in his village as a gaucherie, rather than an abomination. Chances are, he can, indeed, buy his way out of it.

"And Ulrike? What does she do?"

"She won't say." Suddenly tired of the subject, Jutta goes to the bed. I follow, and turn out the light. She snuggles against me. Her skin is cold, clayey. "I don't think she knows."

We kiss for a while, slowly warming up against each other. Then I stop abruptly and ask, "Don't you feel sorry for her?"

Jutta thinks about it long enough so that I believe her when she answers. "No," she says.

But I don't believe what she says next, as justification for her callousness: "I would have left Kurt a long time ago."

☐

I wake up with a face full of piquant armpit hairs. Jutta is reaching across me. "What—?" I ask.

"Getting René," she says.

8:05. Mmrrrmph. Wakemefordinner . . . A loud, cheerful nose honks in the room. *"Bonjouuur, mesdames et messieurs! Maintenant nous avons les actualités d'aujourd'hui—"*

"Bath, Mommy!"

René blabbers, and I run water.

□

"Haven't you figured it out yet, Eric?" Renate asks me indignantly.

"What?"

"Jutta has been this way with most of her boyfriends. You're no great exception."

"But she told me when we first met that she always grew tired of her men."

Renate shakes her head, gripping her medical journal and mug of herb tea as if holding on to reality for dear life. "You're so naive sometimes, I don't know whether to laugh or hit you over the head."

"You mean she doesn't really love me?"

"I mean that this will end the same way all the others have ended. You'll leave and she'll be devastated."

"But I—"

"And more than usual because you've stayed longer. Somehow— I don't know how, but somehow you get along better with her than other men she's had." She makes it sound like an accusation. "That will only make it worse."

"I'm not leaving her."

"You don't think so."

"What am I supposed to say to that? Yes, I don't think so!"

"But you will. You'll see what I mean."

"Renate," I laugh, "that sounds ominous."

"You'll see."

□

"Excuse me, young man, I'm a reporter for television station FS-2. May I ask you a few questions?"

". . . Yes."

"Could you tell our viewing audience what in hell you're doing?"

"I'm building."

"Speak into the mike, please. No, the mike. Here. They don't have microphones where you come from?"

"I'm building!"

"Well that's fascinating. But I'm sure the herds of sheep who watch this program would prefer to know *what* you're building."

"I'm building a building."

"Amazing! What kind of building?"

"A doll house."

"Stupendous! It's going to be a brick structure, I take it?"

"The walls are going to be brick, but the roof will be tin."

"A complete sentence! Fabulous! Where's the tin? Ah, you mean this piece of rusty sheet metal with the jagged razor-sharp edges?"

"Yes."

"Why a house?"

"So Heidi can have a place to stay when I'm away."

"Why does she need a place to stay?"

"She gets lonely without me."

"Why do you leave her, then?"

"Well . . . she's only a doll."

"Ahh, I know what you mean. The weaker sex, always trying to tie a man down . . ."

"But if she has a house, she can play with her own dolls."

"Whoa, careful with that! Where did you find this roof, anyway?"

"Nowhere . . ."

"Come on, where did you get it?"

"Come on, where did you get your face?"

"Onnnh, wise guy, eh? If you don't tell me, I'll electrocute your eyeballs with my television antenna."

"I'll hit you with a brick and hit you with a stick! And you're *weird!*"

"I'm rubber and you're glue. Everything you say bounces off me and sticks to you."

☐

"She's much different with you," Ulrike says. "You don't know what it's been like before."

"It's interesting you say that," I say, "because Renate told me just the opposite. She said all Jutta's affairs went the same way."

"No, no. She seems much more . . ." Ulrike considers and rejects two or three words, "well . . . *stable* with you. Or more secure. Usually there are terrible fights. Forgive me," she smiles charmingly, touches my hand—I think she knows how captivating I find her appearance—"but I'm curious why."

"Simple," I say. "I just don't fight. I refuse to. I radiate calmness."

"Be serious."

"I am being serious." Why should I bare my heart to you? Just because you're beautiful? You've told me nothing about yourself, about Kurt.

I say, "In my family, we—"

" 'In your family'! Do you realize how often you say that? Every time Jutta or Renate or I ask you about yourself you start talking about your family."

Psychology students! They think they are the only ones attuned to these patterns. But all that distinguishes them from other people is that they are tactless enough to talk about them.

"I'm sorry, Ulrike, I don't feel like being psychoanalyzed today." She stiffens, and I regret having spoken sharply. "Ulrike, you have to remember I haven't seen Jutta with other men. I have no idea why she feels better or more secure or whatever with me. I'm just happy she does."

Ulrike is apologetic, too. "So are we, Eric." She leans forward and kisses me sweetly on the lips. "I just hope it lasts."

□

Timo loves to feed birds.

Vienna has turned its pigeons to account. In Stephansplatz, a hundred and fifty feet below the diamond-patterned tiles of the cathedral roof, old raggedy men sell sticks of birdseed for a few shillings.

"This is where it all started," Jutta says, as I hand coins to one of the men. She means Timo's passion. Timo pushes back the hood of his jacket and steps gingerly away from the cathedral, holding the seed-encrusted twig. A bird lands on his arm, and he turns to us excitedly —"Mommy, look!" Then two more, and then ten more, and now Timo is running, covered in birds, a feathered clown or a Hitchcock victim, and from the stumbling running column of flapping wings I can hear, flying back across the pavement to us, Timo's high, hysterical laughter.

□

Among the Iranians, the Turks, the Yugoslavs, the Filipinos of Lazarettgasse, Timo still stands out. Even though he has only been to Ghana once, for a few weeks, even though he refused to speak to or touch the source of what the Viennese consider his most important trait, he still connects himself somehow to that country. In some part of his mind he must realize that if people ever think of him, they think "ah, the little Ghanaian boy"; as if he did not live in Austria, as if he would not one day vote in Austria's elections. By the time I tell Timo I am an American, we are on good enough terms that he wants, the way children often do, to establish a common ground between us, to relate my unknown life to his familiar one. He asks, "Is America in Ghana?"

Typically, Josh assures me he can sympathize with the boy. "I'm a Jew from Atlanta—I know what it's like to be a freak. And now I've moved to a city in which people still call themselves anti-Semites as if referring to a purely political position. But it's even worse for *die Schwarzen*. There are only two places you can find blacks in this city: at night, in the bars on Seitenstettengasse, playing jazz; and during the day, over at the Hilton, opening doors. And the sad part of it is: they're the same people."

□

January 15, 1986

Dear Mom,

I suppose the work has kept me too busy, but I've been *intending* to write for the past couple of days. The weather here has been cold . . .

. . . you asked about my work—but there really isn't much to say about it at the moment. It's going fairly well. Frankly, after a long day in the archives, I find I don't like to think or talk about it much. I suppose I picked that up from you, since you never cared much to talk about your work, either.

It's very late, though. I've got to get to sleep if I'm to get anything done tomorrow. My next letter will be longer, I promise.

Love,
Eric

□

"It's three hours!" she says with shock, looking up from the *Rheingold* poster in the lobby. "You said it was the shortest one."

"It is," I answer. "The others are five hours." Jutta foolishly promised to take in an opera with me, if I endured another morning at the Spanish Riding School with her.

"Don't be a wimp, Jutta," says Josh, who agreed to come when I told him Jutta was coming. He smiles down on her from his six and a half feet. "As Charles Ives once said, 'Goddamnit, take your music like a man!' "

Josh and Jutta love each other's company. Jutta says, marveling, that he can always make her laugh. And Josh is tickled by the way she looks up at him as if she's a fraction of a second away from throwing her arms around his waist. On our way home after the first time she met him, Jutta asked me, "Are all Jews so funny?" Josh was the first Jew she had ever met.

The line has begun to move. "This time I can keep an eye on you," Jutta says, holding my arm. Being around Josh puts her in the mood for banter.

"Oh God not that again."

"What?" Josh asks.

"She's talking about the American woman—"

"What, the one with the firm young tits?"

"I talk to you too much, don't I, Josh?"

"*I* always thought so."

"Is this opera by Richard Strauss?" Jutta asks, trying to find the title page of the program.

Josh glances at me, astonished. He says to her encouragingly, "Right political party."

During the mad rush into the standing room area, Josh vaults a railing and secures us three places in the center. I trot behind, keeping enough distance to dissociate myself from him in case the guards decide to arrest him. Jutta brings up the rear, calmly swishing along in her ratty wool pants.

"You're going to love this," Josh assures her.

But halfway through the first act, she sits on the floor between us. "I can see from here!" she whispers to us reassuringly. Then she opens her shoulder bag and pulls out some knitting. Josh leans down and whispers to her that if she does a single stitch he will take the needles out of her hands and plunge them into her heart. She pouts and puts it away. Within fifteen minutes, she's asleep.

I sure know how to show a girl a good time.

Later, in a wine cellar: "I'm sick and tired of this horn playing," Josh says, over our second liter of violet *Hexenblut:* "witch's blood" wine. "It's giving me an ulcer."

"What's coming up?"

"The worst! Bruckner's Fourth." He fetches his mouth piece out of his pocket and spritzes a couple of licks at me. A passing waiter glares. "It's Bruckner, pal!" Josh yells after him. "Your favorite!" And then to us, "The Viennese puke all over the tables and they say *'Schmeckt's gut, mein Herr?'* but one American Jew-boy buzzes his chops and they jump down his throat."

"So when's the concert?" Josh, on the subject of the Viennese, can be a trifle monotonous.

"Tomorrow in the Musikverein. You'd better not show up. I'm going to be all over the place." He does a loud and uncanny imitation of a French horn aiming for a high note and missing it.

Later still, walking tipsily toward the Ring with linked arms: "I'm going to open a Mexican restaurant. You want to join me?"

"A what?"

"You haven't noticed? There aren't any Mexican restaurants in Vienna. We could clean up."

"What makes you think there's a demand?"

He shrugs. "Everybody loves Mexican food. Right?"

"I've never had it," Jutta says.

"Josh is a terrible cook," I say.

"Who needs to cook? We'll hire a cook, a few Mexican waiters—"

"Where are we going to get Mexican waiters?"

"Aannh, we can use Iranians. What do the Viennese know? A wog's a wog."

"So the cook will be Iranian, too?"

"No, wait—of course! Filipinos. Leopoldstadt is crawling with them. *Someone* had to go live in all those empty Jewish apartments—"

At the Ring, Josh insists on getting a taxi, instead of waiting in the cold for the streetcar. He knows we're broke, so he pays for it. He loves to play the open-handed patron, the master of ceremonies. In the taxi he sits in the middle, his curly head pressed against the underside of the roof, his long arms around both of us, like a father bringing his sleepy kids home from an Adventures in Music concert.

When Jutta and I get out at Lazarettgasse, Jutta leans back through the rear window and gives him a kiss. "Why don't you come up for a while?"

I can't see him in the dark interior, but I can hear that deep, sonorous voice. "Of course I'd love to. But unfortunately, my love is waiting silently for me. Can't treat her *too* badly, you know." The voice rises to address me: "Good night, Junior!" Then he gives the driver a burst of directions in slurring Viennese, and the car takes off. From the open window, I can hear his voice, fading, singing "Homeward Bound."

□

"Bath, Mommy!"

Jutta runs it even hotter than usual. She cries out with pain as she lies down in the water. Her skin turns a frightening dark rose. Later, Timo, splashing around, opens an old cut, and a faint swirl of red appears in the suds. The sight of it makes me shudder. Afterward, I put a bandaid on the wound.

The steam on the inside of the windows has frozen.

□

During these bitterly cold days, the number of folks working Kärntnerstrasse has diminished. The beggars outside the churches have disappeared—to shelters? to subway stations? to morgues?—except for the cadaverous man who stands in the foyer of St. Stephen's holding a cardboard box-flap to his chin ("I'm Christian and I'm hungry"), and stares over it with deep, haunting eyes. Most of the other Christians, the ones with the bullhorns, guitars, the lurid literature, have also gone

102

—to retreats? to seminars?—and like the other beggars, they have left behind a sole representative: an elderly lady with unkempt hair who holds out a fan of broadsides entitled *Wann ist die Apokalypse?* Her eyes glint strangely, and they drift always upward, either because she is comforting herself in the contemplation of her Creator, or because she is blind, or because she is severely retarded. Her vacant, unchanging smile inclines me to the last view. When I speak to her she smiles on, eyes curved upward, without answering. I take one of her sheets and it slides out of her hand, with a tug of friction, like a receipt out of an automatic dispenser.

Curiously, in these coldest days, there are newcomers on the street. The Circus Ziegler arrived in Vienna a week ago, after someone had put up placards along the Ring and the Gürtel promising international stars and elephants and tigers. The Circus Ziegler set up a tent in a snowy field in the tenth district, gave one performance, and promptly went bankrupt. The owner of the field tried to evict the troupe, but it became obvious that the performers didn't have enough money to pull up stakes and go. Articles in the *Kronen* and the *Kurier* making the field-owner out to be an unfeeling bastard brought a change of heart, and he offered to let them stay rent-free until they raised enough money to leave, provided they kept the field clean.

Keeping the field clean has proven to be easy, as apparently there are not, after all, any elephants or tigers to tidy up after. Observers report not seeing much of anything around the tent in the field other than a monkey, a piebald goat, and an old, sick brown bear. The presence of the old bear caused one columnist to refer to *The World According to Garp.* He seemed rather proud that his city was living up to its sad and shabby portrait in the American novel.

While the curious look for tigers in the tenth district, the international stars collect money every day in the pedestrian zone along Kärntnerstrasse. The international stars consist of a single Gypsy family. "International, I'll buy," Josh says. "But the only stars are in their eyes."

Josh is right—it's an oddly naive and stage-struck family. Especially for Gypsies. There's a friendly woman, fattish but still pretty; a husband, thin and tired, dressed in a ringmaster's costume that looks like Spanish Civil War surplus; a boy and girl, both dark, both about five years old; and a strikingly beautiful boy of about twelve, with black hair offsetting a pale, thin face, and arresting gray eyes.

The stars go through their motions. The boy balances on a wooden plank thrown over a cylinder. Then he balances on a wooden plank supported by five plastic cups on another wooden plank thrown over a cylinder. While balancing, he awkwardly pulls a hoop over himself, then under his feet; twirls a hoop on each arm; twirls a lasso over his head. Everything is done with the same serious expression, the stunning gray eyes withdrawn and focused on some inner landscape. The five-year-old boy leads the rotund little goat up a step-ladder and across a raised plank and back, making as if to guide it with a long leather training whip. Josh and I watch this routine for the sixth or seventh time, our hands plunged into down pockets, and Josh observes, "An interesting variation. Most animal tricks consist of training the animal to do what is unnatural to it—tigers leaping through fire, an elephant standing on its back legs, and so on. But nothing comes more naturally to a goat than picking its way along a ledge." The monkey, dressed like a bellhop, is listless. The older boy appears to hope it will perform wild antics on the goat's plank, but it won't even hold on when raised up to it. The only time the animal shows a spark of energy is when the littlest boy accidentally steps on its foot, and it scurries off squealing, and is missing for half an hour. The bear, too, does nothing. It plops down each day on the same warm-air vent and remains there throughout, in a profound stupor. The father and the girl shake cans in which small amounts of money can be heard clinkering. The mother bangs her can like a tambourine. The beautiful boy stands silently during collections, and Austrian women stop to talk to him, drink him in with their earnest eyes. In the late afternoon, the family goes back to its tent. The mother stays behind to sweep up the pellets of goat shit. The bear, apparently, doesn't even shit.

Several times I almost speak to the boy. Where have they been, I want to ask. Who has taken them in, and actually gone to their shows? And where on earth could they have gotten the idea of coming to Vienna? Even in a village, their acts would be unpardonably lame. What fantastic image of themselves, or of the big city, made them think that they would belong here? That is a great part of their fascination: this otherworldly naïveté. The Viennese along Kärntnerstrasse gape at their inexplicable self-possession. And then, shaking their heads, making that knowing turn of the hand that in Vienna suggests gentle derision, they give a little money. And the family Ziegler accepts it as though it were in appreciation of their performances, rather than an act combined of compassion and wonder.

But I never ask the boy. When the women speak to him, his eyes look away. When he answers, he smiles beseechingly, as if to say, I don't mean to offend, but I don't want to talk to you. Whenever I pass I find myself unable to take my eyes off his face as he performs, or stands silent and abstracted, or pets and murmurs to the monkey. I wonder, Where are you going, boy? What are you seeing with those gray eyes? And it seems appropriate to wonder, too: What have people done to you?

And then, one day, the family is gone. The mother was as neat on her last day as on the others: the sidewalk is clean. No one knows where the family went. There is nothing in the newspapers. "He looked like Buster Keaton!" Jutta exclaims. The Albertina has been doing a Keaton retrospective, and he's all the rage in the arty cafés. We went to *Seven Chances* and Jutta fell in love. She has told me she's begun to have dreams about him. Keaton, not the boy. Although perhaps the boy is in there, too, now—I don't know. I've had a couple of dreams about him myself. The boy, not Keaton.

□

"I feel comfortable with you. As if we'd been together for years." She ponders this marvel for a while. "You're so calm. I like that."

"Always happy to please." Renate, Ulrike, now this. I'm sick of this subject.

"You're this way with everyone, aren't you?"

"No, not everyone." I dodge the real question. "The last person I tried to live with drove me crazy." I let her believe I'm talking about a woman. Actually, the last person I tried to live with was Rick. A purely economic decision, and short-lived. "What say we take in *The Third Man?* There's a showing at the Burg Kino in half an hour."

"OK." We jump out of bed and start gathering clothes.

Jutta assumes I've changed the subject out of modesty. She— always so close to tears, her nerves on edge—sees my calmness as a blessing. She would be surprised to hear that most of my affairs (back before the AIDS test) have ended over just this issue. Other women have seen in this calmness a dearth of feeling. I don't admit my doubts, they said. Even to myself. And they were probably right, I reflect, as we head down the stairs, winter-coated, arm in arm. Looking at Jutta, I smile. She smiles back, and a strong feeling of affection surges up in me, an acute concern for her happiness. I am in love with her—those are the words I use to express what I am feeling. But at times, too, I feel as if I'm looking down on her from a great height. "You're not committed!" the old girlfriends would charge. I hated them when they said that. Where did commitment get them? They were committed— until they changed their minds. They "opened themselves"; until they closed themselves again. At least my conscientiousness, my distance, lasts longer. Fortunately, what Jutta wants more than anything else is acceptance. I am a virtuoso accepter.

Emerging from the grimy back streets onto Alserstrasse, we catch sight of the streetcar pulling into its stop. We sprint over the slippery cobblestones. Jutta catches the back door as it is closing and forces it open again. The elderly Viennese women in the back of the car draw away, as if we were roughnecks. Jutta is so pretty, with the flush in her cheeks from the cold, that I kiss her, and she looks happy, and snuggles her back against me, drawing my arm down over her shoulder across her front.

I've never been a haven before. A haven, and the hand of an angry god, too! Oh, brother.

☐

"Who's this little hoodlum standing here?"

" . . . "

"Well, out with it—who are you?"

"Who are *you?*"

"Oonnhh! Feisty little critter, ain't ya? You trying to burn your eyebrows off, or what? What's your name?"

". . . Theodor."

"Don't lie to me, pal—Theodor is the squishy white kid. What's *your* name?"

"I'm not telling."

"You're not *telling?*"

"No!"

"Why, you little . . . all right, all right, I give up—you can get off me! I'll call you Rick."

"I don't like that name!"

"Hey, tough shit, kid, you don't give me your name, you take what you get, see?"

"What's *your* name?"

"Binki Weatherspoon. You laughing at my name, *Rick?*"

"That's not your name!"

"Well . . . you're right. Hey, when you're right, you're right! Right? No, my real name is Timo."

"That's *my* name!"

"No shit! Two people named Timo! Who woulda thought it?"

□

"Eric?"

"Yes?"

"Why don't you ever talk about AIDS?"

"Should I?"

"Aren't you worried?"

"Sure."

"But you never talk about it."

"I suppose not."

"Is that because you're sensitive about it?"

"Not really."

"Because I'll stop asking about it if you are . . ."

"But I'm not."

"Then why don't you ever talk about it?"

"Unnnhh . . . Because you never asked?"

"No, really."

"Maybe that *is* really. I don't know."

"Well, I'm asking now."

"OK."

" . . . "

"So what do you want to know?"

" . . . Ohh . . . I don't know. Whatever *you* know."

"That's not much."

"Well, whatever—"

"You want to hear the sentence I memorized?"

"All right."

" 'The clinical significance of a positive ELISA test on a serum sample from an asymptomatic donor not belonging to any AIDS risk group is unknown.' Ask another leper, and he'll probably quote you something that completely contradicts that."

"But you do belong to an AIDS risk group, don't you?"

"You mean the bumper-car man?"

"Yes."

"Of course, that's what anyone would assume. He's very convenient, isn't he? The signpost on my road to hell. People who knew about him would all heave a sigh of relief—as long as they didn't have bumper-car men in *their* pasts. But actually the one thing I know for sure is that the bumper-car man is not responsible. He was a virgin."

"He must have lied."

"No, I'm sure he didn't. He wasn't like that. And incidentally, I was not a virgin. So the poor guy might have gotten it from me. If I had it then. If the whole damn thing isn't a mistake."

Jutta is stunned. "You mean you might not have it?"

"Who knows? Nobody knows! I'm a statistical curiosity. *And*—I'm armed with my quote. I repeat it to myself every night before I go to bed. You want to hear it backward?"

"When will you know for certain you have it?"

"Please—let's put that in the conditional."

"When would you know if you had it?"

"Short of coming down with AIDS and dying horribly?"

"Yes."

"You want another quote?"

"All right."

" 'Low-risk individuals be advised that until more is known about the status of a positive test result in a low-risk population, that testing the patient's regular sexual partner may provide better or more information to determine if the test result may be a true- or false-positive result.' "

"Which means?"

"If you start testing positive, it proves I really have it. You could be my guinea pig."

"Then why all the fooling around with the condoms?"

"Because fucking guinea pigs is bestiality."

"That's cute."

"Thank you."

"How many people know about you?"

"Practically no one. The more people who know, the more likely

I am to lose my medical insurance, my employment, and all my friends. For example, I certainly wouldn't have gotten a student visa for Austria if anyone had known."

"Not even your family knows?"

"My family doesn't need to know. I have no intention of having sex with any of them."

"So you only tell women who you're going to have sex with."

"No, I only tell women who I *want* to have sex with. The sex never happens."

"Except with me."

"Right."

"Of course."

"Of course."

"And the other women?"

"Ever since the test, they've all been strangers. I became big on the singles bar scene, if singularly unsuccessful. I was looking for quick, anonymous sex; secret and furtive sex; one-night stands. One great thing about carrying the AIDS virus is that you don't have to worry about catching the AIDS virus."

□

A violent lurch: "Whoa! Hold on, Junior! I told the driver I'd give him two hundred extra schillings if he got us there in five minutes." The car roars up Billrothstrasse, into the hilly suburbs, the cobblestones drumming under the tires. A streetcar looms suddenly in the windshield, we are thrown left, then right, and it's behind us. Josh checks his watch. "And he's not doing that badly, either."

"What's the hurry?" I ask, making note of a red light streaking over our heads.

"We're supposed to meet Jun this minute."

"She can't wait?"

"Of course she can—but it's fun to see what these bozos can do. If he makes a left up here, he can shave off a few seconds—" I am pitched into Jutta's lap. "Yeah, I guess he knows that way." We're in a narrow street now, going too fast for surprises—little kids on tricycles, that sort of thing—then bouncing onto the Grinzinger Allee and up the last straightaway. The road is empty and the driver, shooting a collusive smile at Josh, floors it. Fun? I think, grabbing Jutta for dear

109

life—fun on the backroads of Georgia, maybe. The taxi brakes, screaming under a picturesque arch, and we burst into the village square,
braking hard now and swerving to spare a woman's life, and stop
abruptly at the sidewalk. The taxi rocks on its springs. Josh looks at his
watch. "Five minutes, forty seconds. Hmmm." He ponders for a moment. Then he claps the driver on the shoulder. "I think I'd better give
it to him, anyway."

"Good idea."

Jun is waiting in front of the baroque church at the west end of
the square. "Is that driver crazy?" she exclaims, when she sees it was
we who were in it.

"I'm going to report him," Josh says. "The bastard might kill somebody." He takes Jun's arm. "Where to, Bruté?"

"Heiligenstadt. It's too crowded here."

Jun Akishima is Josh's wife. She is Japanese, a violinist, and tiny:
four-and-a-half-feet tall, seventy-five pounds. She and Josh met at the
Salzburg festival, where Josh was subbing in the Vienna Philharmonic
and Jun was giving guided tours of the city to Japanese tourists. "What
can I say?" Josh wrote on my trilingual (English-Japanese-Hebrew)
wedding invitation. "At 27, she's an old maid in her parents' eyes.
Better a Jew-boy *sans* epicanthic folds than nobody at all." And you?
I wondered. "And me?" the invitation went on, "Frankly, I'd started
feeling lonely—a lot of gloomy breakfasts at noon with no one to pour
the cereal. Maybe it's this goddamn gloomy city. And picking up girls
in Viennese just isn't as fun as in English. When I'm drunk, I trip over
my lines. I've had it with one-night stands."

Ha! I thought.

And I was right. But perhaps Josh picked his wife with that skepti-
cism in his own mind. Jun considers herself a European, but she was
brought up Japanese. She doesn't complain. She doesn't, I think, even
blame Josh. Josh calls it "the Japanese resignation bit." Resigned, however, is one thing it is not. Jun has told me privately that she expects
Josh to grow out of girl-chasing. She calls his promiscuity a "disease."
She said she finds it "disgusting"; but then (and I quote), "All men have
a disgusting attitude toward women." (Present company, I had to
assume, not excepted.)

After a ten-minute walk, we come into Heiligenstadt. In the groin
of a fork in the road, a bare yellow lightbulb and a bundle of fir
branches dangle over a wooden door. We enter, cross the empty

Schanigarten under the vine trellises and go through a door hung with streamers and ivy. There is the usual heurige din inside: clinking glasses, bawling waitresses, shouted conversation, drunken singing, Schrammel music. My glasses fog up. "Beethoven lived in this building for a while," comes Josh's voice, off to my right. "He hated it." I can hear in his tone the implied round-off: "Of course." We find a table beneath kitschy wood carvings of pot-bellied hikers and hunters guzzling and pigging out. Josh insists on ordering for everyone: Viennese sauerbraten, liptauer cheese, broiled chicken, marinated white asparagus, hot peppers, cranberry sauce, bread, and *heuriger Wein*—the new wine. He catches me looking worriedly at the food mounting on our table and whispers, "Don't worry about it, Junior. This is my treat." He is especially magnanimous tonight because he has just played a good concert. Jutta and I demur ritually, and are overridden. Thanks, Dad.

Heurig wine is underhanded: it goes down innocently, like scented water, but fans out into the bloodstream brandishing as much alcohol as regular wine. Yearly, the heurigen are the scenes of massive alcohol overdoses by unsuspecting foreigners. The pretty iron lampposts in the wine suburbs show the marks of having been embraced by rented cars. The Viennese overdo it, too, but in a more calculated manner: they just puke in the *Schanigarten* or pass out and urinate, supine, in the hardy mums; then, instead of killing themselves, they take public transportation. I begin, dimly, to remember all this about the time I have knocked back my fifth *Viertel*. Jutta has put herself under my arm and is slouching like a rough beast against me, sucking on my neck. Jun sits straight up, hands tightly on her glass, a spot of red nippling each cheek; she speaks carefully, as if she were picking her way through a minefield. Josh is loquacious. Things have begun to run together on me—my thoughts, my words. Even if I stop now, I am going to get much drunker during the next hour. "So why stop?" Josh asks reasonably, and orders another liter.

Our waitress is sitting with a party of Viennese at our backs, and it takes some coaxing to get her over to our table. She'd rather drink herself and play dice with an old one-eyed man. Her party must have given the accordionist and his fat, florid singing partner with the double-necked guitar a fat tip, because the two haven't budged for six songs running. A huge, hairy dog—half Airedale, half Newfoundland —lies at the waitress' feet, his muzzle resting in a puddle of his own drool. "A cult of over-consumption," Josh is saying. "Look at the carvings. Even the dogs eat themselves into a stupor—"

Ich hab' mir für Grinzing ein'n Dienstmann engagiert,
Der mich nach Hause führt,
Wenn irgend was passiert—

"There are more Japanese in the city this month," Jun is telling Jutta. The Japanese men wear dapper beige raincoats and go around in pairs. The Japanese women move, like geese, in groups of four to six. Both men and women seem lost. Nothing is in their language; they hold guides out in front of them and stand indecisively on unexpected corners, often far away from any of the usual tourist sights. When you try to help them they shake their heads, intimidated, smile, and go back to their dazed indecisiveness. Jun is their only hope. She puts ads in the papers.

"She had to take a *two-year* course for her guide license," Josh exclaims. "Four days a week! How do you like them apples?"

"And how's the business?" I ask.

Meine Seele hängt an diesem Dienstmann
viel viel mehr als an der werten Frau

"I *hate* this music," Josh says. A burst of laughter comes from the next table. "It's all about booze and sex and booze and booze and what a great city Vienna is. The uptight old bitches love the dirty parts." Josh swallows another mouthful of wine.

"Oh, fine," Jun answers. "The money's very good." But she isn't happy. Jun is a musician. Guiding is a desperate stop-gap that has been going on for years now.

"She's a more dedicated musician than I am," Josh has told me. "She's the one who should be in the orchestra. I'd be happier playing the stock market." Josh tried that for a while, starting when he was twelve years old. He studied the market carefully, and bought and sold through an uncle for two years. He made twenty thousand dollars. He spent most of it later on a Triumph Spitfire, which, above fifty miles per hour, vibrated a good deal, and below it, sounded like an incipient earthquake. Josh kept the car so clean that a German friend, evincing the national penchant for scatological humor, sprinkled the car one day with suet so that the birds would shit all over it. The car is currently moldering in Wiesbaden, where Josh had his last job; his license was taken away for driving in Cologne the way he used to on the backroads of Georgia.

So why isn't Jun playing?

"Simple," Josh says. "She's Japanese."

The table across the aisle is crowded with Viennese students. They are sprinkling their conversation with English, which, in the ejaculatory mode, is fashionable among the Teutonic young. "Oh shit!" one of them says, and then lapses back into German.

"*And,* she's a woman. You know the Vienna Philharmonic is the last all-male orchestra in the world? And management says openly that they plan to keep it that way. The Viennese are the biggest pigs around."

"Really weird!" says one of the students.

Jedoch am Ende dieser seligen Partie,
da war der Dienstmann noch viel b'soffener als I'

"You should know," says Jutta, smiling with wet lips.

"He-ey! Mrs. Junior made a joke! Ho ho!" He grabs her face and kisses her. "I like your woman, Eric."

Applause at the next table. The dog picks its head up and looks blearily around, then lowers it again into the pool of drool. Jutta returns to my neck with gusto. Alcohol brings out her abiding exhibitionism. "Someone in the orchestra yesterday offered me a gig and he needed violins, too," Josh is saying. "So I said I knew a really good violinist, this woman friend of mine—I didn't say she was my wife— and the guy held up his hand, said, 'Only men!' That was it. I didn't even *get* to the fact that she was Japanese."

"What an asshole!" one of the students says.

"*Sonst noch etwas?*" asks the waitress, lurching against our table and belching.

"*Noch einen Liter Wein, bitte.*"

"Why only men?" I ask. Jutta is trying to get her hand into my pants. I grip her wrist and immobilize it.

"It's tradition—," begins Jun.

"This place is traditional like you wouldn't believe," Josh cuts in. Jun goes back to her glass. "The Phil still uses single horns, its own kind of oboe, trumpet, tuba, its own fingering systems. And of course, its own piano: the Bösendorfer. I mean, it's a great piano, but they never use anything else. It's so goddamn huge—in the chamber music halls, you'd think someone's going to stick his head out of it, swing it around and blast out the back wall with a forty-pound shell." While he speaks, Josh hangs spoons on his face. It is something for which he has an inexplicable talent. A spoon dangles from each cheek, one from his chin, and one from his nose; the last wavers as he speaks, like a turkey wattle. "This is the only orchestra in the world that still uses *animal* skins on the tympani, for chrissake! They've got to be kept oiled. Look at them, next concert—they're slimy! And they're always going out of tune." The wattle clatters onto his plate; he picks it up and rubs it against his nose again, carefully withdraws his hand and leaves it hanging there. "You'd expect the orchestra to employ a Numidian tympanist. You know, like the gleaming fat slaves who made up the rhythm sections on the Roman slave galleys; except of course they don't allow blacks in the orchestra." Barred from fondling my penis, Jutta tries to hang spoons on her face. They fall under the table. "You don't sweat enough," Josh says. "You need a water seal." The big dog is under there now, bumping against our legs and licking the spoons. Jutta goes under to collect them and bites my leg. Jun is quiet, her little head down on her little hands. Our waitress is sitting on a man's lap with her breasts pressed into his red and perspiring face. "The Tone-killers aren't so bad—we've even got a couple of women, buried in the back of the strings. But it's now management policy to take no Asians. They'll only take *Ausländer* as long as they don't *look* like *Ausländer*. Music in this country is as patriotic as football in America. The head of the State Opera is paid more than the chancellor. The taxpayers in the villages don't like to see their money going for an orchestra full of chinks."

"Well . . . at least they're honest about it."

"Hell, why shouldn't they be? They don't see anything wrong with it."

"Son of a bitch!" one of the students says. The Schrammel musicians launch into another song. Jutta, under the table with the dog, gooses me.

Later, we're back in the street, slipping over the wet pavement toward Grinzing. "I've got the perfect place for that Mexican restaurant," Josh says.

"Oh?"

"We can put it in one of the old World War II flak towers. The Viennese don't know what to do with them. They've *wiederauf-gebaut*ed everything else so they could forget the war ever happened —but the towers would be too expensive to tear down. I bet we could buy one pretty cheap. Paint it, put an enormous papier-mâché sombrero on the roof, broadcast sambas and rumbas from the gun platforms. The city government would be grateful." He's dragging Jun by the hand down the street. An hour ago, she went catatonic. Josh, irritated, threatened to leave her in the heurige to be pitched out by the cleaning crew, but Jutta and I pointed out that in her state she might get taken in by anybody. That brought him around: Josh is driven crazy by the thought of Jun having sex with anyone else.

"Sambas and rumbas are Brazilian and Cuban," I say.

"Make me puke," Josh says.

In the square at Grinzing, Josh spurns the taxis, for once. "We're just in time for the last streetcar. You'll love this, Junior. Biggest mobile party in town." Many of the topers in the village have emptied out of the wine gardens to catch this last cheap chance home. By the time the trolley swings like a great jointed glow-worm into the square, there are several hundred drunks at the stop, singing boisterously, hanging onto each other, crying shamelessly. The doors fold open and this tide of sodden humanity surges in, the first wave diving at the empty seats, the next clutching at the leather straps or draping itself around the metal poles, the last holding intimately onto the coats of strangers who are holding onto the coats of other strangers who have managed a grip on pole, seat, or strap. The streetcar lurches forward, the crowd lurches backward, and we all curve under the baroque arch, back down the long slow hill toward the city, the front half of the car breaking with the driver into a fitful rendition of *"Wien, Wien, Nur Du Allein,"* while the back punctuates it with salvoes from *"Mein Mutterl War a Wienerin."* Meanwhile, Josh stands in the middle, a head taller than anyone else, and hums the *Horst Wessel Lied,* filling in the words wherever he knows them: *". . . Wenn das Juden Blut vom Messer spritzt, dann geht's noch mal so gut . . ."* The beauty of his voice does not prevent a man nearby from rounding on him indignantly—"How dare you sing that evil song!"—and Josh sings placidly back, "Soon Hitler's banner will wave over the barricades . . ."

This is Fasching, the extended Viennese celebration of waltz balls, masquerades, drinking parties, and travesty shows that begins with the most dignified and prestigious ball of them all, the *Opernball* on New Year's Eve, melds imperceptibly into what other countries call Carnival, then grows more and more frantic through the first weeks of February until it emerges, a puffing, overstuffed, exhausted whale of a good time at *Grosser Dienstag,* to blow its final plume of sweat, sperm, and champagne before sinking out of sight under the leaden waves of Lent. Fasching is what the Viennese do best—sing, drink, become maudlin, forget the execrable weather, forget their responsibilities, forget that they too once sang the *Horst Wessel Lied. Schlamperei!* Fasching is the season that most reminds me of that famous old Viennese witticism: "the situation is desperate, but not serious." It was during Fasching that Prince Rudolf, Crown Prince and perhaps Last Hope of the Habsburgs, went out to his hunting box in Mayerling with his mistress Maria Vecera and shot her and then himself in a fit of muddle-headed romanticism combined with despair over the longevity of his autocratic father—who went on to rule for another twenty-eight years. It was during Fasching that the Social Democrats, in a fever from the wine and waltzing, foolishly took to the streets in 1934 and demonstrated against Dolfuss and the "Austro-Fascists," until their demonstration led to streetfighting, and then to armed, pitched battles, and finally to the retreat of the Social Democrats into the Karl-Marx-Hof, one of their model workers' housing complexes, where the Austrian army artillery shelled them and finally crushed them. And the perfect irony: it was during Fasching that Austrian Chancellor Schuschnigg—who haunted my father's dreams more than any other man, whom my father called "a tower of weakness"—on a day after he and his cabinet dressed in their best and waltzed the evening away, took a train to Berchtesgaden and then a car to the Eagle's Nest, where Adolf Hitler bullied him into a series of concessions that he did not have to make, concessions that were to pave the way for the *Anschluss* a month later. The date of the chancellor's humiliation was February 12, four years to the day after the Karl-Marx-Hof was shelled. The chickens were coming home to roost for the Austro-Fascists on this fourth anniversary. A month later, thousand-year-old Austria had become no more than the newest district of the German thousand-year Reich, soon to be designated—with contemptuous disregard for what the Viennese had fatuously believed would be their "special status" in the Reich—nothing more than the Danubian and Alpine Provinces.

Like all other non-Nazis who had played with the Nazi fire, the Austro-Fascists had been burnt to a cinder. They were desperate; but can such asinine bumbling be quite serious?

We are at the Schottentor. Josh drags us into a bar. It is a seedy, sad place of plastic-cushioned benches and linoleum tables. There is a prostitute, looking cold in her thin red dress, but no customers. The bartender is a jowly man with unsettling eyes like porcelain balls. Jun has begun to come around. "We thought we'd lost you, Dorothy," Josh says unpleasantly, in his Auntie Em voice. The bartender regards Jun warily as he brings our wine. As we are leaving, we trade with him the usual *Grüss Gotts*, and then he adds, in a voice heavy with malevolence, *"Sayonara."* Josh, in front of me at the door, turns on his heel and pushes me out of the way, saying "Excuse me, Junior, I'm going to have to break his nose." I grab him, try to hold him back, but he is too big for me, and he keeps walking, dragging me across the floor after him. "Jun, Jutta, help!" I cry, and they come back in from outside, but it's too late, Josh is at the counter and the bartender is looking at him with dangerous calm. But perhaps Josh notices now how big the bartender is—bigger even than he is—and how scarred his face, like a pumpkin begun for a jack-o'-lantern but abandoned; because he holds his hands up, expressively, as if to say, "I'm not going to touch you," and he turns to me and whispers, "What do you think, Junior?" "I think we should back out the door," I say. "Bowing and scraping, if necessary." "I don't think much of that," he responds. But he is wavering, so I grab the back of his coat and pull. "Come on! Don't even give him the satisfaction." That is, of relocating your teeth somewhere behind your uvula. Josh takes a step backward. "That's the way." And I tug him on out. At the door, Josh, still stumbling backward with my hand entwined in his coat, cups his hands around his mouth and trumpets gleefully, "Fascist Austrian Nazi Jew-baiting SS Brown-shirt *Oberreichssturmkommandanthundfängerscheisskopf!"* (Over-Reich's-storm-commander-dog-catcher-shithead.) The bartender's tattooed arms uncross and he vaults over the bar. I don't need to see any more and I drop Josh's coat and bolt, grabbing Jutta and Jun on the way. "What about Josh?" Jutta asks breathlessly, but before the question is out of her mouth, he sprints past us, his long legs a blur of concert-dress black. "See you in the next district!" he shouts back. Fortunately for us all, the bartender is more like a dog than a Hungarian baker, and at the end of the block he stops. His voice follows us, a guttural bark, for the next three.

Across Freyung now, under the square towers of the Schottenkirche, wet snow beginning to fall into the street lights out of the black above. Jun is at last conscious enough to walk on her own. Josh, freed, swoops down from the sidewalk into the gathering slush and then up again and twirls around poles and kiosks. Since the heurige, I have taken his horn in charge. A witch, a beggar, a clown, and a devil appear at the end of the block yelling merry obscenities. They vanish down a side street. The devil runs back for a second, picks up something he dropped, and disappears again, calling, "wait, wait!" In Am Hof, the first whiteness is visible on the cobblestones, on the roof of Mozart's yellow baroque house, on the heads of the adorable and chubby sword-wielding iron putti (frozen halfway through decapitations of evil spirits) at the base of the Mother Mary Column. On to the *Graben*. Snow is coming down thickly now, and covers the paving an inch deep. The emperor Leopold's face, turned up in prayer on the Plague Column, is obliterated by a pile of white, as if God had answered his plea for deliverance with a snowball. The heads of putti stick out of lumpy stone clouds mounting up thirty feet— "EEEyyyeugh!" Josh howls as if struck in the chest by a spear, "it's so . . . UGLY! Like some giant had squatted here after a breakfast of cupids—" and Jutta, on my arm, dissolves into laughter, which turns into choking, and back to laughter, and next thing I know I'm sitting under her in the snow, the neon lights of the *Graben* reeling crazily around me. *"Rambo"* a marquee glows, "the most successful film in American history!" Josh looms over us, and bends down to help us up. We go on. The tower of St. Stephen's, bathed in the white of a dozen klieg lights, drifts into view: improbably elaborate, soot-black with frills and striations of white where the thousands of bulbs and corners and peaks have been rubbed cleaner by the wind; a mammoth cone like the burned trunk of the World Ash Tree. On to Kärntnerstrasse, almost empty in the gathering snow. The expensive stores are closed, locked behind their steel gratings. Someone has spray-painted a swastika and the SS symbol on a municipal trash can. "Notice how they never get the swastika backward here?" Josh asks. A woman walking three dachshunds comes toward St. Stephen's. A young tough in leather and a girl dressed like a Gypsy pass us headed for the Ring. The tough points at the dachshunds and begins to shriek with laughter; the dogs, startled, begin to bark; the tough laughs louder, over the barking, still pointing as he comes nearer to them and turns as he passes, pointing and shrieking like a mad man. The dachshunds go wild with fright and excitement, leap about yipping and snarling, and begin to fight with each other. The woman becomes entangled in their leashes; the tough keeps walking, his Gypsy-girl laughing beside him. As Josh passes the woman, still trying to extricate herself from the leashes, he pulls his mouthpiece out of his pocket and spritzes a "Charge!" at her. She takes a swing at him. "All these war widows," Josh muses to me. "So repressed; so angry." We pass on. The snow falls so thickly now that the next block is invisible. At Walfischgasse, by the opera, we turn left, past a six-story pink stucco building. "It's pink," says Josh, 'because it used to be a *puff*—a brothel." A plaque next to the door memorializes W. H. Auden, who died in the building in 1973. Beyond are the curtained doors and red awning of Vienna's Moulin Rouge; photographs in the display windows show plump, naked women swallowing swords and letting doves out of top hats. And then, farther on, the travel bureaus, peddling the same wares: "TUNISIA!" shouts a poster, under a photograph of a blond woman with her back to the camera, the edges of her one-piece hiked to reveal expanses of creamy buttock. "I get it," Josh says. "Come to Tunisia and bugger beautiful Scandinavians." And we go farther on, through the dappling of whore-cafés and whore-bars that await the walker in the darker sections of every district in the city: bars open until *"Morgengrau,"* bars promising separées, bars whose lit names are flanked by side-silhouettes of women, kneeling armless and naked, pushing forward rounded receptive mouths and almost square nipples. On into darker and darker blocks, as the graffiti multiply: *"Boy sucht boy!"* says one, and gives a p.o. box number—something tender, beginners desired. *"Leider, kein oldies":* sorry, no oldies. And farther on, a balancing sentiment: "Woman—wake up!" inscribed over the lesbian symbol—two circle-topped crosses, joined as if hand-in-hand. Out into the light again, back onto the Ring at Schwarzenbergplatz. *"Fremdenverkehr ist . . . ,"* says a billboard picturing a big yellow daisy: "Tourism is . . . " Black spray-paint obliterates the rest, and below is written the second half of the equation: *"Analverkehr."* "Tourism is sodomy." Across the Kärntner Ring stands a neo-Renaissance building glowing in orange light: the Hotel Imperial, where foreign dignitaries, from heads of state all the way up to guest conductors of the Vienna Philharmonic, all reside on their visits (all, that is, except U.S. officials, who patriotically stay at the Hilton), and where Hitler stayed in 1938 when he came to take control of Austria, and where crowds of Viennese stood cheering in the street below, calling him again and again to his balcony. And next to the hotel, the surest sign that Hitler lost the war: a McDonald's. As we pass, the green-uniformed workers are locking the doors. Not blacks, as in so many McDonald's of American cities, but Vienna's own underclass mix of Turks and Iranians. And more Turks in the heavy snow outside—Turks in orange jackets hawking the *Neue Kronen Zeitung* ("Tyrol Boy Shoots Social Worker!") and Turks in red brandishing its rival, the *Kurier* ("Terror in Tyrol!"). The logos of the newspapers adorn the Turks' caps and the backs of their jackets so that, blowing on their hands, squinting against the snow, the dark men resemble rival Little League teams, dispiritedly trying to raise money for better uniforms. Out of Schwarzenbergplatz, and up the Belvedere hill. The Levantine French Embassy, all curved bays and gilt arches, looms on the right. (The result of a bureaucratic snafu—the architectural plans for the French Embassy in Istanbul were accidentally sent to Vienna, and vice versa. I've always wanted to go to Istanbul and find its French Embassy. Among the mosques and minarets, the arabesques and rounded arches, is it stupidly there, a blunt box of Habsburgian neo-Renaissance excess?) "Who Killed Fernando Pereira?"—that's the banner of the Greenpeace vigil, across Prinz-Eugen-Strasse from the French Embassy. There is a large photograph of the dead man, killed when the Rainbow Warrior was blown up in a New Zealand harbor: dashing, smiling, rugged, with "Save Our Seas" on his shirt. A little flame spits at the snow in its tripod and two figures sit near it, huddled together for warmth, while the snow piles up on their wide-brimmed hats. A loden-coated policeman strolls along the embassy's low Art Nouveau fence, Uzi hugged intimately to his side. On the glass of the shelter of the street-car stop, half-way between the policeman and the protesters, a poster: "The Unborn Live! The Unborn Are Everywhere!" And farther on, past the Swiss Embassy, a long cry sprayed along the Schwarzenberg garden wall: *"Ausländer bleibt! Nazis Raus!"* "Foreigners stay! Nazis get out!" And we go farther up, along the interminable rows of apartment buildings—*Neubauen, Wiederaufgebaute,* relics in the Ringstrasse style—and on the left, there is one last billboard before Josh's apartment building, to crown the succession of foreigner-hating Nazis and Nazi-hating foreigners, of Greenpeaceniks, anti-abortionists, homosexuals and lesbians: a candidate for President of Austria, smiling ghoulishly with a widow's peak and a nose like pulled taffy, sitting with his dirndled wife against a background of Alpine splendors: KURT WALDHEIM, it says, A MAN WITH EXPERIENCE. By Mrs. Waldheim's mouth, someone has affixed a tiny pink-and-white sticker: *"Ich wähle Freda Meissner-Blau!"* "I'm voting for Freda Meissner-Blau!" She's the leftist ecological candidate, and she doesn't stand a chance.

Suddenly, I realize I am not holding Josh's horn anymore. Panic! Where is it? But then I see the case open on the sidewalk. The horn is in his hands. He fits his mouthpiece in it, turns to us, bows, and says, "And now, ladies and gentlemen, members of the press, honored guests, friends, Romans, countrymen, and privileged neighbors—a Fasching recital." "Josh, no," Jun says, and takes his arm. But he shakes her off. "It is Fasching, *mein Liebchen.*" He gestures toward Waldheim. *"Das ist ja meine Pflicht."* He breathes twice and long into the gleaming brass instrument to warm it, then licks his lips, settles them precisely into the cup of metal, closes his eyes, and begins to play. Jun mutters something and goes inside, but Jutta and I remain. I love the soaring, auburn sound of the horn. Its warmth and sadness are perfect for a snowy night. The melody floats up, out over the park, to the rooftops of the quiet dark buildings, into the snow-muffled night. Above, a window opens. A sleepy voice yells down, "Shaddap! Whatinahell you think you're doing down there?" Josh keeps playing, ignoring him, eyes closed. The man—I can just make out his head through the flakes twirling down, three stories above us—yells again: "If I hafta come down there, I'm gonna take your fuckin' head off!" Josh, eyes closed, plays louder. "You fuckin' twerp!" And then something happens that could only happen in Vienna—another sash slides up, another head pokes out, and a second voice begins to yell. Not at Josh, but at the first voice. "Why don't *you* shut up, you gorilla?" I can see the man in the next building over, on the second floor. "Can't you hear the man's an artist?" "I gotta go to work in the morning!" bellows the first. "You're keeping more people up than the music is, with your piggish noise! Just shut the hell up and go to sleep!" "He's not right under your goddamn window!" "Well he can move then! Tell him to come over here!" And a third window flies up: "Is he coming over here? Hey—do you play any Strauss?" "I'm gonna knock his fuckin' head off!" "You say that once more, pal, and I'm calling the police!" "I'll knock their fuckin' heads off, too!" And through it all, Josh just keeps on playing, his horn held high, his face turned beatifically up, so that the streetlight falls across his forehead and his cheeks, so that the snowflakes settle silently on the lashes of his closed eyes and linger there for a few seconds before they melt and drip from the corners of his eyes like tears.

□

Jutta is smiling pensively as we spiral up the stairs.

"What are you thinking about?" I ask.

"Oh," she shrugs, "nothing much." Outside our door, while I'm peering through the gloom to find the keyhole, she says, "I think Josh is a very attractive man, don't you?"

"What, physically? No, not much."

She retreats, afraid that I've spoken out of jealousy. "Oh no, I didn't mean physically." She laughs to reassure me. "I wouldn't want to *lie* with him, or anything."

But that's precisely what she does want to do. I could sense it from the first time I brought them together. I flick on the light inside the door. The kitchen is in complete disarray. Renate has been baking bread again, and the pans and mixing bowls are stacked on top of the usual mound of junk in the sink. "Look at this!" I exclaim, disgusted. "She promised she'd clean up!"

Now Jutta is sure I'm jealous. She embraces me from behind and kisses the back of my neck. "Leave it," she murmurs, contentedly. "Come to bed."

"No, I can't. I can't sleep knowing this will be here in the morning."

"Are you angry?" she asks, into my coat.

"No, not at all." I turn around. "Really."

Jutta drifts happily on toward the bedroom. I roll up my sleeves, reach down into the scummy cold water in the sink and pull the plug. "What am I paying rent for?" I think, for the hundredth time.

I remember Jutta telling me that she usually fell in love with older men: substitutes for her grandfather, who rarely spoke to her, or for her real father, who never laid eyes on her, or even for the middle-aged village landowner who raped her—after all, she had sex with him for two years, longer than with any man after him. Josh is older than I am, a fact accentuated by his graying hair. With his stature, his money, his energy, his love of dominance, he cuts a better father-figure than I do. Look at me—what *I* like best is to put my head in Jutta's lap, like a dog.

I squirt lemon-scented goo into the sink and blast it with hot water. *And* I do all the housework. Like a servant.

Or more damning, like a woman. That is the attitude of Central Europe. I could talk all I wanted to about American men and security in masculinity and all that crapola. But it wouldn't change the fact that here there is thought—by both sexes—to be something wrong, something weak, about a man who can't get his woman (his women!) to clean up, who stays up to scour dough-cement out of bowls, while three certified vagina-holders sleep. Josh, meanwhile, makes his women do everything, and treats them like shit while he's at it. How could Jutta not respect that? All the important men of her life have done the same. But jealousy would be stupid, uncalled for. The greater Jutta's expressed sexual passion for a man, the greater the admixture of hatred in her feelings for him. That is not to say that her hatred predominates or is even very significant. But it does show that her sexual proclivities, like those of a necrophiliac, might be cause for concern, but are nothing to get jealous about.

I've run out of hot water. Down to the silverware. I plow on with cold.

If anything, I'm relieved to know that Jutta has interest in keeping other irons in the fire while we are together. It lessens my fear that I am becoming, over this apparently unprecedented length of her relationship with a man—not counting the rapist—too important in her life. Right? But does that mean—I can hear the old girlfriends—does that mean I am not committed? Does it mean I don't love her?

Love, love, love. I wipe off the table and lock the door. I've only begun to use the word in the past few weeks, and already I'm sick of it. It's supposed to be somehow both ineffable and obvious: like pornography, impossible to describe, yet immediately and in all cases recognizable. But one word cannot mean so many things. Love is our great white whale. We read into it all the mysteries that we cannot fathom, the vapors we cannot hold, and then we harpoon it jollily with that insipid point: a word that sounds like doves cooing.

I turn out the lights.

The old girlfriends said, "You'll know when you're in love; you'll be sure." But I don't trust that: Moonies are sure, and no one is taking that as a sign that they are right.

This is all I know. At the end of the hall, on the left, there is a room. And in that room, on a wooden platform, lies a woman. And I, lifting the blanket and slipping in next to that warm, naked woman, kissing her through her sleep and feeling her, still sleeping, begin to press against me, I—for tonight at least, and I expect for tomorrow night, and probably for some time to come—don't want to be anywhere else.

□

"Bonjouuurr, mesdames et messieurs! Maintenant nous avons les actualités d'aujourd'hui—"

Mrrmf. Wha? "Uuunnnh . . . can you turn it down?"

"—un événement tragique s'est deroulé à Cape Kennedy dans les premières minutes du matin américain—"

"Jutta," I say groggily, "hello, don't you think it's a little loud?"

"Shush! Something about America—"

"Big deal. Another spot on Reagan's nose—"

"Shush!"

"—a eclaté au-dessus de l'océan Atlantique—"

I reach past her and turn the radio off.

"Hey!" She turns it back on—*"Président Reagan a declaré que les sept—"*

I turn it off again and pull her hands away. "I told you it was about Reagan—" I pin her to the mattress to keep her from getting back to it, and she laughs.

"No—it was something about an explosion over the Atlantic."

"If it's World War III, we don't have to hear about it from René." I kiss her.

"But I have to practice my French," she says, now coyly, with slitted eyes.

"I'll teach you French."

"Oohh . . . ho ho ho!"

124

And when Timo comes in to ask for a bath, he has to wait until we're done.

□

January 29, 1986

Dear Mom,

Nothing very interesting to report on the research—it's coming along pretty well. With all the work, I haven't been getting as much sleep as I should, which makes me rather groggy; perhaps that is why I haven't written you as often as you'd like . . .

□

On a cluttered shelf over the children's bed is a home-made book of cardboard pages tied together at the edges with red yarn, and on the cover is written in crayon "Our Favorite Things." Underneath are the authors, each in his own hand: Timo, Theodor (a quavering "T"), Jutta, Renate, Ulrike, and Elizabeth (a thumb print). On the first page inside, there is a photograph of Elizabeth, her face still wizened, red, and solipsistic from birth. Her favorite thing? It must be Renate's breast, which curves hugely from the top of the photograph like a dirigible, narrowing to the beet-red mooring cone lodged between Elizabeth's lips. On the next page is Renate entire, returning the compliment: she stands with a shy, surprised look in a T-shirt and shorts next to the perambulator; summer sunlight makes startling headlights out of her glasses. Her forearms are brown, with a sheen of blond hair. Then there is a photograph of Theodor, in the kitchen, reaching into a jar of hard candy balls. Another of Theodor, watching television. Then Ulrike, beaming proudly with Theodor on one side and Kurt—a big, unsmiling man in work-clothes—on the other. And Ulrike again, at her desk with pen to paper, looking up flirtatiously from under her lush dark eyebrows and smiling, her psychology books opened and disposed carefully in a ring around her. Then Timo, in the park at the Schönbrunn Palace, feeding birds. Then a surprise: Jutta leaning back on her elbows in window squares of sunlight, her legs crossed at the ankles. The surprise? She is naked. She is arching her back slightly, to

125

pull the large breasts higher and to give a delicious curve along the lower back to her buttocks, which, so coyly prominent against the carpet, seem to invite the butt-fucking that Jutta has admitted she dislikes. And then the last photograph: Timo and Jutta standing together by a road in one of the outlying districts, a line of pollarded sycamores dwindling into the bluish city-haze of the background. They're both looking into the camera, Jutta with a slit-eyed expression of tough knowingness, Timo with curious eyes and open mouth, as if about to ask, "Who are *you?*" This is the only photo in which the protagonist is not clear. Who is whose favorite? Jutta and Timo look not like mother and child, but like partners. They have picked each other.

□

We stroll through the shopping district, Jutta on my arm and Timo holding her other hand. Jutta is an avid window shopper, so our progress is glacial. She oohs and aahs at everything: the watches, the jewelry, the fur coats, the sportswear, the Oriental rugs, the vacation posters, the sweaters, the designer jeans, the designer glasses, the loden overcoats, the pastries. We actually buy three members of the last category.

"You have catholic tastes," I remark, stopping with her outside a Matinique store. Here it's all earth-tones and draped fabric. The mannequins' faces are self-absorbed, hostile; their bodies in the last hideous stages of anorexia.

"Well why not?" she responds. "There's something beautiful in everything. Else no one would buy it."

Why not indeed? She wears eight different colors at once, four different patterns. Every day, she clothes herself and Timo in cast-offs from various styles and eras. In New York, I hear, it's some sort of fashion. But Jutta doesn't do it with fashion in mind. And in Vienna she and Timo stand out like two carnies who have lost their troupe. When I'm searching for her in the crowd at a rendezvous point (when she is even more than usually late), I can always recognize her distant figure, walking slow and slew-footed, long before her face comes into focus. I see the bulk of wool, the clashes of color and the winding of scarves and shawls. Then comes the shock of hair. Only last, the dark close eyes and the thick-lipped smile, the wave of a woolly mitten and

Timo's mitten, below, doing the same. "I look like a witch, don't I?" she has said to me. "All these scarves and vests. I have potions everywhere, in my wool pockets." She obviously likes the idea. She reads my palm. She cooks like an alchemist. Being a witch makes her feel powerful. "I'm going to put a spell on you," she says sometimes in bed, cradling my head, gazing down with a rueful smile. "So you'll never be able to leave me."

I point to the mannequins. "Self-absorption and hostility are chic now?"

"I . . . guess so," she says, vaguely, not really listening. "Don't you think that's a lovely scarf? Ohh!" She bites her lip. "Wonderful!" she murmurs.

"It's five hundred schillings!"

"Well," she takes my arm again and we move to the next store, "it's a good thing we don't have to buy it, then." Timo follows, dribbling poppy-cake crumbs in the slush.

I'm only playing the expected male role: professing shock at the prices, feigning ignorance of fashion. Actually window shopping with Jutta is fun. Unlike many who do it, she seems completely unbothered by the fact that she can't afford a thing. To her it's like going to a museum exhibition. And her uniform appreciation of all these things —whose only constant is that they are "fancy," i.e., expensive—is endearing. She sometimes confesses to me that something seems rather ugly to her, but then she goes on to admire it in any case. It is one of the hard lessons of a spare life: that her own opinions don't count. The opinions of rich and beautiful people count.

"*Tiimo!*" she cries, exasperated. He is urinating against the bottom of the store front. She grabs his hand—"No, Mommy!"—he jerks back, and the little spray wavers, dribbling across the front of my shoe. "Am I raising a barbarian?" She shakes his penis dry and hurriedly stuffs it back in his pants.

"I needed to go!" Timo expostulates in an injured tone.

"Well you don't *go* in the *street!*" Jutta whispers fiercely.

"On Lazarettgasse—"

"This is not Lazarettgasse! This is Kärntnerstrasse! And if you piss here the police will arrest you and put you in jail and tape up your whizzer so tight you won't be able to piss and it will explode!"

"General rule, Timo," I said, upending a professorial finger. "Never piss in the first district."

"OK."

"And don't piss on my shoes."

☐

In Jutta's eyes, I suspect, there is something romantic about my condition. Perhaps she even hopes that it is *our* condition, now. That would make it even more romantic, wouldn't it? Virtually a *Liebestod*. Sharing AIDS, like the commission of incest, would bind us together by excluding all others. And she would imagine that she had little to lose. After all, society already will have nothing to do with us—with me sexually, with Jutta socially. Jutta has Timo, and I my one homosexual lover. Neither are causes; but both are the mark of Cain, the emblems of our respective disgraces. If AIDS came to her, she would accept it superstitiously, as her Fate. She has always trusted Fate more than her own weak hand to make the final determination whether she deserves to live or die.

The Viennese satirist Karl Kraus, in *The Last Days of Mankind*, wrote, "Each era gets the epidemic it deserves. To every age its own plague!" AIDS is the disease of our age and thus has the cachet of all potent symbols. One needs only think of the last social revolution before the sexual one and its attendant disease to recognize the enduring fascination of illnesses that seem to go to the heart of a way of life. During the Industrial Revolution, in the midst of great optimism about scientific progress, tuberculosis sounded a warning call from the depths of all that was beyond the reach of science. Today our optimism lies not in progress but in pleasure. We have accepted the fact that we are on the road to hell, but we pave that road with comforts and freedoms unimaginable to previous generations. From what else but our pleasure and our freedom should the scourge come? AIDS is as subtle, as pernicious, as the evils of our time. It responds to a fragmented age by attacking in a hundred ways.

Moreover, AIDS, like tuberculosis, has the advantage—to the romantically inclined—of having a long incubation period during which the victim is presumed doomed but is not yet ugly enough to lose sympathy. Of the various early symptoms, the most noticeable is only weight loss, which just makes victims look like mannequins, and therefore more stylish. By the time the horrors set in—the purple lesions and deformities of sarcoma, the pneumonia, the progressive dementia—AIDS victims are in hospices, where no one has to look at them. Their predecessors were the unseen consumptives, sequestered on mountain tops after long and attractive low-grade fevers, coughing up blood and pieces of lung.

But there is, after all, a problem. I don't believe Jutta *really* wants to kill herself. She only plays with the idea of death, petulantly—like an adolescent. And with me, if we're not careful, she stands a good chance of actually dying. When she used to cut her wrists, what were the odds? Impossible to say, because she could control the odds. A few surface cuts, augmented every few minutes to keep the blood flowing: it is so easy to create the bloody impression of abandon while calculating how far one has gone, how much farther one can safely go. People do die of slit wrists. But more people do not. And Jutta has proven herself, despite all her dramatics of despair, to be a survivor. Her track record stands at eight out of eight: the odds she has set for herself are generous, even loving.

Does she quite realize that in this instance she cannot control the odds?

□

The lunches in Jutta's bedroom are the best meals. The windows there face north and west, but on the rare clear days the sunlight, squeezing between the Children's Hospital and the elevated Stadtbahn station on the Gürtel, actually manages to reach us for about half an hour at mid-afternoon.

So many of my memories of the room are matched with gloomy wet afternoons, reading Kraus or Musil, or a volume from Jutta's collection of Arthur Schnitzler, in a small cone of yellow on the bed; or coming from the dark hall into more dark with Jutta on my arm, fumbling with her clothes until she steps away from the pile, glowing faintly white in the street-light reflected up from the sidewalks; or reclining in even blacker black, back in Jutta's arms, listening at night, with the curtains drawn, to her talk about her grandparents, the only light the red-orange tip of her cigarette, sucked brighter just above my head where her mouth is and flashing down, dying, to my elbow, where she rests her hand, which I even guide sometimes to my own mouth to take a puff, so that I can taste her.

So it is always, for me, a vaguely amazing moment when the

sunlight spills through that western window and falls across the bed, leaps to the floor and reclines against the far wall. It's like one of those moments in a Dracula movie when, after an hour of dark corridors and lightning-illumined cellars, the scene shifts suddenly to a sun-drenched square. One suddenly has hope for those victims who seemed so doomed in the dark, and one wants to yell at them, "Don't move! Stay in the light!" And there, at lunch, in the sun, are our own dark familiars—daunting piles of Jutta's weeks-old dirty clothes, magazines and newspapers thrown long ago from the bed, Timo's bricks and bats and other makeshift toys of destruction left to brood until he finds them again. I am amazed that they still exist in the sunlight. I am amazed to see that the room is as messy as I imagined it was, in the half-light, reading or listening or making love, when I was half afraid to look.

I don't tidy Jutta's bedroom. I tried it once, and she complained that the room looked like a tomb. I think it has been good for me to be forced to live in such squalor and chaos. At my age it is perhaps unhealthy to be too set in my ways. I left one of my own shirts on the floor once, as an experiment. And it didn't even really bother me, lying scrunched up there. But all the same, I was never quite able to forget it, either. Every time I came into the room, I found myself looking for it—ah, there it was, weighted down by random pieces of Timo's wooden jigsaw puzzle (and an enduring puzzle it is, since he can never find more than a third of the pieces at any one time); or there, kicked under the desk with the dust-balls; or there, stretching one supplicant sleeve out from under a pair of stretch-pants, a wet rubber boot (mateless), and a winter coat. I finally realized it was not healthy, either, to be thinking so much about a shirt, so I plucked it up, dusted it off—or was I stroking it, apologetically?—and dropped it in the hamper.

For these bedroom lunches, a card table is brought in from Ulrike's room and set up next to the bed. Kitchen chairs are brought in, Timo always insisting on dragging his own, banging it against doorframes and dropping it at least once with a loud clang. The tradition is that Timo can sit in his mother's lap whenever we eat in the bedroom, so Jutta settles herself cross-legged on the bed, a pillow across her thighs, and pulls Timo up on top of her. She grimaces and exclaims how heavy he's getting, but she doesn't really mind because once he's on top of her she can't move and I therefore become the factotum. In this household, so quickly do patterns (like myths) establish themselves, no longer to be questioned, that soon we have another tradition—and even when Renate or Ulrike lunch with us, which is most of the time, I am the one who runs back and forth from kitchen to bedroom, fetching forgotten sugar, salt, spoons, glasses, or sponges for spills. The women joke about how nice it is to be waited on by a man, for once. Marveling, I realize that they are serious: that they have somehow blocked out the fact that I do nine-tenths of the housework in this apartment as a matter of course.

But I don't mind. With them all in the sunlight, eating hungrily, and more than usually gabby and gossipy with me out of the room half the time, the lunch turns into a noisy party—a happy female *Kaffee-klatsch*—as if they were treating themselves to a lunch on the town. This, too, becomes a tradition—the festive nature of these meals. And the first couple of times, I was surprised at how happy I was to be trotting in and out, keeping the table supplied, listening mutely to the conversation about jobs and men and babies and men and parents and men. But I'm no longer surprised. I notice how much Jutta enjoys these boisterous afternoons, cozily sandwiched between her bed and her son, with her lover bringing her whatever she wants, and it seems perfectly natural that I should be happy. So *this*, perhaps, is what love is. Doing what someone else wants and yet not resenting it. Is this how my father thought I felt through all those years when I did his bidding?

□

When the lights change, Josh flashes a Hitler salute at the green walking man in the fedora and goosesteps off the curve.

"It drives me crazy the way nobody jay-walks in this city," he exclaims. "Have you noticed how long the pedestrian light stays red after the traffic has been stopped?"

"No."

"It's a deliberate test of mindless obedience! And the Viennese pass with flying colors! Standing there with their eyes fixed on that little red man, without a moving auto for half a mile. Turns green and whammo! off they go. *Jawohl, mein Kommandant!* Do you think if some practical joker switched the light-template at night, from a walking man to a green tableau of a mob lynching a Jew—do you suppose when the light changed they'd wheel around and string me from the nearest lamppost?"

□

"Bath, Mommy!"

I fall out of bed and crawl across the floor. Timo climbs on my back. He hangs on tight as I clamber up the steps to the faucets. "Biggest tub in the world!" he yells. He reaches far across the green abyss and lets the water fly. The steam is copious. "His cough is gone," I say to Jutta.

"So it is," she says.

"It must be all these baths, all this steam." Timo splashes water everywhere, and sings a song about Knecht Ruprecht. He beats his chest like King Kong. I'm relieved.

"And all your worrying for nothing," Jutta sniffs.

"And all my worrying for nothing," I concede. It is our way of closing the subject.

□

It is hot in the #52. Timo stares at a black-clad woman with purple spiked hair. Then he kicks the seat in front of him until Jutta threatens to pull his ears off and sell them at a discount in Zimmermannplatz. Then he draws lines in the condensation on the window. Outside, the wet snow falls. The new white only makes the street-muck look dirtier.

We trundle up toward the outskirts of the city, between bars and pizza parlors, shoe stores, bakeries, and brothels tastefully fronted by cafés. (The best apple strudel to be had between the West Bahnhof and Penzing is sold by a madam along Mariahilfer Strasse.) The enormous Schönbrunn Palace complex, with its ghastly piss-yellow façade ("You'd expect it to steam in this cold weather," Josh says), floats for a few seconds into view like a baroque aircraft carrier, before our streetcar swings beneath the railway lines and on to Linzer Strasse.

I don't know where we are going. Jutta said this morning only that she wanted to show me a house that she liked, that she wanted to live in some day. "I can't stand the thought of staying in this apartment," she has often said. "Broken windows and doors, and nobody responsible for fixing anything!" Somewhere out here, far away from the Ring and the university, is a house that she has seen, and for some reason this house, out of the thousands of buildings in Vienna, immediately seemed right to her.

The street is wider now. The trees have disappeared. The buildings are all inter-war *Neubauen*. (The German word, with pronunciation appropriately reminiscent of the word "noisome," means "new constructions.") They are blank-faced, blank-eyed, unpainted. These are the famous housing projects of Red Vienna, which for decades were models for European socialists. They have not aged well. "It's hard to imagine," I say, feeling depressed, "how this bleak style was once welcomed as a breath of fresh air. Now we have entire cities of this, looking like penal colonies. If Adolph Loos had seen this neighborhood, wouldn't he have thrown away all his drawings?"

"At least they have bathrooms," Jutta says. "And showers. At least they aren't heated by coal stoves that coat everything with dust and give you black lung disease." She is watching the street signs. She stands up. "We should get off here."

Walking away from Linzer Strasse, we leave garages, bakeries, and cafés behind. The snow has stopped. We come into an older area, of block-filling apartment buildings from the turn of the century. Here, Loos' revolt is suddenly understandable. The complex neo-Renaissance façades are pompous and oppressive.

The streets and sidewalks are vast, but there are still no trees, there is no grass, only dented and rusting automobiles parked head on to the curb, some of them trapped by weeks-old drifts of snow, crusted and blackened. The sidewalks are broken, with slabs of concrete jutting up like ice sheets in a frozen river. "I always forget until I come to the outer districts," I say, "how poor this city is. Even the center is much shabbier than Salzburg, or Linz. But out here! Out here, we could be in Eastern Europe."

"We *are* in Eastern Europe," Jutta retorts.

"Mm."

"Vienna has nothing to do with the rest of Austria. My parents, everyone I know in Innsbruck—they hate Vienna. They hate the Viennese. My living here—" she laughs bitterly, "they think that's just perfect!"

In 1918 Vienna became an imperial capital without an empire. That old, lax Viennese cosmopolitanism had for decades attracted those who were at loose ends, or unpopular, or on the run. Thus, the city was a mélange of Germans, Slavs, Hungarians, Jews, and other peoples from all over central and southeastern Europe. The rest of Austria, made up almost entirely of Catholic Germans, wanted nothing better than to unite with the German Reich and to leave its overblown, under-financed, mongrel imperial capital to collapse under its own weight and sink out of sight forever.

Meanwhile, the tensions of Vienna's cosmopolitanism produced citizens like Georg von Shönerer and Karl Lueger, and their young admirer, Adolf Hitler. And when Hitler returned to Vienna in 1938, tolerance disappeared, along with, eventually, over a quarter million Jews and other scapegoats. Misfits are most clannish, once they have found a niche; mongrels conceive the most violent rages against perceived impurities. The Viennese tried horribly to cleanse themselves, and in so doing wiped out the one thing they still possessed even after they had lost their power and their money: the most illustrious culture in Europe. In front of the whole German people, Hitler could point with pride to the city of his adolescence.

Now Vienna is like an emptied ballroom. Its ghosts are identified on red-and-white plaques next to the doors of the buildings they haunt. There is virtually no living culture. *The Third Man* is shown in the cinemas for the sole reason that it includes background shots of Vienna. An excited rumor circulates that the city will be the setting for the next James Bond movie. One Austrian director makes one minor movie, which does not even take place in Austria but rather in Los Angeles, with American actors, and the city goes wild to celebrate it. The Theater an der Wien, which once premiered *The Magic Flute* and *Fidelio,* is now showing *Cats.* On Blue Danube Radio, Barry Holtzman jabbers on for twenty minutes about Christopher Isherwood's novel *Prater Violet,* only to conclude, disappointedly, that it's not really about Vienna's Prater, but about the making in England of a movie of the same name, and that Isherwood, although he *did* live in Berlin for a while, actually only spent one afternoon in Vienna and didn't remember much about it. Only classical music flourishes, and classical music is the celebration of the dead. The only current Austrian writer of note lives in Carinthia and roots his art in a near-psychotic hatred for his country and his countrymen. And the only politician of note is a foolish moral cripple and former Secretary General of the United Nations who is now running for the presidency by denouncing Jewish conspiracies in a country without Jews.

It has become hillier, and a few bare trees have reappeared. We begin to pass gaps between the buildings. There is a feeling of irresolution about this neighborhood, of opportunities not yet taken. The city

134

is coming to an end. At the top of a knoll, we cut across a park. Half a dozen teenage louts are hanging about a grade-school swing. They heckle us as we pass and Jutta calls them a bunch of shitheads, while I hurry her on. They won't beat *her* up if it comes to a fight. Farther on, we turn up a small street. Timo is tired. "We're almost there," Jutta assures him. And we are. She touches my arm. "There it is!"

My first thought is that it looks like her.

My second thought is: She didn't tell me it was a *ruined* house.

It is small—a concrete shell with a peaked tile roof, crouching between two apartment houses. It commands an eighth of an acre, and is drowning in weeds. We came all the way out here for this? "I think it could be beautiful," she is saying. "Don't you?" Lost in thought, I don't answer. I am wondering, why does it look like her? We wade through the high, over-bending grass, following the remains of a concrete front walk. It is a thick-bodied structure—as hard and thick as Jutta's stomach. The unpainted stucco is a pale yellowish white, the color of her skin. Brown bushes with dense spindly branches have grown up its walls within a foot of the eaves—sere and bare, prickly and unruly, they look like her hair.

Timo has run ahead. He pauses to report: "Mommy, look! The door is open!" There once was a screen door, but now only hinges. The second door is wedged open by weeds growing up through a great crack running diagonally across the floor of the interior. With some difficulty, I push the door further open, tearing away the tough weeds, and we step in, crunching on broken tiles and a drift of dirt and sand.

It is a mess. An unbelievable mess. More than anything else, *that* is why it looks like her.

"It needs some work," Jutta is saying. "But that's the only way I could ever afford it. I would fix it up myself."

This from a woman who never washes the dishes. "It would need a hell of a lot of work," I counter. The ground floor has two rooms, with no door between them. A cloak of black and dimpled mold is spreading from one corner. More work than you would ever do, I think. "Have you talked to the owner? Do you know how much it might cost?"

"Oh, no." She obviously hasn't even considered it. "I don't know who the owner is."

In the back, there's a long narrow area lined, waist-high, with steel-framed windows. For some reason, none of the windows are broken. "This would make a lovely kitchen," she says hopefully. "The sunlight comes in these windows all day long." She hugs herself. "I've been here when the sun was out—and it feels wonderful!"

I find it rather hard to believe the sunlight comes in all day long, since the windows face west. Through them, there is a view of weeds and, beyond, trees sloping up. We are at the very edge of the Vienna woods. It occurs to me that Jutta has picked a house about as far out of Vienna as she can get. I look along the floor and walls of the kitchen-to-be and see no electrical outlets, no pipes, no sealed-off gas lines. Nothing but concrete. What could it have been? We come back into the main room, where Timo is rooting around in the scattered junk. No outlets here, either. "What is the age of this house?" I ask her.

She shrugs. "I have no idea," she says, dismissively, as if to imply she's not interested in technical questions.

But I wonder—has the damn thing got any wiring? Has it got any *plumbing?* "Where's the toilet?" I ask.

She glances around. "It must be on the first floor."

We walk up the enclosed stairs. Timo abandons his digging and comes to stand at the bottom. "Mommy, it's dark up there!"

"No shit, Timo," I say. I'm getting irritated. The door at the top is locked. "You've never been up here?" I ask.

"No. But you can see in a little from the outside."

"Great. So you don't know if there *is* a bathroom."

She is surprised by my tone. "Well . . . there must be."

"Oh, yeah? I don't see any pipes anywhere."

"I suppose they're inside the walls."

We come back down. The light on the ground floor seeps through two bush-clogged windows set high in the back wall. "The ground must slope up around the back of the house."

"Yes, it does."

We return outside and circle to the back. I try another exterior door, which gives access to the upper floor. It, too, is locked. Through the windows, I see more debris, in rooms as featureless as those below. "There isn't any toilet in there, Jutta," I say testily.

"Well . . . I'll have to put one in, then. That isn't too hard, is it?" She speaks sweetly, hoping to appease me but not, I think, understanding why I need to be appeased. I don't answer. "I don't see how the people who used to live here could have done without a toilet," she ventures. She doesn't want to cast doubt on my opinion any more directly than that.

"I'm not sure anybody ever lived here," I tell her. "I don't think it was built for that."

"Well—that's even better! Then I'll be the first person to live in it, and it will really be my house!"

I turn and glare at her, smilingly wrapped in her dream-world, and feel words rising toward my mouth. This is a completely new feeling to me, this unstoppable uprush of anger. "This is never going to happen, Jutta—buying this house, or fixing it up, either. Face reality, for once. There isn't a chance in hell."

We're both stunned. Is this, I wonder, what being in love is like? This sudden urge to be cruel?

Jutta's eyes are filling with tears. "Why?" she asks. "Why are you saying that to me?" She peers into my face, bewildered.

Why, indeed? My anger has drained utterly away, and I feel empty, guilty. I have struck at her most cherished and vulnerable possession: her store of pipe-dreams. I reach for her hand. "I'm sorry if I hurt you, Jutta."

She snatches her hand away and lashes out angrily. "You? *You* didn't hurt me. I'm not that easy to hurt!" At least she does have her reflex of pride. Like burying the cigarette in my hand, or turning over the kitchen table—she does try to hurt back. But then she flees. As she does now, turning blindly and disappearing around the corner of the building. That flash of pride *is* only a reflex. The fleeing is not a rejection of me but a form of submission—she wants me to follow her. Like the weaker wolf that bares its neck to the stronger and is thereby spared, she allows me to become the aggressor again, chasing her, so that I can soften and be magnanimous. This, regardless of the fact that I am to blame.

After a moment, I do follow, and find her some yards away. She is seated strategically, facing away from me, on a wall skirting the road. I am carried suddenly back to my childhood: that long-dead little boy, exhausted from a tantrum that had achieved the opposite of what he had had in mind. "I don't know why I said that, Jutta," I say to the back of her head. "It was stupid and unkind."

"Can't I have hopes, too?" she exclaims. "I thought you believed in me!" She is crying. And it comes as a shock—goddamnit why can't I learn this?—how frighteningly easy it is to make her cry. I've always been so nice to everybody, so careful with them—and I half dislike that veiled part of myself. I have a grudging admiration for people who say what they think, take what they want, who have great and violent and emotional fights with their mates and then make up later with equal violence and emotion. Saul Bellow characters. I envy them. But I don't like this at all, making her cry. I would rather spend a lifetime saying nothing.

I come around the wall and sit with her, while the clouds rise and the light grows brighter and brighter, until it has become a blinding white streaming out of a sunless white sky. Eventually, Jutta forgives me. With much effort I convince her that I don't really believe what I said, that my remark came purely from annoyance that had been building up in me for weeks from having to do all the housework all the time at Lazarettgasse. And I find I am very happy and relieved to be back doing what I do best: comforting people with half-truths.

It is not utterly lost on Jutta that when she lay in bed after burning me I sat and waited patiently for her to relent, but that here, on the wall, I pleaded with her.

We stand up and look around for Timo. My eyes have always been too sensitive to light, and I shield them with my hand. "This light is giving me a headache," I say.

She takes me by the crook of my elbow and hugs my arm to her coat. "Why don't we go home, then?" she says.

"Yes, let's."

Timo has disappeared in the whiteness—he flees from his mother's fights, too, but honestly, not like a bird faking a broken wing. After we call and search through the high grass, Jutta spots him in the woods. She calls, "Tiiimo!" And after a pause, again. *"Tiiimo!"*

And I think: I *do* love that voice. And I love the pressure of her arms around my arm. And I love the kind way she looked into my face when I shielded it—both from the white light, and from a sudden shocking tremble on the verge of a sob.

☐

Lying in the dark. Jutta is asleep beside me.

She chose that building because it is ruined, yes. But not for the reason she gave—that it is therefore more affordable. For Jutta, nothing is affordable. The fact of the ruination is itself the reason. She has found the image of herself in a house: one small part of the world that could belong to her, that she could redeem with her labor.

People whose lives are disorderly find this dream the most enchanting: that someday they will make over everything in their lives, from what they do for a living and how they take care of themselves, down to what time they will get up in the morning, how many sit-ups they will do each day, and where their toothbrushes will unfailingly go. They desire to build everything again on a more solid foundation so that eventually, after deliciously steady effort, they will find themselves at the top of a glorious edifice, from which they can at long last see their lives spread out, like limpid and unruffled seas, at their feet.

I think of those Chekovian dreamers who fill up their leisured, empty afternoons with talk of living a better, more meaningful life in Moscow—without, of course, ever going there. Or who look forward to some bright future in which they will "work," in which they will find fulfillment in this selfless and meaningful "work," without having any idea what the work might be or stopping to wonder how they will manage to do selfless work when they are, in fact, selfish and self-absorbed people. Jutta wants to buy a house, using no money, from an owner she can't identify. She wants to fix it up with no knowledge of tools and no expenditure of energy. And then she wants to live there, a neater, healthier life, as if the coal stove and the hall toilet in Lazarettgasse were the sources of all her problems. She wants to live there by the steel kitchen windows, where the sun both rises and sets in the west.

I am angry again. I look indignantly at her sleeping form. In the little concrete house, she would still smoke two packs a day, the dishes would still never get washed, Timo would play with bricks and lighters and pieces of broken glass and have colds that lasted for months, and a string of men would come through the house like presumptuous boarders, for a few weeks fucking the mistress of the house, patting Timo absently on the head, and then leaving them both to their mess, and their loneliness, and to the hostility, at least in an arc of 180 degrees, of their neighbors.

I glare at her. I am tempted to shake her roughly awake and ask her: why do you still need to take refuge in this fantasy? Why can't you be happy in Timo? In me?

That, perhaps, is what infuriates me most of all. She spoke of life in that concrete house, of fixing it up and moving in, without a mention of me. I know she still doesn't believe I will stay. I suppose I don't believe it myself. But I thought she was glad to have me here. Shouldn't her dreams of the future include me, at least until I leave?

☐

February 4, 1986

Dear Mom,
    Nothing much to report on the research—it's going pretty well. I've been fighting a cold the last few days . . .

☐

"Kurt called this morning, while you were asleep," Jutta says.
    "What did he say?"
    "He wants Ulrike to come home."
    The weather is frigid and dead-calm. Crusted snow covers the grounds of the Belvedere Palace and forms rakishly tilted berets on the heads of the stone sphinxes. The reflecting pool is an acre of ice, Timo a darting patch of powder blue. "And what did Ulrike say?"
    "She said she already *was* home."
    "Good for her."
    "I don't know . . . I think she's being too hard on him. She was arrogant on the phone."
    "You never liked Kurt before."
    "I still don't. But he's really sorry."
    "Sorry he got caught, you mean."
    "I just don't see where Ulrike gets off being so high and mighty with him."
    "Some day you should try taking a woman's viewpoint, Jutta."
    She laughs, turning and tweaking me painfully on a cold ear. "Oho —who's lecturing? Are you such a feminist? Or just jealous?"
    "Please—not concerning a thirteen year old." I rub my ear.
    "Well if not that, at least it's pleasurable to take Ulrike's part, *nicht wahr*? She's so beautiful—"
    "It's not only Ulrike. I take *your* side more than you do."
    "Yes, but against who? Against yourself! Some lesson." I can't deny the irony. I am trying to get her to take more umbrage at mistreatment; and at the same time I am worried that I will end up mistreating

140

her. "There's no difference between us," Jutta goes on. "I take the man's part because I like men. You take the woman's part because you like women. We're both titillated by it."

"Very clever," I say, a trifle snidely. What else can I say? She is basically right.

Timo is out on the ice, scattering bread crumbs from a plastic bag. The terns, little gulls with orange bills, wheel above him and then fall to the ice and patter after the crumbs in an accelerating run, like wind-up toys gaining purchase. They seem so appealing, so vulnerable, as they run with their necks stretched out, their heads lowered greedily. The carrion crows remain aloof. Shiny black and feathered like burnt books, they glare red-eyed down on the boy from the branches of box-cut trees. "And Renate?" I ask.

"What about her?"

"She's been looking down, of late."

"She's going to run out of paid leave time for the baby pretty soon. She's got to go back to work. She can't afford not to."

"So what happens to Elizabeth?"

"Well that's what she's worried about, of course."

"Mm."

"But all three of us can take care of her. In the apartment and at the day-care center. She can go on formula, or be weaned. She's old enough."

There is a touch of defensiveness in her voice. Has there been an argument about this? "That's what Renate wants?"

Jutta looks away, shielding her eye against the sun. "Timo!" The boy is running on the pond. The ice is a captivating color, the deep steely blue of rifle barrels, or of the Atlantic, brooding through a watercolor storm. "Timo, be careful!" He is chasing a lone crow, which has landed among the terns like a puffed-up bull among velvety cows. It hops ahead of him and then, annoyed, unfolds its wings and lumbers aloft.

"That *isn't* what Renate wants?" I try again.

"Ooh—" Jutta exclaims with such sudden exasperation that she stamps her foot. "Renate doesn't *know* what she wants!"

A smack sails across the ice. Timo has fallen, hard. "I told you to be careful!" By the time we reach him, he is on his feet, groaning deeply: he has knocked his wind out. But he doesn't cry. It occurs to

me, brushing powdered ice off his new jacket, that I have never seen
him cry.

□

"So where's the Favorite Thing in this picture?"

"Hm?"

"This."

"I like having my picture taken."

"Naked?"

"Yes, naked. Especially so . . . What's the big deal?"

"It's porn."

"Aren't I allowed to feel attractive?"

"Of course. But do you only feel attractive this way?"

"Eric, don't be such a jerk. As I recall you couldn't take your eyes
off my tits the day we met—"

"But I didn't know you then."

"And you wouldn't know me now, either, if we hadn't fucked that
very afternoon. You wouldn't have bothered."

"That's not true."

"Yes it is! This sentimentality of men is so hypocritical. You treat
us like sex objects and then are angry when we treat ourselves the
same way."

"No, I—"

"Oh shut up! You want it both ways. You meet me on the street
and the first thing you want to do is fuck me! Well that's fine, that's
the first thing I wanted to do with you, too. So what's all this namby-
pamby crap? You make noises about women being more independent
so you can feel sensitive and so on, but if a woman really refused
herself to you, you'd resent her. If you're ashamed of porn pictures it's
just because you're ashamed of yourself."

"I—"

"All men are the same! Italian, Austrian, American. They've got
this little portrait they carry around in their pockets and they want to
make their women over to it. Italian men and their obedient, quiet
mistresses; Austrians and their tidy wives or carousing whores; 'sensitive' American men and their masochistic ideas about liberated

142

women. But when it comes down to it, what makes all of your cocks stand on end, what makes you all chase around like a bunch of loony birds is spread legs and a big inviting smile. So why are you knocking me? I spread the legs and I got the smile! Enjoy it!"

"You make us sound pretty foolish."

"You said it."

□

"God Almighty, that's the last time I'm going to let you get within a mile of the Musikverein. Just try to forget you ever heard it!"

"Come on, Josh. It wasn't so bad—"

We're crossing Schillerplatz toward the Ring, Josh striding forward as if trying to get the afternoon well behind him, and me hurrying after. Behind us is the Academy of Fine Arts, which once turned down an eager young applicant named Adolf Hitler, who came down the steps into this same Schillerplatz dazed, disappointed, and wondering, now that his dream of being an artist was thwarted, what he might do instead.

" 'Bad'? Are you kidding?" Josh swings around for a moment and fixes me with a suspicious glare (as in: perhaps you don't know anything about music, after all). "It was *terrible!* It couldn't have been worse if I'd stuck the horn up my ass and farted through it!"

"Most of it you couldn't even hear—really!"

He reaches the wide promenade skirting the Ring and heads across it, waving back dismissively at me. "What's the point of even having you come if you're not going to be straight with me? You only tell people what they want to hear—"

The car traffic on the Ring runs one-way: clockwise. As you cross into the Inner City, the cars come from the right. But the streetcars, slipping quietly along both edges of the stream of cars, run both ways. Josh glances right and steps off the curve. "Jesus!" I grab the collar of his coat and haul back on it as hard as I can. My feet, in the slush, go out from under me and I fall, Josh and the horn crashing down on top of me, as the warning clang of the streetcar washes over us and the windows whip by, startled faces close, peering down at two men on the ground. "You can get off me now," I gasp, wondering how far away my breath has been knocked. Josh rolls on to his hands and knees. We're both in about two inches of filthy wet snow.

He gets slowly to his feet and bends down to hand me up. "You look like a steam-roller went over you, Junior." He brushes some of the slime off my jacket, while I look around for my breath. He fetches the horn case out of the snow and carefully wipes it dry. His face is white. He catches my eye. "Thanks, Eric."

But of course we are both embarrassed. (I say "of course," as if this recoil would be universal. But when I recount this to Jutta later, she snorts and says, "That's so like men!") So Josh retreats into jocularity, saying, "Junior—my life is yours! In the tradition of primitive peoples everywhere, I am now your slave. Do with me what you will!"

"You have to do whatever I say?"

"Yes."

"All right—let me come to your next concert."

"Ooof!" Josh looks genuinely pained. He appears to debate whether or not to back out of the joke. But then: "Yes, master." He adds ruefully, "Being a slave isn't going to be as much fun as I had thought." At the next corner he looks both ways with exaggerated caution, and then with a cheerful and booming *Heil und Sieg!*, goose-steps off the curb.

□

Jutta spots a new boutique on Kärntnerstrasse. It's Italian. It's Nower than Now. The mannequins—women—look like concentration camp victims. Their expressions suggest they would gleefully beat the shit out of the Matinique mannequins across the street.

The store has that Italian conformity to the Milan party line. Last year, the word from on *alto* was red, black, and gray. This year, it is solid black (shirt, jacket, and tapering pants, ending above the ankle) with accessories flashing bright colors. The Italian tourist season in Vienna is cranking up, and hundreds of Italian teenagers move through the first district in tight packs like Roman turtles. Or they walk abreast, arms linked, stopping for no one, like riot police scouring the streets of rebellious citizens. When they knock into you, they tell you in bad German to get out of their way. "Every single goddamn one of them wears black," I say. "With a bright red scarf, or a bright green handbag, or a bright yellow tie. They might as well be in the military, with such uniforms."

"Perhaps so," Jutta answers distantly.

"And shades! They all wear shades! On days as gray as Timo's underwear!"

"I know."

"I know you know. But it drives me crazy! Lemming hordes!"

I'm waving my arms. She puts out a restraining hand. "Why are you so excited? I think the way they dress looks nice."

"But it's all the *same!* It's a tyranny! You get the feeling that if one of them wore powder blue, the rest of them would string him up."

"That sounds like something Josh would say."

"Well it's a similar tendency—"

"Fascism and fashion? That's a novel idea!"

"Hmp . . . I think you could argue—"

"Let's not." She takes my arm and turns me up the street. "You're being silly." She gestures at the line of display windows, receding toward Stephansplatz. "What do you think fashion is for?" She shakes her head, displeased. Perhaps I am overplaying the role of the per- plexed male. "I've dated Italian men, remember. *Everything* they do is for show. Everything!" She shrugs, noncommittally. "Some people find that charming. At least I don't think it's ominous." We bump up against another window. Leather goods. "Italian men are the only ones I know who will drag you *into* the light when they want to kiss you. At night you will see them lined up with their girls, under the street lights: like Burgtheater stars, lit by spots."

"Well, it makes me sick. How can anyone base their sense of self-worth on the Burgtheater? On appearances to that extent? On such conformity?"

"Pff!" Jutta puffs, exasperated. "Believe me, if I could conform to that extent, I would. You think I like standing out like this, in these ratty clothes, with the black boy—and him pissing on the stores?"

I kiss her. "I wouldn't have you any other way."

"Ach!" She pushes me roughly away and throws up her hands. "Next time somebody spits, then, *you* tell him what it means!"

□

"What are you standing here for?"

"I'm waiting for my friend."

"Oh? You think that gives you the right to stand here?"

"It doesn't?"

"Take your hands out of your pockets. Come on, take them out—look at this!"

"What?"

"Your hands are empty!"

"They are?"

"Where's your boy pass?"

"I don't have one . . . "

"What? A boy without a pass? You're in big trouble. BIG trouble. What's your name?"

"Timo . . . "

"Timo! What kind of name is that? It sounds like a German sausage —*Timowurst*. Are you sold with mustard and onions?"

"No . . . It's a Ghana name."

"Ghana? Where's that?"

"Where is it?"

"Yes, where is it?"

"It's . . . it's . . . My father lives in Ghana."

" 'Father'? What's a 'father'?"

"What?"

"Is it a bird, a plane? Superman?"

"A father is like my father in Ghana."

"What does he do?"

"He doesn't do anything . . . He's dead."

"That's no excuse."

"Theodor has a father."

"Well whoopee for him."

"He's my father, too!"

"Who?"

"Theodor's father."

"Kurt is your father?"

"Yes."

"You don't look a bit like him."

"I don't?"

"So Theodor is your brother."

"He is?"

"I'm asking you."

"No."

"I'm sorry, you're a boy without a proper boy pass, and now you're contradicting yourself. I'm going to have to take you in for torturing."

(Merciless tickling ensues.)

□

"Did you know Timo says that Kurt is his father?"

"What? That prick?"

"He—"

"How can he think that? I've told him all about Joseph—"

"I don't think he really knows what a father is, actually."

"He doesn't know what *Kurt* is, anyway. Still, why would he think that?"

"As far as I can tell, his idea of a father is simply a male who pops up now and then. If Kurt is Theodor's father, why not his?"

"Ohh . . . but it's—it's important that he know . . . how can he? . . . I know it's not good to raise him this way . . . "

"Hey . . . I wouldn't have brought it up if I knew it was going to upset you."

"Poor Joseph!"

"Yeah, poor Joseph. Poor me."

"Poor you?"

"Well, sure . . . "

"What?"

"Oh . . . I don't know . . . "

"What?"

"Well . . . Why Kurt, anyway? It seems like he could have mentioned me . . . don't you think?"

"You?"

"Is that so ridiculous?"

"But . . . no, of course not. But you're too young—"

"Oh come on, Timo doesn't know that."

"Eric, you really seem hurt by this."

"Wouldn't you be? I mean, what's wrong with me? Am I such a babe in arms? What makes Kurt such a father-figure?"

"Um . . . "

"Because he works? Drives a tractor? Fucks thirteen-year-old girls?"

"Now you're joking."

"But what *is* it?"

"Well . . . you said he thought of a father as someone who was away most of the time. I think that's right. You're here all the time."

"Mm."

"Eric, I know he likes you."

"Yeah . . . I know that, too."

"He didn't like Joseph, you know. I would imagine it's a good sign that he doesn't consider you a father."

"Then what does he consider me?"

"Why is it so important to you?"

"Ohh . . . habit, I guess."

"I think it's wonderful you care so much."

"You needn't say it so condescendingly."

☐

February 9, 1986

Dear Mom,

The research is still coming along all right. I wish there were something specific I could say about it, but it would take pages and pages to fill you in, and I haven't got the time.

Josh and I were at the opera the other night and we ran into a couple of blah blah fart twirl bend stretch kick blbllbbllbllbllbbllblllllbllbllblbl . . .

☐

Another night in a goddamn booze cellar. Altogether too many nights . . . I'm not used to this. All Josh's idea. I think he's an alcoholic. Hm? This is a strange place. I didn't know Vienna had new-wave wine stubls. Corkscrew neon lights . . . If he filled out one of those AA questionnaires, he'd have to answer half of the questions yes. Jutta looks great tonight. I wish we were home right now. I'd love to take

her to bed. The people in here are so *thin*. Upswept hair . . . loose
sweaters, black mascara rings . . . pale and thin and big-eyed. Do you
drink alone? Yes, I know he does. Or at least alone with Jun. Why isn't
Jun with us? Josh treats her inexcusably. Jutta really is beautiful. She
really is. I just have to kiss her. She tastes so good. She laughs so much
with Josh. Do you drink to relieve tension? Shit yes. He hasn't played
a concert in his life when he didn't get blotto afterward. That man
over there is bronze. I mean, really bronze. Like a trophy with a
flat-top. She doesn't laugh as much with me. Well, why should she? I'm
not a comedian. All this drinking can't be good for you. I can feel the
brain cells dying—fifteen per ounce of alcohol, they say. He's holding
her hand. Well, it's good they're friends. Flesh of my flesh, friends of
my friends. How can anyone know if it's fifteen or fifteen hundred? I
can't believe how hot it is in here. These cellars are amazing. Geother-
mal? This wine would freeze solid out on the street tonight and I'm
sweating like a pig. Do you feel like you have to drink to have fun?
That one, too. Poor Jun, at home. Why does she put up with this? She's
probably drinking, too. No gigs, no husband. Listening to tapes of
herself from old Japanese concerts. Don't look now, but two brides of
Frankenstein just sat at the next table . . . If he could get her a job,
he would. He could quit and get rid of his ulcer. God what this alcohol
must be doing to his stomach. "Junior, I've been thinking some more."
"Yeah?" "About ways we could make money." "Mm." "The Mexican
restaurant idea is basically sound, but we need some way to attract the
clientele." "It seems like a flak tower with a Mexican hat on it would
attract anybody." "That's just a gimmick." "OK, so what do we do?"
"Simple. We combine the restaurant with a whore house."
"Pllplplplp!" "Don't be so dramatic. Here's a napkin. I'm serious."
"Who's going to come to our whore house when there's already a
hundred to choose from?" "This city's crying out for a really high-class
institution." "I wouldn't know." "Well, la-di-da. As it happens, I do. We
got the scuzzy Gürtel girls and the middling *puff*s. All the high-class
girls work through the newspapers." "What's wrong with that?" "No
paraphernalia! I've been reading *The Balcony* and I think Genet's on
to something. A fantasy palace! Something extravagant. American-
style. Look how popular the American bars are! We could have a
Dallas room—rawhide whips, cowboy boots. A *Miami Vice* room—
magnums, stiletto heels, coprophagy. A bit of the old Hollywood

149

magic. The Viennese would line up around the block. We could charge maybe four hundred dollars an hour, pay the girls fifty dollars, and we'd have it made! And then the Mexican restaurant would be right downstairs whenever anyone got the munchies." "But what about Jun?" "Jun?" "You know—your wife?" "Oh—well, I don't think she'd be interested—prostitution's not her line." "That's not what I meant." "How about me?" "You're game, Jutta?" "Sure." "That's a girl!" "But you'll have to pay me more than fifty bucks." "Don't even joke about it, Jutta." "Where's your sense of humor?" "I got it. It's just that's not funny." "You're such a goddamn wet blanket." "Loosen up, Junior." Loosenup, schmoosenup. Go jump in the Danube. And there they go, gabbing and laughing. Fantasizing together. They're on the same wavelength. Just have to face that. Josh is the perfect pimp—a big guy, a charmer, a lot of power over women—Jutta fits him hand in glove. He should be having an affair with her and then going home to lie to Jun. Jutta could yell at him and throw fits and he could knock her around and tell her what a bitch she was. She could cry about how she was breaking up a marriage and what a worthless whore she was and how Jun had every right to hate her, and she'd only deserve it when Josh finally dumped her. She'd love it . . . What am I doing here? Who wants such a wimp around when they're all being self-destructive and Byronic? Look on the bright side. It probably does Jutta good to see you jealous. How many other men have cared so much? Are you looking, Jutta? Look, I'm turning green . . . Oh, are we going now? And Josh paying the bill. Of course. "Really, I think it's our turn—" Hopeless. All right, pay it, then. Why not? It's your fucking party.

□

Oooh God. Pphhheww. Isn't it kinda bright in here? Should get it off, though. Late, late, late. Pat'll be wondering where it is . . .

February 10, 1986

Dear Committee,
    The work is going pretty well.

Oof. That's what I always say to my mother. Anh, who cares—

However, I've had one big setback, in that the archive
depository on Kandlgasse burned to the ground three
nights ago—

Wha-at? You wish, pal. Try again . . .

February 10, 1986

Dear Committee,
    Happy Shrove Monday! Good news! Last week, a
contact I'd established through Oberbichler in November
got me in touch with an old, old Viennese family; I spoke
with the scion over coffee at the Hotel Sacher last week,
and I think I'm going to be allowed access to the family
archives—

No major breakthroughs, please. Looks too good. "Over coffee at the
Hotel Sacher"?—sounds Euro-fag. Make me puke.

February 10, 1986

Dear Committee,
    In last month's report, I talked about the *Schutzbund*
and the *Heimwehr,* the private militias of the Social
Democrats and the Catholico-Fascists, respectively—

"Catholico-Fascists"? I've got to be kidding. What was that party really
called? Christian Socialists? Christian Democrats? Christian Techno-
crats? Christian Autocrats?

February 10, 1986

Dear Committee,
    I was in the Kandlgasse archives Friday, poring,
fascinated, over the manifests of the second-string kitchen
staff of the Austrian army's 3rd division, drawn up in the
days immediately prior to Hitler's invasion, when this tall
blond bitch-goddess dressed in jack-boots and black fish-net
panties pulled me out of my chair and forced me with the
butt of her rawhide whip to go down on her—

151

O—K. . . . Getting a little punchy. Do we want to get this done or don't we?

February 10, 1986

Dear Committee,

Happy Shrove Monday! I'm deep in the middle of work on the Nazi infiltration of Austria after the brief civil war of 1934.

Last month, I was talking about the *Heimwehr* and the *Schutzbund,* and it is interesting to see how the effective crushing of the *Schutzbund* and the Social Democrats in '34, and with it, the indefinite perpetuation of the virtual state of siege that Dolfuss initiated in 1933 (when he dissolved all political parties), opened the way for the Austrian Nazis (still an illegal party) to begin undermining the Austro-Fascist institutions of government (in particular, the police) . . .

Much better. I do like the effect of parenthetical remarks. Makes me look so knowledgeable. Let's see . . .

. . . I have finally come across a useful manuscript in the National Library. It details the research of one Gerhardt Baumann, who went through the city archives in the fifties compiling data on Schuschnigg's police. He also spent some time in the national archives, doing the same for the army. Baumann is a fascinating figure, and as far as I know, completely unknown.

And, I might add, for a very good reason . . .

He was a fifth-generation Austrian and a Jew who considered himself completely assimilated. A professor of linguistics at the University of Vienna, he lost his job during the *Anschluss.* Young Nazis poured into the university even while Hitler was in Linz—the day before he arrived in Vienna—and announced that all Jewish professors were fired, all Jewish students were expelled. Three Jews were thrown from the second floor balcony of the grand entrance of the university onto the stone steps below. Two of them died.

I got that last image from the movie *Julia*. On second thought, better get rid of it. Pat's a movie nut.

Baumann didn't need many hints. But he was still trying to get a visa for himself and his mother from the American consulate when the SS arrested him and stuck him in Dachau. He was "offered" expulsion in exchange for all his money (the money would pay for the expulsion of other Jews). He agreed, and found himself back in Vienna. But he still couldn't get a visa for his mother, who was ill and "likely to become a public charge," as the consulate put it. Eventually both of them were shipped back to Dachau and then, in 1942, to Theresienstadt, the Nazi "relief camp" (Baumann was too well known in European academia to be sent to a death camp). But of course, Theresienstadt was not a relief camp at all, but a processing center for sending Jews east. Baumann's mother, for example, was forwarded almost immediately to Auschwitz, where she was apparently taken directly from the train to the gas chamber (well, there was a five-minute stop to get her to write a cheery postcard back to her son in Theresienstadt— "weather's fine, wish you were here," that sort of thing). The same thing would have happened after a while to Baumann except that he assumed the identity of a Danish Jew who died one night of pneumonia. (Living skeletons tend to look alike, and the numbers of the two men were identical except for a "1" on Baumann's arm where the dead man had a "7." With a clout nail and some shoe polish, courtesy of a former concert violinist who shined the officers' shoes, Baumann turned his "1" into a "7," and when the Dane was dumped in one of the mass graves, the name crossed off the camp manifest was "Baumann.")

Baumann hurriedly set about learning Danish from two other Danish Jews. All this was worth the trouble, because the Danish government actually tried to save the lives of its Jewish subjects (it was unique among European

governments in this effort), and the Nazis actually paid
some attention to the Danish government since Nazi racial
ideology placed the Scandinavians above even the
Germans. The government in Copenhagen kept virtually
all Danes from being shipped out of Theresienstadt to one
of the death camps, and it also sent packages of clothing
and vitamins (the Germans forbade sending food or
medicine, but vitamins, for some reason, were allowed)
which duly arrived in the morning post with the prisoners'
names on them. (Throughout the war, the *Deutsche Post*
continued to deliver packages to the inmates of the camps,
as it would to someone at a normal street address—you
know the motto, *weder Schnee noch Regen, Krieg noch
Rassenmord . . .*)

That stuff about the post is actually true. I read it somewhere. Not the
motto, unfortunately . . .

So Baumann survived, learned to speak Danish flawlessly,
and was bused "back" to Denmark with the other Danes in
the early months of 1945. As the dead man had had no
family, Baumann's real identity remained a secret until the
day the German army laid down its weapons in Denmark,
when he attacked and maimed a *Wehrmacht* soldier with a
hacksaw, and was shot in the leg for his trouble by a
Danish policeman. By the time he got back to Vienna in
1948 (in the meantime he had married and separated from
a Danish woman, another Jew, to whom he always referred
later as "that bitch monster from hell"), Baumann was
rather nutty. He became obsessed with the idea that he
could explain the inexplicable—that he could unearth, if
only he dug long and hard enough, the reasons for a
convulsion that had murdered 200,000 fellow Austrian
Jews. He actually believed he could make some sense of it.
So he spent the next six years doing erratic, rather suspect
research. He would work only on Saturdays, would touch
the records only through rubber gloves (which he filled first

with cortisone ointment, to fight terrible bouts of eczema on his hands), and he filled dozens of notebooks with wildly ungrammatical text (this from a former professor of linguistics), about a third of which was real information (of course I check everything I can), another third an elaborate, chicken-scratch system of cross-referencing in his own code which, once I broke the code and started chasing references down turned out to be (or certainly appears to be) utterly random, and the last third a text mixed with drawings—classic schizophrenic art: swirls and complex, repeated patterns filling whole pages, with words written very small around the edges or cross-hatched like Keats' letters, and tiny tiny sketches of what appear to be fornicating animals. Well. It *is* a subject that tends to defeat its practitioners. Baumann's work was cut short one day in 1955 when he looked the wrong way on the Ring and stepped in front of a streetcar and was run over and chopped into little bits. He was buried at city expense in the *Zentral Friedhof,* utterly forgotten. All that is left of him are his early articles and books on linguistics—which no one reads anymore—and this stack of spiral bound notebooks with faded red covers, which I found in a cardboard box at the back of a wire cage in the basement of the university stacks. The sad remnants of a wasted life! Who is willing to learn the lesson Baumann inscribes in his books—that we are all capable of far worse than we dream possible? That the little weaknesses, the quailing turnings-away-of-the-head in all of us can come together in a scaffolding of evil that sprawls across a decade, a continent? And this Jew who considered himself an Austrian first, who was driven crazy trying to figure out how Austrians could be genocidal toward other Austrians, was buried in the *Israelitische* section of the city's cemetery, in one grave among a vast matrix of graves spreading across a huge flatness—each with its little slab, each stamped with that six-pointed star like the print of God's finger, which even here, where it is supposed to be an honor, is also an accusation. And the same night-people who leave swastikas and SS symbols on the trash cans of the Inner City have been to these outskirts, and over these somber stars they have daubed yellow paint.

I rip the page out of the typewriter and pound it into a ball. My chest hurts, as if something vital has been removed. I find myself fighting back tears of rage and grief.

WE HAD A LIGHT SNOWFALL during the night, but sometime early this morning the east wind blew the clouds away and when I woke there was a new dusting of white on the windows and bright blue sky behind it. The air in my bedroom was frigid. But our kitchenette takes the first sunlight on a dark-tiled wall, and the room was tolerably warm by the time rolls and tea were ready. During breakfast we listened to the wind buffeting the kitchen windows. Now, an hour later, I look down at my hands on the typewriter, unsure how to go on, half-hypnotized by that same violent sound.

Comparisons are inevitable, I suppose, between the two winters —that is, the one I am waking to each morning and the one I am remembering. I cannot recall such relentless wind in Vienna. There, when it blew, it was blustery, gusty. Here it comes steadily out of the northeast, as fast and merciless as the hell-bound train. Even our apartment, which is supposed to compensate for its bland and cramped modernity by offering conveniences such as insulation, seems to mutter with each blow of the wind, and in muttering it lets in drafts that creep in the corners like icy cobwebs.

I am not sure why I mention all this. Except that it seems strange to write of one winter and to live in a different one. In describing those Vienna days, I have to be careful to keep this vacant blue sky out of it, for the winter sky of Vienna is never this blue. I must not forget that these towering mountains—beautiful but dumb, as Virginia Woolf called them—properly belong on the north and south sides of this valley, not in the pages of this book. This city is basically bright and cheerful, even in winter: tanned skiers clump energetically up the steep streets, and under the lemon sun the pastel buildings of the Old Town beam like birthday cakes. The airport hasn't had a terrorist attack. There is no synagogue to blow up. There are as few submachine guns here as there are prostitutes. To recapture the atmosphere of Vienna, I often have to draw all the curtains and work under a lamp, or close my eyes for long stretches and think of one familiar street of the Inner City after another, black and glistening under the lowering sky, vaporous at the ends from the dank air. I have to picture the old apartment in Lazarettgasse, the clothes and dishes everywhere, the coal dust, the up-curling linoleum, the empty halls and dark wet bathrooms; and the old rooming group, now shattered. Some days, Vienna feels very far away, and the life we lived there far away with it. I hesitate to mention how sad that makes me . . .

Perhaps the jousting of then and now is especially in my thoughts today because that beguiling nexus that all memoirists know—but perhaps it interests only me—has occurred: that is, the lines of my writing and my living have crossed at a date. Today is February 10, and today I am still taken up with that other February 10. I balled up the letter. But later I spread it out again, and even laughed a little at it. The historian's habit reasserted itself in the end, and I put the letter away, with my books. As a curiosity, I thought to myself. And now I have it, rather yellow and frayed, in front of me. What might I have thought, had I known that some day I would rummage these words out of a box, smooth them once more by a typewriter, and insert them into an account of that lost winter? I think I would have felt a chill. I would have wondered, what does that future Eric know that I do not know?

February 10. For some reason that I have never understood, dates have always been important to me. I love to lie in bed at the end of a day and see if I can remember with certainty what I did, where I was, on that same date the year before, two years before, three, four, and on back until my memory fails me. As artificial an alignment as this is, it still seems to me a meaningful form of stock-taking. Like a spinning wheel, a life, when viewed under a strobe light, may reveal patterns never seen before. Failures and triumphs; friends lost; mistakes made and repaid. The correspondence of dates makes the past seem more real to me. The fact that today is February 10 somehow helps me to believe that there really was that other February 10. Even on this bright howling morning, I can better feel that gray, subdued one. I feel closer today than I have in a long while to that Vienna winter, and to that other Eric, my protagonist.

That other Eric was lost on that morning, and surprised at his own unhappiness. My heart goes out to him. This story takes him to me, so that at the end the protagonist will be myself, typing out the last sentence in an Innsbruck spring.

□

Jutta was still asleep when I flattened the crumpled letter with my hands and pressed it between the pages of a notebook. No one else was in the apartment except for Timo, who had poked his head into the common room while I was typing, and disappeared again when he saw I was busy. I decided I couldn't bear to try another letter for the time being. I felt that need of company—a symptom of vulnerability—one often feels after being upset, so I went off to find Timo, stopping in the kitchen first to wash my face.

Homing in on a dull clonking sound, I found Timo in the children's room. He was gathering wooden blocks into a pile. I squatted. "What are you doing?"

"Playing." Terse, as usual. I was getting tired of doing nearly all the talking.

"Can I play, too?"

He shrugged. "Sure."

"What should I do?"

"Help me gather the blocks." So I did. They were in the bed-clothes; under the bean bag chair; under Ulrike's bed. There was a blue cylinder up in the bathtub. "How did it get *there?*" I asked. "I don't know." There was a green parallelepiped in Elizabeth's crib. "Elizabeth was sucking on that one," Timo said, helpfully.

"Now what?" I asked.

"The chair has to be up."

"What?"

"The chair has to be up!"

"Show me what you mean."

He dragged the bean-bag chair to the wall and tried to lift it. "We put it up!" he said. "On the wall."

"Like this?" I pulled it up so that it sort of stood on end, leaning against the wall.

161

"Yes!"

I let go, and it collapsed, slid out along the floor again. "I don't think it's going to work."

"We'll use boards." He hauled a one-by-six off brick columns in the corner. Then he scattered the bricks with a few savage sweeps of his arms and took another board from underneath them. (The boards had appeared weeks ago. Timo had dragged them up from Zimmermannplatz, where a new stall was being built, and I'd found him one morning walking across one of them from the kitchen table to the stove. He'd been inspired by the circus goat he'd seen in Kärntnerstrasse. When I moved him out of the kitchen, he started to set up from the top of the television to the back of the sofa. "I won't hurt myself!" he yelled, when I stopped him. "I'm not worried about you," I said. "You're liable to break the TV." I took the boards, a few of Timo's bricks, plus two cinderblocks the women were using as doorstops— and good riddance, in the dark I'd nearly broken a toe on one of them —and made shelves in the children's room, where Timo and Theodor could put their toys when they weren't playing with them. The shelves had remained empty ever since.)

Timo stood one board on end and leaned it against the wall.

"So what?" I said.

"The boards hold up the chair."

And as it turned out, he was right. With their bottom edges wedged against a rolled-up throw rug, the boards were heavy enough to pin the chair to the wall. It sagged there, like a tortured prisoner, held up by guards. "Now what?" I asked.

Timo produced a long rubber strap. Where *did* he get all this stuff? "Hold this end," he said.

I took it. Timo moved away with the other end until the strap lifted from the floor and became straight between us. He kept walking back, stretching it. He reached the door into Ulrike's room and kept going, backing now, pulling against the strap with both hands. The pull of the strap in my hands became quite strong. Then it suddenly slackened. Timo's end came whipping back into the room and snapped me neatly in the groin. *"Tiiimo!"* I howled, bending double. *"Scheisse! Was ist denn los mit dir?"*

He reappeared at the door. "I'm sorry. I didn't mean to let go."

I did the duck walk around the room.

"Are you all right?"

"Ohhh . . . nnnh . . . I guess so." I flopped onto one of the mattresses. "I'm not supposed to use 'em, anyway."

Eventually I found out what he had in mind. He had wanted to tie his end of the strap around the doorknob of the door into Ulrike's room. I pointed out that the door, which stood wide open, would just have slammed shut as soon as he'd attached the strap to it. And anyway, why didn't he tie the strap when it was slack, and *then* have me pull on it? "Oh," he said. "Yeah."

"Duh," I said.

We closed the door, doubled up the strap, tied both ends around the doorknob, and I stretched it out from the middle. Timo selected a blue cube from the block pile and placed it against the strap. He retreated into the corner, pulling the strap and the block with him. Then he let the cube fly. It missed the bean-bag target by a meter, smacked loudly against the wall, and left a dent and a tear in the wallpaper.

"Whooopsa!" Timo cried. He shot me a worried glance. "Sorry!"

Enh—what were a few dents in the walls? I remembered Renate saying, months ago: *"Our* walls, Eric." OK—your walls, girls. "Try again, Timo. Watch out for the window." He shot a red cube. It missed, too. "They've both gone too high. Don't go back so far."

Timo hovered over the block pile. "Which should I pick?"

"Try the green pyramid. It's heavier." The green pyramid missed, as well. It hit the wall point on and hung there for a second, before falling. A shower of plaster followed it.

"That was your idea," Timo said.

"It's because you're still going back too far."

"I am not!"

"Suit yourself." The next one arched feebly and fell to the floor. "OK, we're getting our range, now. Try again." He followed with a red-cube grounder and a yellow-cylinder pop fly. I started doing physics in my head: trajectories, elasticity, gravitational constant, air resistance. Meanwhile, Timo hit the exact center of the bag with a green cube. "According to my calculations," I said, "that shouldn't have happened." The next three blocks flew to the same place. "This is too easy!" Timo exclaimed. Perhaps it was overconfidence, or simply boredom, that led him on his next shot to pull as far back as he could, squat, and hold a cylinder to the strap pointed forward, like a cannon. He

163

snapped it, the cylinder pinwheeled, and the ceiling light shattered into a thousand pieces.

□

Timo made breakfast: a bowl for each of us, brimming with Day-Glo tori called "Ring-O's." The side of the box said the tori had all the vitamins known to man mixed in. They certainly had all the sweeteners. "Nutra-sweet causes brain damage, you know. And saccharine causes cancer. And sugar causes hyperactivity, tooth decay, and obesity."

"Mmm." (Slurp, crunch.)

"I wonder how they got to be this remarkable color? With Day-Glo Dye #2?"

"Don't know." (Gulp, munch.)

"Where's the surgeon general's warning?"

"Huh?"

"Never mind. So where are Renate and Ulrike and Theodor and Elizabeth this morning?"

"Ulrike and Theodor are at the *Koppel.*" That's what the women called the day-care center. The word meant "paddock."

"And Renate and Elizabeth?"

"Don't know."

"Out for a stroll?"

"Don't know. Can we get Mommy up for breakfast, too?"

"Let her sleep," I said. "She needs it."

"Oh. I *know!*" The last word was loud. Timo looked pissed off.

"Oh? How do you know?"

"You were both drunk last night," he said.

"I thought you were asleep."

He shook his head, matter-of-factly. "Nope. You were both really drunk."

"Come on, we weren't *that* drunk."

He shrugged, and returned to his eating. One spoon. Two spoons. Quietly: "Yes, you were."

"Were not!"

"Were too!"

I pulled his knit cap down over his eyes. But he wasn't in the mood to fool around. He rearranged the cap gravely. "And you and Mommy were having a fight."

This reminded me of certain episodes from the old *Dick van Dyke Show:* squishy white blond Richie cutely confronting Daddy D. van D. and Mommy M. T. M. (later, a production empire). So I answered smirkingly, with the classic sit-com line. "No, Timo—Mommy and I were having a *discussion."*

"It sounded like a fight, to me."

That's exactly what Richie used to say, to an explosion from the laugh track. "So you've seen those old shows, too, huh?"

"What?"

"Only we really need someone to do the laugh track—" I imitated canned laughter. Oh-HA-HO-HEE-Ha-ha-heh-heh . . . oh-HA-HO-HEE-Ha-ha-heh-heh . . .

"You're weird!" And then he laughed. Timo rather liked weird people.

But he deserved a better answer. Not this smirking. The sit-com answers were revolting pabulum: discussions, not fights; control, not chaos; squishy white blondness and normative parents, not mulatto bastards, slatternly mothers, and diseased boyfriends. Besides, Timo was most sensitive to this, of all subjects. Once the fighting started— he must have been thinking—how long would I stick around?

"Oh, all right—we *were* having a fight."

He ducked his head. "Mm." It was a sullen murmur, bubbling through the milk in his spoon. Then silence. He wasn't going to ask.

"Do you want to know what it was about?"

He shrugged. His eyes were distant, worried. "No."

"Are you sure?"

"It's none of my business."

No doubt he'd been told it many times. "Well, let's *make* it your business. Your mother and I had a fight because I was jealous."

"Jealous?" He was all ears. "Why?"

"Remember Josh? The very tall man, with graying hair? He's been here a couple of times."

"Yes."

"I like him a lot."

"I do, too."

"Good! Well, so does your mother."

"Oh." He was sullen again. He had an idea what that meant.

"Don't misunderstand me. Josh isn't going to take my place. Your mother likes Josh, but she doesn't like him *that* much."

"Then why were you jealous?"

Ah, yes. Good question. "I'm . . . not sure. I was feeling rather unloved and useless last night. Like my life was pointless."

"But why?"

"I seem to have staked everything on your mother. And your mother hasn't been as kind to me recently as she was before. It hurts my feelings, and it scares me."

Timo seemed not to know how to take this. According to Renate and Ulrike, Jutta's boyfriends always left her. Perhaps Timo found it hard to believe that his mother could hurt someone else. "Mommy's been mean to you?" he asked, wide-eyed.

"No, not mean—I . . . don't know what the matter is. I have to ask her. I *will* ask her." And who knows? She might even tell me. "Don't worry, Timo. We'll work it out. It's no big deal."

He twirled his spoon slowly in his deconstructed cereal. He was mulling something over. Then he looked up at me. "Is that why you looked so sad this morning?"

"Oh, you noticed that, did you?"

He nodded.

I sighed. "Yes, that's why." Partly why, anyway. "Actually, I thought for a minute I was going to cry."

He gaped at me, wonderingly.

"Not only your mother cries, you know."

"I know. Renate and Ulrike cry, too."

"Not only *women* cry."

"I don't cry!" he said proudly.

I gazed at him. I know the feeling, kid. I never cry, either. Does it give you the same hollow pain in your chest that it gives me? As if someone has punched the backside of your sternum? "I've noticed that," I said.

□

We heard rustling from the bedroom. Then padded feet crossed the hall, went through the children's room and Ulrike's room, on to the bathtub. Running water. "What do you want to bet she didn't even notice the broken light?" I asked, conspiratorially.

Timo giggled, happy, like most kids, at the opportunity to mock a parent. "She never notices anything!"

A silence followed, during which we could hear the tub filling. Then a splash, and the sound of ripples subsiding. Then nothing. "She's soaking now," I said.

"The water is very hot," Timo said.

"I'll say."

"She's boiling herself like a chicken."

"BAAAWK, bok-bok-bok!"

Another silence.

"I *will* ask her, Timo," I said, to reassure myself.

He looked at me, grave again. "She won't tell you anything," he said sadly.

A key scratched in the apartment door and Renate kicked it open, holding Elizabeth in her arms. "Whhew! My arms are tired!" She sat Elizabeth on the bench and took off her coat. She looked drained and disgusted. "I've had to carry Elizabeth all morning. Someone stole the perambulator."

"No! When?"

"Ohhh," she collapsed in a chair, "I don't know." She pulled Elizabeth into her lap, began to take off the baby's things. "Someone took it from the downstairs hall. It was gone this morning. I just don't understand how people can do things like that." I rescued a spoon splattered with fluorescent sugar headed sideways for Elizabeth's mouth. "It's not like anyone living in a dump like this would have money to spare." She lifted Elizabeth over her head and sniffed her bottom. "And Lizzie needs her diapers changed. AGAIN!"

She sounded close to the end of her rope. "Let me do it," I said. "Relax for a few minutes." I took the baby.

"Deal." She slid forward and nestled her head on her forearms on the table. Timo reached across and patted her head solicitously. A muffled "thanks" came up through her arms.

Elizabeth burbled happily as her clothes came off. A lot had gone down one leg of her body suit and collected in the foot. "You've been a productive little girl, haven't you?" (Blup, blup, gub.) "Yes—I'll bet you're proud of yourself, aren't you? Aren't you?" (Blbllbbbl!) I put a pinky in her mouth and she clamped down blissfully. Yeeow. Two top and two bottom teeth were just beginning to come in. Timo appeared

167

at my elbow. "Timo, could you throw this in the bucket?" He carried it as if with tongs. "It's not a smallpox blanket, Timo." He dropped it.

"Sorry."

"Well pick it up—"

"It's dirty!"

"*You* are talking to *me* about dirt? Looked in your room lately?" Then came the wet towel, and Elizabeth began to wail. "Your shit doesn't smell so good, now you've started to eat rolls."

Jutta padded in, her hair in a towel. "Oh, you're a darling, Eric!" She kissed my shoulder. "Really—it's wonderful. Who would expect a man to be willing to change diapers?"

Certainly not you. "I don't mind," I said.

"Is there any coffee left?"

"I didn't make any."

"Oh." Pause. "Why not?"

"Timo made breakfast."

"Well do you want any coffee or don't you?"

"Sure."

"Tea, Ren? What's the matter?"

The muffled voice: "I'm tired."

"Is that all? You look terrible."

"Somebody stole the perambulator," I said.

But that wasn't all either. After Elizabeth was clean and dry and back at the breast, Renate told us that she had left the baby for an hour at the *Koppel* and gone to the hospital. She'd tried to extend her paid leave. No luck. If she didn't return to work next month, her salary would be cut off.

She said, "I don't know what to do. I've got no money saved up. I can't go two days without a salary."

"What about your parents?" I asked.

"Don't be ridiculous. They wouldn't support me. Not on account of Elizabeth, anyway. Hell . . . "—she waved despairingly at the air—"they haven't got the extra money, anyway."

"Can't we help?" Jutta asked.

"With what?"

"Well, Eric has money coming in—"

"No, I wouldn't think of it."

"But it's the least he can do—"

"No, it's simply out of the question."

"But why? I'm sure he'd be glad to help. Wouldn't you, Eric?"

"If you'll allow me to inject some reality into this discussion," I said, "we're spending all of the grant money as it is. The next check won't come until March 10th or so, and we're going to be scraping to make it."

"What? How can that be?"

"Don't ask me. I put it in the household fund and it magically disappears."

"Can't you ask for the next check earlier?"

"Oh, sure. Just what I need. Attention from the department. I could call up and say, 'Ah, hello? Yes, the research is going fine—but I'm afraid the baby's mother just lost her job.' "

"Just make something up, as usual."

"And then what do we do for the next check? Or do you want me to demand a raise?"

"No, stop," Renate pleaded. "I wouldn't accept it, anyway." Ha! I thought. You're already accepting part of it through the household fund. "It's simple. I'm just going to have to go back to work, that's all. God knows what I should do with Elizabeth."

Jutta shot her eyes heavenward, exasperated. "Let's not bring *God* into it, of all people! If you're determined to get back to work, then we can all take care of Lizzie together."

"Oh, no," Renate said vaguely. "No . . . much too much bother for you. With Theodor and Timo already . . . "

"We've already gone over this, Ren—"

"No, Jutta," Renate said more firmly. "It's not possible. I won't ask you to do that."

I guessed Renate had another reason for objecting. Jutta guessed, too. "Why don't you drop the pretense," she exclaimed, aggrieved, "and just say you don't trust us to take care of her?"

"Jutta!" Renate was horrified. "How can you say that?"

"Ohh!" Jutta blurted out angrily. She stood up so fast she jarred the table, and her coffee spilled. *"Scheisse!"* She grabbed a shirt someone had left on the bench and dabbed at the coffee furiously. "How can I . . . ?" The shirt was too dirty to be absorbent, so it simply painted swaths of coffee on the table. "How can I . . . ?!" She made a final swipe with the shirt, balled it up, and threw it at the sink. It landed with a clatter among the medicine bottles. "How do you *think?!*" She whipped up her cup with its remaining coffee and stormed out. Down the hall the bedroom door slammed.

"Bitch," Renate muttered, embarrassed.

"Bitch," Timo echoed cheerfully.

□

"Who does she think she is? Her precious little bastard is too good for us? Or just too fragile, maybe? I notice she never worries about Timo or Theodor! I can't believe she's got the nerve—"

"I think you're making too much out of it—"

"And *you!* Why don't you ever defend me? You never take my part! You never take *anybody's* part! You just sit there behind your schoolboy glasses and murmur 'oh, I don't think' and 'oh, maybe this' and 'maybe that.'" She spoke simperingly, mimicking my *Hochdeutsch* pronunciation. "And then you stick around afterward and sweep the floor. You think you can tidy everything up so you can forget about it—stick everything back in the cupboards and close the doors and go read a book. But whenever anything happens you just sit there like a little schoolboy hoping the teacher won't pay any attention to you—it makes me sick!"

"I make you sick?"

"Ohhh! . . . " She pressed both hands to her forehead and closed her eyes, then spread her hands, tugging her hair slowly and powerfully to either side. "Noo . . . You don't. Don't listen to me! I'm mad at Renate, not at you." She tossed her hair back. "I suppose . . . I'm being a bitch."

"Funny, that's just what Renate said."

"Did she?" Jutta laughed. Doing a bit of yelling often put her in a better mood. "Well, she's a bitch, too."

She reached up to the shelf over the bed and rummaged through the piles of junk for her cigarettes. Two empty packs came down and were thrown on the floor. A third, crushed, yielded two cigarettes, both bent. She lit one and drew the smoke sharply, deep into her body, and held it, waiting for the drug to help her. A concentrated silence. Then: phheeewww! A wedge of the stuff spurted from her mouth across the room. "I needed that." I looked curiously at the haze. Exhaled smoke looked so thin—so different from the heavy thread drifting up from the end of the cigarette. Did it leave so much behind in the lungs? And that coating of sludge actually made life bearable?

Jutta read my thoughts. "Of course you didn't defend me. You're a clean-living type like Renate. I'm sure you agree completely that she shouldn't let poor Lizzie live with smokers and coffee-drinkers."

It's not just the smoking, I thought. She's afraid you'll forget to feed her. Or will never change her diapers. Or will simply *lose* her under the vast piles of discarded cigarette packs. I said, "I drink coffee, too."

"My question is, though—where *is* she going to put Lizzie if she doesn't want us to take care of her? She's going to find a nice old couple who don't charge much and who drink herbal tea and who will push her around the Vienna hills every day? They better lock up their perambulator!" She crowed gleefully.

"Why not the day care center?" I asked.

"Her hours are irregular. At the hospital, she has to work all night every third day."

"They won't even take her off rotation?"

"Her boss is a prick. He's told her to her face—he's got no sympathy for unwed mothers." She lit the second cigarette from the first, looked for an ashtray, and then stubbed the butt out against the metal edge of the shelf. "He'd have even less, if he knew who the father was."

"Who was the father?"

"No, I just meant if he knew the father was black. No one at the hospital has seen Lizzie, you know. Renate made sure she was out of Vienna for the delivery. And since Renate has never brought her to the hospital, everyone there assumes something's wrong with her. Retarded, or something. Ren's getting a lot of undeserved sympathy at the moment. Except from the prick."

"They'll have to know sometime."

"Of course they will. It's terrible the way she hides the baby. She may get all high and mighty about us, and the smoking, and all that, but—" a brief, happy look flitted across her face "—but it's just insecurity. You know, she's really ashamed of Elizabeth."

"Oh?"

"She would never admit it. But *I*—for all my problems, all my smoking and all my boyfriends—I never hid Timo."

"Still, you'd be happy if he were white."

She turned on me angrily. *"No!* That's wrong! I've never wished that he were white! I wish that the world were a good enough place for him. Far better he be black than have a father like Kurt, looking down on everyone different from himself. Or like my own father, who shames only himself by refusing to look at the boy. Only the misfits have any compassion in this world."

And if only you could really believe that. "But now I'm curious," I said. "Who *was* Elizabeth's father? How did Renate meet him?"

She had already sucked her second cigarette down to a butt, and was rummaging on the shelf for another one. A dollop of ash fell from the glowing tip to the bed, where a dozen others had fallen—they lay scattered about, crumbling, some smeared into gray streaks, like the fine granular shit of a lung-burrowing worm. "Where are all the goddamn *cigarettes?* Oh—" a shoe-box full of seashells tipped off the shelf as she pried behind it, flipped over, and scattered ribbed calcium bits across the bed and floor—"here they are." She grabbed the nearest scallop shell and turned it cup-up. Then she lit a third cigarette and stubbed out the second in the shell. "Elizabeth's father was an intern," she said. "At the hospital."

"And even so, the hospital doesn't know Elizabeth is half-black?"

"Christ, no. They kept their affair a secret. There'd have been trouble, otherwise. And besides—" (Suck. Hold. Ppphheeww! Smile.) "—Renate was ashamed of that, too. They used to go to Wiener Neustadt when they wanted an evening on the town. Imagine loving someone and yet being ashamed of him!"

Imagine.

"At least I was open with Joseph. *And*—I suffered the consequences. I was ostracized. People would not talk to me. Literally. They would turn away. I was willing to do at least that, for him."

Well, that was one interpretation. But it seemed more plausible to me that Jutta's openness—her flaunting of Joseph, really—stemmed from more shame than Renate had, not less. Her affair with Joseph had to be open because it was less a love affair than a self-inflicted punishment. A debasement. How could she not, on some level, share the racism of the couple who raised her? I could imagine Renate—quiet, undramatic Renate—being surprised by a passion which she could not suppress, but which she could, out of a dislike of attention and trouble, at least hide. And, too, she would hide it out of self-respect: that part of self-respect that ignores conscience and declares, "Whatever I may privately feel, I do *not* deserve ostracism." And opposite her, I could imagine Jutta picking out Joseph: devoid of passion for him personally, but with an eager and accurate eye for the pariah. If it had been 1938, she would have picked a Jew.

"Where is this intern now?" I asked.

"Back home, presumably. Rwanda. Renate hasn't heard a word from him since he left Austria."

"Does that bother her?"

"Well . . . ," she shrugged. "It doesn't surprise her. He broke it off as soon as she got pregnant."

□

I lay in the dark, mulling things over, as Jutta lay asleep beside me. How often I did that! When I was asleep, did she ever stay awake and think about me?

I had broken my promise to Timo. I had not asked her. But I could hear the delighted laugh, the high rasping voice: "What? Something the matter? Of course not, Eric!" She would feel no need to answer. The fact that I had asked would say enough.

What was going on? Fights had begun to happen between us. For example, this morning. "Schoolboy?" It was true enough; in fact, I couldn't think of a better epithet, myself. But she would not have said it a month ago, two weeks ago. I say the fights "happened" because they seemed to come from nowhere; they condensed out of the air like violent summer storms. Enough of them happened in the apartment so that Ulrike had said, "But Eric, you know, it's still not like old times." "What do you mean?" I had asked. "At least the other boy-friends fought back." No, I didn't fight back. I could not fight what I did not understand. Instead, I retreated. And retreating just seemed to make Jutta bull forward more. So I retreated more. I absolutely would not fight blind. Then her anger would disappear. Just as abruptly. Some need had been satisfied. But only temporarily.

The fights were not all. She had never been punctual, but her unpunctuality had begun to take on an aggressive character, as if she were testing me, whenever we had agreed on a rendezvous, to see how long I would wait for her. When she finally appeared, walking so slowly, so unconcernedly, she would say nothing. "What kept you?" I would ask, and she would respond, shrugging, "Oh, nothing; why, am

I late?" Once, she failed to show at all. I came home to find her taking a nap. She had decided not to go after all because she had felt tired. I had passed her test with flying colors. I had waited two hours.

And the body language. She didn't *cling* to me any more when we embraced. It felt distinctly as if I was clinging to her. That little smile of triumph that I had seen on her face the first day, as I agreed against Timo's wishes to come home with her—that smile had come back. And with it, a new hesitancy. I could feel it in her body, a momentary stiffness as I took her in my arms. The smile seemed to say that she was happy to be able to feel that hesitancy. Proud to be able to think, "Oh, this again; but why not,"—the stiffness dissolving graciously—"if it is so important to him?"

I could just make her out in the gloom. She was curled on her side, turned away from me. Even in the beginning, when she had seemed so frighteningly dependent on me, she had slept that way, and I had spooned with her. I hadn't thought much about it. But then I noticed the way she slept with Timo. Sometimes I was the first up, and coming back into the bedroom with a cup of coffee for her and a buttered *Semmel* for Timo, I would find she had turned in her sleep, so that she and the naked boy were facing each other, his face pressed suffocatingly into the soft flesh below her shoulder, and her face bent down, in his hair, her hand protectively cupping his buttocks. That, I would think, is the sleep of lovers. Something in her, perhaps, had always balked at an ultimate acknowledgment of my presence, even though she undoubtedly needed my presence. The same way she undoubtedly needed sex, but balked at the ultimate surrender. In the honesty of the frantic seconds before climax, and in the honesty of sleep, her fear and loathing surfaced.

When Timo plodded in, I lifted the bed clothes for him. "Goodnight, Timo," I whispered. I was happy to see him.

"Goodnight, Eric," he mumbled, crawling in between us. Like his mother, he turned his back to me, and I kissed him through his curly hair.

□

"She's afraid of being happy," Ulrike said. "She has never had a stable, healthy relationship before, you know. She can't blame her problems on her boyfriend if he is too understanding, and that scares her. She resents you for forcing her to confront the unhappiness within herself."

Ulrike tended to favor interpretations that made me look good. Unfortunately, I suspected her motives. Ever since Kurt had been caught with the thirteen-year-old girl and Ulrike had left him—temporarily or not, she still, apparently, did not know—she had shown more interest in me. I still remembered vividly her sudden kiss, and my sudden delight, my desire to return it. Perhaps it had occurred to her that having a fling with another man would be the best way to get back at her husband. And who better than me, who was not only proximate, but so clearly attracted to her? Moreover, Ulrike knew that Jutta thought she was being insufferably high and mighty with the repentant Kurt. I could imagine her thinking: we should see how *she* likes it. (Remarkably, Jutta had never told either Ulrike or Renate that I was quite possibly an AIDS carrier. I had asked her not to, of course, but I had not expected her to listen to me. I think she had refrained because she feared that if they knew, they would be unlikely to let me stay. The parallels to a young girl bringing home a sick puppy are a mite chastening.)

"But what *does* she want?" I asked Ulrike.

Ulrike sat curled up on the sofa, stroking Ziu in her lap. She wore thick red socks with articulated, multicolored toes, and she looked very cozy. "She wants something to cry about. She wants to be punished. It may sound odd, but you have been too good to her."

So if I were to take that cat out of your lap and lay you down, everyone would be happy. Right? I sighed. "Perhaps she's just not used to quiet men," I said, pursuing a related line. "She may associate true love with a lot of raw, bleeding emotions and screaming—if that's always the way it has been for her. She may have decided this can't be love because we get along too well."

"Perhaps."

"In which case, I'm simply the wrong man for her. If she needs passion . . . "

"But if you really think that"—she said it as if to suggest that I really couldn't—"why don't you just *be* passionate with her?"

"I can't turn it on like a faucet, Ulrike. At least my feelings for her make sense. Which is more than I can say for her feelings for *me.*"

"Her feelings make sense to me—"

"If she wants me to hurt her, that's sick."

"You're being judgmental. That is the way she is. You're dealing with a woman with very low self-esteem."

"No kidding."

"Well, act like you know it."

"How in hell am I supposed to raise her self-esteem by treating her badly?"

"Are you really in love with her?"

I got excited. "Let's not talk about love, OK?"

"All right," she said mildly. I could see her ears prick up. She sensed a "revelation" coming.

"I think about her all the time. I don't want to be anywhere but with her. When she's good to me, I'm happier than I've ever been in my life. I'm also willing to admit that she's really fucked up. But that doesn't mean I'm going to do what's not natural to me, just to give her what she, in her fucked-upness, might want!" Put *that* in your pot and stir it.

Ulrike stroked Ziu for a few moments without responding. Then she looked up again and said, "You're a puzzling character, Eric. I think you would benefit from analysis."

□

"You're too weak," Renate said. "You don't defend yourself. Jutta doesn't like that."

"Defend myself how? If she told me I smelled, I'd show my soap to her. If she said I was stupid, I'd multiply numbers. But how am I supposed to defend myself when she blows up at me for no reason?"

"You've got to find the reason."

"She won't tell me. I don't like playing guessing games. Ulrike says I've been too good to her."

Renate ran a finger thoughtfully around the edge of her cup. (All my conversations with Renate seemed to occur at the kitchen table; with Ulrike, on the common-room couch. I remember Renate from those days always with tea, sitting up straight, in fluorescent light. And Ulrike curled up among the cushions, in softer yellow light, playing, cat-like, with me.) "That's one way of putting it, I suppose. It's not so much that you've been too *good*, though. It's that you've shown her too much that you care."

"That's a problem?"

"You haven't been with her that long, Eric. You don't know what she is capable of. If you start caring about what she does, she'll squash you."

"Why is it that every time I talk to you, the conversation turns threatening?"

"You're really not very perceptive. That's a common trait among Americans, isn't it?"

"I'll claim my blockheadedness as my own, thank you."

"Do you honestly think Jutta can accept someone—anyone—on an equal footing? Do you really think if you love her and try to understand her, she'll love you and understand you back? All she has learned from the time she was a baby is that the only answer there can be for love is contempt. She loves—she worships!—the people who despise her. You must know at least that. And she'll despise anyone who loves her."

"Well," I said peevishly, "next time she gets out of line, I'll turn red and scream obscenities at her. Then everyone will be happy."

"As long as you joke about it, nothing is going to get better."

Rick had always despised me for being too closemouthed, too camouflaged. For the first time in my life, I had tried to open up to someone. And I had managed to pick someone who despised me for *that,* instead. The conversation had depressed me immeasurably. "It's all a fucking joke, anyway," I muttered.

"There!" Renate exclaimed encouragingly, "why don't you say things like that to her?"

I felt the blood rush furiously to my head. "Why don't *you,*" I spat out, "make a recording of it and broadcast it from the four fucking walls?"

☐

The days went by, and we went on, and I didn't fight back, and Jutta and I settled more and more into an emotional arrangement no more unhealthy or destructive than the great majority of them, I suppose.

I realized that Renate and Ulrike, in their different ways, were right. But I could not agree with them that I owed it to Jutta to reestablish my dominance over her. I gradually came to see that Jutta's having someone she could despise a little was doing her good. Here, at last, was a male who did not openly judge her, but who simply

177

accepted her and wanted her. In the light of my admiration—which was stronger now than ever—she blossomed. There was an appealing abandon in the way she lashed out at me; an intriguing, almost delightfully child-like aspect to her sudden, explosive aggression. She was so much feistier! So much more assertive! So much more alive! For the moment, it was unthinkable that she would curl up in bed and whimper apologies about how despicably weak she was. Nothing she could do to me could possibly make me as sick at heart—or more accurately, as sick to my stomach—as those earlier feats of self-degradation. Moreover, having found herself at last in a role of power and cruelty, perhaps she would conceive a certain understanding for the powerful and cruel people who haunted her life; and perhaps, in understanding them a little more, she would fear them a little less.

In other words, I imagined that my relationship with Jutta had become therapeutic for her. This, of course, was an old and much-used formulation of mine. It had always held the attraction of elevating me, during those times when my self-respect was threatened, into a superior position: that of the mentor, the psychiatrist. My behavior was therefore not quite as masochistic as it might at first appear.

☐

One day Jutta came up with something she called The Flirting Game. We would go to a bar or wine cellar, she said, and both of us would try to ensnare other people. We would have a friendly little contest to see which one of us had more luck. Then at the end of the evening we would disengage ourselves, go home together, make love, and talk about the foolish people whom we had lured on.

A silly idea. But I thought I understood the impulse behind it. The game would reflect her new sense of self-confidence, of power. She was quite an attractive woman, in her way, but most men had come to her as I had come: as creatures on the prowl, who took her because she offered the least resistance. Now, it seemed, she trusted herself enough to essay a more aggressive role. *She* would pick out the stranger in the bar, and by the force of her attraction would make *him* change his plans for the evening. And of course, there was something else: although she presented the game to me as a joke played on strangers—on the world—it would also be a joke on me. That "friendly little contest" would only thinly disguise a bare-fisted attempt to make me jealous.

But as they say, forewarned is forearmed. And she had to get the nonsense out of her system, somehow—better, then, when I was expecting it. So I agreed to go along with the idea. I even thought the game might provide a little kinky fun, if taken with the proper amount of spirits.

That very night Jutta led me to a popular single's joint near the Josefstheater where the picking, she thought, would be pretty good. We split up at the door. "Good luck," I called to her, through the crush of bodies, and headed toward the bar to get appropriately soused.

Jutta found herself a partner quickly enough. I turned from the counter to find that she had maneuvered the man to a stool near me. I thought I had been prepared, but I almost dropped my drink. I had pictured her, I suppose, on the arm of some taciturn hunk in a polo shirt, with sandy hair and coconut pecs; she would be draped over his shoulder and would be talking non-stop to him, while he lifted the wine-glass to his face as if he were curling a dumbbell. I would intervene and have the shit kicked out of me. Jutta would break a chair across the hunk's back in order to save me. Something along those lines, anyway. So who was this ugly, obnoxious, adolescent geek? He looked like something out of the nightmares of Sheriff Clark: greasy strings of hair dangled to his shoulders; the pimples on his cheeks and forehead seemed as angry and sour as his expression. He had the beaky, lumpy sort of nose that makes one think of the slick white cartilage inside it. And it wasn't Jutta, but he who did all the talking. She listened to him as if enthralled.

Aghast, I edged closer to hear what he was saying. " . . . I warn you, don't get into an argument about the theater with *me!* I am very opinionated!" He laughed grimly, as if it were a fine and terrible thing to be so opinionated about the theater.

"Are you working on something, yourself?" Jutta asked deferentially.

"Oh . . . " he waved the question down as if it were hopelessly obtuse, "it is not a time for writing in the theater; it is a time for revolution! Only the machines keep turning out play after play, the automatons with their safe and self-satisfied middle-class audiences; the last writer of any consequence was von Hofmannsthal; he is exquisite! I am something of an expert on von Hofmannsthal—"

"Excuse me," I said, breaking in.

"Who are you?" he exclaimed.

"I'm her brother," I said, grabbing Jutta's arm.

"What are you *doing?*" Jutta hissed.

"Come on," I whispered, "just for a second—you can come right back." I guided her out of the geek's earshot.

"So what is it?" she demanded.

"You're asking me? What is *that?*"

"What?"

"That thing you're talking to. Where did you find him? Stuck to the underside of a table?"

Her eyes glittered. "You're supposed to be looking for somebody. You're not supposed to be hanging over me."

"Hanging over you? You practically sat the guy down in my lap. He looks like a California condor—"

"—and now you're jealous."

"Appalled, maybe."

"You're not playing the game!"

"No, *you're* not. You're just trying to gross me out."

"I haven't seen *you* pick anyone up, yet."

"Come on, Jutta. You're a good-looking woman. You can do better than that."

"Oohhh," she groaned, furious, "this is *ridiculous!*"

"Get rid of him," I said. "He nauseates me."

She pulled her arm out of my grip. "I'll do what I want." But when she returned to the geek, I followed her and heard her say—her anger already replaced by elation—"I'm so sorry, I can't talk to you, anymore. My brother is *terribly* conservative; so bourgeois—"

She returned to me. "Satisfied?" she demanded.

"Yes."

"Go find someone else, then. And leave me alone."

But of course, she wouldn't leave *me* alone. She herded her next pick within a few feet of me and arranged him along the bar so as to give me the best possible view. Then she conducted their conversation at a shout. He was a blond man, chubby, in a leisure suit, with big plastic-rimmed glasses on a little nose. He laughed delightedly at everything she said. When she pressed his hand, his face turned so red that he tried to hide it by taking a gulp out of his wine glass.

"Excuse me," I said, breaking in.

Jutta rolled her eyes. "Again?" She was high, now: so excited, her voice quavered.

"I'm her brother," I said to the chubby man.

"Say!" He held out a hand like a hot mitt. "Glad to meet you! Hugo!"

"Hello, Hugo. Eric."

"You've got a charming sister—"

"Yes, isn't she? Could you excuse us for a moment?"

"Sure—" And I dragged her away.

"*Jutta . . . ,*" I began angrily.

"You haven't found anyone *yet?*"

"How can I concentrate when you keep cattle-prodding these charity cases under my nose? Butterball is hardly the type to arouse my competitive instinct."

"You're being so childish. I really wouldn't have thought this of you."

"Don't give me that. At least admit that you're loving every bit of this. You think I didn't see you looking over at me every couple of seconds?"

"I was just wondering if you were ever going to stop staring."

"I'm staring because I'm flabbergasted. First you pick a pimply Bunthorne, and then the Goodyear Blimp. It's insulting."

"To who?"

"To both of us. Can't you at least come up with someone worth getting jealous over? Or are you trying to tell me something?"

"Yes," she said and grabbed the lapels of my jacket. "You want to know what it is?" She pulled the lapels toward her until our noses touched and she hollered, "LEAVE ME ALONE!" Her breath smelled pleasantly of witch's blood.

"Fine, fine! No problem!" I made my way into another part of the bar. I found a lone seat at the counter and ordered a *Viertel.* Five minutes later Jutta was there, too, with the butterball.

"You still haven't found anyone," she said with motherly sympathy, threading her way to me.

"I thought we were going to leave each other alone."

"But you're just sitting here, doing nothing."

"I haven't seen anyone yet who deserves me."

"Don't be a sore loser."

"I'm not."

"You are, too."

"I'm not. I'll prove it: I concede, you win. Congratulations! Well played, old man! Now let's go home."

"Already?"

"All right, we'll stay, then." I certainly wasn't going to beg. "You go back to the Graf Zeppelin, and I'll sit right here."

"But it's no fun if you don't try—"

"I'll try! I'll try!" That is, not to murder you when we get home. "I'll tell some young leggy thing that I'm researching the *Anschluss*. They always love that." *Toll!*, the young things say, when you tell them about the research: "Crazy!" Austria's war guilt is a trendy subject for the rebellious, aged 14 through 19. They all get over it around the time they start having sex regularly.

Jutta squeezed my shoulder and disappeared again into the crowd. But she contrived to keep herself and her consort more or less visible to me. All right, all right. I *was* jealous. Not of the butterball—I wasn't foolish enough to believe that the man was more than the merest tool —but of my former self. She would not have done this to me a few weeks ago. Knowing that this was coming hadn't seemed to help a bit.

Nonetheless, I had always thought it better for all concerned—not least myself—to be able to step back from any ugly situation and view it as if I were watching strangers. Some situations required less a "stepping back" than an acrobatic back-flip; but those flips got easier a lot faster than one might think. I had done so many of them since childhood that I could usually land high on a platform out of everyone's reach without batting an eye. And looking down from my platform into that cacaphonous Josefstadt bar, at the girlish, gleeful woman—riding the crest of her fortune, hardly daring to believe her power—and at the blockheaded American, reminding himself that the experience was good for her, all the while slowly getting angrier in spite of himself—looking down, I had to admit that the situation was pretty funny. And if it had been a scene in a novel, I would most certainly have been on the woman's side. She was colorful, active; it was a cute and gutsy game she was playing. The man, by contrast, was distressingly passive. He was a ruminant. A dud. I decided I could learn a thing or two from Jutta's abuse.

"Excuse me," I said, breaking in.

"I'm not going to go with you again, Eric!" she burst out, exasperated.

"Fine," I said. "I don't want to talk to you, anyway. I want to talk to him."

I put my hand in the small of his back (if it could have been called that) and propelled him gently in front of me. "I don't want to intrude into a family quarrel," he objected, his soft brow wrinkling with concern.

I held up my hand. "Not at all. We're not having a quarrel. There's just something you should know about Juttli, that's all. It's why I stay near her—to make sure people who need to know, will know."

"What?" His eyebrows were high and rounded. He had a completely open face. He looked as if he would believe I were an android if I told him.

"She's got AIDS."

The blood began a general retreat from his face. "AIDS?"

"Oh dear—I hope you haven't kissed her yet, have you? She does so like to kiss people—"

"No, no—"

"She hasn't licked you?"

"No—"

"Bitten you?"

"God, no—"

"Well, that's good."

"But—" he cast his eyes around, as if looking for an escape route —"but what should I do?"

"You mean, now? Oh . . . well . . . Do whatever you want. I just wanted you to know."

He looked back at her. He was frightened. But he was torn between his fear and his reluctance simply to abandon her. But if he went back, what could he say to her? Finally, with a look of regret, and perhaps of shame, he turned away from her, toward the door. "I'm sorry—" he blurted out.

"Oh, no need to be," I assured him. "I understand. I don't even use the same bathroom she does. I'm surprised they let these people out in public." He fled. I glimpsed him at the door, struggling with his coat. Then he was gone.

I returned to Jutta. "He seemed like a decent, kind fellow," I said.

"Where did he go?" she asked, mystified. "What did you say to him?"

I picked up the glass of wine that he had left behind and took a sip. I suddenly felt like laughing. But instead, I kissed her.

She, intrigued, kissed back.

And we went home, after all, and made love, and talked about the two men as if they were the fools, and not we.

□

The next thing I can remember is buying potatoes. I was in Zimmermannplatz, in the shadow of the Children's Hospital. A city ambulance had been at the door, and two men had gone back and forth between the building and the automobile, with a bottle on a stick, with a stone-faced parent, with a small stretcher. The ambulance had driven slowly up Lazarettgasse toward the General Hospital, its lights blipping, the siren off.

"Perhaps that means it's not serious," I said.

Ali shrugged. "Perhaps that means the child is dead," he countered.

Ali was like that. A tall, gaunt man with hands and feet like platters and a mustache so wide you thought of it in terms of wingspan, he preferred the pessimistic view. Why not? He had fought hard and paid a lot of baksheesh to get his stall on Zimmermannplatz, and now he sold his vegetables only to a piddling number of Turks and Yugoslavs. The Iranians bought at the Iranian grocery store on Pelikangasse. All the Viennese bought from the Viennese woman who ran the stall across the walkway. Ali was not making enough money to support his subdued, silent wife and their four children.

The Viennese woman was the enemy. "She is a bitch, I'll tell you that," Ali had said to me. "She fooled me, all right."

"How so?" I had asked.

"She was joyful when I came on the platz. I thought she was a friend. But you know why she was joyful?"

"No, why?"

"The man I replaced was Viennese. Her competition, you understand? As soon as I was here, she raised her prices. You know how much?"

Ali had a weakness for dialogue in the form of call and response. "No, how much?" I asked.

"Half again as high. Look at her stuff—her cabbage is fifteen schillings a kilo, mine is eleven. Her carrots are twelve a kilo, mine are eight. And she still gets most of the business. As far as the *Wiener* are concerned, she's got the only vegetable stand on the platz."

"Yes, but you get all the Turks."

"Turks can't afford prices like that. And no matter what they say, there aren't so many of us after all."

That was long ago. Today I said, "Haven't you got any fatty potatoes?"

"No. Got some good dry, though. Lots of grainy and red, too." Central Europeans distinguish about eight different kinds of potatoes. It keeps them from feeling like they're eating the same thing every day.

"Unfortunately, Jutta wants the fatty ones."

"Ahh," Ali said. There was a note of disparagement in his voice; as in, when she squawks, I jump. "How is Jutta?" he asked.

"Fine," I said, poking the winter squash.

"Everything's fine?"

"Yes, fine."

I never told Ali anything about our squabbles, although he would have loved to establish a man-to-man bond with me in that way, and give me some rough-and-ready advice. Ali was so utterly and unthinkingly a male chauvinist that there seemed something benign about his chauvinism. He had none of the malevolence, the ugly babyishness, of men who fear for their traditional territory. There, at least, Ali had never been challenged, and he loved women as any decent person would love children who had never disobeyed him, nor broken his windows, nor mocked him.

"That Jutta is a good woman," Ali said. "I like her."

"So do I."

"But she is a little unfair with you, isn't she? She is a little . . . " He searched for a word that would suggest her untoward independence without also suggesting my untoward weakness. He gave up. "You get angry with her, but you don't act. That's not good. The situation will only get worse, Eric. You must listen to your anger."

I never told Ali anything, and yet he often knew what was going on between Jutta and me. Of course, Jutta told him. Telling him enabled her to bask in his paternal disapproval; she liked Ali's view of her as an errant child, with nothing wrong in her nature that firmness wouldn't correct.

I tried to return to the matter at hand. "No fatties at all?"

He shook his head, pitying me. "None. She really won't accept anything else?"

"No. I'm afraid I'll have to buy from the bitch," I said. Concerning women, it was the only man-to-man bond we had made: we both disliked the *Wienerin* across the walkway.

By now, I would have long forgotten those potatoes—and with them, the trip to the market, the queries about Jutta, the sick or dead child—except for the fact that, circling up the stairs of our frigid *Zinskaserne,* I slipped on a patch of ice. I shot my hands out to keep from falling, the bag ripped, and the potatoes tumbled down the stairs. And then, squatting and picking them up at one level and another, no longer deafened by my own shoes gritting on the stone, I heard a commotion floating down from the top floor. Screaming. I froze. I remember my exact position—doubled over, three potatoes cradled to my chest with the left hand, the right holding the ripped bag and reaching for a fourth potato against the damp wall—as the adrenalin poured into me, feeling like a hot cloth on the back of my neck, as I recognized Renate's voice: "No! No!" and Jutta's: "Get out!" Then there was a crash, and the cackling of breaking glass. I dropped everything and ran up the stairs.

The door to the apartment was open and through it, in the kitchen, all I could see was the table, overturned, and a tangle of bodies. I rushed in. A big man stood with his back to me; he was staggering backward, toward the door. Renate was beyond, livid, screaming "no!" and then, "Eric! Stop him!" Jutta flew about like a harpy, her hair wildly disheveled, her silk bathrobe billowing. She jumped toward the man and clutched his arm, digging in her fingernails. He shoved her away with his fist and she thudded into the sink. As he had turned to push her I had seen why he was staggering—Ulrike was on the other side of him, on the floor. He was dragging her toward the door by her wrists. Her eyes were closed. Blood was pouring from her nose.

"Kurt!" I yelled.

Surprised to hear a man's voice, he glanced over his shoulder. "Get out of my way!" Ulrike wasn't fighting him. She lay limp; she might have been unconscious, except her lips were moving. She was whispering. On her knees, with her arms raised up to him, her wrists

gathered in one big hand, she looked like his worshipper, or his mana-
cled slave.

"Kurt, let go of her!" I said.

"Get out of my way!" he repeated. He backed into me.

"Renate, call the police!"

He was twice my size. I held on to the doorway, my face pressed
into his back, but he just kept coming. My hold broke, and I went
down. He overbalanced and fell, too. He didn't put his hands out, he
didn't do anything, to break his fall. He kicked up his legs and landed
on top of me. I do remember thinking, as the black-bloody light
swirled over my eyes: my God, he's even heavier than Josh. It seemed
to take him an eternity to get off me. He rolled foward and back again,
digging me with his elbows, doing a certain amount of damage to my
gonads. Then he put a callused hand on my throat and pushed himself
up, jamming my adam's apple. I thought: this man likes to hurt people.

But if he had fallen on me intentionally, it turned out to be a
mistake. He may have thought that I—the only man—was his only real
opponent. But Jutta was as big as I, probably stronger, and certainly
a better fighter. I was told what happened, later. In falling, he had let
go of Ulrike. Renate ran forward, grabbed her, and dragged her back
through the kitchen, into the hall, and then into her room, where she
locked the door. At the same time, Jutta, who had been thrown against
the sink (and who also, as I knew, was not always averse to hurting
people), reached blindly behind her for something she could use—
behind the sink, where all the medicine bottles were kept. Her hand
landed on the tallest object: a liter bottle of economy-brand bile-green
mouthwash. The bottleneck fit perfectly in her hand. As she put it
later, Kurt and the jug full of bile were simply meant for each other.
As Kurt went down, the bottle came up into her hands. As he rolled
gleefully on top of me, the bottle sloshed cheerfully toward the door.
And as he came up, gripping my throat and pushing, the bottle swung
down. At the time, I was aware only of being unable to breathe. Then
I heard a bonk (from the bottle), a grunt (from Kurt), and the bottom
two-thirds of the bottle and about half a liter of mouthwash landed in
my face.

("How did it all land on *me?*" I asked later—the post-mortem for
this fight went on for days—"Where was Kurt?")

"Well," Jutta said thoughtfully, "the bottle didn't break. It only
cracked. Then Kurt rolled sideways. With this very unhappy look on

187

his face. So I lifted the bottle to hit him again, but the crack split open and the end of the bottle fell on top of you. What were you doing down there, anyway?")

Kurt was swaying on his knees like a holy-roller, clutching his head. I was trying to get the stinging green fluid out of my eyes. There was a sharp pain in my side. I heard the apartment door close and lock.

("Why did you lock me outside?"

"It was my only chance. You were too slow. Besides, he was only after Ulrike. I knew he wouldn't hurt you."

"He already had."

"Well I didn't know that, did I?")

Kurt grabbed the stairway banister and hauled himself to his feet. He teetered. He bent over the railing and held his head in his hands. "Fucking BITCH," he muttered, in a croaking voice. "Fucking BITCH fucking BITCH." I sat up. I groped for the shaft of the spear buried in my side, but I couldn't find it. "Fucking BITCH fucking BITCH."

I noted the locked door. "Are you all right?" I asked. It was time to appease this wounded bull. They say the only other option with a wounded bull is to kill it, and I had a feeling I wouldn't be able to do that.

"No I'm not fucking ALL RIGHT!" he ground out. "I'm gonna kill that fucking bitch."

"Which, uh . . . which fucking bitch might that be?"

"All three of 'em." He felt in his straw-colored hair for blood. There wasn't any. "That slimy cunt Jutta first."

("Jeeesus, where did Ulrike pick up that guy? At a dog-stomping contest?"

"No, their families were neighbors. Kurt inherited the farm."

"So Ulrike cried all the way to the altar, while her family laughed all the way to the bank?"

"Something like that.")

"Who are you?" he asked menacingly. "Are you Eric?"

Uh-oh. What might Ulrike have been saying about me? "Uh . . . " It was rather hard to think with a crushed rib cage.

"Are you or aren't you?"

"I . . . suppose I am."

He grunted. "So *you're* this goddamn fucking cunt-smelling Eric."

That's me! I looked at the door. Nope, still locked.

Kurt abruptly became calmer. "So Eric," he asked, almost in a matter-of-fact tone, "tell me—what's your problem?" He was slowly getting his senses back. He had turned toward me and was leaning against the railing, his shoulders slumped. A hand picked vaguely in his hair, as if searching for grubs. There apparently weren't any of those, either.

"What do you mean?"

"I mean," he said impatiently, "I want to know what your fucking problem is."

"Uh . . . " I was watching the railing bow outward. The next floor was twenty feet down.

"I'm really curious. What are you here for? You got a thing for sluts, or what?"

"I can't really answer that." Just lean back a *little* more. . . .

"No, tell me. I'm curious. Do you have a different one every night? Is that it? Or do they all get in bed with you at the same time?" His voice was ragged with hatred.

"Um . . . "

"I mean, you're a good-looking boy. Why else would you resort to such trash?" He stood up. (Damn.) He took a step toward me.

"You've got it all wrong," I said quickly. I couldn't let him believe I had touched Ulrike. He looked like the homicidal husband *par excellence*. "I haven't had anything to do with Ulrike, or Renate either. I'm just Jutta's boyfriend."

He chuckled acidly. "Is that so? Well then—the more fool, you. She's the worst of the lot, you know—Jutta." His voice became smarmy, confiding. "*Jutta* . . . She'll give you a little something to remember her by. She's taken men from every third-world country on earth between those legs. I wouldn't be sticking *my* peter in that slimy cesspool."

I didn't answer.

("The man is the most repulsive creature I've ever met."

"Oh, he's not so bad," Jutta objected. "He was angry, that's all. Wouldn't you be? Well, no, I guess you wouldn't be."

"Gimme a break.")

Kurt smiled unpleasantly. "But if I did, I think I'd at least have the guts to stand up for her."

I searched for something dignified to say. "She doesn't need to be defended from you," I said. No, that wasn't what I was looking for.

"I could break you in two," he said slowly, bemusedly. He flicked a glance at the apartment. "I could also break down that door."

He sounded like a schoolyard bully. I felt like saying, "I dare ya! I double dare ya!" I often lean toward levity, when any serious consideration of a situation would only humiliate me. It's a bad habit. I said, "I'm sure you could. But why don't you just go away, instead?"

"You'd like that, wouldn't you?"

"Everyone would like that."

"Including my wife?" he asked with a sneering smile.

I couldn't help smiling back. *"Especially* your wife." Real bad habit.

He balled his fists and took another step toward me. "You're a fucking wise ass, aren't you?"

I picked up the broken bottle.

He laughed. "You can put that down, pretty boy. I'm not going to touch you. I only came for my wife."

("You see?" Jutta exclaimed.

"Purely rhetorical," I said.)

"And for your son, presumably." It hadn't escaped my notice that he talked as if Theodor didn't exist.

"Yeah . . . For him, too. Is that too much to ask? That a man should be able to have his wife and son with him? Ulrike belongs with her husband. Not with these bitches and their ideas." It sounded like received wisdom. He was probably quoting his cement-headed friends —who had egged him on in the Wolfsberg bar, perhaps? They would have been quoting other cement-heads from time immemorial. Beware people who actually believe clichés! Their faith can destroy continents. "They've changed Ulrike," Kurt said. "Out of pure jealousy and spite, they've changed her. Because they couldn't have husbands of their own." Theodor seemed to have dropped out of the picture again. Why? Too much of a wimp? Or was Kurt only interested in little girls? "They've turned her away from me," he muttered.

I searched for something to say. If I could just keep him talking, keep him off his guard—then perhaps he wouldn't go ahead and break down the door. And kill Jutta. Ulrike, I didn't care about as much. I blamed her for marrying a man who clearly belonged underneath a rock. "I've never heard either of them say anything bad about you."

Kurt grunted and hung his head. One hand gingerly patted his crown— I could see the lump swelling there. "You're lying," he said unhappily. "You're a fucking liar." Then he added, his voice heavy with self-pity, "Jutta hurt my head." He winced as he probed the spot. "She'll be sorry." But he didn't move. Perhaps he was having second thoughts about this rescue mission. He had nothing to fear from me; but Jutta was another story. She had no doubt armed herself with a pair of eight-inch steak knives by now, and the possibility of a jail term for manslaughter would only encourage her. In the Wolfsberg bar, it would have seemed so easy!

From below came the sound of the street-door opening and then slamming shut. Footsteps gritted up the stairs. Kurt looked over the railing. "The police," he said. He sounded dumbfounded. Why would the police show up over something as natural, as right, as a man wanting his wife back?

□

Of course, the police were impossible. Basically, they agreed with Kurt. It *was* natural and right for a man to want his wife back. Especially if he had reason to suspect an unhealthy influence on her. Neither the shade of two-thirds of our children, nor the fact that the apartment was conspicuously lacking in husbands, went unnoticed. Another fact—that Kurt had broken Ulrike's nose—seemed trivial by comparison.

Ulrike did not help matters by refusing to press charges. She insisted her nose had been hit accidentally in the melee, and not by Kurt. Jutta would not press charges, either. She considered the clout she had already given Kurt on the head to be his just desserts. And faced with Ulrike's and Jutta's indifference to any legal action, Renate said that she wouldn't press charges, either.

The policemen turned to me. As with poor Giancarlo, the lover I had displaced so long ago, the main question in their eyes was, "Where do *you* fit in?" They, too, may have been wondering whether I slept with a different woman each night, or with all three simultaneously. I saw in their eyes, too, an edge of hatred. "And you?" one of them asked. "Do you want to bring charges?"

What could I charge him with, without the women's support? Falling on top of me? Failing to block half a bottle of mouthwash? "No," I said. "But can't you at least get him out of the building?"

"We can escort him to the street," the man said. "But the front

191

door is open. Unless you bring charges, we can't keep him from coming back." The thought of his department's impotence in this matter seemed to please him.

"And I *will* be coming back," Kurt said. "I'll get what I came for."

"Didn't you hear that threat?" I demanded of the police.

"And *I'll* give it to you, big man!" Jutta laughed. "I've got more bottles than I know what to do with."

"We heard both of them," the man said. The two officers led Kurt out into the hall. The one who had spoken all along turned back toward the door. "Let me give you girls some advice," he said, looking over my head. "Don't be so quick to go running to the police for help over every little family matter. We're not marriage counselors."

Jutta closed the door. "Why did those assholes show up, anyway?"

"I called them," Renate said.

"Ren! What for?"

"It was Eric's idea."

Jutta threw up her hands. "Oh! Eric! No wonder." She kissed me affectionately. "I could have told you they'd be no good, Eric."

I felt very distant from her. They were only no good, I thought, because no one would press charges.

"Let's get Ulrike to the hospital," Renate said.

Her pretty little nose was under her left eye.

□

"Distance has its dangers," I said absently to Timo, handing him bricks.

"What?" he asked.

"I mean, if you're always back-flipping out of situations, there's likely to come a time when you just can't return."

"Return?"

"Into the fray."

"Huh?"

"Back to caring again. About anything."

"What are you talking about?"

"I'm talking about your mother and me."

He was silent. Why on earth was I talking to *him* about it?

"You and Mommy get along pretty well," he insisted.

Now I was silent.

"You do!"

"Your mother is a wonderful person," I said. Even my admiration for her is distant. I consider her more and more like a case study: a neurotic depressive, showing signs of improvement. And yet there is still this burning in my chest when I think of her; the desire to be with her, to be loved by her. "A relationship is a constant balancing act," I said to Timo. "Like that circus boy standing on the cylinder. You remember him?"

"Yes."

"Relationships are changing all the time." Timo was the last kid who needed to be told that. "Your mother and I love each other, Timo." And perhaps it was true. "We're balanced together; like two people on a see-saw." Or rather, like two people pulling on either end of a rope. And in tugs-of-war, the person losing holds as much power as the person winning. "What looks simple and stable is in fact a complex interplay of forces." The winner takes a great risk every time she hauls on the rope. The loser just might drop his end. When that happens—it bears pointing out—only the loser is left standing.

"I still don't know what you're talking about."

"That's all right. Neither do I." But none of this answered my first question. Why Timo?

"Don't put that there!" Timo said.

"Why not?"

"Because it goes here!"

"How can you tell?"

"It just does."

"Listen, how am I supposed to learn how to do this if you don't give me any reasons?"

"*That* side is for the wood. *This* side is for the metal."

"Ahhh. And why is that?"

"This is the morning side. The sun on the metal warms up the house." Timo had seen a program on television about solar energy—something of a joke in Central Europe, where direct sunlight is about as common as a lunar eclipse.

"What about the evening?"

"The house doesn't need sun in the evening. It's warm already."

"Wouldn't it be better to have the metal side facing south? That's where the sun usually is."

Timo conceded the point graciously. "OK. The morning side will face south."

I laughed. "Deal."

Answer: Nobody else would listen. Renate and Ulrike would interrupt me and assure me they knew what was wrong. Josh would say welcome to the club and drag me off to a whorehouse, where I could drown my sorrows by infecting all the whores. Only Timo was a good listener. "What did you think of the fight yesterday?"

"It was noisy," he said.

"That's all?"

"Mommy locked Theodor and me in the bedroom. We couldn't see anything."

We worked on for a while in silence.

"That Kurt scares me," I said.

Timo said matter-of-factly, "He said he was going to slit you up the middle like a hanging pig."

I was startled. "What? When did you hear that?"

"When I was on the farm."

"During Christmas?"

"Yes. Ulrike said she didn't know if she would come back to the farm and Kurt said he would make her and then Ulrike said you would stop him and then Kurt said he would slit you up the middle like a hanging pig."

"Timo remembers everything," Jutta had told me once. "It's frightening! You think he's lost in his own world, but those black ears are open all the time. God knows where he stores it. Anything you say may come back and haunt you."

"Why did Ulrike say that?" I asked.

"Well—you *did* stop him."

"Oh yeah? Who says?"

"Mommy." And then: "It's done!" Timo sat back to contemplate the structure.

"It is?"

The house was made out of Timo's usual mixture of refuse: wooden fragments, bricks, sheet metal, burr-ended iron tubing. Timo built dozens of houses. Until I started helping him recently, I hadn't realized that; after all, none of his creations *looked* like houses. In the absence of nails or glue, he piled them up out of parts leaning against each other. The tubes supported the roofs from points on the floor

194

outside the brick foundation, like flying buttresses. The finished products were barely distinguishable from the waste piles at construction sites from which Timo spirited the materials. But in there somewhere, hidden by the crazily leaning walls, was a space—and that space made it a house. And when Timo was done (only he could recognize this subtle slipping into rightness), he would fetch Heidi and carefully insert her into the space, making the house a home. As often as not, the whole thing would collapse from the trauma of the tenant moving in.

"Why don't we just build the house up around her?" I asked.

"She gets bored," he said. "She has other things to do."

I was learning about Heidi, too. (An amazing discovery, this other world! I had thought the boy impenetrable; but that was only because, instead of asking him to let me into his fantasies, I had been trying to coax him into mine.) Heidi was quite a spirited little girl. Although she got lonely when Timo was not around, she was pretty fresh with him when he was. If he wasn't keeping her properly amused, she told him so. She liked to be swung around by her hair. She *loved* to be dropped down the stairwell. If she made it all the way down (instead of bouncing off a railing and landing on one of the intermediate floors), you could hear her laughter floating up. Every other word she said was "shit." She tended to eat too much, so Timo had her on a diet of milk and vitamin pills. (He popped them far back into her mouth, clamped her mouth shut, and rubbed her throat. Meanwhile, she tried to bite him.) She didn't care for Theodor. She thought he was creepy. She regarded Elizabeth maternally.

I also learned, to my immense pleasure, that she liked me. "Why does she like me?" I asked, reluctant to let go of such a gratifying subject.

Timo shrugged. "She just does." He swung her around by her hair and let go. She sailed through the open door, out of the room. From the sound of the crash outside, I inferred that she had hit something unbreakable. "Dolls are like that," Timo said, wisely.

□

Jutta had a truly marvelous way with anger—with that abandoned, cathartic, vein-popping, sclerotic fury that convulses the body and squeezes the eyeballs out of the head. She surrendered to her anger in a way she never quite did to sex. Her *grande passion*—like many *grandes passions,* indulged in rarely—was not I, nor Timo, nor love for me or Timo, nor love at all, nor fear, nor contempt: but rage. Rage at herself, at her "parents," and at every substitute for her parents; in short, I suppose, rage at everybody.

I remember thinking this, when I came home from the opera one night and found Jutta and Renate fighting in the kitchen. Poor Renate had been provoked beyond endurance; she looked angrier than I had ever seen her. But her anger was a burning column: self-contained, defensive, it appealed to above and below. It was no match for Jutta's anger, which was a bristle of needles, a sunburst. Jutta was moving, always moving: circling poor Renate like a wolf, or like a peasant woman, with the peasant's uninhibitedness, her long and loose wool skirt flaring to left and right; bent at the waist, arms and hands jabbing at the air, her witch's hair an exploded bush of static like some electric conductor drawing rage out of the air and channeling it through her body and out through her wool-socked feet which pampammed emphatically, almost dancingly, against the linoleum as she circled.

I edged my way to Ulrike, who sat at the kitchen table, her head in her hands. The middle of her face was lost in a crisscross of gauze and bandages. Her rose-milk complexion had died out of her days ago. She looked drawn and ill. The doctors had told her she would need several operations on her nose.

"What's going on?" I asked her, awed, not taking my eyes off the other two.

"Oh, God, I'm sick to death of it!"

"What? What?"

Suddenly, she was sobbing. My question had broken a dam. "I just —I just can't stand it!" The tears trickled into the gauze, and were soaked up by it.

"But what? What?"

"The *fighting!*" And she fled from me, from the room.

I followed her. "Ulrike! Fighting about *what?*"

Just at that moment, Jutta ended with a flourish and turned to stalk out. We crashed into each other at the door. "Let me through," she demanded. She was so unhinged by her fury, I wondered if she even recognized me.

"Jutta, calm down," I said, holding her arms. "It's me."

She sneered, and pulled her arms free. "I know it's you." She hauled off and belted me. "Now let me through!"

She had caught me in the stomach, unprepared, and I doubled over, mouthing at the air. Then I was on my knees in the hall. Jutta was stepping around me. "No—" I croaked, "you can't—" and I grabbed her leg. She exploded. It was an amazing sensation. The leg convulsed in my hands, as strong as a heifer; I was punched in the head, the ear, the neck, pounded on my shoulders. I tried to hug the leg to me and bring her down but she kicked and I lost my grip. She kicked again, and again, and I curled up on the floor, shielding my head with my arms. Then suddenly, she stopped; as if a switch had been turned off. I didn't move. I heard footsteps. Her door slammed. The fit had lasted only two or three seconds.

I uncurled. Renate was in the kitchen, banging things and muttering to herself. Timo and Theodor were gawking at me, like frightened birds, around the door jam of the children's room. I found there was a word still in my mouth, and I pulled it out to look at it: "can't." Ziu, excited and curious, came to rub his winter-electric fur, one side and then the other, in my face. I said, "For reasons unknown to this reporter, Lazarettgasse 17/8 is turning into a war zone."

"Oh, shut up, Eric," Renate said, and stepped over me into her room. I turned my head to watch her shut the door. The crib next to her bed was gone.

"That's right, blame the victim!" I called through the door.

"Just shut up," she called back.

I sat up, groggily. I poked myself all over. Well—there wasn't too much damage. Other than to my glasses, which were bent all to hell. Jutta had been flailing too fast to hit very hard. Still, this was becoming a mite hard to take. Even *I* wasn't this masochistic.

Timo and Theodor had come into the hall, gripping their dolls like shields. They faced me, wide-eyed, in their pajamas. I assumed they were waiting for an explanation. I settled the skewed glasses back on my nose. "Gentlemen," I said, "I suppose you're wondering why I've called you to this meeting on the hall floor. Well I assure you, there is a perfectly reasonable explanation . . . Which I'll think of in a moment." No response. Timo looked scared. I sighed. I patted the floor. "Why don't you two come here?" I suggested. Timo came, and Theodor trotted doggedly after. They sat on either side of me. Theodor, as always, was deadpan. Ziu climbed up and curled in my lap.

"Timo," I said. "First of all, could you please tell me what's going on? I came late to this party."

"Renate took Elizabeth away," Timo said. "Mommy is very angry."

"Yes, I noticed that."

"Why did she hit you?" he asked.

"I'll get to that. Do you know where Elizabeth went?"

He shrugged.

"None of your business!" Renate hollered through the door.

"O. . . . K. . . . Here—" I said, "pat this," and put my hand on my stomach. The two boys obliged. "Now this," inclining my forehead. "And this," exposing my neck. "Feels OK, right?" They nodded. "No damage done. It probably looked much worse than it really was. I wrestled with a heifer once on my grandparents' farm in Wisconsin and it was much worse than this." I smiled to reassure them. What a nice guy I was. The heifer had broken my arm.

Theodor was looking sympathetic. Then he surprised me. He actually spoke up. "It doesn't hurt?" he asked.

"No. Jutta would never really intend to hurt me, Theodor." Hahahahahaha . . .

Theodor nodded. "It doesn't mean she doesn't love you," he said.

"That's right. She was only very excited. Do you boys know why she was so excited?"

They thought about it. Theodor spoke again: "You were noisy?"

"No—"

"You were messy?"

"No-o . . . "

They shook their heads.

"Because she loves you two." They looked doubtful concerning the connection. "Because she loves all children. Elizabeth, too."

"She wishes Elizabeth were here," Timo said.

"That's right."

"So do I."

"But Elizabeth's *not* here!" Renate hollered through the closed door. "She's somewhere safer—"

"Goddamnit, I'm not talking to you!" I hollered back.

"—somewhere where men don't break down the door and start beating everybody up!"

If she's lucky, she's somewhere where women don't beat everybody up, either.

"But why did Mommy hit *you?*" Timo asked me.

"Oh," I assured him, "nothing important. I just shouldn't have been in her way." I smiled again. I was getting better at it. Timo seemed much more upset by the violence than Theodor was. It occurred to me that Jutta, for all her eloquent threats on Timo's person, never actually hit him. And Theodor? I gazed at him. Why this sudden response? This understanding? He was such a quiet boy, so seemingly unimaginative—never messy or noisy, never in the way . . . The pale blue eyes looked blankly back up into mine. The mouth was a little pursed thing, like something trying to hide. And the soul down in those blank eyes, it was trying to hide, too. You have been beaten by your father, I thought. Regularly. Haven't you?

"I think it's time to go to bed," I said. We all three got up. Ziu dug in his claws for a moment, then gave up his bed for lost and jumped to the floor.

□

"If he did, she never told us about it," Jutta said, curled up in bed. She hadn't taken her clothes off. She'd done nothing since coming in except sit, as small as possible against the wall, and smoke.

"He broke her nose into a dozen pieces," I said, undressing. "With one calculated punch, while he had both of her wrists caught in his other hand. You said so yourself. The man is accomplished at mayhem. He's been practicing on *somebody.*" I folded the clothes I would be wearing the next day and stacked them on a chair. I examined myself in the mirror. A little stiff here, a little soft and sore there. Nothing that a truly contrite woman vowing never to do it again on pain of death mightn't correct.

"I've never seen a mark on Theodor," Jutta said.

"I have."

"Oh? When?"

I climbed onto the bed, naked, beside her. "I was with Ulrike when she dressed him one morning. He had a bruise as big as my hand on his lower back. Ulrike said he'd fallen out of a tree on the farm."

"He probably did."

I shrugged. "Maybe . . . But it's time we really thought about it: Theodor in a *tree?* We can hardly get him to climb up in his chair."

"He's always more active on the farm. Ulrike says so."

"Of course she says that. His being more active would explain bruises, broken limbs."

"Ohhh," Jutta exhaled, stubbed angrily, and pitched the butt onto the floor. She had taken to doing that lately. I had counted six scorched places on the linoleum since she'd started. As my father had been, I was morbidly afraid of fires. Jutta knew that. "Maybe you're right." Another cigarette was cocked jauntily between the whitish lips. "But why is it so important?" A match-flame hissed, was sucked down to a mercurial ball. Without looking, Jutta flicked the match, still lit. She had taken to doing that, too. "Everybody's got their troubles," Jutta said. "Everybody solves them their own way."

I could see the smoldering match out of the corner of my eye. I lifted the bottom of Jutta's sweater and unfastened and unzippered her pants. "Or ignores them," I said.

She smiled roguishly at me: "Or hides from them." Her dark eyes, gleaming and challenging, seemed especially beautiful.

I nudged her backward. She held the cigarette high and straightened her legs obligingly. I gripped the pant cuffs and tugged until the pants slid from under her buttocks and rustled thickly into my hands. "Hides from them, then," I said. "As long as they can; until they pop up and punch them in the stomach." I hadn't intended to say that. I didn't want to get onto that.

But Jutta said, "Oh, that. I'm sorry, Eric."

"It's all right—"

"No, I really am."

"There's no need to assure me, Jutta."

"I was so angry at Renate I didn't know what I was doing."

"I understand completely." She was wearing knee-length wool socks. Thick, dark, smelling sweetly of sweat. I began to roll one down. As they appeared, the moist brown hairs on her calves pulled away from the skin, twitched and dried. They smelled not only of sweat, but of cigarette smoke. "Why *were* you so angry with Renate? You knew she was not going to leave Elizabeth here."

"But I didn't really believe it."

"Still . . ." I rolled the sock around her heel, detached it from her foot. I blew softly on the sole to dry it.

"And I really thought she had sense not to send Elizabeth *there.*"
She was flat on her back now, speaking to the ceiling. Ash from the cigarette fell on her sweater.

"And where is 'there'?"

She lifted her head to look at me. "You don't know? No one told you out there?"

"Renate wasn't in the mood for conversation."

Her head dropped back out of sight. "To her parents' house."

"Her parents' house? I thought they wouldn't have her." I began to roll down the other sock.

"Oh, they'll have her, all right. Little Elizabeth is their cross. The girl hardly weighs 4 kilos, but you'd think she weighed a thousand, the way their shoulders bend, their faces turn anguished. I've seen them, the poor things." Jutta's other sock was off. I kissed the warm soles of her feet. "No, they're glad," she continued. "They've been trying to get Elizabeth for months."

"But what for?" I began to massage her feet, pressing the soles with my thumbs, flexing the toes inside my closed hands.

"So they can hide her away. They still *love* Renate, Eric." I heard the irony of the contrast in her voice. "They hate it that she's outside with Elizabeth all the time, letting good people see this black—this black *mistake* in her perambulator. This is like being able to take your child's stutter, or her hunch-back, and lock it in the back room. Wouldn't any parent be happy to do that, to suffer for that?"

I worked gradually up to her calves. I could feel the tight muscles, almost quivering. Jutta, talking of parents and bastards, would be in a frenzy by now if I weren't keeping her down, turning her mind to more sensual things. As her frenzies had taken more and more to turning against me, I did it for my sake as much as hers. I kneaded the muscles vigorously, pressing them up against the shin-bone, rubbing the skin and hair with my palms.

"And Renate caved in. She's weak, she's weak! She's always been weak with her parents. That poor girl will get no more fresh air. She'll be stored away in a room with the curtains drawn—like a death room. She'll be fed and changed by a woman who can hardly bear to touch her. How terrible that must be."

She sat up suddenly. The panic had grasped her. "Don't you see how terrible that is?" she demanded harshly.

"Yes, of course—"

"Well why don't you say something? Why do you just listen like that?"

"Like what?"

"Like—like—some sneak!" Her eyes stared sightlessly.

"I do think it's terrible. Jutta, I didn't know until just now—"

"Ohhh . . . *goddamn* you!"

I grabbed her shoulders. *"Jutta.* There's nothing we can do. It's Renate's decision." She tried to wave that away. "No—no. We're getting nowhere. You've got to calm down. Please," I coaxed. "Please lie down." She resisted for a moment. Then she let me push her back. I returned to massaging her legs. For reasons unknown to this reporter, I thought, Lazarettgasse 17/8 is turning into a loony bin.

I moved up to her thighs. For a couple of minutes, there was silence. When I raised my head to look at her face, I saw that Jutta's eyes were squeezed shut. The last cigarette had burned out. Eventually, she said, "I'm sorry, Eric. That's twice tonight, isn't it?"

"It's all right," I said.

" 'It's all right,' " she repeated, laughing drily. "Everything's always 'all right.' "

It was true: I could no more keep from blurting out "all right" when someone apologized to me than I could keep from gagging when my throat was swabbed. Apologies mortified me, and I tried to bury them with "all right"s. I said nothing. Her thighs wriggled and rippled beneath my hands.

"You never *do* get angry, do you?" It wasn't an accusing question. I had calmed her enough so that she sounded merely curious. The distant curiosity of one species about another, of a terrestrial about a Martian.

"Sure I do," I said. I patted her hip. "Turn over."

She did. I slipped her underpants down from her hips to her calves. She caught them against one toe and kicked them off. I began to massage her buttocks.

"So what do you get angry about?"

"Oh . . . Unimportant things. Inanimate objects."

"Like what? Mmm. That feels good."

"Good."

"So like what?"

"Well," I stopped massaging for a moment to kiss one of her buttocks. I loved how big and fleshy they were, dimpled a little lower

202

down—warm jiggling dough to sink my fingers into. The Turkish sol-
diers in *Candide* could have lived a year off one of these. "Like when
I smashed my toes against one of those cinderblock-doorstops. I got
angry at the cinderblock. You have a bruise here."

"Where?" She was beginning to sound dreamy; thick-voiced.

"Here. Where did you get that?"

She turned back to look. "Hm. I don't know. I suppose when Kurt
pushed me." She lay down again.

"Or if I'm stacking magazines, and the stack keeps falling over.
Then I get mad at the magazines." I kissed her buttocks again. I did
not return to the massaging. I kissed her between the buttocks.

She spoke indistinctly, into the bed. "You wouldn't have to express
your anger that way if you let it out when you're angry about something important."

"But I don't *get* angry about important things." I licked the top
of the cleft between her buttocks.

"Mmm?" she murmured, more and more indistinctly.

"I don't consider anger an important emotion."

She laughed softly.

"I'm serious."

"Oh? What *is* important, then?"

I had worked down between her buttocks. I was licking her anus.
Even here, she smelled and tasted of cigarette smoke. It was as if her
body were embalmed in tar and nicotine. "Protection," I said. "Unassailability."

"Ohh." Her hips had begun to move beneath me. "What does *that*
mean? That's not an emotion." She lifted her buttocks from the bed,
urging me to move farther down.

I stopped, lifted my head. "You're right. It's better than an emotion. It lasts."

"Don't stop!" she commanded. "It's too late to stop now!"

"Unassailability means when people do things I don't like, I burn
the bridges. Then there's nothing to get angry about. Anger betrays
you."

"Just don't stop."

"There's an old saying in English: don't get mad, get even."

"It sounds like you don't do either."

I laughed. "That's right. I get away."

"Oh," she moaned mock-pitifully, almost laughing herself. "But not now! Not now!"

"No." I spread her legs and returned to her, lower. The first salty taste of her vagina flared at the tip of my tongue. Her legs squirmed beneath my hands. I held her down. I could feel the breath go out of her body, as it had out of mine when she punched me. I would be kinder, though, and smarter. I would be careful not to go too far.

Her vagina was warm and open, smelling of salt, of soil, of sea. Here was one power I still had over her.

□

So for once, I had actually spoken a little truth. After taking Jutta's anger upon my head, after sitting with the boys and comforting them, after calming Jutta and then serving her even as she tried to provoke me, I felt—an unaccustomed, heady feeling!—that I was a Good Person, dispensing only goodness where others wrought evil. I felt as if I stood on a high moral plane, above pettiness and anger. And in that self-congratulatory mood, I felt that to say anything but the truth would be unworthy of me.

But even in that mood, I would not have spoken if I had known Jutta would listen to what I said, would remember it practically word for word. In my more level-headed moments, I didn't like to tell the truth any more than I liked to get angry, and for the same reason—it made me vulnerable.

But Jutta did remember. Like Timo, she might close her eyes, but her ears were always open. She lay in my arms in the darkness and she murmured sleepily, "You won't always be so alone."

"Hm?"

"Such a loner. So 'unassailable.'" I could see from the streetlight along her cheek that she was smiling. "Don't forget, Eric. I am a witch."

"Not that again."

"I'll bind you. I'll put menstrual blood in your coffee. You will never be able to think of anything afterward but me. You will pine for me. You will die of love for me."

You might have had that, I thought. You were the first woman to get me to ask myself what love was. You might have also been the one to teach me how to stop asking. If only you had treated me better. It was you, not I, who introduced contempt into this damn affair.

"I *will* bind you," she repeated, and kissed my hand. She bit a finger softly. I fell asleep with the uneasy feeling that she had had to restrain herself from biting harder.

I dreamed that night of my sister, Helga. She had come home with Jay. She wanted to marry him, she said. My parents looked at the man sitting on the sofa as if he were a Martian. "I may be black," Jay said, "but at least I'm not blind." "I know that joke," I exclaimed, very excited, "but it goes the other way." My father cut me off with an impatient gesture. He stood up. He filled the entire room. He swooped down over Jay and covered him like a storm cloud. "But can you have fertile offspring?" he asked in a rumbling voice, blowing great smoke rings that bounced like plastic tubes off the walls. "I want grandchildren." "On that question," Jay answered, "the answer must wait for the results of continuous experimentation. Wouldn't you agree, professor?" And he sucked on the ear-piece of his broken glasses. Then Helga was in her room. She was locked in. I intervened. "Give me the key, Father," I said. "I haven't got it," he said, shrugging, utterly unconcerned. "I lost it." I went to the bedroom door and kicked at it, yanked on the knob. The door sprang open. Helga ran to me and flung her arms around me. I fell over backward and she landed on top of me. She kissed me sensuously on the lips. "Come with me, Eric," she said. "Please come with me!" "No," I said. "I'm sorry. I've got too much to do." "But I need you—I need you!" Yes, I was going to say—yes, I'll come. But she ran from the house before I could open my mouth. "I'll give you my telephone number!" she called over her shoulder and she reached up as she ran, dwindling down the street, she reached up and wrote something illegible in the sky. Jutta was standing next to me, shaking her head. "What a bitch!" she said. "What . . . a . . . BITCH!" I was seized with rage and I grabbed her, forced her to her knees. "She's a bitch, Eric," Jutta repeated. "A slimy bitch. Face it." I gripped her by the hair and pulled her head back. With one careful punch, I broke her nose.

Then I woke. There was a blue-gray light in the room. Jutta was still asleep. Timo had snuggled between us.

I was convinced for the first couple of minutes that I really had helped my sister, when she had come home to say she was engaged. Then for a few more minutes, I was less certain—had I helped her, or hadn't I? Then, gradually, I realized that the opposite was true, although it seemed, so early in the morning, barely credible: I had done nothing to help her. My father had locked her in the house for two days. For two days he had kept at her, arguing, bellowing, threatening; and my mother had let him. Helga did exactly what he would have wanted anyone else to do: she defied him. She screamed obscenities through the door. She threw the food brought to her against the walls. It only enraged him more. This happened before his grosser eccentricities had developed, and I was shocked at his behavior. I was revolted. But I did nothing. And I hated this Jay, this man I had never met, for reducing my father to this state of indignity, of uncontrol. At the end of two days, my father opened the door. He would not speak to Helga, nor she to him. She was white with fury, and perhaps with revulsion too. She had come home with only her coat, and she took up that coat and ran out of the house. I could remember her running to her car, pulling on the coat as she ran. Later, she would not talk to me on the phone. Then she moved to Jay's apartment. I did not know where it was. Eventually I heard in a roundabout way that Jay and Helga had married. I hadn't seen her since.

Morning thoughts. And somehow you get up and get dressed, anyway. Perhaps you hope, as you pull on the clothes, that you are taking on a new personality: a social, presentable personality. Some stronger thing that has no need of wish-fulfillment dreams, or of apologies cried out down the lines of sleep to people long out of patience, or out of earshot, or both.

March 9, 1986

Brigham Fellowship Committee

Dear Committee,

Hi Pat—why am I even addressing this damn thing to the committee when I know they're all too frigging high-and-mighty to read it—pardon my French—you're the only person who *does* read it, so why should I fill it with a lot of historical garbage about Hitler's monorchism when you couldn't care less—so let's forget the Brigham— between you and me and the filing cabinet, I've got myself a fancy lady and a few dependents and bills up to my neck and troubles up to my baby-blue eyes—I'm researching the

Viennese under-class, actually—the despised, the weak, the
confused, the self-destructive, the thoroughly untogether—
the horror! the horror!—not a pretty sight, let me tell you—
lot of field work involved, crawling around in the bush, har
har har—damn expensive, too—maybe I could have a raise?
—perhaps you could bring it up with the chairman, if he's
gotten himself upgraded lately to *compos mentis*—how are
you doing, anyway?—didn't you tell me once that your
ex-husband used to slap you around a bit?—what did you
do about it?—immediate divorce, castration, the silent
treatment, slow torture, poison in his coffee, magnanimity,
understanding, forgiveness, self-debasement?—a purely
academic question, I assure you—but I'd appreciate an
answer immediately—by the way, the March-April check
hasn't arrived yet—now don't give me that not-on-your-life
bullshit—I'm trusting you to be confidential about this—
burn before reading, right?—I'll submit a report every bit
as well researched and valid as the one on departmental
file about the effect of Arabic culture on Russian sacred
music—be a friend and get the $$ here before my creditors
break my knee caps—I'll be forever in your debt, your
slave for life, your chattel, and so on—don't send it here,
send it *poste restante* (*postlagernd,* auf Deutsch), Wien
1080.
Mit herzlichsten Grüssen und vielen Dank,
Eric Repeatedly

As in, one who never learns, I thought, groping in the kitchen
cupboard for some money. Repeatedly Ripped-Off. *Wiederholt ab-
gerippt.* I had said the money was short, but I'd had no idea . . . Where
did it all go? Or a more intriguing question: why did I keep putting
it in here?

I trudged two blocks to the post office and dropped the letter
through the outside slot. It was a Sunday morning, so all the stores
were closed, by law. But Ali would probably be selling surreptitiously;
I went around to the back of his shed and knocked. "I'm closed," he
called from inside, and then opened the door.

"Just me, Ali."

"Hey, Eric. What do you want?"

"Bread."

"All right." He ushered me inside. "Anything else?" he asked, stuffing the disk-shaped loaf into my jacket.

"Nope."

"How did you get the bruise on your forehead?"

"Oh—" I blushed. "A little fight."

"Eric!" He dropped a spatulate hand on my shoulder and regarded me with chagrin. "She didn't—"

I couldn't stand to listen to this. "No, Ali, no. It wasn't Jutta." Not this early in the morning.

"Ah."

"It was a group of men."

Ali relaxed. "I see, I see." He waved reassuringly. "An unfair fight. The cowards—" He broke off for a moment to contemplate their baseness. Then he asked gently, "And how . . . ?"

Why not? It would give him such pleasure. "They were pulling me off Jutta," I said. "I was beating the shit out of her."

A moment of stupefaction. Then his face broke into a beatific smile. His hand came down on my shoulder again, this time with a great manly clap. "Bravo!" he exclaimed. He pronounced the vowels with a rounded fullness, a chivalric sound: "*Bravo*, Eric!" He was gratified—a barrier between us had dissolved. "And she is happier this way, not so?"

I demurred. "We'll see."

"She *is* happier, Eric. Trust me. I know." He waggled a finger at me. "But you must keep it up! You must follow through!"

"Yes, yes—"

"You promise me?"

"Yes, of course—" I held out a bill. Ali pushed it away. "No, Eric. The bread is my gift."

□

"What are you doing?" Timo asked.

"Looking for money," I answered. "You want to help?"

We crawled around the apartment. I came across a hundred schilling note hidden in the folds of the beanbag chair. Another one lay drowned in a pool of ambiguous liquid behind the toilet. Timo found a fifty actually inside the television set. "Wow," I said, snapping it, "what made you look there?"

"Heidi told me to."

I puzzled over that for a few minutes, while Theodor joined the search. Timo found a twenty in a tampon box in a drawer, and I found seventy-eight schillings in change spread around the back of a shelf at the top of a closet. Theodore contributed a Life-Saver bristling with Ziu hair. Then nothing. Coins espied in a narrow-necked glass on Renate's dresser turned out to be Bulgarian leva, good only for putting on dead men's eyes. I knew Timo had tired of the search when Heidi came streaking through the door and whapped me on the shoulder. She lay on the floor, shaking with laughter.

By the time Jutta fell out of bed, Timo, Theodor, Ziu, and I were having breakfast. The parti-colored sweeteners this morning came under the name of "Kablam!" "Where are the others?" Jutta asked, turning on the radio.

"Ulrike's still asleep," I said. "Renate took the early train to her parents'. There's coffee for you on the stove."

Barry Holtzmann on Blue Danube Radio was conducting a phone-in. This week's topic was the Reagan-Gorbachev summit. I waited until Jutta sat with her coffee. Then I asked, "Where has all the money gone to?"

"What money?"

"*My* money."

"It's not in the cupboard?"

"There was only fifty there, this morning. I scrounged up another three hundred and fifty around the apartment. As far as I can tell, that's all we've got."

Barry was apparently getting pretty desperate for calls. "C'mon folks, I know you're out there! The number again—" Last week, the topic had been rock 'n' roll, and the phone lines had been jammed for two hours.

"Perhaps Renate took some for the train this morning."

"Why is she taking *my* money for things like that?"

"She doesn't have any money. She only started work again yesterday—her first paycheck hasn't come yet."

"This is an important issue, folks. I'm trying to bring you serious radio, here—"

"That doesn't account for it all, anyway."

"Well, Ulrike may have taken some for her medicine."

"What medicine?"

"—intermediate nuclear weapons reduction. So if someone will just call—"

"Can I turn that idiot off?"

"No, I need the practice—"

"Shit, I can't even think straight." I switched it off.

Jutta switched it back on. "—and if no one is interested in these crucial issues, I'll just have to go back to the same old—" I switched it off again. "Don't be a baby—" Jutta switched it on. "—in this era of possible global conflict—" I grabbed the radio, yanked it out of the wall, and sat on it.

"Now goddamnit, what medicine?"

"Pain-killers, I suppose; for her nose, remember? Now can I have the radio?"

Ulrike had had her first operation on Friday. The doctors said that they might never succeed in getting her to breath normally through her nose again. But they would try. And try. "Why doesn't Kurt pay for her nose? He's the one who pulverized it."

"Kurt has stopped supporting her. If she wants money from him, he says, she has to come home and get it."

"She can force him to support her."

"What, you mean legally?"

"No, I mean telepathically."

"Ulrike refuses to take legal action against Kurt. You know that."

"But I don't understand it. If she wants so hard to believe he didn't break it, why is she having all these operations? Why doesn't she just crawl back and kiss his feet and keep her nose flat and bent over to one side for the rest of her life, like a badge of honor?"

"That's a very cruel thing to say."

"Shit. Timo, cut that out. So I'm supporting Ulrike too, then?"

"We're both supporting her. I get money too, you know."

"Oh, that's right. I think we bought a pair of socks with it last month."

"Will you just put the radio on, please?"

It was a ludicrous situation—to be talking so angrily about money, when I didn't earn a cent of mine, and Jutta earned only about a third of hers. We were like children, playing adult. Except that there were no real adults to come save us from ourselves. "Timo," I said, ignoring her, "do you want more milk?"

"No," he sulked.

"Toast?"

"No."

"What in hell's the matter, then?"

"Nothing."

"Well could you please stop banging your spoon on the table—"
He threw it in the corner. "Very nice. Could you pick it up, please?"

"No!"

I lifted him by the seat of his pants, carried him to the corner, and held him horizontally over the spoon. Jutta grabbed the radio and turned it back on. "—I just can't believe the lack of interest; I'm really disappointed—"

"Pick it up."

"No!"

"I'm not going to allow you to distract me from my argument with your mother, Timo. If you don't pick it up, I'll just drop you on your head and go back to fighting with her, anyway." He picked it up. I sat him back in his seat. "You're a good kid." He threw the spoon again.

I turned pointedly to Jutta. "Listen," I said. She turned up the volume on the radio. "Listen!" I shouted. "Everyone is welcome to the last four hundred schillings. You can lose it again, or stick it in your ears, or flush it down the toilet for all I care. But after that—" I felt Timo's gaze, and I looked at him. My words stopped in my throat. "After that . . . we'll have to work out something different."

"—I'll have to switch to music, then—" I felt myself blush. "It's not working this way." Timo was sitting quite still, those trusty black ears of his at full throttle. "—but if anyone wants to call in, we'll break for it—" "Now Timo," I said, "if you don't pick up that spoon, I'm going to rip out your fingernails and scratch you to death with them."

Jutta, cradling the radio, went off into gales of laughter. "That's the most ridiculous thing I ever heard!"

Timo picked up the spoon. Jackson Browne wailed.

□

"I want you to walk to the hospital with me."

"All right."

"I want you to get a blood test."

"All right."

"For the AIDS antibody."

"All right." I called the hospital. "What for?" she asked.

"Isn't it obvious?"

"I mean, why now?"

"No use talking about that until the results come."

Timo went with us. A male nurse sat Jutta in a padded chair, swiveled a tray in front of her, swabbed her arm with alcohol. "What's the matter with Mommy?" he asked, as the man drew back the plunger on his syringe. Jutta watched, fascinated, as the leech-colored cylinder lengthened.

"Nothing," I said. "This is just a test."

"Are you and Mommy going to have a baby?"

"No, this is completely different."

"Oh."

"That was a very wilted 'oh.' "

"What?"

"You want Mommy and me to have a baby?" I asked.

Timo didn't answer.

"Men don't like babies," Jutta called from her chair.

"They don't?" Timo asked.

"Babies scare them," she said.

The boy looked hurt. "You're not a baby, Timo," I said.

"Elizabeth is a baby!"

"Yes, and Elizabeth is very nice. Elizabeth doesn't scare me at all. But Elizabeth is not *my* baby."

"Why does your baby scare you?"

"Any baby of mine would be a poor little baby that would always be sick and wouldn't live very long."

Timo was struck with wonder. "But why?"

"Just my luck, I guess."

Before leaving, we filled out some forms, and were told we would be called in a few days. On the way out of the building, we passed a gurney being pulled in the opposite direction. On it lay a bald young boy. His eyes rested on us fleetingly; lacking eyebrows, they looked gelatinous, like raw eggs, in his bright white face. The body outlined under the sheet was a skeleton, curled fetally. Timo, holding my hand, turned and slowed, watched the gurney roll silently away. When he consented to walk with me again, I expected him to ask me what was the matter with the boy. But he didn't say a word.

□

Why now? Because I would perhaps leave Jutta soon. And I could not leave her until I had made sure she was still all right. Surely she was still all right. All those goddamn rubbers. Making love through an industrial curtain. Touching the world fearfully through plastic bags, like my poor nutty father. Condoms made sex feel so solipsistic, so lonely; surely they had protected her.

But what if she *did* have the virus? Would I be able to go? I could only assume that she would not change her sexual habits, and I would be indirectly responsible for every man she infected. I would have created a monster, and then loosed it on the world: a one-woman AIDS epidemic. A terrifying thought. It would be better, perhaps, to stay with her, no matter how badly she treated me. Keep her chained to the bed. Shoot her. Surely she was still all right.

And there was another fear: Jutta having the virus would prove conclusively that *I* had it. I could not know exactly how much comfort I had taken all these months from that statistical uncertainty—from that splendid little quote. But I would quickly find out, if that uncertainty was ever removed. I had an idea it would not be one of my better days. Surely she was still all right.

The day the hospital said it would call came and went, without a word. I called two days later, and was upbraided for my impatience, for my assault on the staff's tidy routine. We would be informed as soon as possible, they said. The delay frightened me. It suggested retests. I began to have trouble sleeping. But this is Austria, I told myself. Everything is late here.

Ulrike was drugged much of the time. Or at least, she acted as if she was. Her classes had begun again at the university, but she didn't go. She had a second operation, and a third. The doctors kept pulling things out of her nose, trying to unblock the passages that Kurt had so easily collapsed. It had been such a small nose, anyway. I wondered how much would be left by the time the doctors were finished. The gauze was augmented by wooden stiffeners like popsicle sticks; the contraption had as grotesque and hopeless an air about it as one of Timo's houses. Two huge black eyes made her look like an insect.

Renate would try to cheer Ulrike up. She would sit with her in her bedroom and make jokes about free nose jobs, and relate, or perhaps make up, outrageous gossip about the doctors who were treating her. But then Renate herself would break down and cry, at night, in front of the television. Jutta would hold her, and say "Elizabeth can be brought back any time, Ren," at which point the crying would stop and another argument would begin.

We all watched television now, in the evenings. The children had always been drawn to it, as all children are, like some different, unhealthy species, some videotropic variety of plantlife. Or perhaps children are extraterrestrials, programmed to become entranced by the flickering blue messages, which are actually codes sent by their own race, instructing them on how to subvert the planet Earth. How to ask for so much material satisfaction that their parents will go bankrupt, and the world economy will collapse. How to become so stupid, so passive and empty, that they will grow up to vote so stupidly, so passively and emptily, that the political system will collapse.

We all watched television now. It was our substitute for talking to each other. There was little we could say any more that would not be recrimination. I wondered, having grown up in a home in which television was reviled and locked in a closet like a secret, idiot child, I wondered, is this what it does for other families? Solves problems so magically by getting members to forget each other?

During the day, and often at night, Renate worked at the hospital. Her paycheck came, and the next trip to her parents' house in Eisenstadt she paid for herself. Ulrike read mysteries and slept a great deal. Jutta, too, sometimes sat with her, and the two of them would drink coffee and chain-smoke cigarettes until the bedroom was a cozy place, a warm fog-bank of carcinogens. Kurt did not come back. He called once, but Ulrike would not come to the phone. He made a few threats, a few obscene remarks, and then hung up before I could suggest that he send money.

Jutta was going to French and English classes again, so René and Barry jabbered at us whenever she was in the apartment. I had grown more aloof with her, and the change had not gone unnoticed. "For godssake, I *said* I was sorry!" she exclaimed. "For hitting you!"

"I've forgotten about that entirely," I assured her.

214

"You're just trying to be unassailable again."

"Believe me, I'm sorry I ever brought it up."

"You will be."

"Bind me, O Witch, and make me sick of love." Ere I, by dumping you, a blackguard prove.

On her way to class, Jutta sometimes took both boys to the day-care center. Other times, Ulrike found the energy to play with her son, who had grown even quieter and more listless. Meanwhile, I would spend the day with Timo, either depreciating the value of the apartment, or seeing the youth-oriented sights of the city: the Sea House; the Circus Museum; the Watch Museum. And of course, the Prater. Some of the Prater rides were just starting up again, for the spring. Two of the six *Autodromes* had opened. I didn't see my old lover. I had learned from him that pretty girls were employed to ride the cars all evening, so that men would pay for the opportunity to ram them. Timo and I bought tickets, got in the same car, and chased the pretty girls for hours. The octopus had opened, too, and every day at dusk its million colored lights would come on; it looked wonderfully gaudy, spinning and tilting in the night like the mother ship from a Steven Spielberg movie. I rode it only once and got sick; Timo stood by me while I retched in an alley and he said, "We won't try that again!" We went into the Zombie house, but it was a bust; Timo wasn't scared. His favorite activity was throwing away money on chances to knock milk cans over with a rubber ball; I couldn't figure out whether the cans were actually nailed to the table or just weighted with material from a neutron star. I never got up the nerve to ask the ex-con who ran the game. Not everything was for kids. There were casinos, too. There, the clientele never varied: cancerous little men in snap-brims and pudgy peroxide blondes, all of them alcoholics. Then, between the casinos and the *Autodromes,* next to the Lilliput train, stood the sex video booths, each with its screen, its bench, its wastebasket. The Sex Museum nearby declared itself the only one of its kind in the world. A sign in English said, "Strip Tease, 100%. No consummation." "Actually, they mean 'no drinking,'" I told Timo. "What's a 'strip tease'?" he asked. "The saddest thing you'll ever see," I said. "Can I see?" "Not legally."

And the Ferris wheel had begun again too. And one day when we bought tickets for it, during the dinner hour, we were the only ones at the turnstile when the next big red-and-white car swung down into the berth, so we were locked in and lifted into the sky alone in the car; and when the car stopped at the top and was rocking in the wind, I stood with my hands on Timo's shoulders, seeing below me the same hazy corrugation of stone and noise that I had seen as a child, when I had stood at the same vantage point, with my mother's hands on *my* shoulders. And I thought, how strange life can be, how unruly. When I was last here, I stood touched by the center of my world. Everything was safe, everything made sense—I would never leave that center. Then I did leave it. And now I was here again, elliptic, eccentric, inexplicably adult, with the sly and slippery old city almost unchanged below me; my mother thousands of miles away, unhappy, betrayed by her children, my father dead, his life's work unfinished, my own life a shambles. And here was this lonely boy in front of me, this boy whom I had not known five months ago, who had had nothing to do with me or my life or whatever dubious, anxious image of a future life I had imagined for myself, and yet who already, somehow, felt natural, felt right, as he stood in front of me, his slender shoulders beneath my hands. Of course I wasn't the center of his world. But astonishingly, I wanted to be.

Which did nothing but complicate matters.

□

I was checking the *postlagernd* window at the post office every day. Six days after I had written to Pat, a letter arrived from her—not at the post office, but at Lazarettgasse. It had crossed mine in the mail. Pat referred to some budgetary tangle that had only just been re-solved; she apologized for the delay that had resulted; nested inside the folds of her letter was the Brigham check for March and April. It had only been the purest luck that I had found the letter before Jutta. Without showing the check to anyone, I took it to my bank first thing Monday morning.

My habit had been to deposit about two thirds of each check, and bring home the remaining one third in cash, as household money for the next two or three weeks—invariably two, as it turned out. But this time, I deposited the entire check. With the money safe, I then spent a few hours looking for the right pension. It had snowed eighteen inches since Sunday evening—an unusually heavy snowfall for Vienna—and the walking was difficult. Many of the streetcar lines weren't running. I hopped on a double-decker bus heading for the south station and I and about fifteen other passengers watched through the windows as the bus pulled away from the curb, attempted a turn, and promptly slid into a row of parked cars.

But I persevered. I didn't really know if I would leave Lazarettgasse, or when, or what I would be doing exactly, afterward, or whether I would keep in touch with Jutta, or instead would have to hide from her, and what effect it would all have on Timo, and whether that would end up being the decisive factor for me rather than anything Jutta might say or do. I didn't know any of that. But I did need to know of some place I could go to on short notice that I could afford, that I could be reasonably sure would have an empty room, that was far away from Lazarettgasse, but perhaps not too far away. And by trudging through snow and knocking on doors and hopping on every streetcar I saw moving, I eventually found a quiet and run-down place in Favoriten, near the autobahn, in a neighborhood of small brick churches, sporting fields, and warehouses. It was run by an ailing old man in a back brace who had all but given up the business, confining it now to two rented rooms, both of which were usually vacant. The last time he'd had both rooms filled simultaneously had been in July 1984. He told me this over a cup of rum-coffee in his lace- and antique-filled sitting room, where the walls were checkered with photographs of family members, each with its black bit of ribbon crossing the bottom corner, and Schubert lieder played quietly on the record player. Two hundred and ten schillings, or about thirteen dollars, a day, including breakfast and—in the evening, he said, in exchange for conversation, whenever I might feel like it—the finest apricot schnapps anywhere, made and sent by his brother *aus dem Land.* No dogs, please. Cats were fine, as long as they were fixed and could get along with his six cats. By the time I went through his curtained cut-glass door and waded up the hushed street, I wondered why I hadn't moved in immediately. Thank God, I thought, the money is safe. Now I have only to wait for the test results. But as I drew closer to Lazarettgasse, the quiet pension and the lonely old man seemed less real; I passed the flashing lights on the Fox Club marquee, the posters of women being sodomized by animals, the construction junk around Zimmermannplatz from which Timo got his toys; René was announcing a clearance sale on dildos in the window of his sex boutique; the trash hadn't been collected in weeks and the new snow made a mal-

217

odorous Fuji out of every mound; this was the sort of neighborhood where kids felt like they could piss on the storefronts. I thought: Good old Lazarettgasse.

Jutta was back from class. "Where have you been?" she asked.

"What?"

"Where did you go?"

"I was at Café Hawelka."

"All day?"

"I was reading the newspapers."

"Must have been pretty interesting."

"Yes, it was."

"Any news?"

"Nothing very interesting."

"You didn't read the new stuff about Waldheim?"

Jeeesus, what is this, a murder trial? "Waldheim? No, I skipped over the current events. Too depressing. Where's Timo?"

"Somewhere."

"*Timo!* You want to go out?"

"Where are you going?"

"I don't know."

"Just for a walk?"

"I don't *know.*"

"Eric, what's the matter?"

"I just want to take a walk with Timo."

"I'm not invited?"

". . . No. Not this time . . . Don't worry—we won't say insulting things about you."

"You don't have to be snide about it—"

"Sorry. I was just joking. You ready, Timo?"

"Almost."

"Get your gloves."

"I can't find them."

"One of them is on the floor under the desk in your mother's room. On the right. The other is at the foot of the bed."

"So why aren't I invited?"

"Just this once, Jutta. I promise."

"A man-to-man talk?"

"Sort of. You found them, Timo?"

"I'm ready."

"Let's go!"

Outside, the sidewalks were unnavigable, so we kept in the street, running and sliding along the tire tracks. The parked cars were buried under the plowed snow. We played King of the Trash Mountain until I managed to bang my head on a Mercedes' side-mirror. We rode on an empty streetcar with snow in our pockets and left snow-stars on the back seats. On Prinz-Eugen-Strasse, we watched a huge crane lift the parked cars, one by one, while a team of orange-jacketed men furiously shoveled out the snow from under each car and tossed it up onto the bed of a truck. Many of the men were elderly, swinging kettledrum bellies, looking forward to a meal of beer, pork, and dumplings. I wondered if their chances of dying in the next three or four years were even greater than mine. We bought bread in a Turkish store near the Turkish Embassy and trudged through the Belvedere gardens to feed the birds. The reflecting pool, which had melted in February, had filled up with milky slush and was freezing again. The terns were thin, and they crowded around us kerruking piteously. "We need more bread," Timo said.

"That's all the money I brought."

We walked away and the hungry birds followed us. We had to run to get away from them.

"What's that?" Timo asked, pointing to a statue on the stone balustrade of a terrace.

"You haven't seen one of those before? They're all over Vienna. It's practically a symbol of the city. That's a sphinx."

"What's a sphinx?"

"A lion with tits."

"I can *see* that. But what is it?"

"A mythological beast. The child-eating mother. It asks questions that cannot be answered. Then when you can't answer, it kills you and eats you."

"That's not very nice."

"Not at all. But as JFK once said, 'Life isn't fair.' "

"It isn't?"

"You haven't noticed that before either?"

I showed Timo how to make an angel in the snow. A little girl stopped to watch until her preoccupied mother dragged her on. We went out through the wrought-iron gates. On Fasangasse, a grizzled man in shabby clothes with epaulets of snow did more than just give

Timo the fish eye. He jabbed a finger at me and said, "Raiding the zoo?"

"I beg your pardon?"

"Anh . . ." he lifted his chin several times, knowingly. "Anh . . . Anh . . . I know your type."

"My type?"

"Arrogant young son of a bitch. You think you can get away with anything."

"What are you talking about?"

He gestured at Timo. "Eh?" He chuckled mirthlessly. "Eh?" His expression became obscene.

I steered Timo past him.

"Where are you from?" he called after us. "Germany? Holland?"

"Where is *he* from?" I asked Timo, winking. "The moon?"

"We know what to do!" he yelled. "We're not helpless you know!"

"He's weird," Timo said. He looked intrigued. "What did he mean?"

"He's like the sphinx," I said. "His questions can't be answered."

We wandered around in the third district. I hadn't any clear idea why I had brought Timo along. Guilt feelings had made me want company, and Jutta would only have irritated me. I felt as if Jutta owed me something, although I didn't know what. And I felt as if I owed Timo something, but I didn't know what that might be, either. An apology? But what possible good would an apology do him? Apologies are like Bulgarian leva—coins with no value; they serve only to obscure, to keep eyes from opening. If people weren't allowed to apologize, perhaps they would treat each other better.

We came to a park, bounded by nineteenth-century row houses. "Castles!" Timo exclaimed. That was what he called the old flak towers. There were two in the park. Before the war this had probably been a pleasant little green space. Now, it was mostly flak tower. The towers, throughout the city, were hideous. They might have been made by Le Corbusier, had he ever embraced the International Style: they were fortresses of reinforced concrete, enormous pus-yellow blocks, ringed, above the level of the surrounding roofs, with gun emplacements. Rising hugely from the grass and trees, they looked like props for a Hollywood dystopia, some futuristic vision of a totalitarian government in a garden-like setting. One could imagine the windowless towers being called Headquarters, or The Administration.

One could imagine post-neo-peasants in improbable costumes paying quasi-religious obeisance to them. But actually Viennese children sledded irreverently down the concrete slopes of their colossal bases; adolescents played wall-ball against them; graffiti aficionados went wild on their vast, blank, and porous surfaces.

Timo ran around the base of the nearer one. "Fuck off!" the wall said to me, in English. A woman went by with a baby in a stroller. "It's not open!" Timo reported on his return, disappointed.

"None of them are open," I said. "The city would like to pretend they're not here." I followed Timo around the corner. Two hearts were joined on the wall. V. M. and B. W. Underneath: "Fuck off!" again.

"What does 'fuck off' mean?" Timo asked. He pronounced it "fook oaf."

"It means 'go away,' " I said. Then I stopped short. "Timo! I didn't know you could read."

"Only a little." He seemed disappointed that I had found him out.

"Got any other secrets?"

"No."

"I'll bet you don't."

We strolled to the next tower. It was different from the first—squatter, with two fat cylinders rising out of the top—as if the builders had not wanted Vienna's defense system too monotonous to look at, too Levittown-ish. Flak towers in three styles! 100 rms, gr vu, blt to last! Easy credit! Yes, but did the zoning laws allow restaurant/bordellos? "What are they, really?" Timo asked. Like his doll, who spoke to him but who was still "only a doll," these castles had a different, adult reality that he recognized.

"*Fliegerabwehrkanonentürme*," I said. "Towers for shooting down planes that attack the city."

"Really?!" Timo was astonished, pleased. He had never suspected that the adult reality would be more fun than his fantasies. "How?"

"There used to be powerful guns on those platforms. When the planes came over, the guns would swivel around and fire shells at them."

"Why would planes attack Vienna?"

"You should ask Josh that some day. He'd be more than happy to tell you. He wants to turn one of these things into a Mexican restaurant."

"Hier darf gesprüht werden—Der Bürgermeister," the wall said: "Spraying allowed here—the mayor." Beneath, happily, "Fuck off!"

We threw snowballs for a while, as high as we could on the wall. After much effort, I managed to get one to land on the lower gun platform. I turned around to accept applause and was hit in the face by a snowball. "I'm tired," Timo announced shortly afterward, as I pulled him out of a snowbank. I lifted him up and sat him on a ledge next to one of the locked steel doors. I brushed him off. Letters were spray-painted here, too, but through a stencil—much older letters. *"Wehrmacht,"* they said. An arrow pointed to the right, around the corner. And lower, over an arrow pointing to the steel door, "women and children." It was getting dark.

"Are you cold?" I asked Timo.

"No. Just tired."

"We'll take streetcars home."

"Eric?"

"Yes?"

"Are you mad at Mommy?"

"No."

"You're not mad because she hit you?"

And kicked me, and punched me, and insulted me. "No."

"Mommy didn't mean it."

"I know, Timo."

"Mommy wants you to stay."

"Yes, I know."

"You're not going to go away because of what she did, are you?"

"No, of course not." I'm going to go away for other reasons. "Timo, can I ask you a question?"

"OK."

"What do *you* want?"

"What?"

"Doesn't anyone ever ask you that question? What do *you* want?"

He poked at the snow with a finger, not answering. Then: "What do you mean?"

"I mean anything—what do you hope will happen? What would make you glad? If you had a choice about one thing or the other happening, which would you choose? You talk about what Mommy wants, and Mommy talks about what Mommy wants—you're a person, too. What do *you* want?"

Silence.

"You can be honest with me. I won't tell anyone else if you don't want me to."

Silence.

"For instance, do you want to grow up soon? Would you rather never grow up? Do you want to live in a different house? Do you want to have more toys? More ice cream? Do you want to have a brother or sister? Do you want to have a girlfriend? Do you want to be in school?"

He shrugged, intimidated.

"You don't know what you want?"

He looked at me dumbly. His eyes were big and round. If he'd been any other child, I would have thought he was on the verge of tears. He shrugged again. He looked down. "I want to go home."

I picked him up from the ledge. "Well," I said, "that's not a bad answer." I kissed him consolingly on the cheek. "A much better answer than a lot of us can muster." I carried him on my back out of the park. "Oof! You're pretty heavy."

"I have big bones," he said.

I laughed. "That's what fat people say."

"That's what Mommy says."

I turned to give the huge ugly structures a last look. "They're a mess, aren't they?" I said.

"I like them."

"You like messes. Some castles! The kings are gone, and the queens are lousy housekeepers. And the princes, out of control, bounce cannonballs off the walls. Oh-HA-HO-HEE-Ha-ha-heh-heh . . . oh-HA-HO-HEE-Ha-ha-heh-heh . . ."

"You're weird," Timo chirped.

On the streetcar, he poked me in the shoulder and said, "I want Mommy to be happy."

□

The next morning, there was a knock on the door. In the cold hall stood a uniformed man, stamping the snow off his pant legs. He held a telegram. "Eric Wiederholt?"

"Yes."

He handed it to me. "Almost didn't make it," he said. "The streets are still in a terrible way." I closed the door and ripped the envelope open. I could feel some gland dumping anaesthetizing chemicals into my bloodstream.

3-18-86

Eric
    Warning stop ma has blown whistle stop got dept to
issue stop-payment on mar-apr check stop if act
immediately withdraw all funds may get $ anyway stop
don't say never helped you
Rick

"What is it?" Jutta asked. I was throwing on my coat. I couldn't think of a good lie so I didn't say anything. "Where are you going? Eric, has something happened?"

"No, it's news from Rick."

"Rick?"

"My brother—of all people—I've just got to check something right away—I'll explain when I get back." I bolted down the stairs. Ten minutes later, having pushed and stumbled through a dozen blocks of the conquering snow, I was at the bank, out of breath. The lobby was empty. One teller, engrossed in a crossword puzzle, kept the bank in business. Perhaps she had come to work on skis. Maybe there *was* a chance as Rick had thought. The international banking connections could be slow, and Austrian banks were especially slow.

But I was too late. The woman behind the thick glass turned from her terminal—dreadful how the computers keep working, across oceans, when the traffic is stopped and even the messengers can hardly make it through the streets—she turned with a curious, dubious look and told me there was a hold on my account.

A "hold"? What did that mean?

It meant I couldn't touch the money. Not the recent check nor even the few-odd schillings left from the last check.

How could they do that? I asked.

She shrugged. She clearly was not interested in helping someone whose account was being "held."

But I knew. I had only forgotten: Harvard can do anything.

□

And that was that.

I was ruined. My mother had found out. The department had found out. Had Pat told on me? Perhaps. But I didn't think so. My mother could have figured it out for herself. I could see her growing more and more suspicious of my letters to her. I could see her barging into Professor Drury's office—they were friends—and demanding that the Brigham Committee examine my file. I could see her and Drury walking to Pat's office and asking for the goods. God, I could see all *three* of them now, parading into the chairman's office with the evidence, and telling him he had to take action. "Me?" he would have wailed, the fly-blown white hair quivering on his liver-spotted pate. We would have been no match for my mother; and even an incipient case of Alzheimer's disease would not have blinded him to the utter balderdash that was being sent back by one of his remote charges. But even then, he would have preferred to forget it, "to adopt a wait-and-see attitude," as he always said, before lapsing back into the 1930s. But my mother would have insisted, and Drury would have backed her. It was her way of getting me to come home. Harvard had been forced to act.

Outside the bank, on the empty street, I asked myself, while the snow fell thickly on my shoulders, my eyelashes, why I had written those letters, when just a tiny bit of effort would have better hidden me. Perhaps—like Dostoievski's criminals, or Batman's would-be nemeses—I had wanted, down deep, where none of us make much sense, to be found out.

If that was true, then it was pretty goddamn far down deep.

Just think. I was only the second student in university history actually to *lose* the Brigham funding. To do that, you practically had to mail photographs to every professor in the department, showing yourself holding a lighted match to the money and cackling gleefully. It was not the sort of distinction I had had in mind for myself. And now what? A question, startlingly, for the rest of my life. Charles Wigginton Whitehouse III, the student who had gambled away his Brigham, had simply joined his father's investment company—simple, because in the business world unethical conduct and irresponsibility are, if not the norm, at least respected exceptions. But my family's business was academia, which for all its chicanery, its stupidity and politicking, actually did have higher standards. I would never again be able to show my face in a university, study in any subject. Not even hotel management. Worse, infinitely worse—my parents' names, their reputations, would be connected to the scandal. My father's, especially. I had been awarded the fellowship because of him. To be precise, I had gotten it because he was dying, and the faculty had made it a bedside present to him. He had not asked. But that was a detail certain to be lost on everyone.

Then there was my mother. At least my father's opinion of me now had the fortuitous characteristic of never changing, of hovering imperviously around a qualified approval. But my mother, presumably, would never forgive me. Not only for wasting Harvard's money, not only for tarnishing the reputation of the family firm, but also because I had never confided in her. She had never forgiven Helga for that very reason—not because Helga had married a black man, although my mother had thought it a dreadful idea, but because Helga had reacted to my father's two-day diatribe with such lasting fury, because she had cut ties with the family. My mother's family had always been close, as she was fond of stating. (Like all people who have grown up in "close" families, she was good at making barbed comments, one of her favorites being that very statement.) The only "close" family left after my father's death had been she and I. I, the good son. Honest Eric. Her outrage at my betrayal could be intimated by the method she had chosen to strike at it—by going to the *department.* She had, in effect, denounced me publicly: something ex-bedfellows in politics do, or injured parties in palimony suits.

I was chilled to the bone. I began to walk back to the apartment. I didn't have enough money to go anywhere else.

What I had joked about had actually happened. The only person I knew in the U.S. who would have anything to do with me any more was Rick. Who, to be fanciful, was like my alter-ego, the unabashed truth behind my dissembling. Who, for all his faults, was never one to abandon a failure and a loser on his day of reckoning. Who would take me into a room scaffolded with adjustable ring-stands holding bunsen burners, bubbling reagents, and graduated cylinders, and ask me to tell him exactly which part of my brain I wanted to fry.

Rick. Who in the end had tried to help me.

I turned onto Zimmermanngasse and walked to the telegraph office. I counted my change.

Rick

    Too late thanks anyway big bro

Eric

"Ach, Herr Wiederholt," the sender said to me. "We have a telegram here for you. We were about to send someone out with it."

Eric

    Please call collect

Mother

Not on your life, I thought. Thank God I never told her Jutta had a phone. The last thing I needed at the moment was a confrontation with her, with her opinion of me. I could not bear the thought of trying to explain. What was there to explain? I was simply not the person she had thought I was.

Then who was I?

I had asked that before, hadn't I?

Then why hadn't I come up with any answers?

□

"What was it? Where did you go?"

"To the bank."

"What for?"

"The telegram was from Rick. He needed money pretty desperately."

"Oh?"

"Yeah. It's not unusual. He's always getting himself in a corner. He needed a lot, unfortunately. I had to send him everything I had."

"But I thought you didn't have anything."

"Didn't I mention it to you? The Brigham check finally came a couple days ago. I had to ship the whole damn thing to Rick. I haven't a clue how we're going to get by for the next few weeks."

"We can manage, Eric." She got up impulsively, and hugged me. "That was very generous of you, to help him like that."

"What are brothers for?" I muttered.

□

I hadn't seen Josh for over a month, not since the night I'd found myself jealous of him and Jutta. He had called once or twice and we had talked vaguely about getting together, but nothing had come of it. Now I went to his apartment and asked, as he opened the door, if I could borrow some money. "Well, sure," he said, "you can have anything I've got." I gave him a figure. He shook his head. "I haven't got that." He was puzzled. "What's the matter, Junior? Are you in some kind of trouble?"

"Financial trouble, obviously," I said drily.

He led me down the hall to his kitchen, and put on some water. He was still in his bathrobe, although it was mid-afternoon. He squinted at me as if I were training a klieg light on his eyes. "How'd the concert go?" I asked, assuming that was the reason for his condition.

"Great. I blew it away. Standing ovation. Why didn't you come?"

"Didn't know about it."

"Yeah, you've been off in your own world for weeks now. I wouldn't have let you come, anyway. It was *Till Eulenspiegel.* I was shitting bricks." He opened a cabinet, took down some stomachic tea. "What *has* been going on with you, anyway?"

"Oh, problems. With Jutta. And Harvard."

"Sounds like a bad combination, Junior." There was a pause while we both contemplated such bad combinations. Then: "You been reading the papers? There's more and more out about Waldheim all the time."

"Oh?"

"Now he's sure to win."

"Oh come on, Josh—"

"I'm serious. Simon Wiesenthal says the same thing. Look at Waldheim's slogans: 'A Man With Experience.' 'His Experience For Us All.' Sure—murdering Yugoslav partisans and deporting Jews. That's experience Austrians can sympathize with. The death threats have already started to pour in. One of them promised to blow up every Jewish-owned business, every Jewish home, every Jewish magazine, if Wald-heim doesn't win on May 4th."

"If they can find them, you mean."

"I'm thinking of leaving Austria."

"As a protest?"

"Fuck protest. For myself. It's just masochism for a Jew to live here. We could move somewhere where Jun might have a better chance to get a gig or two." The kettle whistled. "Antarctica, maybe." He pulled two mugs out of a drawer. "So Harvard has taken away your fellowship, has it?"

"Yes. How did you guess?"

"What other problems with Harvard could you have, at this dis-tance? What kind of tea do you want, anyway? You don't want this stuff I'm drinking, it tastes like dandelions. Some Japanese green tea?"

"Sure."

Josh cleared crumbs, glasses, and two empty champagne bottles off the table. "Don't look now," I said, "but there's a man with a submachine gun in your courtyard."

Josh looked. "Yeah, that's one of the guards from the Turkish Embassy. He's been wandering around in here, the last few days, looking up at the windows. Something's up. Terrorists in one of the apartments, maybe."

"Doesn't it make you nervous?"

"Enh. I figure if a firefight starts, I can always crawl into the refrigerator. The door closes with a magnet, so it's safe."

We sat. Josh leaned over his mug, stretched his left eye wide open with thumb and forefinger, and held it in the rising steam. Then he did the same with his right eye. He looked up, both eyes watering, rimmed with mucus. "Gets the gum out," he explained.

"Mm."

He groped blindly for a napkin, and I guided one into his hand. "Well—listen, Junior," (wipe, honk) "I wish I could help out with the money sitcho. But I have this habit of spending every cent I make. What about your mother?"

"She's the one who got my fellowship canceled."

"You've really gotten yourself into a mess, haven't you?"

"Afraid so."

"I won't ask for the sordid details."

"Thanks."

He sipped his stomachic tea, looking a little hurt that I didn't offer them. "Normally, I could just lend you some of Jun's money—this tour business really rakes in the bucks. But unfortunately, she just blew everything on a round trip ticket to Japan. She's there now, visiting with her parents for Easter."

"Easter? Already?"

"It's early this year. You didn't know?"

"No."

"The Tone-killers are giving a special concert for Good Friday. That's Friday next week. That reminds me—" Josh got up, "I've got a couple of tickets around here, somewhere." He went into the pockets of a tux that was draped over one of the kitchen chairs. I noted a petite jacket crumpled in the corner; a bow tie on the floor; pearl cufflinks on the window sill. "Here they are—" he squinted at them. "Strange program—incredibly long—*Kindertotenlieder, Tod und Verklärung, Das Klagende Lied;* pretty grim stuff. Death, death, death."

"Not so surprising for Good Friday."

"Certainly not for the Viennese. More of this cult-of-death crap. I suppose this concert is supposed to hold them over until next All Souls' Day, when they can troop back into the cemeteries wearing their *Totenkopf* insignias and dance on their relatives' graves. We should be doing the Resurrection Symphony for Sunday, but of course playing Jew music on Easter would be out of the question."

I shrugged. "Well, you've got two Jew-pieces on the Good Friday program."

"Of course!" He laughed hoarsely, then trailed off into a coughing fit. "Strauss is where he loves to be—on the fucking cross—and poor Mahler is on either side, nailing him there."

"Touché."

"I've been playing so well lately, I'll even allow you and Jutta to come. Assuming you're still speaking to each other. You say there have been problems there, too?"

"Oh, yes, you know," I waved it away. Talking with Josh about love problems was like complaining about peeling paint and leaking pipes to a man whose specialty was dynamiting buildings.

"Well, I'm not surprised," Josh said. "She's a very likable wench

—I'd toss her in the hay myself for a quick one-two, if you weren't a friend. But then I'd boot her. She's trouble."

"Remarkable how many people say that."

"Well it's obvious, Eric. You're the only guy I know who could walk into a gaping man-trap like that with your eyes open. For someone who's supposed to spend his days discovering things, you're amazingly oblivious."

"Remarkable how many people say that, too."

"That night she was giving me the eye—you shouldn't have sulked like that. Women don't respect that. Any bitch that did that to me would find herself walking home."

"But unfortunately, her home happens to be my home."

"That's your biggest mistake. *Never* move in with a woman, Junior. Make her move in with you. Then when it comes to locking doors, you're on the inside and she's on the outside."

"Well one thing's clear. You and Jutta would make a perfect couple."

"Don't get ruffled—"

"I'm not ruffled. I'm absolutely serious."

"Joshua?" It was an accented voice, calling sleepily from the bedroom.

"In the kitchen!" he called.

"Hello, Joshua?" Tentatively, in the hall.

"It's all right," he called, irritably, "you can come in."

An abundant mass of tousled black hair appeared at the door. There was a small, young woman with a fine-boned white face beneath it. She was wearing a kimono. "Eric," Josh said, "this is Alika. She's Hungarian. Alika, Eric." He winked at me. "Alika has a thing for Western men." He drew the woman to his chair and squeezed her ass. "Isn't that right, Alika? You like their *very* hard currency, don't you?" Then he patted the chair next to him. "Before you make breakfast, kiddo, have a seat. Try some of my wife's tea, it's good."

Seeing me out at the door later, Josh handed me a few bills. "This is all I could find—about eight hundred schillings."

"No," I said. "You need your rock-hard currency for Alika."

He pressed the bills into my hand. About fifty dollars. "I insist. She'll live." He grinned: "This is *my* apartment, remember? For godssake, don't look so hangdog."

"Aren't you worried about getting AIDS?" I tried to tease him.

"AIDS?" He said it as if his next question would be, "what's that?" But he laughed, and went on, "They don't have trouble with AIDS in the East Bloc. Didn't you know that? All the carriers are shipped to the Gulag." He pressed for the elevator. "It's what they should do with them here."

"You might be right," I said. "Keep them out of trouble."

"Damn straight."

☐

Eight hundred schillings wasn't enough to move out with, so I hid it in the bedroom. Perhaps I would be able to add to it. From what source, I hadn't the slightest idea. My mother would wire me money, of course, as long as I was willing to subject myself to a phone conversation with her—but it would come, no doubt, on the condition that I use it to return to the U.S. Poking both my eyes out with a sharp stick struck me as a more attractive proposition. Rick? Actually, I knew he would send me some if he could. Rick had always been generous with money. But for just that reason, he never had any. And Helga? It is to laugh. I wondered just how many drafts of her letter she would write, trying to hit on the most exquisitely sardonic way of telling me to go fuck myself. Helga was a riot.

I called the hospital again. They were even ruder than before. "What's wrong with you people?" I demanded. "What in hell is taking so long?" They hung up on me.

Jutta started to miss her classes. She wanted to spend the time with me, she said. But you'll always have time for me, I said. I walked her to class, and all the way we would argue about whether or not she would actually attend when we got there. In the decrepit halls of the Ringstrasse university basement, students at folding tables would be handing out pamphlets supporting Freda Meissner-Blau for president against Waldheim and Steyrer. Graffiti on the wall said *"Sozialpartnerschaft: Verrat!"*; *"Volksdemokratie: Verrat!"* Betrayal! Amid the swirl of hurrying students, I would hug Jutta and kiss her, so that she would feel comforted enough to go to lecture. And then I would stand there alone, and feel exhausted and empty. And guilty. And angry, too. How dare she become dependent on me again!

Sometimes Timo came to the university with us, and then it was even harder to convince Jutta to go in to class. The sight of the two of us together, waving her on in unison, made her feel as if she would be missing out on something. I kissed her, and soothed her, and assured her, and kissed her again until the gorge rose in my throat. After she finally went in, Timo and I would wander through the labyrinthine halls, taking in the posters, the pamphlets, the graffiti, the conversations. Only here was Meissner-Blau in much evidence. The students at the tables looked desperate; Meissner-Blau was going to lose the election by a huge margin. Of course. Hers was an honest, dignified grass-roots campaign for social justice, ecological responsibility, respect for women, economic fairness. Has anyone ever won any election for any post in all human history in such a way, on such a platform? Moreover, Josh had been right—Waldheim's support had risen steadily since his Nazi past had come to light.

Timo and I would eventually pop out the back of the university and take a circuitous route to the apartment, playing in the still-deep, blackening snow. At Lazarettgasse, we would build houses, or pick through a book together. Timo's level of reading comprehension, I discovered, was at a second or third grade level. Conversation was not the only thing that he had understood far more of than he had let on. "Where did you learn this?" I asked him, increasingly amazed.

"Heidi taught me."

I looked at the doll. She winked.

□

3-22-86

Eric

Did you get my last message stop please please call collect stop letter coming stop love

Mother

□

Monday and Tuesday of Holy Week, I walked Jutta again to class. She had been paid over the weekend for part-time work at the day-care center, and she insisted on spending the money on the two of us—without Timo—in organized afternoon jaunts. That meant I had to stay in the area so that I could meet her again after lecture. I collected Meissner-Blau literature at the basement tables. Then I went through the Inner City, carrying handfuls of the cheap little squares that said "I'm voting for Freda Meissner-Blau!" and stuck them on lampposts, on storefronts, on municipal trash cans. One Meissner-Blau square was just big enough to cover one front tooth of the ghoulish grin in Waldheim's posters. Kurt Steyrer, the dull-as-dishwater Social Democratic candidate—the man who had actually stood a chance of beating Waldheim before the Nazi stuff came out—wasn't smiling in his posters, so I had to content myself with affixing Freda's square to his enormous chin, like a mole.

On the afternoon jaunts, Jutta was back to playing the bimbo, the girlish devotee. She held on to me constantly. She laughed at everything I said. She would not sit on the other side of a café table—she sat next to me and captured a hand. She smiled at me greedily. She said things to the waiter such as "he likes his *Melange* with a lot of milk," as if, by showing how much she knew about my tastes, she could assert her claim to me. Wherever I turned, she turned, where I stopped, she stopped, where I looked, she looked. She seemed to think this smothering attention, this choreography, would work on me like a spell. One of her witching fantasies. "You're trying to bind me," I said.

And in a way, through my dread and annoyance, through my fatigue of it all, the spell began to work. Bereft of my family, my self-respect, whatever reputation I might once have had, I realized gradually that the warm feeling that came to me as she hung on my words, or as she leaned against me and put her cheek against my cheek, was gratitude. Someone still wanted me. For reasons, perhaps, that did not bear looking into—all right then, I would not look into them. But someone *did* still want me. I could feel myself turning toward her again, like some poor plant that had no choice but to turn toward the source of light. Her smell began again to entrance me, to pull at my desire. I began to daydream again of taking her pale moist skin in my mouth and swallowing it like unbaked bread. Perhaps she really *had* put menstrual blood in my coffee.

But I hid this. I knew now that I had to hide it. I remained aloof. How long, O Lord, how long?

□

Eric
     Can't understand silence stop terribly worried about you stop need to talk to you about the funding stop what has Rick said to you stop do you need money stop please please call collect stop will explain everything stop absolutely must hear your side stop sure everything can be worked out stop letter coming stop love you
Mother

□

At long last, the hospital called. A cool male voice: it would speak only to Jutta. I insisted that she let me listen in. We held the receiver catty-cornered between our ears. Under the enzyme-linked immunosorbent assay (ELISA) technique, the voice said, her serum sample had repeatedly tested positive. Following the department of public health guidelines, the hospital had then subjected the sample to the Western Blot test which, the voice explained, was generally believed to have higher specificity than the ELISA test, although probably lower sensitivity, and—"What?" Jutta said. "Shhh!" I said—of that test had also been positive. The ELISA tests were covered by the state health care system, but the Western Blot test (a more expensive procedure, we were to understand) was not. A bill would be sent to us. The voice suggested that Jutta come in for counseling (not on the bill, presumably, but on her health). It told her that if she had a regular sex partner, she should urge him to come in for a blood test, too, and did she realize that she was putting him at risk? In the meantime, she should have him use condoms. The voice gave her a couple of numbers to call, and hung up.
     "So this means what I think it means?" Jutta asked.
     I had sat down. It took me a moment to answer. "It means," I said

at length, "that you're infected." And it confirms—the thought nau-seated me; I choked on a constriction in my throat—it confirms abso-lutely that *I* am infected. My God, I have it. I really do have it.

"Well," Jutta shrugged, her expression of curiosity unchanged, her spirits undampened, "we figured that was going to happen anyway, didn't we?"

I gaped at her. "Jutta . . . what are you talking about? What—why —what do you think we've been using those rubbers all this time for? That was supposed to protect you." Where did I get it? I don't deserve this. Even with condoms, I kill people. There is no escape.

"Oh," she said dismissively, "protection doesn't work. My feeling is, if you're going to get it, you're going to get it."

"Very scientific."

"It's not like we've been kissing through plastic baggies."

"Kissing isn't supposed to transmit it."

"Who says that? I thought no one knew."

I blew up. "Of course no one KNOWS! Nobody knows shit! I'm sure they'll know more after about a million of us die. But somehow I don't think I've got the patience to wait that long. It's thought, anyway—as of the current body count—it's thought that kissing is all right—"

"Well, apparently it's thought wrong."

I put my head in my hands. ". . . yes, apparently. Or there's some other reason."

"Like the condoms didn't work. That happens."

"Yes. Or something else. Something no one knows about yet. Al-though I'm sure we could find a quote for this too, if we wanted." This is it. The last. I will have to be celibate for the rest of my life. I cannot do this to people. I just do not have it in me to kill people.

"What does it matter how it happened? It happened." Jutta put a comforting hand on my shoulder. "Eric, I accepted this when I first met you."

I was bewildered. "If you were so sure the condoms wouldn't help, why did you put up with them?" I asked.

"To oblige you. All that silliness—" she giggled. "It was the only way I could get you to screw me." I just stared at her blankly, uncom-prehendingly. "Eric," she exclaimed, exasperated, "don't mope so much. You're such a worry-wart!"

Can I ever leave you? I thought. Am I trapped? Oh my God, what am I going to do?

□

That night we made love for the first time really touching each other, not separating ourselves by a film of rubber. It was an incestuous feeling, but one in which the taboo was reversed—in all the wide world, I could have only Jutta, and she only me. Had this been Jutta's fantasy? We were bound by our sickness. We were Olympians: gods who alone enjoyed the right of incest, whose attentions meant death to humans. "You've kept to your pills all this time?" I asked her.

"Of course!" she said, with a full-throated laugh. "You think I would trust those stupid rubbers?"

And the sex began almost as if it were the first time. It felt so different. So . . . *intimate*. I was naked with Jutta at last. I had trouble —that night, and again on the last night, Thursday. "I can't help feeling," I said into the heavy silence, "that it's a syringe—a syringe with the wrong compound in it—some terrible mistake made by the hospital! It's supposed to give life, but instead it kills. I inject it into you, and it goes to your spine and paralyzes you, it goes to your brain and makes you insane, it goes to your heart and plugs it up until you die. I know—I know you already have it. But if I had shot you, and you lay dead on the floor, that would not make me feel right about pumping more bullets into your head." Jutta became frantic for me to continue. I couldn't. The tangible sign of my need for her, the only evidence she had ever believed, was slipping away. Now we both struggled with demons during the act. "I'm losing you," she said, daring me to agree with her. I said nothing. And she worked on me, and I concentrated as hard as I could, and after a long while I injected into her more of that wrong, deadly compound, the result of some hideous mistake. And Jutta cried, she was so relieved.

The second night, I got out of bed afterward and went to the wardrobe. "I forgot to tell you," I said. "Rick already wired some of the money back to me." I showed her the eight hundred schillings. "I'll put it in the kitchen cupboard tomorrow." I stood over her. She was stretched out on the bed, naked, looking up at me along her forehead the way she did when she wanted to be sexy. I ached with the thought of how beautiful she was.

I climbed back into bed and clung to her. I do not know this woman, I thought, and I do not know this man. I am done with asking questions. None of it makes sense any longer.

□

3-27-86

Eric
    I have done nothing to deserve this stop am frantic with worry stop have pity on poor mother and call collect immediately stop fellowship career and history mean nothing stop your silence is inexplicable and childish stop I love you

Mother

EASTER

JUTTA'S GRANDPARENTS called on Good Friday, and within a minute she was in tears. In the kitchen the words were inaudible, but I could hear the cadence of her voice, falling and shattering, like a pane of glass, again and again.

"What happened?" I asked, when she came in. She sat at the table and sobbed. "Jutta—"

"God I hate them, I HATE THEM!" She sprang up and pulled away from me. "They never let me do what I want to do! They make me feel like shit, like nothing, any time I do the slightest thing—it's like I'm still five years old and they've got me locked up in the back yard." A swift, savage look distorted her face—"I could just *kill* them! They deserve it for what they've done to me—" The grandparents had forbidden Jutta once again to bring Timo to the Easter get-together. They would also not allow her to bring me. "She said I could just stay in Vienna if I couldn't get such ridiculous ideas out of my head."

"And your grandfather agreed?"

"Are you kidding? My father *never* talks to me on the phone. My mother said horrible things about you."

"Spare me. Why don't you stay in Vienna, then?"

"Oh, Eric!" She started to cry again.

"Jutta, you've got to buck up a little—"

"It's easy for you to say," she snapped. "You haven't got them in total control of your life!"

"Jutta . . . they're not in total control of your life."

"They could make me do anything they wanted—"

"All you have to do is say 'no.' "

"If they told me to murder someone, I would, I know it, I wouldn't be able to—"

"That's total, complete, utter nonsense. They don't support you; they have no claim over you. You don't need them. You don't—have —to go—"

"*Oh!*" she shouted in exasperation, "you don't understand a *thing!*" And she barged out.

I guess not.

Jutta was due to take the Saturday afternoon train to Innsbruck. Renate and Ulrike were also heading off to respective parents. No one would be back until Monday night, so Timo and I were to hold down the fort over the weekend. I tried to argue with Jutta about her grandparents later in the day, but she would have none of it. "You're just trying to make me feel guilty," she yelled.

"How do you figure that?"

"You're trying to make me feel guilty about how *weak* I am—how I go crawling off to them every time they whistle. Well I know that! I don't need you to tell me that! I'm not *stupid.* "

I sighed. "No, you're not stupid." Fucked up, yes.

"And don't give me that placid martyr look, like I'm just too-fucking-much for you—why don't you say what you're thinking, huh?"

"I'm thinking that you're fucked up."

"Brilliant! It's taken you this long to figure that out? I could have told you on the day we met and saved you a lot of trouble. But I've got two pretty good reasons for being a basketcase and they're waiting to get their claws into me as soon as I step off the train. And *no* I can't not go—you don't know how they'd torture me over that—God, it would be horrible—everything would be infinitely worse if I didn't do what they wanted. Eric, I just can't turn my parents off in my mind, the way you do with people who are beneath your lofty attention." She sucked a half inch off her cigarette and gulped the smoke down. I started to clean up. By the end of the butt, she had calmed down a little. She lit another one and began to suck on it. I opened a window. She smirked. "Actually, it's too bad my mother wouldn't let you come. You might have liked my father—the two of you could have sat together in the study like a couple of machines, murmuring at books and ignoring each other." I ignored her.

We tried to celebrate our last night together before the holiday by going to Josh's Good Friday concert. But Jutta was on edge again, and would hardly speak to me. I mustered as much patience as I could; I knew she was terrified of the coming weekend. I was hoping that Josh would go out drinking with us afterward. He could always charm Jutta out of her depressions better than I could. And perhaps she would transfer all her attentions to him. After a day of her terrors, her defensiveness, all I wanted was a respite. But Josh, in *Tod und Verklärung*, went for an exposed high A and did an unlovely little dance on several other notes instead. So after the concert, he was both inconsolable and unsociable. "You'll never see me again!" he swore, as he kicked his horn case across the warm-up room. "Never!" He sounded as if he meant it, too. The fine-boned, pale Hungarian was there, and as Jutta and I left, I could hear him abusing her.

So we wandered. Jutta was pensive, and I was weary, numb. Eventually, we found ourselves south of home, in the eighth district, in a light rain. The eighth is an old and run-down part of Vienna, a grid of narrow and dark streets, dark stores, sidewalks black and slippery with the by-products of internal combustion. As everywhere in Vienna, the streetlights are strung between the buildings on a web of cables; they form a dashed line over the middle of the pavement. Here among the narrower streets, the lights gave me the feeling of being in conduits, specially illuminated for observation. We went from one corner to another, down the dirty close streets, until I was turned around, lost. The streets were the conduits of a vast maze, the research project of some superior and supremely indifferent being. A research laboratory for world destruction? Karl Kraus' epithet for Vienna crossed my mind that night. But that was history, even in my father's days. The city's importance had shrunk. It would never again teach the world how to be weak, how to embrace weakness with a glad cry. Its stage now could only accommodate the dramas of its inhabitants. I imagined that night, turning under the fluorescent lights from one identical street to another, that the city was a vast and brutal laboratory for the study of dreams; the dreams of white mice, caught in the maze; a study of how dreams are wrenched, bawling, out of the unconscious; how they sicken and die in the squalid air.

I will always believe that Jutta led us to the place on purpose. She knew the streets in that part of the city better than I did. What motivated her, I still don't know. Although one reason must have been a desire to connect with me, and in doing so to chase away the bad dreams of the nights before: our failed sex, our fights, our disease. And to chase away, too, the image of her "father," waiting for her at the end of the next day's train ride, unspeaking and uncaring, in his study.

I will always believe she led us there on purpose. But what she said that night, as we scuffed around the last corner, was meant to sound like an exclamation of surprise. And she pointed. And I looked. And I suspected.

In the block stood the single's bar where Jutta had once played The Flirting Game. "What luck!" she said brittlely. "Why don't we have something to drink before we go home?"

"All right."

As it was a Friday night, the place was hopping. We inserted elbows into a tiny space along the bar and ordered wine. Through our small talk, I waited patiently. I had always been more patient than Jutta. And so, too, tonight. She turned perhaps a little too early, too abruptly, to the subject that really interested her. She spoke of the last time we had been there. I listened mildly. ". . . but it never really got going that night," she was saying. "You weren't in the mood, remember?"

You mean, do I remember how jealous I was? I thought. How angry? Yes indeed I do. I was shocked that you would want to hurt me so much.

"I've played the game with a lot of my men," she said. "And it isn't fun unless both people are really trying." She expanded on this theme. I waited. She stopped, drank from her glass. She looked around the room, jutting her lower lip out judiciously. She pretended to be thinking, to be running what she had been saying over again in her mind. Then she pretended to have an idea. "I have an idea—" she began.

"You have an idea," I confirmed.

"Why don't we play it again, while we're here? It really *can* be fun, Eric. Aren't you willing to give it another chance?" She looked searchingly into my eyes. She interpreted my silence as reluctance, and hastened to encourage me. "You know, in a way, you *won* last time. You really showed me."

"We can play again, if you'd like. Sure." Things were different now. I really would win this time. Because all she wanted to do was make me jealous again, make me angry. And that would be impossible now. I had grown completely accustomed to how much she wanted to hurt me.

I gave her a long kiss. The delicious feeling of her open lips, the taste of smoke on her tongue. "This is a pretty stupid game, Jutta."

She laughed. I felt as if I were listening to that husky voice for the last time. "I know it's stupid. It's silly. But you'll play it for me, won't you? It's no fun if you don't want to."

"I want to."

We separated. I watched her disappear through the smoke and bodies. She turned back fleetingly and waved, her close-set eyes manic, and then, with a swirl of her long skirt, she was gone. I will never understand you, I thought. But I do believe, I do believe, that I love you.

I looked around for someone to talk to. There were a great many unaccompanied women. I settled back into my place at the bar and spoke for a few minutes with a couple of teenage girls from a suburb: silk scarves knotted around necks, stark make-up, tangy perfume, quick delight, histrionics with wine-glass and cigarette. *Der Anschluss? Toll!* I ran on automatic. Then I got into an argument with an older woman—a thin, nervous professional in soberskirt, blouse, and fem-tie—about Chancellor Sinowatz. I said his nose looked like a zucchino, she said like a penis. Her conversation stayed on this frank plane, and I parted from her with the feeling that I could infect her with deadly viruses any time I wanted to. Farther down the bar was a blond goddess: one of the strapping, high-breasted, long-legged *Überfrauen* that only the Teutonic race seems capable of producing. She was two inches taller than I and wouldn't give me the time of day. I went back to the teenagers. *Der Anschluss? Toll!*

Jutta sidled by conspicuously with a man on her arm. Not bad looking, actually. Small, like me. Moved like a boxer. A bit hairy. At least she was setting her sights higher.

The teenagers had to leave, or they would miss the last streetcar home. They took down my name so that they could keep an eye out for my book. I waved them out the door and watched them go up the street, head to head, giggling, sharing the secret of a man in the bar, an American, *Der Anschluss.* What an age, I thought. And to think I'll never have a child to reach that age, to help me relive its excitements and disasters. To think that I'll never have a child at all. "I want grandchildren!" my mother had often said to me. She hadn't said it to Rick or Helga. Only my genes would do, she seemed to think. Rick's offspring would have God-knows-what sort of mutations from all the drugs he had taken. Helga's offspring, of course, would be half black; and my mother had always liked Helga least. I was the only decent copy. "I don't want children," I lied. "Why not?" she asked, surprised and hurt. I came closer then to telling her than at any other time. But I restrained myself.

"Lost your young friends, eh?"

I turned. A man at my elbow had spoken. He smiled conspiratorially. I had a feeling we were suddenly in man-to-man territory. "Got to catch 'em faster than that, eh? They're all safely home by midnight and no way to get 'em out again." He laughed snortingly, like a horse neighing.

"I suppose not." Jutta and her man drifted into my line of sight. She caught my eye for a moment. I ignored her.

"But it's an easy enough game, eh?" he said. "Start early enough, a few drinks. Compliments go a long way at that age."

I felt the blood rush to my head. "Yes, I should think they would," I said. He was a big man, earthbound as a sack of potatoes, hands as big as my face. I could see that hand fumbling with stockings; covering a mouth bright with too much lipstick. "After all, they're so eager to hear it," I said.

Jutta floated into view again. I turned away.

"Yes, eager," the man was saying.

"They're so vulnerable, so innocent," I said.

"Vulnerable, yes—"

"They're sitting ducks, aren't they? For a grown man, anyway."

"Yes, yes!" He laughed again, his eyes disappearing momentarily behind sphincters of folds. "Just so! Ripe for the plucking, eh?"

"Yes. And so clean!"

"Clean?"

"You know—virginal. No diseases there, hm?"

"Yes, that's true."

"I mean, it's awfully nice to know that those tight little cunts haven't been host to all sorts of diseased third-world pricks, don't you think so?" I asked.

"Uh, yes—"

"I mean, you never know what you're getting with the prostitutes, what with God-knows-what-kind-of-germ-infested spoff still draining out of them from the last john, barely ten minutes ago and there the wog is, still buttoning up his filthy work pants in the hotel foyer. Nice

246

to know you're boldly ramming your way where no man has gone before, right?"

"Uh—"

"I mean, so what if there's a lot of blood? That's the guarantee, right? Of the goods, I mean. Good lubricant, too. I always rape 'em with a towel on the bed, so I don't mess up my sheets."

"Rape?" The laughter had died away. The man looked rather unhappy with me.

"Sure. Call a spade a spade, right? No point in talking about consent at that age. 'After a few drinks,' as you say. After a few drinks, they're rag dolls; they're not even there. It's a bit like fucking corpses, don't you think? Only more fun, perhaps; a little resistance—gives it that *soupçon*, that *frisson*, that *je ne sais quoi*—"

"You—" he interrupted me, sputtering, furious at being mocked. "You swine—" Spit stippled my glasses.

I deliberately misunderstood. "Oh? That disgusts you?" I found I was very excited. The customers in our vicinity had quieted and shifted slightly, to sneak looks at us. "Why should you be disgusted?"

"Well!" the man puffed out, and stopped. He appealed to the people around us. He put down his glass and raised his hands palm up; a gesture of innocence. "Well!"

"So you were joking, then?" I demanded of him. "You aren't a child molester, after all?" His face turned red. A couple behind him exchanged an alarmed glance. "You don't get girls drunk and offer to drive them home and then take them out into the forest and rape them?"

The red darkened to an extraordinary shade of purple. The man lurched away from the bar and looked for a moment as if he would fall against me. The crowd tensed. (*Kronen:* "Child Molester Murders Neat Freak in Upscale Bar!"; *Kurier:* "Falling Pedophile Flattens Foreigner!") But he managed to keep himself upright by jabbing me painfully in the chest with his index finger. "You are crazy, my young friend." He appealed again to our audience. "Crazy! Why is he talking to me?" He broke the circle and hurried away. The circle closed after him. Everyone looked at me expectantly.

"Show's over folks!" I said. "No need to get excited. The rapist is gone." The audience wavered. I went back to my drink. The people turned away slowly.

Jutta appeared. "What was that all about?" she asked irritably.

"Nothing," I said. "Go back to your boyfriend."

She shrugged. Of course she was irritated. I had started my own ring in this goddamn circus. "Go on!" I said, sharply. She gave me a slow, resentful look and disappeared.

I ordered another *Viertel*. The woman with penises on the brain settled against the counter where the child molester had been. "You lead a complicated social life," she remarked, letting her shoulder press against mine.

"Oh, not so much," I said, taking a long pull out of the new glass. "The woman is my sister. The big man was an old boyfriend of hers. She dumped him when she found out he was fooling around with ten-year-olds, and now he bears a grudge against the whole family."

"You and your sister don't look a bit alike." She made it sound suggestive.

"Different mothers," I said. "Mine was in the foreign service. A beautiful woman. Brilliant scholar. Small, like me." I sighed. "She was killed in Rome." The woman pursed her lips and made a sympathetic noise. "Oh, that was years ago. An old story. She was riding with the ambassador from Ghana—her lover at the time—and somebody's liberation organization blew the car two stories high."

"That's horrible!"

"You're telling me. Something to do with the Ghanaian civil war. I hear there's even a song in Ghana about it, which starts 'Whoops! there he goes!' Doesn't mention my mother. Can I buy you a drink?"

She inclined her head graciously.

I downed the rest of my glass and ordered two. "Now Jutta's mother was Viennese. My governess first, and then my stepmother. I had a rather sordid affair with her myself after my father died. I was tubercular, and she nursed me for months. One day she just crawled into bed with me. I was only fourteen. She had a weakness for real thin boys. She was a nymphomaniac, poor thing."

"Jutta is—"

"My sister, right. Jutta is quite a handful. Like mother, like daughter." I winked.

"Mmm," she said, not knowing whether to believe me, or if not, whether to show it. She was a good-looking woman, forty-ish, strong-featured, dark, with a handsome streak of pure white hair dividing the black on the left side. She wore gold bracelets on her bony wrists which clanked together with the sound of distant cowbells. Her name

248

was Marietta. Hey Marietta, how would you like me to shorten your life expectancy?

My glass was already empty. I ordered another *Viertel* for myself. The child molester had gotten me rather depressed. The only course of action, under the circumstances, was to get drunk.

Marietta and I exchanged bios. Hers, presumably factual, included three divorces, the last from a man whose weekend pastime turned out, as his trial revealed, to be throwing matchbooks, lit and tied to stones to make them carry farther, from his automobile into the woods. One of his fires destroyed three thousand acres, two houses, seventeen deer, and all the body hair on a firefighter. I described my youth in Southwest Africa, my disastrous stint fighting the Angolans (getting lost in the jungle, surviving on grubs, etc.), and the death of my brilliant brother, whom I worshipped, from a massive drug overdose. Meanwhile, Jutta and her hairy friend (black beetling eyebrows, an awl-hole in his chin) commandeered two stools at the counter six feet down and cooed at each other. The childishness of the "game" made me almost physically sick, and I exchanged places with Marietta so that I would have my back to them. How could I have gotten involved with someone so infantile? I ordered another *Viertel.*

A familiar face caught my eye in the crowd. Round, bland, good-natured. It took me a few seconds to place him. Then I remembered —it was the chubby man whom Jutta had picked up last time we were here. I waved to him and he took a step toward us, hesitated. "Another of Jutta's old boyfriends," I explained to Marietta. "One of the nicest, most decent men I've ever known. A bit reserved. Naturally, she treated him like shit." I beckoned vigorously, and he made his way over to us.

The name came back to me just in time. "Marietta, this is Hugo."

"Very pleased," he said, politely. He took her hand in the old style, palm down, and bowed. The gesture looked good on him. "Your sister is not . . . ?" He looked warily around.

"No, she's here." I jerked a thumb over a shoulder. "Busy, as usual. Can I buy you a *Viertel?* A beer?"

Marietta regarded Hugo sympathetically. He had lost some weight since I'd last seen him. Or perhaps my eye was being fairer to him. I bought another round with Josh's money, and Hugo squeezed in with us. "How's the hunting?" I asked him.

He glanced sidelong at Marietta and colored slightly. "Oh . . . you know." He mumbled something into his glass.

"Isn't it terrible?" Marietta chimed in. "It was so much better a decade ago. All the good men now are either married or homosexual."

"Present company included?" I asked. Bisexual, maybe.

"Oh no! Of course not."

"I don't envy you, though," Hugo told me.

"Hm?"

"Keeping an eye on your sister."

"Yes, Eric told me she treated you badly," Marietta said, pursing her lips again sympathetically.

Hugo blushed deeply. I decided it was rather fun to watch Hugo blush. "Well—not *badly*, really," he objected. "It was a close call, that's all."

I touched my ring finger and winked at her. "Oh," Marietta said. "I understand that *very* well."

He looked surprised. "You do?"

"As she said," I pointed out, "all the good men today are either married or *homosexual.*"

"Oh, of course," Hugo murmured. The special danger to women hadn't occurred to him.

"It makes the pickings pretty slim," Marietta said, shaking her head sadly. "You're not careful, you pick a wrong number—"

"You have to protect yourself," I said, with the air of quoting a maxim.

"Oh, but I have!" Marietta insisted. Hugo looked relieved. "I've gotten pretty tough, believe me."

"I suppose you *have* to be tough," Hugo said. A doubtful look came over his face. He clearly didn't believe in his ability to be tough. "These are bad times," he added, vaguely.

When Hugo excused himself to go to the restroom, I followed him a ways. "Hugo—" I said, "Marietta doesn't know about the AIDS. I only tell those who need to know."

"Oh!" He clapped a hand over his mouth. "I'm terribly sorry! I mentioned it, didn't I?"

"No, you didn't. You were fine, just fine. Marietta thought you were talking about relationships in general."

"Thank God!"

"By the way, how do you like Marietta?"

"Oh . . . very nice, very nice." He said it as if it were a compliment to me.

"She's not my girlfriend, you know."

"Oh. No?"

"Not at all. Just an old friend. One of the nicest, most decent women I've ever known."

"Really? Mm."

"But she's had a succession of disastrous men—an arson, a child molester, a necrophiliac, you name it."

"That's awful!"

"Absolutely." I took his elbow, spoke confidentially. "She's looking for a good, quiet man, Hugo. I promised her I'd keep my eye out."

"Aah." The seriousness of this proposal appeared to deprive him of words.

"She's a wonderful woman, Hugo. Promise me you'll think about it." I squeezed his arm. "She loves Chinese food and dancing." I headed back toward the bar. Halfway there, I ran into Jutta. "Where's your hairy friend?" I asked.

"In the men's room."

"What a coincidence."

"Why don't we head home?"

"What? Why do you want to do that?" I was genuinely surprised.

"Oh . . . I don't know. This is boring."

Am I doing such a good job of ignoring you? "But I can't leave now," I objected.

"Why not?" she snapped.

"I'm in the middle of a bit of matchmaking."

"What?"

"The chubby guy, Hugo, and this woman—I'm trying to set them up."

"Eric!" She was really angry now. "What kind of idiot do you think I am?"

"I'm serious. Give me fifteen minutes."

"With that anorexic bitch? You *shit!*"

"Now, now—"

"You're making fun of me!"

"Listen. This was *your* stupid idea. *Your* stupid game. Give me fifteen lousy minutes, and then we'll go."

"I don't think you *have* fifteen minutes!" She spun around and walked off.

"Don't be so snooty!" I called after her.

"What was that all about?" Marietta asked when I got back to her.

"Oh, God!" I spoke as if exhausted. "Jutta hates to see me talking to Hugo. She's sure we're talking about her."

"She looks like a fiery one."

"She is, bless her heart. And not a bad person, really. She's touchy about Hugo, I think, because she feels guilty, deep down, over how badly she treated him."

"Was it so bad?"

"Terrible. And he's such a sweetheart."

"He does seem nice."

"You know, it goes on, even now. Why do you think Jutta's sitting so close to us with her new boyfriend?" I pointed. The hairy man was back from the john and the two of them were talking intimately, leaning into each other like a pair of teepee poles. Jutta was gripping the man's knee between her legs. "It's because she's trying to make Hugo jealous. She follows him everywhere, with her men."

Marietta was outraged. "What a bitch!" She stopped herself. "Oh —excuse me. But really! That doesn't sound like guilt to me—"

I shrugged. "Guilt makes people do the strangest things." I confided in her, "Her main problem is—she's got a low self-image."

Marietta sighed. "Who doesn't?"

"Yes, but I mean *very* low. I mean rock-bottom."

"It must be hard for you."

"Oh," I waved it away. "Not as hard as it was for Hugo."

"But you've had to put up with her your whole life."

It certainly seems that way. "Still—she's pretty decent to me, on the whole."

"Hm."

There was a pause. A rather pregnant, thoughts-moving-in-the-same-direction sort of pause. Marietta ran her finger around the rim of her glass, and the gesture had the deliberateness that was supposed to focus my attention on her finger, on its light, sensual movement over a surface that could as easily be, say, my body. Where the hell was Hugo? "Would Hugo mind much, do you think," she asked, "if we left him here and went to my apartment?"

Well you bold thing, you. And if I weren't the fourth horseman, I'd be mighty tempted to take you up on that. But one victim a year is enough. "Oh dear," I said. "I would love to, I really would—except . . ."

"Except what?"

"Well, what was it you said? You think I'm a good man, right?"

"Seems so."

"And I'm not married. So I'm afraid that leaves . . ."

"Oh nooo!" she cried, disappointed. "You're homosexual!" She struck herself on the head. "I've got all the luck, haven't I?"

"Sorry."

"You know, I thought you might be."

"You did?"

"Oh, there's a certain something, there."

"Really."

"Oh, I don't know. A little . . ."

"Je ne sais quoi," I offered.

"Yes. Like talking about your 'beautiful mother,' or saying 'she was a nymphomaniac, poor thing'; that kind of talk." Then she blurted out, "Well goddamn it, what were you flirting with me for, then?"

"Heavens, I wasn't flirting with you at all."

"What were you doing, then?"

"Well . . ." Well, smart guy? How about it? "Well, you know, I'm —I'm afraid I'm an inveterate matchmaker. I couldn't help thinking that you and Hugo would make a wonderful couple."

"I and Hugo?"

"Sure. He's a wonderful man, he really is. Steady, considerate, loving. And—" I whispered, "even Jutta admits he's great in bed. And she's mighty hard to please."

Marietta colored. "You mean you planned this whole thing from the beginning?" Then she laughed. "You . . . you . . ."

"Rascal," I offered. "Scamp. Devil."

"I'll think about it."

"Please don't tell Hugo. He'd be terribly embarrassed if he thought I was trying to set something up. Here he comes. Please *do* think about it." Hugo slipped in beside us. He had apparently spent some time grooming himself in the bathroom mirror. Even his eyebrows looked combed. I whiffed a generous splash of cologne. He had also gotten thoroughly tongue-tied. The conversation lurched awkwardly for a few minutes. Hugo ordered a round. He stared into his glass a lot. He swallowed a lot. Now was the time for me to bow out and go home with Jutta.

Hugo's eyes widened. "Oh!" He tapped my sleeve. "Oh!" He was looking past me.

"What?" I asked.

"But they're kissing, now!" he said, alarmed.

"Oh, you poor thing," Marietta murmured. "Don't look."

"Shouldn't you warn him?" Hugo asked me. He glanced at Marietta, remembering not to mention AIDS. "You know, about the, about the . . . danger he's in?"

"That's all right," I assured him. "I've already spoken with the man. He knows all about Jutta. He says he doesn't mind."

"But they're kissing with open mouths!"

"I'm sorry—that woman is just a *bitch,*" Marietta exclaimed.

"Is that what they're doing?" I turned to look.

"B-i-t-c-h, bitch!"

"Hmm," I said. "So they are."

"How can you still care about such a bitch?" Marietta asked Hugo.

"I don't care about *her,*" Hugo answered. "I'm worried about *him.*"

Who cares about him? I thought. Let the hairy bastard die of AIDS.

"Don't you think that's overly noble of you?" Marietta asked Hugo.

If it's good enough for me, it's certainly good enough for him.

"Why?" Hugo said. "He may say he doesn't mind, but he can't really know what kind of trouble he's getting into."

"Well he *should* know. That woman has trouble written all over her," Marietta said with finality.

"Yes, she's real trouble," agreed Hugo.

No, she's *in* real trouble, I thought. Big trouble.

"I *do* think it's remarkably good of you to be concerned about that other man, when he's certainly done you no favors," Marietta was saying.

Jutta and the man had gone into a clinch. I knew her well enough to be able to tell that she was about to lose control. Right in the middle of the bar. She'd drag him down on top of her any second. "Excuse me," I said, "I'm going to have to break them up." Is there a pitcher of water in the house?

"Before they fornicate right on the floor," Marietta said. Hugo blanched at the thought of all those AIDS germs flying. "Oh, I'm sorry, Hugo!" she exclaimed. "Look, why don't we get out of here?"

"Out of here?"

Don't be such a dope, Hugo. "Yes, take him away," I told her.

"There they go!" Hugo yelled.

I turned, wildly. "Where?"

"Over there!"

I saw them heading through the crowd. Or rather, I saw Jutta dragging the man through the crowd. "Well, kids—gotta run!" I pulled Marietta aside and whispered, "He loves Chinese food and dancing."

"Oh good!" she whispered back. "So do I!"

"*Auf Wiedersehen*, Hugo, Marietta!"

"*Auf Wiedersehen!*"

(Who *was* that masked man?)

I pressed through the crowd in the direction Jutta had gone. Up three steps, into a smaller side room. There was a door beyond, to the outside. I ran out to the alley. The rain had turned to snow. There was no one there. I ran to the corner, and looked up and down the street. It was 1:00 A.M. The street was empty. A taxi? So quickly? Not bloody likely.

I went back down the alley, back into the sideroom of the bar. After the streetlamps, the bright new snow, it was very dark inside. I peered into the corners and saw strangers. From the top of the steps, I scanned the main room again. Nothing. Then I noticed, right beside me, the two doors. Restrooms.

Would they be in the men's or women's? Men's, of course. Women would shriek, cause a fuss. Men would only shake their heads and smile, trying not to be shocked.

I pushed through the door into more gloom. I switched on the light. Blue tile. Two sinks. Two stalls. A silence that sounded like waiting. A stillness as of motion stopped. Two sinks. Two stalls. Two feet.

I pulled at the stall door. It was locked. But it was flimsy construction, and when I kicked at the jamb and yanked on the handle, the door popped open. Inside, Jutta was sitting on his lap bare-assed, her knees pressed around his waist. Her pants were over the back of the toilet. Between her buttocks, I could see the rigid base of his penis, disappearing upward.

She was looking around at me. Her mouth was twisted into a rigid smile. The whites of her eyes glistened, opalescent, like mackerel skin.

I took a step backward. I paid no attention to the man. I saw only her eyes, her crazed smile. We stared at each other. I took another step backward. "Sorry to disturb you," I said. My voice sounded ghastly. Why did I say that? I wondered. Was that supposed to sound ironic? Bitter? Was it supposed to bring her to her senses? Bring her back to me?

I retreated to the door. My eyes remained locked on hers. She, in her turn, seemed fascinated by me. The other man might not have existed. Except that he was in the process of fucking her. I turned out the light. I felt numb. I turned to go. Deep, down deep, down in the pit of my stomach, I could hear a voice, commanding, "Don't care; don't care; don't care." I can do that, I thought. I can arrange that somehow. I opened a door that seemed a mile away.

But no. It was no good. The hollow place at the back of my sternum was blooming, mushrooming through my whole chest. I felt as if I would implode if I walked through that door. I would leave a corpse like a crumpled piece of paper. I turned back, into the gloom. The stall door was still open. I reached in and grabbed Jutta. "Is this what you want?" I asked her calmly. I grabbed her by the hair. I grabbed her by the hair and pulled. Like unspitting a pig, I pulled her by the hair off the man's penis, off the man's lap. "Is this what you want?" She hit the floor. Her hands scrabbled at my arm. I tightened my grip on her hair. "Is this what you want?" I hit her in the face. The sound of the smack echoed in the room. "Is this what you want?" My voice roared in my ears. I hit her again. The man loomed, fumbling with his pants. He lurched past me. I lifted her by her hair. "Is this what you want?" I hit her again. She kicked me. She screamed. Her scream roared in my ears. "Is this what you want?" I hit her again. The lights snapped on. Shouts. Men poured into the room. They grabbed me. The walls lurched, tipped over. The floor banged up against my nose. Someone kicked my wrist and the hand holding her hair went numb. Jutta was shrieking. The hairy man was on top of me. He said, "What in the hell—?" They picked me up again, gripping my arms. A man was handing Jutta her pants. He was smirking. I caught sight of myself in the mirror. I was bloody from nose to chin. Someone, far off, was crying. Then the room blazed and twinkled with stars. I realized it was me.

□

She would talk only to me. But I ignored her. The hairy man tried to comfort her, but she pushed him away. It began to dawn on him that he had been a tool, and before long he looked as if he wanted to beat her up himself. Then he tried to commiserate with me, but I ignored him, too. I kept trying to leave, but the other men wouldn't let me. They were waiting for the manager, or for anyone who might tell them what one was supposed to do when one found strangers fucking and beating each other up in a public bathroom. When the manager appeared, he ordered everybody out of his bar. Witnesses included. The men tried to explain what had happened, but he didn't listen. He herded us roughly out to the street. In the snow, men offered to escort Jutta home. Hers or theirs: theirs, in case hers was also mine. Or in case she wanted to fuck them in their own bathrooms. But she said she would go only with me. The hairy man called her a crazy bitch, lost control and all dignity, kicked snow on her, and tramped off. I headed in the opposite direction. Jutta ran after me, but I shoved her away. She faltered. I left her. Several blocks on, a taxi slowed down beside me. The back window rolled down. "Eric? Eric?" It sounded like a voice trying to break into a dream: needling and far away. I turned and walked in the opposite direction. The taxi stopped. It began to back up. "Eric? Won't you come home with me?" I turned again. The taxi stopped and drove forward again. I felt like an animal hunted from a Land Rover. This was not sporting. I stopped. The taxi stopped. "Eric?"

I had not intended to get in. But I found myself getting in. The back of the taxi smelled of plastic seat-covers and cigarette smoke. "Lazarettgasse, please," Jutta told the driver. "Near the Gürtel." We sat in opposite corners. All I could see of Jutta was the slow wink of orange at the end of her cigarette, and her hair, caressed once a second by the liquid slide of streetlamp light. Neither of us spoke. At the end, I paid. Jutta had no money. "You terrified me," she said, on the stairs. "I thought you were going to kill me. You wanted to kill me, didn't you?" I didn't answer. "You hurt me, what you said about getting away from me, 'burning your bridges.' That was cruel. I had to hurt you back. I'm sorry."

The angry marks of my hand covered her face. In the bright light of the apartment, I regarded them curiously. I had never hit anyone before. She would have a black eye, bruises on the cheekbones and forehead. But nothing had been broken, nothing had bled. I had been disgusted, even at the time, by the thought of touching her nose. Between my thumb and forefinger I still carried the scar where she had burned me. This is the only way we can communicate? I wondered. This is how we will remember each other? "You don't seem to understand," I said. "This is not an issue between you and me. You and I are plague carriers, Jutta. We can actually kill people by having sex with them. Your vagina now, your anus, your blood are diseased."

"Eric, I know that—"

"No you don't. This is not the fanciful morality your grandmother taught you. This is clinical, incurable disease. This is screwing someone and two years later they've got purple lesions all over their bodies, or they're drowning in the fluid in their own lungs, or they've got a stinking fungus in their mouths—this is condemning people to intense pain over months; to progressive dementia, until they're staring vacantly around the terminal ward and drooling like babies born without brains."

"I know that—"

I looked at her curiously. "Do you think it's right to get back at me by killing someone else?"

"I was trying to get your attention."

"You know, I even thought I had to stay to protect the world from you. Another one of my Atlas fantasies, I suppose. But my presence doesn't protect anyone—not even a few yards away."

"You're still angry at me," she said simply, with some satisfaction. "I can understand that."

"I am going to try once more. I did not give you death, Jutta. I gave you celibacy. This is not something that just happens to you; this is something you do. This is harder than death. It requires strength. Believe me, it's going to drive you nearly insane—the frustration, the masturbating, the taunting dreams. It's only if you're very lucky that you will find someone with a death wish who will agree to put up with you for a while."

"But I've got you. I can't hurt you."

Me? I thought. You've got *me?* This failure? This floundering, lying nonentity? You've got the man who has ruined you, who has taken away from you the one thing that comforted you, that got you to feel that other people loved you? You've got a man who hid behind his words and his fears until he despised himself so much that he had to purge himself—which he did by beating you in the face? "Do you honestly think this is a healthy relationship?"

"Healthy?"

"You know—not sick. Not repulsive. Not perverted."

"Oh come on, Eric," she stamped her foot. "I said I was sorry!"

"Yes, I know. You're sorry. Very good. Your apology is accepted." I began to stack the clean dishes on the table. "And now you'll have to accept my apology."

"Oh God, don't clean up now! Let's go to bed. I want to make it up to you."

I put the last plates on the table and picked up the empty suitcase. "Some other time. I'm moving out."

She followed me into the bedroom. "You don't mean that—" I put the case on the bed and took the backpack out of the closet. "Don't be so melodramatic. This isn't like you." I didn't answer. She sat down on the bed. "You don't mean it," she repeated.

"The advantage of being neat," I told her, "is that you can move out very quickly. Note—" I opened two drawers in the dresser. "Here are all my clothes, neatly folded." I put them in the backpack. "None of this running around, looking under beds, crying hysterically, and that sort of thing. Everything's ready to go." I pulled open the drawers of the desk. "Here are my papers, neatly stacked, separated by subject: letters to and from my mother; letters to and from the committee; papers from my Harvard days; I've even got a few *Anschluss* notes I took in October." I loaded them into the suitcase. "And my books," I pointed out, "are all together, right here—" I removed them from the end of a bookcase, and put them in with the papers.

"Eric, stop. This is ridiculous!" She took a pile of shirts out of the pack.

"Please," I said, going to her. I removed the shirts gently from her hands. "They'll take up too much room if you mess them up." I returned them to their place. "Now, if *you* were leaving, it would take you hours to get ready. You would never get out the door. You would change your mind, first. You would come back for another beating, which would no doubt excite you sexually, and you and your father-figure could then fuck each other's brains out." I put the typewriter in with the books, and closed the suitcase. "*Voilà!* Elapsed time, four minutes. And you thought my tidiness was pointless."

"This whole thing is some sort of joke," Jutta said, weakly.

"I'd agree with that." I shouldered the pack. "Oh—I'll leave the money I've got with you. There's enough for a couple of days, anyway." I put the bills on the desk. I picked up the suitcase and headed for the door. Jutta ran to the kitchen and blocked my way. Her face had turned dead white.

"Eric—not this weekend! Any time but this weekend!"

"Hm?"

"No one else is here. Renate and Ulrike are gone for the holidays. I can't stand to be alone!"

"You've got Timo—"

"GodDAMNit, Timo doesn't count!"

For the first time, I was angry again. "The least you can do is say it in English," I hissed in English. "So if Timo is listening, he won't understand."

"*Fuck* Timo!" she spat out in German. "You hypocrite! If you cared about him the slightest bit you wouldn't be leaving—do you have any idea what this is going to do to him?"

"You're not going to be alone, anyway," I said. "You're going to your grandparents tomorrow."

"My parents? I can't go to them. Not like this. They'd see right through me. They'd tear me to pieces!" Her eyes had become wild.

"They're not lions, Jutta."

"What do you know about it?"

"Well then *don't* go see them!" I said and shouldered past her, went through the kitchen and out into the hall. "I'm sick and tired of hearing about your goddamn grandparents—put up with them, or stay away from them. But don't fucking *bitch* about them all the time!"

"Eric, I've *got* to go—if I don't go, my mother will never forgive me."

"My mother would happily throttle me if she ever got her hands on me—do you see me getting hysterical about it?"

"And what will I do with your beloved *Timo,* if you're not here?"

"Give him to me for the weekend. I'll pick him up tomorrow."

"Oh yes, so you and Timo can be together having a great time while my parents pick me apart—"

"Jutta . . . It was your idea, remember?"

"In this apartment, yes—but if you're going to run away from me,

260

you don't get Timo, too—God knows what you'll tell him—you've already tried to turn him away from me—"

Revolted, I turned down the stairs. She followed me. "Don't follow me!" I shouted.

She stopped. "I can't go there alone! I can't go there if you're not here for me! *Please*, Eric, *please!* Just stay this weekend, this week when I come back! I'll be good, I promise! I won't say a thing about my parents! Not a word! Then you can leave, and I won't say a thing! I'll be good! I won't bitch! You can't leave me now! It's the worst time! My parents will kill me!"

Enraged, chagrined, frightened, I stood on the landing below and looked up at her. I didn't trust her anymore. I didn't recognize her anymore. "It will always be the worst time," I said. "You should stay here with Timo, who loves you more than anything in the world. You should let your grandparents, who don't love you at all, go to hell— where apparently they belong. If you can't see *that*—" I stopped, searching for words. "If you can't see *that*, then you don't deserve him." I continued down the stairs. At the bottom, I was stopped by a deafening scream: *"ERIC!"* I went on. The word was still reverberating in the stone stairwell when I closed the street door on it.

I went out to the middle of the pavement. I looked up at the windows. The light in the children's room was off. I prayed, against all logic, that he was asleep. Beyond that, I could not bear the thought of him.

□

As I had no money, not a schilling, I went to Josh's apartment. He was still out. I sat in the hall outside his apartment. At 4:00 A.M., he came home, drunk and alone. At some point during the evening, he had lost the Hungarian woman; he could not remember when. I lay down in his guest bedroom, which looked over the garden of the Schwarzenberg Palace, and listened for the rest of the night to the wind-driven sleet outside and Josh's retching in the toilet.

Saturday afternoon, the phone rang. "Answer it," Josh yelled from his bed. "It's Jun." I answered it. It was Jutta. Before I could say a word, she had put on Timo. "When are you coming back?" he asked. "Timo, put your mother on—" "Yes?" Jutta asked. "How dare you use him—" She gave it right back to Timo. "Mommy wants you back, Eric." "I know Timo, I know—could you please put her on again?" "Yes?" Jutta asked. "This is dirty, Jutta." "I can't tell him—you tell him." "You go to hell." I could hear the receiver being passed again. "Timo?" "Yes," he said. "Last time, I promise—could you please give the phone back to your mother?" There was a pause. "She doesn't want it," he said. "Tell her I'll listen." There was another pause. "Yes?" Jutta said. "What do you have in mind?" I asked. "I told you—*you* explain to him why you're not here. He's been asking for you all day. I'm sure there's something very intelligent and reasonable you can say to a five-year-old boy you've just abandoned—" "Goddamnit, Jutta—no, don't give it back, don't—! Hey, Timo. I don't know about you, but this is one of the weirder phone calls I've had. Could you tell your mother that I have something intelligent and reasonable to tell her?" Another pause. "Yes?" Jutta asked. "Jutta, I can't do it over the phone." "Well you'll just have to come back to Lazarettgasse and do it." "And have you all over me?" "Eric—*you* left. This is your responsibility. It's pure cowardice to ask me to explain. All I'm asking is that you come back for a couple of hours. That's all. Is that so much to ask? I promise I'll be good. Just come back and talk to Timo. Perhaps somehow—I don't know how, but somehow—you can help him understand what you've done to him." I sighed. She was right. I had left her to do what I could not bear to think of myself. In a way, she was being uncommonly generous; she was allowing me to tell Timo my side of it. "You promise that's all you've got in mind?" "Promise." "All right. When should I come?" "Tonight." "But you're going to Innsbruck—" "I've already missed my train. I'm going to disconnect the phone, so that my parents can't reach me. My mother will go to the station, but no one will be there." She laughed. It was an odd, unpleasant sound. "What time tonight?" "8:00." "All right. I'll be there." "You promise?" "I promise."

Josh got up at 4:00. He took aspirin, made tea, ungummed his eyes. "What do you think?" I asked him.

"She's going to booby-trap the apartment," he said. "You might find a couple of old boyfriends there. Who knows? Perhaps she used the rest of my money to hire Kurt as an assassin."

"That could be the beginning of a beautiful relationship. Speaking of money, I need some more."

"Whatever I've got, Junior."

That turned out to be two hundred and fifty-seven schillings. I took a hundred, as pocket money. "I should be back by 10:00."

"If not, I'll call the police."

From Lazarettgasse, I could see no lights on in the apartment. But the kitchen wasn't visible from the street. I went up the stairs slowly, listening for movement, for a man's voice. Or the sound of sharpening knives. Or of a weighted baseball bat being swung. On the second floor, I stopped. I had heard something. Then it came again. It was Timo's voice. It was coming from the apartment of the Jordanian, Rashid. Now and then, he watched the women's children for an hour or two, when the *Koppel* was closed. I knocked on the door.

Rashid greeted me when he opened up and said, "You changed your mind?"

"What?"

"About Timo."

"I heard his voice through the door."

"Well of course, he's here. I thought you knew."

"No."

"Oh . . . Jutta asked me to take care of him for the evening. She said you and she were planning to spend the night out. Did you forget?"

"I guess so."

He chuckled. "Naughty boy! It's good you talked to me, then— you'd be in big trouble! Six months together, eh?"

"Oh . . . that's right." No, that wasn't right.

"Not good to forget those things, Eric."

"No. No, of course not. Where's Timo?"

Timo was angry, and would not speak to me. He pulled his hand away. "I think I'll take Timo, Rashid," I said. "He belongs in this party, too. Will you come with me, Timo? Please?" It took some coaxing, but he finally agreed, with a curt nod. "Sorry for the trouble, Rashid."

"Oh, no problem! Jutta is a very dear friend of mine! Anything I can do to help!" He shut the door.

I took Timo back down the stairs. "Where are we going?" he asked.

"For a walk," I said. I was livid. So she *had* been lying. She had used Timo to lure me, and then put him callously out of sight so that she could confront me alone. Well, now she could sit up there and stew in her own juice. I would explain myself to Timo without her. We turned into the bright commercial lights of Alserstrasse. If only I could think of what to say to him.

We got onto the first streetcar that came along and rode it to the terminus at Schottentor. Then we switched, again to the first car, which happened to be a D. Timo sat with his face turned away from me. A woman across the aisle directed her young daughter's attention to him: "Look at the cute little Negro boy!" she said, as if Timo could understand, say, Swahili, but surely no German. The five-year-old girl, dressed like her mother, cooed like her too. "Where could he be going, alone at night?" her mother wondered. I tapped Timo's shoulder. "Look at the middle-aged lady and her squishy white daughter!" I said. Timo did not respond. But the smiles across the aisle vanished. "Let's go," I said, standing up. "He's with me," I told the woman, who looked away. "And a dozen years from now he'll be dating your daughter."

"You're a pig," she sniffed.

I snorted like one. It was an excellent imitation—a talent I'd had since junior high school. The streetcar stopped and I led Timo off.

We were across the Ring from the Volksgarten. It was a warm, clear night. "Would you like to walk in the garden?" I asked Timo. He shrugged, silently. "Sure you would." We went through the wrought-iron gates. It occurred to me that we had inadvertently taken the same path, in reverse, that we had taken that day a little over five months ago, when I had followed Jutta and Timo from the Volksgarten, to the Schottentor, to Alserstrasse—where Timo had seen me and kicked me, and had started everything. Now, in the Volksgarten, the pollarded trees along the gravel paths were as bare as before, but the autumn leaves were gone from underfoot; instead of hoar frost on the grass there were the scattered, melting remains of the last snow; and the spade-shaped tips of the branches showed where the new buds were forming.

We walked, saying nothing. Timo let me hold his hand, and it felt small and fragile and cool in my hand, like a bird's egg. "Look!" I pointed. The full moon was rising, a cream-colored button on the navy blue sky, over the lit façade of the Hofburg. The newly sand-blasted stone of the old emperor's palace was just the same color, not black as it had been when Hitler, in a different March, had stood on the balcony and proclaimed the *Anschluss*. "That's why Easter is so early this year," I told Timo. "Tomorrow is the first Sunday after the first full moon after the vernal equinox." And the crowd assembled for the proclamation had stretched all the way back through this garden, through the iron gates, across the Ring, and up the driveway and the steps of the Parliament building. Somewhere on this field, forty-eight years ago almost to the day, Heinrich Bechtler had met his future wife, Marianna. And now they lived in Innsbruck, wondering, presumably, why their granddaughter Jutta had not been on the afternoon train.

"What's the vernal equinox?" Timo asked.

At last. He had spoken to me. "The first day of spring."

"Is it spring already?"

"Yes, and Easter, too. This is supposed to be a very hopeful time of the year—a new beginning, a new birth, a new chance—all that crapola." I pulled down a low branch. "That red-tipped swelling at the end—that's a new bud. It was beaten up by the last storm, but it's still alive. Buds are hardy critters. In another month, all these trees will be in bloom."

We followed one of the paths to a small stone Doric temple. The temple had been built in the nineteenth century to house the Canova sculpture *Theseus and the Centaur;* but that was now more safely kept on the main staircase in the kunsthistorischesmuseum. All that was left by the temple was a distinctly Nazi-looking bronze, dated 1921, of a young Aryan athlete. The plinth read, "The strength and beauty of our youth."

We sat on the foundation of the temple, between two Doric columns. "You're mad at me," I said.

"*Mommy's* mad at you," Timo said.

"You're mad at me, too."

"No, I'm not."

"You're afraid I'm mad at you."

"No."

"What then?"

"Mommy's mad at you."

I sighed.

"She's been saying bad things about you all day," he added.

"And you agree with them?"

"She won't be mad at you anymore, now that you're back."

The bronze youth faced away from us. His wiry, muscular body glinted in the moonlight. I stood up and walked around to his front. He had a flattish face, wide-set eyes, a nose that descended in a straight line from a point directly between his eyebrows. Thin lips. Skin taut over high cheekbones. The Nazi ideal. The strength and beauty of our youth. No Viennese I had ever seen looked remotely like it. "She told you I was coming back?" I asked.

"Yes."

"When did she say that?"

"After she talked on the phone with you."

"What exactly did she say?"

"She said everything was all set. She said you wouldn't be leaving us again. She said you realized you had been a stupid jerk."

Timo remembers everything.

"Why didn't we go up to Mommy?" he asked.

"Because I was afraid."

I had placed myself so that the eyes of the bronze Aryan were staring directly into my own. There was the hint of a curl in the thin, upper lip. The mouth was slightly parted, as if about to say something derisive. In 1921, at the height of the popular perversion of Nietzsche's work, perhaps this expression was thought strong, and therefore beautiful. But today, to me, it seemed merely cruel, intolerant, impoverished.

"I don't know what to say, Timo," I said. "I'm sorry for everything I've done."

"But it's all right now, Eric. You're back."

"I'm back," I echoed.

"She didn't mean what she said."

"What?"

"That you were a stupid jerk."

"Mm."

"She talks like that all the time."

"I know, Timo."

The face reminded me of a schoolyard bully. It was a good, realistic piece of work. I could imagine it coming to life—those almondine, wide-set eyes assessing me, then glancing away and spitting provocatively. Or the figure stepping forward to put a hand on my chest and shove. This boy would torment schoolmates who admitted to fear, who did not, on some minor point, conform to the group—his group. This boy would admire strength and hardness. He would test himself ruthlessly for the same. This boy would hate misfits like Jutta or Timo as he hated parts of himself that were not strong or hard. He would be as ruthless with them as he was with himself.

266

"Was she really so upset today?" I asked.

"She was crying." He said this as if offering a minor point, indeed. How could I tell him now that his mother had been lying to him —that I was not coming back? Or was I? Could I really leave Timo? What were a few fights, a few hairy bastards, to abandoning him? Could I leave him to the schoolyard bullies, the brutal and narrow-minded people of the world? The expression on the bronze face looked cruel to *me*. But the same expression could be seen the length of Kärntnerstrasse; it was the expression the mannequins wore. Cruelty and inhumanity, contempt for the weak, were back in vogue; only now, the farce following the tragedy, they were in the service of the fashion industry. The strength and beauty of our mannequins. I touched the cold metal cheek. I would never have another son.

I turned back to Timo. "I don't know, Timo."

"You don't know what?"

I lifted him up and put him on my shoulders. "I don't know what I don't know. You know? Let's go!" I scrunched down the path, back toward the Ring, holding Timo's knees against my cheeks. "Maybe Mommy knows," I said. My forehead was warm under Timo's hands. "Maybe Mommy knew all along."

I was filled with nervous energy, so I decided to walk all the way back. I carried Timo the whole way. We reached Lazarettgasse at 10:30. I looked up at the building. There were still no lights on in the apartment. "She's probably gone out," I told Timo. To look for me with a grenade launcher. "We'll have to wait for her." I pushed against the outer door. But it was locked. Of course; it was always locked after ten. And last night, I had left my key behind. I buzzed the apartment. There was no answer. "Yes, she's out," Timo confirmed. I buzzed Rashid, and he let us in. In the perpetual gloom of the top floor, there was a bright square of light in the glass above the apartment door. The kitchen light was on. The door was not locked. I went in. I put Timo down. The rest of the apartment was dark and quiet. Puzzled, I went through the rooms, turning on lights. The apartment was empty.

"She left the door open because she remembered I didn't have my key," I said. I picked up the phone to call Rashid, but the line was dead. The cord had been ripped out of the wall. I went downstairs. "Jutta's not down here, is she?"

"No," Rashid said. "You've lost her?"

"Temporarily."

"How was your celebration?"

"Fine, thanks."

Upstairs, Timo was yawning. "You should go to bed," I said. "I'll wait up for Mommy." If you hear me scream for help, come defend me. I made sure he brushed his teeth.

"Can I sleep in yours and Mommy's room?" he asked. He didn't like to sleep without Theodor in the children's room.

"Sure."

I sat on the bed with him and took up Jutta's latest book. Another Arthur Schnitzler. I read to him until he fell asleep. Then I went back down the hall to the kitchen. It was so quiet! During all these months, I had never been in the apartment alone at night before. It was usually such a noisy place. I found the stillness unsettling. I read the Schnitzler for a while, but the quiet of the apartment kept disturbing me. I went around again, turning on lights, looking under beds. Nothing.

Sometime after twelve, I thought I heard someone on the stairs. I opened the apartment door to listen. It was just the wind. Taped to the outside of the door was a folded piece of paper. Had it been there before? I must have missed it in the darkness. I took it down and opened it. "Eric—I have thought for a long time about this, and it is the only way; everybody will be better off—"

Dizzy, I held on to the door jamb for support. The light in my eyes was very bright. Where? Where had she gone? The river? I snatched at the phone to dial the police—the line was dead—read the note!— I ran my eyes over the four lines—there was no mention of place— the river was not her way—not since the first time—after that she had always cut her wrists—

cut her wrists

cut her wrists

oh God I bolted down the hall oh God and through the children's room I snapped on the light in Ulrike's room oh God please I ran to the curtain I ripped it back I saw nothing the huge green tub I climbed the steps I grabbed the side of the huge tub I hauled myself up my heart burst in my throat

Jutta

□

A cool, misty morning, incandesced by sunlight. I had forgotten how appealing Vienna could be on a sunny day; like an ugly man with a rare, startlingly beautiful smile. Moist air filled the lungs satisfyingly with young spring. April weather. Lovely weather.

A #71 stopped. There were empty seats for Ulrike, Renate, and the two boys. Josh and I stood. The car swayed out of Schwarzenberg-platz and rattled into the third district. Automobiles, stone façades, signs: all blackened, greasy, with filth. Through a gate, a second's image of the Belvedere gardens, like a dream of French classicism among the Viennese grime; then gone. "But why is it so dirty?" I asked, of no one in particular. No one answered. Past the cloisters. On the right, a few village houses, with yards and trellises fenced by wire: surprising survivors amid the city's debris and noise. On the left, the St. Marx slaughterhouses—suppliers of the whole city—acres of ware-houses. A plywood wall alternating posters, like a comic strip, of Kurt Waldheim and Kurt Steyrer. Not a trace of Freda Meissner-Blau. "Is that Saint *Karl* Marx?" Josh asked. On, under the concrete pylons of the autobahn, onto the Simmeringer Hauptstrasse. Small shops. Then gas works, far off to the left, spitting flame. In the middle distance, gargantuan apartment complexes, buildings sliding menacingly to-ward and away from each other as we moved, like jousting behemoths. All those people! Numerous, negligible human life. On. Fewer build-ings. Now and then, a café or store, like a lone tooth, among overgrown lots. Then gray fields with oaks and poplars, dusted green. Stone-mason shops, behind gardens of marble slabs. "We're here," Josh said.

We got off. I had been here only once before, on All Saints' Day. I had gone with Jutta and Timo. We had been together for a week, and I had not yet even noticed the scars on Jutta's wrists. But today we turned away from the cemetery, and instead crossed underneath the street, through a passageway smelling of urine and carbon monoxide. Graffito: "The unborn live!" On the other side, a pretty drive led us under a linden canopy to the main gate of the crematorium. Josh went into the administration building. A sign by the gate said *"Kremations-feier"*: "cremation ceremony." The words could also mean, "crema-tion celebration." Had there been a party here, too, on November 1, dancing among the dead? I could not remember.

Jutta's grandparents, as next of kin, had had the authority over the disposal of the body. But they had relinquished it to us. There had been only one phone call. Ulrike spoke for three minutes, while I stared out of the window. Across the room, the receiver murmured pointedly, but I could not bring myself to listen. Do they frighten me so much? I wondered. Ulrike put down the phone. "She said they would call the police to get the real story. But they won't be coming to Vienna. They want to have nothing to do with it." "That's all?" "That's all." That was all—Jutta's childhood, reduced to a curt voice over the telephone and a final, dismissive click.

There had been no will, of course, so it was all a guessing game. Jutta had believed in organ donation, and she had even made out the paper for it once, in the presence of a witness; that was shortly before one of her suicide attempts. But she had lost the paper years ago. Characteristically, it had never occurred to her that her charity would come to nought if she was a suicide: that a death alone, undiscovered for hours, left a useless corpse. Not to mention the legal requirement of an autopsy.

Jutta had said once to Ulrike that she liked the idea of having her ashes strewn somewhere. Where? Ulrike had asked her. I don't know, she had said, I'll think about it. They had never spoken of it again. "At the ruined house," I said. "By the windows facing west." But when I rode the streetcar out there, I found that a planking wall had been erected around the site. The little house, viewed through a knot hole, looked the same; but orange-tipped markers showed where a larger foundation would soon be dug. The house was going to be demolished. On one of the planks hung a forlorn sticker: "I'm voting for Freda Meissner-Blau!"

Josh came out of the administration building. "Everything's all set." We went under an arch into a large courtyard. To the left and right were open galleries, in which slabs of marble set in the walls marked where ashes had been placed. Only a foot deep, these final resting places were cheaper than the graves across the road, as the crematorium staff had pointed out to us. But we had ignored them. At the far end of the courtyard stood the fortress-like *Feuerhalle:* the Fire Hall. "It looks like a Temple of Death," Josh said. "The abode of gruesome 'celebrations.' " "Josh, will you shut up?" That was Renate, who had proven impervious to Josh's charms. But Josh was right. Like the flak towers, the Fire Hall—with its monumental staircase leading up to a central Gothic arch flanked by flaming cressets—was the cheesy stuff of sci-fi flicks. Strange sacrifices went on behind its Art

Deco, neo-Dawn-of-Time façade. A man with the appropriate pallor and scent met us beneath the Gothic arch. He led us into the Family Waiting Room, a large, cold space with chairs. The body was beyond, he said, ready for viewing in Ceremony Hall Three. Would we like to see it? No, we wouldn't. Very well. We could wait here, while the cremation was taking place. It would not take long. He left us. Josh flipped through a brochure he had picked up in the administration building. It talked about pipelines, brick enclosures, and degrees Celsius. The gas came from the gas works we'd passed on the streetcar.

I had called the ambulance on Rashid's telephone. Then I had returned to the apartment and picked up Timo, sound asleep, and carried him down to Rashid's, so that he wouldn't see anything. Rashid followed me back up, and became hysterical. The ambulance crew arrived in ten minutes, saw that there was no need for hurry, and waited around telling jokes until the police came, some while afterward. To the police, I identified myself as a boyfriend and a student, only the latter of which I could prove. Rashid said he was a friend; on account of his skin color, he appeared to become a prime suspect. A photographer was all over the place, flashing everything. There was blood on my left hand. He flashed it. He flashed the damaged telephone. The razor, handled with a glove, was inserted gingerly into a plastic bag. Rashid and I were told, in a tone that suggested this concerned us vitally, that there would be a check for fingerprints. A stranger appeared. He looked angry. I asked him who he was and he retorted by asking me who in hell *I* was. My answer only made him angrier. He was the *Hausbesorger*—the superintendent. He had come because the Viennese woman on the second floor had called him to say there were police in the building. And now he had found not only a murder, but an American in residence about whom he had known nothing, the door to one of the bathrooms locked and the key snapped off, and a bathroom in the flat, built without a license, without his being notified, that made use of an illegal hook-up from the sink in the hall. He wanted to know if I had any idea of his responsibilities. He wanted to know how long I had been living in the apartment and what my name was. He was interrupted by the police, who told me I was coming with them. The body was driven off to the morgue. Rashid and I were driven in the opposite direction, to the police station, where we were fingerprinted and questioned. It was only after Ulrike and Renate were reached, and their separate defenses of us found to match, that the police allowed us to go home. Timo was still asleep. I carried him back upstairs. Then I went into the bathroom to clean up Jutta's last mess.

I ran out of the waiting hall, into the sunshine. Timo followed me. We sat on the steps. The thin white haze had blanketed Vienna for days, making the sun easy to look at, a lurid disk of varying and unnameable colors—mixtures of red and orange, saffron, magenta, blood, mauve, purple. Wisps of steam drifted across the face of the disk, like gliding birds. Bloated, lazy, eerily beautiful: was this what a post-nuclear-holocaust sun would look like? As Timo and I sat, the haze seemed to thicken. I looked around. A chimney at the back of the *Feuerhalle* was belching smoke. I thought of Jutta's grandfather, his Einsatzgruppe, his duties at Mauthausen. If he were here, what memories would be waked?

The ashes were given to us in a plain box that might have contained cigars or birdseed.

I had read the coroner's report. Jutta seemed to have made successive cuts over a period perhaps longer than an hour. The coroner conjectured that she had had some difficulty getting the blood to flow —not an uncommon problem when there was so much scar tissue. The approximate time of death: between 9:00 and 10:00 Saturday evening. She had probably first cut her wrists between 7:00 and 8:00. I reached the coroner by telephone and asked if he thought perhaps she had misjudged; that she had cut herself more seriously than she had intended. He said, "That is possible. A relatively small loss of blood may induce mild shock, well before there is a threat to life. That shock might have inhibited her ability to gauge what she was doing. I should say, however, that people who have employed this method several times, as is the case here, have of course proved themselves adept at overcoming such inhibitions."

"So you would say that it's possible, but unlikely."

"I would say it's possible, but *unusual.*"

From Schwarzenbergplatz we walked to Karlsplatz and got on the subway. I spoke to Josh in English. "She had promised she wouldn't do it again unless she meant it," I said. "How do you know she didn't mean it?" Josh asked. "Perhaps she did," I said. "In a way. The situation would have appealed to her; to her trust in a moral working of Fate." "Hm?" "After all, doesn't guilt suggest some trust in an underlying order? Jutta had a boundless capacity for guilt. She believed every detail of her suffering was deserved. Nothing happened to her by chance." "So what?" "So no one else was in the apartment. I had promised to come back to her. If I kept my promise, she would want to live, and she would live, because I would find her at eight o'clock. If I broke my promise, she would want to die, and she would die, because there would be no one else to discover her until Rashid brought back Timo the next morning." "Assuming the deeper cuts weren't an accident," Josh said. "Well, yes." "Quite an *amor fati*." "Yes, but an automatic Fate," I said. "A debased, vending-machine sort of Fate. Just the thing to appeal to someone who was superstitious; who didn't trust herself to do anything, not even to kill herself." "Nothing in her life became her like the leaving it," Josh said. "And of course it struck at *me*," I said. "It made me, in breaking my promise to come to her, responsible for her death. She would thus succeed, at the end, in doing what she had always threatened to do. She would bind me to her. As her killer." I stared at the rushing blackness outside the window. "Smart plan, huh?" I said. "Smart wench," Josh said. We rode on in silence. The subway sprang out into the light. "This is it," Josh said. "Only it didn't work!" I exclaimed. "It was too clever by half —a booby trap, as you said. And booby traps don't just kill burglars, they kill neighbors coming to look for their dogs. I happened to hear Timo; a mere accident! I *did* keep my promise! I came to her with more than she could have hoped for!" Josh gently took my arm and guided me toward the door. "Of course you did," he said. "You always keep your promises." "How could she do this to me?" I asked. Josh shook his head, propelled me up the stairs. I could hear her answer. The high breathy voice: "You hurt me, Eric. I had to hurt you back." Goddamn you.

I had learned something else from the coroner's report: Jutta had been pregnant. So she had lied about the pills. I understood then why there had been a special urgency to her love-making after the blood test, after we had stopped using the condoms. She had had one back-up plan after another for binding me: anger, disease, death, a child. But an AIDS baby? If she believed it. But why not? A sick child would hold me even better than a healthy one. It was only when I read the report a second time that the full truth dawned on me. She had been four weeks pregnant. She had conceived three weeks before we stopped using the condoms. Something clicked. I had puzzled over her AIDS-virus infection. I had been so conscientious with the condoms, so typically goddamn careful. How? How? I went into our bed-room and rooted out the remaining condoms. I spread them out on the dresser. The square wafers of plastic wrap looked normal. I felt along their edges; they were still sealed. I held one up to the light, and tilted it slowly around. Something sparked in the center of the square. I held up another. The same. I peered at all of them, feeling more and more like a fool, like someone who had been utterly outclassed by his oppo-nent. Jutta had driven a needle through the center of every package, and thus, through the tip of every condom. She had been running circles around me for a long time.

We had taken the subway to the Donauinsel: an artificial island in the Danube about a hundred yards across and some twenty-five kilo-meters long. Jutta and I had come here to walk now and then, on the warmer days. There was always a big, blustery sky, a wide-open view of both banks, and the wooded hills beyond. The city itself was mostly hidden by the high quay, which may have been why Jutta had liked to come out here. On the clearest days, when the mountains felt close and the sun on your skin was convincing, you could regain out here the feeling that you really lived on the planet Earth—you know, rolled round in its diurnal course with rocks and stones and trees—and were not whirling through cold space on some stucco and dirt moon named Vienna.

We walked away from the subway. There were bicycle paths, young planted trees, sculpted hillocks and ridges. Two kilometers out, we had left other strollers behind. We made our way down a steep slope; the spring grass was still short enough to show the concrete meshing that kept the hill from sliding into the river. We reached a low embankment. There was a shelter here, where the rockers hung out, and sometimes fought with the police. One graffito: "Away with the arms industry!" And another, more modest proposal: "More horses!" There was also a viewing pier, an arm of the embankment jutting thirty feet into the river. We walked out. The river curled under at the end of the arm, slipped quickly away. Renate had the box. "Does anyone want to say anything?" she asked. We looked at each other. Nothing. Ulrike, who had been crying since we had left the subway, said "Just do it, Ren." Renate flipped back the lid and re-versed the box over the water. Out came white dust. It was caught by the wind and it slanted away, roiling across the water, dispersing. It looked for all the world, as it thinned, like cigarette smoke.

Goodbye, Jutta.

In a moment, every trace was gone. We stood dumbly, and the river curled past us.

☐

I wondered, clutching the strap on the streetcar and staring at Timo, who was staring at the floor, I wondered what her grandparents were thinking in their cuckoo-clock home in Innsbruck. Could they so easily turn off her existence in their minds? Had they eaten their breakfast with the newspaper this morning, buttered *Semmeln* and trepanned soft-boiled eggs with the utter detachment, the impregnable self-possession in which Jutta's imagination had always cloaked them? Or were they angry? Bitter? They had lost something that they had seemed to need. Having lost it, did they themselves feel lost? I was sorry they had not come to Vienna. I could not imagine them. I could not imagine how they would move, how they would speak, what they would say to people who were not their poor, guilty granddaughter. They remained in my mind as ogres; not a healthy image, nor a complete one. Yet the totality of my contact with the grandparents had been appropriate: a murmur in a telephone line, coming from nowhere—like the soft, bland breath of a menace that startles you, but too late, always too late, startles you only after it is gone.

"Timo," I said. He looked up. "Let's get off here." To the others I said, "Timo and I will walk the rest of the way." We climbed down to the street. We were at the Burgtheater. We crossed the Ring and went into the Rathaus park. Timo trotted in silence, an expressionless little man keeping his eyes rigidly to the front. He had not spoken many words since Easter morning, when he had waked to find that no one had gotten into bed with him, that I had spent the entire night cleaning and picking up around the apartment until it looked like no one had ever lived there, nor ever could, and that his mother was nowhere to be found. I sat with him at breakfast and regarded those eyes and nostrils in an utter panic. Jutta had to go away for a while, I told him. I would take care of him until she got back. To her parents, after all? Timo asked. Yes, I said. Timo was used to upended affairs, unexplained changes of plan, and he nodded, went back to his bowl of sugar. He spent a quiet Sunday morning building a house for Heidi while I, with a raging headache, made phonecalls, spoke in English, shat a tan-colored mucus, and vomited five minutes after I ate anything. After Renate and Ulrike arrived in the evening we had to talk about how to break the news to him. On Monday, when I sat with him, he had already clammed up. I told him that Jutta was not going to come back. I told him that she had not meant to leave him, that she would never have left him if she had had a choice. But she had been forced to go. And didn't he understand that she loved him? That I loved him? "She's dead," he said. I had not used the word. "Yes," I said. He reproached me: "I know what death is, Eric." "I'm sorry, Timo." I couldn't tell from the blank eyes if he had already known, if he had picked it up with those vigilant ears from the chaos around him (who knew? perhaps he understood English, too), or whether the knowledge was hitting him for the first time now, sinking into those brown eyes and vanishing. In any case, he stopped talking. He took to following me. He would only sleep in Jutta's bed, and only when I was with him. I lay waiting for him to fall asleep, and sometimes beyond, counting his breathing into the hundreds. Then I got up again to arrange, to clean, to throw things away. I threw away the condoms, the cigarettes, the shells, the photos of Jutta naked. I threw away the Riding School stubs, the opera booklets, the Jackson Browne tapes. I threw away dozens of volumes of Schnitzler. All his stories ended in suicide. I didn't sleep at all at night. I walked from room to room, in the dark. Ulrike told me to stop behaving like a ghost.

We walked on, into the streets beyond the Town Hall. I knelt down to button Timo's jacket, as it was growing colder. I turned the collar up. Something green on the fabric caught my eye. I thought it was lint and I tried to brush it away, but it wouldn't move. I looked closer. It was a bit of embroidery, clumsily done. I had to turn the collar half way around and peer at the design before I recognized what it was. It made my heart ache. It was a sprig of thyme. Perhaps Jutta had hidden it under the collar because she had feared I would laugh at her. I stared into Timo's grave eyes and he stared back into mine. I hugged him. Now I was the only person in the world who would do that. I remembered the long fingers with the cheap thin rings, the long skirts. She would hug him fiercely to her legs and he would almost disappear in all that wool. Now there was only me. I would not have laughed. He would need all the strength he could get in this crusade.

We went on. None of us knew what Timo understood, or what he believed, or what he was thinking. Most children would have cried, whined, needed attention and caresses. Most children would not have understood. But Timo had learned to keep his own counsel. He had also learned, from the beginning, that when people disappeared, they disappeared for good.

Children are flexible, some people say. They are hardier than we think; hardier than we *are*. But I know also that children can be quiet in a very frightening way. Perhaps because they are aliens in an adult world, because they haven't lived long enough to believe that the external world is the only choice of worlds open to them, they can remove themselves to a great distance. A form of autism . . . You can sense them retreating from you and laying waste the land in between. You cannot follow. You are afraid to try. Timo would be six this month. He had another sixty years or so to live. How do you reconcile a child to this world?

It was something I would need to figure out. I had gotten in touch with a lawyer as soon as the Easter holidays were over. I had asked him what my chances were of getting legal custody of Timo. "You aren't an Austrian resident, are you?" he had asked.

"No."

"Then no chance. Zip."

"How about if I were?"

"Is that a serious question?"

"I'm just curious."

"No one else wants him?"

"No."

"No family?"

"All dead."

A pause. "It might be possible, then."

On Zimmermannplatz, Ali shook his head at us. "You must have faith," he said, enfolding me in those long arms, weighted at the ends with hands like dumbbells. "You cannot take this on yourself."

"Allah will provide," I said.

"Whatever you want to call Him," he said.

Back at the apartment, Ulrike mentioned a visitor. Renate showed me a note left by the *Hausbesorger*. It threatened legal action if the bathtub were not immediately dismantled and removed. "Fuck him," I said, and ripped the note up. "Fuck the goddamn son of a bitch."

"Eric!" exclaimed a familiar voice. "I've never heard you speak that way." I turned around.

A small trim man glided into the kitchen like a contented cat. He was blond. His thin hair was parted on the side and combed close and neat. He had wide-set eyes and thin lips curled in a mocking smile that seemed to say, "Now, how did I get here?" He looked very German, very aristocratic, like a World War I flying ace. He looked remarkably like the bronze youth by the Doric temple in the Volksgarten. He also looked exactly like me.

He was my twin brother, Rick.

He made an exaggerated bow, like an emissary arrived at a foreign court. "Mother sent me," he said to the floor, and held out a letter.

EPILOGUE

TIMO IS EIGHT YEARS OLD today. I called in sick and kept him out of school. My students were happy to have a day off, and no doubt Timo's teachers were just as happy to be free of him. We put on hiking boots and shouldered rucksacks filled with food I prepared last night. We caught a bus to the edge of town and hiked out: up the slopes, through thick woods, along an old logging road. At eighteen hundred meters, the trees fell below us, the road dwindled to a track, and we crossed alpine meadows lurid with daffodils and crocuses. Soon those, too, fell behind us, and the way grew steep. We entered a bowl a couple of miles across and picked our way across its inner face, halfway up the wall. At times, the path became so narrow that the local alpine club had bolted a guy to the granite; to keep our traction, we had to lean out, press our boots against the dissolving stone, and work across hand over hand. At our backs, the ground fell a thousand feet before curving away to cup pine forests. At a place where the path widened, we climbed on top of a boulder and had lunch. The stone was warm from the sun. Far below, past where the pine forests, too, dipped out of sight, we could make out the fields and houses crowding the valley floor. A glider crawled down there—a bright piece of origami on the wind. The mountains beyond were gray and piled high, like storm clouds.

Timo was a city urchin when we came here, a year ago; he had thin limbs, a thin chest, and that look of having coal dust behind the ears. But he took to the outdoor life avidly, as he had always claimed he would when he talked about going to Kurt's farm and becoming a farmer. He walks everywhere. He sometimes skips school to do it. He is often out for hours during the violent storms, and we begin to listen anxiously for his return, until he finally appears, soaking wet and dirty, with a long and confusing story of where he has been. He knows all the hill paths, all the old overgrown roads. Whenever the two of us go out, I let him lead. He has put on muscle, and he leads me on long hikes, especially ones that turn sharply up. He loves to get as high as he can, far above and away from the world. He likes the silence up there, the feeling of purity, the feeling of security. Today's walk was my birthday present to him: a day out of the hated classes, alone with me on a rock in the sun, everything else so distant that the haze made it seem unreal. He sat like the genius of the mountain, drinking it in, small and dark and watchful in all that vastness. I like to think he was happy.

We came back into Innsbruck when the sun was going down. We walked through the Old Town. The gift shops were closing and the wine and beer halls were beginning to fill up. The tops of the colorful Rococo buildings were flushed with pink. Then we crossed the river and followed it east toward the newest section of town. Still blocks away from home, we could see lights on in the apartment, high up, against the violet sky. "She's home," Timo said. "Perhaps she has even made dinner," I said. In fact, I knew she had. She had had to arrange a week ahead for this evening off. In the elevator, Timo asked, "What are we going to tell the school tomorrow?" "Why don't we just say you were sick?" "Frau Wieland knows today is my birthday." "I'll write a note saying we had an enormous bash last night for your birthday and you ate so much you pulled a muscle in your stomach and couldn't walk today." We came to the top floor. I opened the apartment door and said, "Oh, my." Inside everything was ready. The table was set; flowers and balloons were everywhere; from the kitchenette came the smell of food. Timo looked nonplussed. "I guess we're going to have a party," I said. My wife came out with the birthday cake, her two-and-a-half-year-old daughter in tow. "Happy Birthday, Timo!," little Elizabeth yelled and jumped around him, clapping her hands. "Thanks for all the work, Renate," I said.

☐

On the day of Jutta's cremation, Rick had brought more than the letter from my mother. He had also come with two plane tickets, and orders to get me on a flight to the U.S., even if he had to hit me over the head to do it. He phoned a report to my mother that day, to assure her that I was alive and well, if not exactly in my right mind. Then he stayed for a week, mostly partying with Josh and crashing on the futon, while I put my affairs in order. Then I went home with him willingly enough. On the plane, he smiled to himself and fell into a deep sleep. The night before, Ulrike had at last revenged herself on Kurt.

I went home to do only two things: to give my mother her due, and to lay the groundwork for my return to Austria. I knew I had no life in the States any longer. At long last, I knew something. I belonged with Timo.

My mother was more easily dissuaded from violence against my person than I had thought possible. Not that she had forgiven me; or that she ever will, really. She said she would never be able to think of me in the way she used to. I could understand that, I said. Neither would I. But she had changed, too. She seemed more willing to accept Rick and me on our own terms. No doubt that was because she had become resigned, because she knew she had no choice; but still, she did accept us, to a degree, and resignation brings its own peace. She even relaxed and joked with Rick—something I had not seen in a decade. I learned that he had come to stay with her during the week when I was not answering her telegrams, and the experience had brought them closer. "You nearly sent her around the bend," Rick told me. "Now you know what it's like," I said.

She understood nothing of what I told her about Jutta and Timo. Jutta had not been the sort of woman she would have liked; she divined that instinctively. And Timo did not have the right genes (i.e., he had none of mine) to render my devotion to him comprehensible. Here it would perhaps have made sense to tell her I carried the AIDS virus and thus had no prospect of my own children. But when the time came, I could not say the words. First I committed myself to a major revelation; then I slid away at the last moment and told her I had donated once to a sperm bank and been told I was sterile. For destruction, that was also great, and would suffice. At least, until symptoms appear.

The only thing she actually *forgave* me for was botching up the fellowship. That—the vacuous letters, the bare-faced balderdash I was dishing out while pocketing my bi-monthly checks—that appealed, deep down, to her earthy Bavarian sense of humor. She would not have found it funny while my father was still alive; his seriousness had a way of tainting the groundwater of all our emotions. But now, she allowed herself a certain satisfaction at the discomfiture of the department that would not hire her, that had always looked with condescension on the faculty of a seething, cacophonous school like U. Mass., Boston. In snitching on me, she had killed two birds with one stone: she had punished me for intolerable academic and filial behavior, and she had embarrassed Harvard. How could she stay angry at me when her revenge had been doubly sweet?

The history department, for its part, was so relieved to learn I had no intention of groveling for readmittance that it was generous, giving me the one thing I did ask for: a job recommendation. Drury, no doubt remembering the familial connection, even pulled a few of his international strings, and the possibility of a minor, dead-end position danced like a marionette at the other end. I flew back to Austria at the beginning of May, impressed the interviewers with my unmistakable passion, and clinched it. I would teach German and English as second and third languages to Turks, Yugoslavs, Poles, Iranians, Filipinos, Pakistanis, Jordanians, Syrians, and Egyptians at a municipal "education center" in Vienna's twenty-second district. On the fourth of May, the day Kurt Waldheim won a plurality in the Austrian presidential election, I married Renate. My "affairs" during the week Rick was in Vienna had included proposing to her, getting the license, and catching the priest.

Renate was the logical choice. After all, Ulrike was already married. And Renate, being a nurse, could take a calmer view of my AIDS infection, since of course I had to tell her of it. Furthermore, I could actually offer Renate something concrete in return for permanent residence and custody of Timo: I would take good care of Elizabeth. We were married just outside Eisenstadt, in her family's parish church, with Timo, Ulrike, Theodor, and Renate's parents in attendance. Renate wore blue and I wore black, and in the wedding pictures I am still surprised to see what a handsome couple we make— both of us slim, blond, pale, and bespectacled; oddly like siblings. Timo assured me that he understood what we were doing. Renate's parents were happier than they had been in years. They had long since given up on *any* husband for their disgraced daughter, let alone a tidy blond one who spoke polite *Hochdeutsch* and who looked like Baron von Richthofen. They told me privately it was clear Renate loved me more

284

than anything in the world. Renate and I laughed over that later, wondering if they had really thought it, or had said it only to add their cord to the net that Renate had somehow, miraculously, cast over me. At the close of the ceremony, I kissed her with my mouth tightly closed, and she winked. I was very grateful to her. We had an excuse for not going on a honeymoon—Renate had to work at the hospital the next day. That night we took the train to Vienna with Elizabeth asleep in a bassinet next to us. Timo exclaimed, "She's gotten bigger!" I said, "Not much." Renate gazed at her baby for a long time and then said, "Well, she takes after her new father."

Timo had spent the last month in a legal limbo. A bureau had been granted total control over his life the moment his mother died, and this bureau decided to put him in a foster home. The fact that he wanted to stay at Lazarettgasse and that all the adults at Lazarettgasse wanted the same, and that no one else on the planet Earth wanted him at all, seemed to make no difference. What actually saved him was the fact that the foster homes were overcrowded. So his case was postponed week by week, while I fought for an Austrian job in the U.S. and we counted the days to the wedding. A social worker came to the apartment to judge whether it was suitable as temporary lodgings for the orphan. "You need to clean up much more," she scolded. "Tell that to the orphan," I said. Even after Renate and I had married, the award of custody took some time, during which we feared that Timo might be taken away from us at any moment. Now there is a law in Bavaria requiring all foreigners applying for residence and all persons applying for a marriage license to get tested for the AIDS virus. Austria is considering a similar law. Had that law existed two years ago, we would never have gotten custody of Timo. I would not even be allowed to live here. As it is, my condition is still a secret, known only to Renate, and I intend to keep it that way. I trust myself to act fairly responsibly about it, which is not something I can say for any government.

Of course, new AIDS studies keep coming out, each one insisting on its own interpretation of my life, my actions, my culpability. It's an odd feeling, to read what complete strangers think of me. One recent book claims that the virus is far easier to transmit than anyone else is admitting. This book assures me that the Vienna prostitute, the bumper-car man, mean nothing. I perhaps picked up the virus from a toilet seat or a glass of water. I am, the book says, a far more hapless

—and far more dangerous—fool than I had realized. But soft! What light through yonder window breaks? An even more recent article says no, not at all: in fact, the virus is much *harder* to transmit than anyone thought. Meanwhile my life expectancy keeps changing. They used to say that a third of us carriers would eventually come down with AIDS, with the real thing. Then they said half. Now, as I understand it, there is doubt that any of us can reasonably hope for a normal life span. Out here, on the cutting edge of global catastrophe, we live from one newsflash to the next.

We had to move last year. Evictions had finally begun at Lazarettgasse 17, and at about the same time, Renate—along with a quarter of the nursing staff—lost her job at the General Hospital in the middle of a new scandal concerning the embezzlement of millions of schillings. She could find a decent replacement only in Innsbruck. After we arrived, I even landed a better job than what I had in Vienna: I teach English literature and language at one of the *Gymnasien*. We live in a high-rise by the river, where the wind is strong. We can actually feel the building flex during the storms. The motion nauseates Elizabeth —who is a frail little girl—and then Renate talks about moving. But we are both busy, and nothing ever comes of it.

I cannot forget that this is the town in which Jutta grew up. I have often wondered which of the toy-like houses belongs to her grandparents. Whenever I pass an enclosed garden, I imagine Jutta trapped inside it, a strange little girl spending her childhood alone. I look at the people in the streets and in the stores and I think, "Is it you? Or is it you?" I lived in the terror, while we waited for custody of Timo, that the Bechtlers would also apply. After all, they had done it before with Jutta, and their revenge, perhaps, was not complete. But no word of it came. Still, when I walk with Timo, I often imagine a pedestrian turning suddenly and asking, "Where did you get that boy? He's my great-grandson—he's mine!" And the figure would descend on him, coattails flapping like wings, claws outstretched.

Josh is still living in Vienna, despite the fact that Kurt Waldheim is now president. And Jun is still married to Josh, despite everything. A recent letter from them tells me the city has just put up a bronze apology near the opera house: a life-size statue of a Jew, being forced to scrub the street. It's the Austrian answer to the international repercussions of Waldheim's presidency. "The passersby love it," Josh reports. "For them, it's just like old times!"

Ulrike divorced Kurt last year and took up with an artist in Leopoldstadt. We visited some months back on the occasion of an exhibition opening for his collective; he looked the classic bohemian, with sallow skin, beard, dirty sweater, beret; Ulrike had bloomed again, and looked as bohemian as he did; unkempt hair and bare feet suited her; Theodor had actually brightened a little. The opening crowd drank white wine. The walls of the exhibition were dappled with nude Ulrikes. Afterward, we went back to their apartment and sat on the floor between crates and canvases, drinking coffee Ulrike had brewed on a camping stove. Kurt, Ulrike said, still worked the farm; he was drinking more, and had gained weight. Ziu had been brought to Leopoldstadt. But someone had accidentally let him out before he had grown used to the new place, and he had never come back. Ulrike's eyes were starry. She was pregnant.

While we were in the city, we swung by Lazarettgasse. Our building and its neighbors had been torn down, and in their place stood the skeleton of a hospital annex. About where Jutta's bedroom used to be, a porcine construction worker sat on a plank and riveted, stopping every so often to take a swig of Coke. Ali's stall was being run by a stranger, who told me that Ali had gone out of business. No one could tell me where he had disappeared to. I have read recently that the construction of the annex has fallen into litigation, and is liable to be delayed for years.

And we in our nauseous high rise? We get by from month to month. Renate and I have become better friends than either of us expected. We don't have the fights that lovers have, we don't suffocate each other, and of course, we need each other. Gratitude predisposes us to affection. Sometimes, late at night, if we are sitting together and talking—we talk mainly about Timo and Elizabeth, as co-workers will do, getting together after hours and talking only about work—sometimes then, that gratitude begins to feel a little like something else. Perhaps Renate feels the occasional nudge as well, but as we are alike in many ways, she would be as disinclined to make mention of it as I. Of course, the marriage has not been consummated. I have found since Jutta died that I do not even have the desire. One victim really is enough for a lifetime. Now if someone took a cue from the safe-sex dating services and started one exclusively for AIDS carriers, perhaps I would be interested. There are enough of us now to make such a thing feasible, and no membership would be more self-regulatory. We would make a cozy clique, as exclusive as Mensa; we could call it "Mors" . . . When Renate cannot bear the celibacy any longer, she goes to Vienna (this is a little Catholic town, and we are ostracized enough as it is), where Ulrike sets her up with one of her new circle of friends. As she leaves on these jaunts, I say, "For godssake, make sure the man uses a condom." And Renate kisses me on the cheek and says, "You're cute when you're worried." I sleep alone. For some months after his mother died, Timo would not sleep except with me; and I would have let him do that as long as he wanted. But I was relieved when he grew out of it. My father used to bar his door at night and dream about getting infected by the weak, treacherous world. Now his son dreams about infecting it.

Timo will probably never be whole. Jutta took too much of him with her. He will probably never really trust anyone. His response to her betrayal has been to become even more of a loner, more self-reliant. His main reason for hating school is that he has to associate with other children. He is not disliked by his classmates so much as held in awe, for his silence and his nonchalance. He hides in the back of the class and reads. I do not know how to say he is brilliant without sounding like just another proud father; but he is brilliant. His latest passion, ironically, is World War II. His grades are terrible. At first, he was my little ruined house. He was the one small part of the world that I wanted to redeem, in order to compensate for my failures, my betrayals. But of course he belongs to himself and I have not redeemed him, I have only watched him grow. Now I try only to keep a quiet place around him so that he can grow in relative peace. I wonder sometimes if I will ever be able to read those unruffled brown eyes. In the meantime, I can only believe what he tells me.

As I said, we get by. We don't expect much and we aren't disappointed. The Austrians have a word for this sort of life: *fortwursteln.* "Muddling through." It is the other side of *Schlamperei,* the humane and appealing aspect of the Austrian character that my father could never see. It describes a life of half measures and improvisations; a talent for salvaging workable situations out of thoroughly botched jobs.

I keep a photograph of Jutta on my desk. It is the one from the book called "Our Favorite Things," in which she and Timo are standing at the edge of a street, looking together into the camera. I like the photo for Jutta's expression in it: a slit-eyed, knowing glance. That glance makes her look tougher than she really was, and wiser, and more able to take her own Fate in her hands. That is how I would like to remember her. On the day she was cremated, I thought that she had carefully worked the suicide out; that she had set things up so that the outcome, whatever it was, would be appropriate. But I no longer believe that. Josh said on the subway that I keep my promises, and he was right. (About the small promises, anyway—a bookkeeper's way of balancing out the big ones that have been broken.) Jutta knew that. Jutta knew I would keep my promise to come to her at 8:00 on that Saturday evening. She knew I would save her. Jutta did not want to die. It was all a mistake; a world pivoting on a pin-head; a copper-oxide globe crushing its weary Atlas. Her death was as meaningless as that microscopic glitch in my bloodstream. Yesterday, I dreamed a dream: the pedestrian turned and recognized Timo, came to clutch him to his evil breast. I snatched the boy up and leaped. With a push of my legs and an intake of air I soared over the garden wall. And I kept on going. I flew upward and upward with Timo on my back. How easy it was! How light he was! I would be able to fly forever with him and never grow tired. I looked back. It was not Timo on my back, but Jutta, holding tight.